WELCOME TO WIMBLY'S

Misfit Magic

A.B. Bradley

Skull & Crosspens Press

www.abbradley.com

Cover design by: AB Bradley.
Back cover design by: AB Bradley.
Interior design template by: David Haden.
Author photography by: Dustin Vyers.

ISBN-13 paperback: 978-1505630442

AB Bradley
www.abbradley.com
Email: authorabbradley@gmail.com

Acknowledgements

Writing a book is only one part of creating the novel. It takes a team of people to build something worth your time and money, and without their expertise I'm certain this dream of mine could have never become reality. So, thank you to everyone who walked this journey with me and who will walk it with me in the future.

Thank You

Thank you to everyone who has supported me on this journey. Writing a book isn't a sprint, it's a marathon, and I couldn't do it without the support of my friends and family.

TABLE OF CONTENTS

1

Oh, What Wonderful Watkins

Quinn's third family came first by bent manila folder, second by five-minute call, and third by long and quiet drive to the edge of Tupper Lake. Sighing, he slid out the squeaky sedan's worn leather seat, his fingers dancing over its web of cracks like a spider angling for a fly. His caseworker shut the car door behind him, gently rocking the tired car. A crisp breeze whistled through Quinn's hair. A sky so blue it could have made sapphires jealous yawned over rolling hills blanketed by trees, their leaves tinged with autumn's rusty colors.

His caseworker shivered, clutching the puffy down vest hanging over his sloping shoulders.

"You should zip up, Tony," Quinn said with a wide grin. "You'll catch your death out here."

"I lost the stupid zipper and it's busted now." He sighed and adjusted the pack slung over his shoulder. "Welcome to your new home, Quinn. Ready to meet your foster parents? I know you'll like them. They're very nice."

"I guess so." Quinn buried his hands in his pockets and pointed his chin down the drive. "Lead the way."

Meeting his first foster parents had terrified him. Being introduced to his second ones made him a little nervous. Now that he'd be on his third foster family, he couldn't care less what they thought about him.

Tony kneeled, resting hands with hairy knuckles on Quinn's shoulders. Quinn smiled. The caseworker wasn't a bad man. Not many who worked in his line were. Still, Quinn could tell the job drained him, wore Tony out like a weight he could never shrug off. The man's eyelids drooped into deep lines along his temples, and his bush of curly hair thinned more each time they met. But despite his stress and troubles, Tony smiled and flashed a front tooth that angled just slightly the wrong way.

"You're gonna be okay," he said. "Will you behave for me? You really need to be good with these people. They're nice, just like I know you're nice."

Quinn shrugged and glared into Tony's eyes. "The first two weren't my fault. You know that."

"I know, I know. But I can only do so much, and despite what you might think, I really do care about what happens to you. There are rules. You break too many and I can't keep you out of harm forever. This is your third strike, your last chance. A boy as bright as you can't end up in youth detention. It'll ruin you, Quinn, and we both know it." He stood, and his double-knotted hiking boots squeaked with each step he took over the cracked drive. "C'mon. They're waiting."

Quinn's new home was a solitary box with a wide, covered patio. Paint peeled from the house's lifeless siding like an old snakeskin while its narrow windows watched him with unblinking eyes. Like most other homes in Tupper Lake, it's heyday passed long ago.

He hated that town. It might have been a nice place once, but time had abandoned it years before he first came there, and now it was a place people passed on the road to better things.

They reached the patio. Tony pressed the rusted doorbell, and it rang a tired tune. Tony rocked on his heels and nudged Quinn's shoulder.

Quinn swatted him away. "I think you're more nervous than I am."

"Just remember your manners. Oliver and Patty Watkins are nice people but they really do appreciate kids with good manners. I can't stress that enough."

"Really? Seems like you're stressing it just fine. I get it, they're nice."

Quinn decided then that the Watkins must not be very nice. The door unlocked with a loud click. Quinn swallowed. It creaked open, and a man appeared behind the mesh screen. Tony stepped back to avoid being smacked in the face as Oliver Watkins stepped onto the patio.

Oliver was a pencil of a man with a scarred jaw and a forehead too large for his hair to hide. He greeted Tony with a handshake, ignoring the caseworker's mumbling apology about being in the way, and turned to Quinn.

"Good afternoon, Mr. Lynch." Oliver extended a hand. "And welcome home. I just know you'll love it here."

"You can call me Quinn. And I hope I do." He shook Oliver's hand. The man had a strong grip. Too strong. Quinn flinched and wriggled free of Oliver's bear trap of a hand and flexed his throbbing fingers.

Behind the man, a woman jiggled through the doorway, nearly knocking Tony over for a second time as she bounded onto the patio. "Is this Quinn?" Her eyes beamed and her hands clapped. "Oh, he's such a charming young man!"

Ms. Watkins must have been eating her husband's meals. She curled her dark hair and plastered it with hairspray into little plastic waves while her makeup could make a doll cringe. Her efforts at beauty ended at the neck, though, because the worn grey sweat suit that clung around her wrists and waist defied any attempt at looking decent.

Quinn forced his lips into a smile. Mirroring his own smile, she squatted and pinched his cheek with her caterpillar fingers. "Hello, Quinn."

"Nice—nice to meet you," he said.

Tony nodded approvingly.

"Wonderful to meet you too," she cooed. "My name is Patty. You're going to have a marvelous time here. I'm certain of it. We take very special care of the blessed little boys and girls who come under our roof. You'll see."

Even though her breath reeked of butterscotch, and her honey-coated words landed sweetly on his ears, her hard eyes turned his stomach. Oliver cleared his throat and squeezed his wife's shoulder. "Let's get inside. It's chilly for this time of August and I don't want you catching a cold."

Patty tittered and stood, brushing her hands against her sweater. "Ollie, don't be silly. You know I've got more than enough padding to keep me warm."

Quinn snorted, the laugh ripping through his nose. He smiled at them, blinking. Maybe they weren't so bad. At least Patty had a sense of humor about her size.

Oliver glared, his jaw set. Patty pursed her lips and shook her head just enough for Quinn to see. "I've got enough padding because my *sweater* keeps me wonderfully warm. Please, come in."

Oliver and Patty walked inside. Tony flashed Quinn pleading eyes.

Sorry, Quinn mouthed.

Be nice, he answered.

Quinn followed Tony into the Watkins' home. It smelled of pine cleaner mixed with cheap lavender incense, both of which couldn't hide the musty scent seeping from every panel and floorboard in the house. They walked into the living room, and Quinn took a seat on a croaking plaid couch.

Tony pulled Quinn's case file from his satchel. He thumbed through it until he found a few papers from the State of New York that summarized Quinn's life in neat, soulless letters along with an official release form for his new foster parents.

Oliver whipped a pen from his pocket and clicked the cap. He snatched the file from Tony like it would lead him to a pot of gold and signed with a quick and eager hand.

Tony cleared his throat, halfway reaching for the bundle. "Usually we go over the papers first."

Oliver's lips bent in a practiced smile. He twisted beyond Tony's reach like the caseworker was a filthy puppy begging for a table scrap. "It's all the same, don't worry. We've done this before."

Quinn buried his hands into his lap and scanned his new home while Tony handed Quinn's life to another master. While Quinn surveyed the room, he noticed a staircase opposite the couch. A boy leaned against the top step, a dark silhouette that teased only the barest details from his body. He leaned against the wall like a lazy statue, and Quinn knew the strange boy watched him even though he couldn't see his eyes. Tony chatted with Oliver and Patty for a few more minutes, and for each and every passing second, the mysterious boy stared from his dark perch.

Quinn hated Tupper Lake. He had a feeling he really wouldn't like the Watkins family, either.

It's a Hard Knock Life

Quinn missed Tony terribly. Watching his caseworker leave the Watkins' home in his ratty sedan marked the beginning of Quinn's miserable life with his third miserable foster family. One awful chore after another dripped from Oliver's lips like poison. The man woke Quinn before sunrise and hovered over him until the sky turned into one great black bruise around the moon's eye. Oliver's wife put all the good things she had to say on a fork and ate them and instead peppered Quinn with an endless buffet of leftover insults and snide remarks. But neither of them compared to their son, Ryley Watkins.

"How's it going, Quinn?" the boy asked.

Quinn swallowed, his fingers trembling on the tragically scarred school desk in the corner of his shoebox of a bedroom. He stared out his single cloudy windowpane at the gold and red leaves carpeting the early autumn landscape and prayed that when he turned around, Ryley Watkins would poof out of existence, or better yet, never have existed in the first place.

But of course Ryley would be there when he turned around. For a heartbeat, Quinn considered jumping through the glass. He couldn't. For one, he'd hurt himself. For another, Oliver would punish him. And Tony said he had no more chances. If he wanted to survive, he'd have to accept the Watkins and all the gleeful evil they showered on him.

"What do you want, Ryley?" Quinn asked.

Ryley rested his forearms on Quinn's shoulders. His breath toyed with Quinn's hair and tickled his ear. "Did you finish my homework like I asked?"

Quinn slowly nodded. "And you promise not to blame me, right?"

Ryley's chuckle washed over his neck. "I promise, don't worry."

Relief rushed from Quinn's lips, carried on a sigh. He slouched and smiled at the desk face. "Thank you."

"Don't thank me. Not yet, at least."

Quinn spun around. Ryley grinned. Quinn's foster brother parted his hair with mathematical precision, and his eyes glittered with a hunger that would always want more than their share. His skin was taught over his pointed jaw, and his cheeks were sun-kissed from days spent making trouble while Quinn picked up the slack.

"Why?" Quinn lurched from his chair, his pulse racing. "What did I do? You promised. I—I can't get in trouble. Please, Ryley. I didn't do anything. Not a single thing."

Ryley rushed him. He grabbed Quinn's neck and squeezed so hard Quinn's pulse throbbed against his fingertips. "Keep it that way. Know your place, orphan boy, and you won't get in any trouble."

He laughed and let go. With a wink he sauntered into the hall and whistled a tune that made Quinn's skin crawl. Quinn rubbed his throat and glared at the empty doorway. Ryley had something planned. He always had something planned.

Quinn finished Ryley's homework but hadn't touched his own. He propped his elbows on the desk and buried his face against his palms, listening to his hot breaths wash over his cheeks. Ryley had demanded Quinn handle each and every subject, quiz, and paper Patty assigned them. At first, Quinn chalked it up to Ryley being just as lazy and mean as his parents. It turned out, though, that while Quinn did Ryley's schoolwork, Ryley studied something else entirely.

Ryley would lock himself inside his room early each afternoon, his desk lamp bleeding light from the crack beneath his bedroom door until stars twinkled and the moon shone high over Tupper Lake. And even though the Watkins rained praise and attention on their son, they still believed children should live simple lives and as such should never have a TV or toys or games distracting them while inside their rooms.

Quinn wondered what might keep Ryley up so late in a room so sparse, and so he kept his eye out for any hint of what treasures might hide inside, patiently waiting for the day Ryley forgot to lock the door. A few weeks after Quinn's first day with the Watkins, it finally happened.

Ryley's door hung ajar, a crack as wide as Quinn revealing the interior. He crept to the doorframe and peeked inside. Ryley had a desk much like Quinn's, but instead of textbooks on Algebra and US History, old and dusty tomes piled high on Ryley's desk. They wore their leather covers like they'd circled the globe on sailboats and passed through many hands, and they bore titles of people and places Quinn had never heard before.

Quinn would have opened one of the books and peered at its ancient pages had footsteps not interrupted his sneaking. He dashed back into his room just in time, and from that day on the mystery of Ryley's studies teased Quinn's thoughts until sleep overcame him.

In a weird way, Quinn enjoyed the double schoolwork. The more time Ryley spent in his own room, the more time Quinn had to himself. He loved losing himself in his books, too. Homework was a fortress with walls none of the Watkins could climb. Ryley, Patty, and even Oliver let him be while he worked on the piles of mathematics and geometry lessons that were as numerous as snowflakes in Antarctica.

But most of all, homework was an escape hatch from the life he lived. Nobody believed in him in Tupper Lake. Nobody expected he'd ever amount to anything. Spend enough time buried in books, and one day he'd show them all.

"Ryley!" Patty shouted, jerking Quinn from his studies. "Quinn! Dinnertime!"

Ryley's footsteps pounded downstairs. Quinn waited for a moment, taking a peaceful second to stare at the bare walls. He thought about putting something on them once, but changing a single piece of the room more to his liking would make that room his, even if it was just the tiniest of part of himself, and he could never accept that. He would never accept that. Sighing, he scooted from his desk and trudged downstairs.

Quinn joined his foster family in the kitchen. They sat around an old oak dining table, none of them caring to wait for Quinn before they started dinner. Patty had picked up fried chicken with potatoes and green beans from the store. The food smelled like rich butter and honey, and they'd been charitable enough to leave a drumstick for Quinn along with the bowl of oatmeal he typically received for dinner. He asked once why he couldn't eat what they ate. Oliver replied cold as ice that a good meal was earned and he hadn't earned it. Despite how many chores Quinn did or how perfectly he did them, he never earned what they ate.

Quinn quietly took his seat. He grabbed his drumstick and munched on his dinner with his head down while Patty chatted about her day.

"...I can't believe it's finally time, Ollie. We've been waiting so long to see how our little man does. To think, all these years are finally going to start paying off. I just don't understand why they want both of them—"

"Hold on, Hon," Oliver said. Patty flinched.

Quinn looked up from his meal. She quickly recovered with a smile and sealed her lips, her dark eyes flicking toward him.

"What's happening?" Quinn asked. "What're you talking about?"

Ryley grinned, cocking his head. "It's nothing for you to worry about."

Oliver cleared his throat. He propped his elbows on the table and rested his chin on the hammock of his fingers. "You've been disappointing me lately, Quinn. You know that?"

Quinn closed his eyes and wished himself away. "How's that, sir?"

"You haven't finished your chores, so of course you'll do double duty tomorrow to make up for the slack. It baffles me how you can be so lazy. Ryley gets his chores done early every day. What's so hard about finishing a few simple things to show the appreciation for all the blessings we've given you?"

Quinn glanced at Ryley, clenching his jaw. The boy had a smear of a smile on his face. It didn't hurt that Quinn really had finished his chores—and most of Ryley's to boot. It hurt that no matter how hard he tried, they never let him think for even the blink of an eye or the beat of a heart that Quinn Lynch was part of the Watkins family.

"I'm sorry," he murmured.

"Excuse me?" Oliver's jaw clenched, his eyebrow sliding up his rounded forehead.

"I'm sorry, *sir*."

"That's better." Oliver leaned back, his tongue sliding across his teeth. "Patty says your homework is subpar at best. So that means you've got no work ethic or book smarts. How do you think you'll ever get ahead in life without one or the other? Luck? The world ran out of luck a long time ago."

"I don't know. Honestly." The only future Quinn cared about was the one that got him out of that house. Everything after would be icing on the cake.

Oliver grabbed his fork and jabbed it at Quinn. "You aren't going anywhere fast. Your case file said you were intelligent, but you haven't showed it in the least. We didn't even want you, not with Ryley being so special and all, but they practically demanded it. Don't ask me how, but that caseworker of yours knew how to jump through hoops of red tape better than any acrobat I've ever seen at a circus."

Patty took a chunk out of a chicken thigh, and bits of greasy batter stuck between her teeth. "That caseworker of his probably forged his documents. In fact, the more I think about it, the more I'm sure that's what happened. Probably wanted to get the little snot out of his own hair as fast as he could. You know, Quinn, if you could just try and be more like Ryley your life would be much easier."

Quinn shuddered. Be more like Ryley? If Patty knew how Ryley tortured the bugs in the yard, she might rethink her opinion. Or maybe she'd sprinkle her worries on a scoop of ice cream and bury them deep inside her belly.

"He can't help it, Mom," Ryley said, addressing the table like a politician. "You know how foster kids are. They're just not like us. Their parents were trash, not like you guys. Not like real parents."

Quinn slammed the table, red edging his vision. "My parents were not trash! Don't you ever call them that again!" He hated the hot tears swirling in his eyes, but calling his parents trash, saying they were anything but the best thing that ever happened to him, that was something Quinn would never take.

Patty gasped. Ryley shook his head. Oliver cut a piece of chicken and savored the bite, his glare nailed to Quinn. No one spoke. They simply watched Oliver eat his food and waited.

Mr. Watkins swallowed his bite and wiped the corner of his lips with a paper towel. "How dare you raise your voice at this table," he said, his voice terrifyingly calm.

Quinn blinked. He clenched his fists in his lap to keep them still.

The man left his seat and circled the table until he stood behind Quinn. Quinn sucked in a breath, the weight of Oliver's eyes like railroad spikes hammered onto his shoulders.

Oliver pinched Quinn's ear with his crab's claw of a hand and yanked him from the seat. "You are a degenerate, you know that? We offer you a home, feed you, teach you, and you throw this disgustingly inappropriate tantrum at dinner? How dare you. Even after Ryley convinced us that you could have a drumstick tonight, that maybe you finally deserved it."

"I apologize, sir." His glare shot to Ryley. The drumstick was no peace offering. It was bait to drop Quinn's guard so Ryley could set him off with an insult he knew Quinn hated.

"You better." Oliver dragged him from the kitchen. Ryley tossed another wink Quinn's way just before Quinn turned the corner.

Oliver and Quinn reached the upstairs hallway. Oliver shoved him in his room and grabbed the dingy brass knob. "You're on thin ice, mister."

"I'm sorry. It's just my parents—"

"Are dead. Died in a fire, a fire some suspect you set. You realize that, right? So when that temper of yours flares up, it doesn't exactly make you look like an angel."

Quinn's eyes watered. His chin trembled. "I did not start that fire."

"That's not my point. You want to prove your parents weren't trash? Stop acting like it and learn some manners." He straightened, scowling down his pointed nose. "We could ruin you. At any moment, I could pick up the phone and send you straight to youth detention. You think I want that?"

"No."

"Good, because I don't…But I'll do it if I have to. Don't forget that."

Quinn met Oliver's glare with his own. "Do you care about me?"

Oliver recoiled. He blinked, laughing. "What kind of question is that?"

"I mean do you care? Do you like me at all? It's hard but—I am trying. I want to be something more one day. I really do."

"Hm." Oliver twisted the doorknob, pursing his lips. "Good luck with that. The odds aren't in your favor, Quinn. That's just the card you've been dealt and the system you're in. You wake up at six tomorrow and get started on the list I'll slip under the door."

He slammed the door and locked it from the outside. Quinn tucked his legs against his chest and buried his face into his knees. Tears threatened, but he swallowed them and straightened instead. A geometry textbook lay open at the foot of the bed. He grabbed it and lost himself in the beautifully perfect patterns and shapes decorating their pages. They were cold, hard things, but they spoke a language that never lied and explained the world in ways that always made sense. If he could learn it well enough, maybe he'd find out how to put Tupper Lake and the Watkins behind him.

Surprise!

The following days at the Watkins' terrified Quinn more than the entire time he'd spent so far at his third foster family's home. Not because Oliver worked him any harder or Patty needled him with any more insults, but because Ryley had been sweet.

Ryley's words were maple syrup slathered on buttered pancakes, and his smiles a cinnamon roll fresh from the oven on a frosty morning. He even offered to help Quinn with a few chores here and there. But at night, the boy would still lock himself inside his room, light washing the floorboards in a warm glow. Quinn heard odd sounds, too, and every so often, he swore an odd light would flare from Ryley's room and paint the hallway in different colors.

Quinn frowned and closed his bedroom door, catching a fleeting flash of red brightening the border of Ryley's. Oliver would come to lock Quinn's door any minute, the only sign of the man's passing the floorboards croaking like a fat frog beneath his footsteps.

Quinn grabbed his notepad and began sketching shapes, reclining against his old metal headboard. He scrawled geometric patterns so perfect they would impress anyone who might see them. Squares formed neat, ninety-degree angles with sides straighter than a desert horizon. Triangles ended in perfect angles. Lines curved in smooth, consistent paths until they connected in interlocking circles. It made sense to Quinn. It all made so much sense. Shapes were constants. He could look at any object in the world and see the geometry that formed it. From the bend of a grasshopper's legs, to the splaying branches of an old oak, to the sun's rays bursting from behind a rumbling thunderhead, it all made sense through geometry.

A familiar rhythmic squeak alerted him to Oliver's approach. Quinn watched his door, waiting for the lock to click. It didn't. Instead, the knob twisted, and the door parted with an irritated creak.

Quinn straightened, his heart rapping against his ribs. Oliver had never come into his room before unless he'd angered the man, and for the life of Quinn, he couldn't think of anything he might have done.

"What can I do for you, sir?" Quinn asked, casually trying to straighten the mess of schoolwork before Oliver noticed.

Oliver noticed the mess almost immediately. The man scowled at the textbooks and doodles carpeting Quinn's bed and desk. "You're room's a disaster. And what's this you've been hiding? Why are you drawing these shapes? How did you learn to draw these?" His voice rose with each question, the trembling rage frothing in his throat coloring his cheeks red.

"Sorry, I, uh, I just do," Quinn said. "It's my favorite subject, and I—"

"Give me your books and drawings. Give them to me *now*."

"What?" Quinn flinched, eyes darting over his nest of papers. "All of them?"

"Yes. And you'll be staying up until midnight cleaning. Maybe then you'll learn how to keep a room."

"But—"

Oliver's face tightened. "What did I say?"

Quinn rolled off his bed. He gathered his notes, his drawings, and his worn textbooks. This wasn't fair. They were his only escape, his only hope, and now a suspicion slithered up his spine like a snake up an old oak that he might never see them again. "Please, if I'm good, can I have them back? I'm trying to make myself something, like you said. Just—I'm trying to learn, and my books, they mean so much to me."

"If you're good, you can have them back. I'm not a cruel man, Quinn."

But Oliver *was* a cruel man, and believing Oliver would ever return Quinn's books was like believing a thief who said he just wanted to borrow a treasure to polish the coins. Quinn collected all the books and notes and drawings into a teetering paper tower cradled in his arms. He sniffed, the faint scent of worn laminate kissing him goodbye.

"Now," Oliver said, "follow me downstairs. You'll scrub the floors until midnight."

Downstairs Mr. Watkins locked Quinn's life, his treasure, and his secrets of the world inside a metal cabinet. The man sat in a dining chair and watched Quinn scrub the graying grout between the milky kitchen tiles. Hours lumbered on until Quinn's arms throbbed and his nose burned from the vinegar cleaner bubbling between his red and raw fingers.

"It's midnight now." Oliver stood, his shadow falling over Quinn. "Follow me to your room."

"Can I wash up?"

Oliver laughed. He bent and clenched Quinn's shoulder. The man yanked him to his feet and shoved Quinn toward the stairs. "Get into your room."

The lock to Quinn's bedroom clicked. Quinn sighed. He stared at the pathetic emptiness of his walls. He had nothing now. No books to read, nothing to draw, and only the reek of his vinegar fingers burning his nostrils. He buried his head into his pillow and fell into a deep, exhausted sleep.

* * *

"Get up." Ryley's voice drifted into Quinn's ears like a slow poison. "You'd better not make me late. Mom has breakfast waiting for you. It's your lucky day. I hope you're ready!"

Quinn blinked. Ryley came into focus. The boy sat at the foot of Quinn's bed, hair parted with the cold perfection of a plastic doll and smile to match. He wore a pressed scarlet button up and navy slacks, and he oozed bargain bin cologne.

"Wh—what?" Quinn glanced out his narrow window. The sky lightened to a pale grey, the last bright stars snuffed out by a sun stirring just below the horizon. "Why are you dressed like that?"

"Because it's test day, dummy." Ryley smacked Quinn's leg, and he flinched at the hot flash and throbbing echo the boy's palm left behind.

"Test?" Quinn rubbed sleep from his eyes and blinked. "What're you talking about?"

Ryley cocked his head and pouted. "Oh, you mean you didn't know? We've both been selected to take a new test, a very special test for very special students—or at least for students who might be a certain kind of special. We've got to take it today, both of us. Mom and Dad tried to get you out of it on account of you being you and all, but they said there weren't any exceptions."

Quinn shot up. "Test? Today?"

In that moment, everything that had happened to Quinn made complete, cruel sense. Why lately Ryley had been something less of a monster, why Oliver barged in and took his books the night before, and why he made Quinn clean until midnight. They knew about the test, and they worked together to make sure Quinn failed miserably when he took it.

Ryley hopped to his feet and made his way toward the door. "Better hurry. We get picked up in fifteen minutes." He bowed, backing into the hallway before darting out of sight.

"No, no, no…" Quinn's heart raced. His walls shrank. Sweat beaded on his temples. There was only one reason he could think of that the Watkins would do this to him. Whatever this test was, whatever it determined, it meant freedom.

Quinn clenched his fists, digging them like drills into his blanket. Nothing the Watkins did would keep him from breaking free of that horrible, evil place.

He bolted to his dresser and pulled out a change of clothes. His only clean shirt was so wrinkled it could have been papier-mâché, and the armpits and collar had rings of yellowed stains from long, sweaty days of cleaning brush and trimming hedges throughout Oliver Watkins' unhappy kingdom. Quinn struggled into his shirt and slipped into his jeans. His pants were so old they'd lost most of their blue and settled into a shade of old lake water. Any day now he'd wear a hole completely through the right knee.

He struggled into his hoodie and zipped it up. He smoothed the sweater, inspecting his reflection in the small mirror above his dresser. His hair was tangled like an old bird's nest above eyes ringed with puffy circles. His outfit screamed second rate. He shook his head and memorized that reflection. The Watkins wanted him to fail, but if he passed, it could be the last time he ever saw the disappointing boy staring at him through the mirror.

Quinn brushed his teeth and wet his hair. He sprinted downstairs and found Ryley finishing a breakfast of cereal, bacon, and eggs. A small bowl of oatmeal glop waited for Quinn. Knowing Patty, it had waited awhile.

Patty grinned like a witch who'd just trapped a child in her candy cabin. "You better hurry, Quinn. The van's almost here. If you'd just gotten up at a decent time like dear Ryley, maybe you wouldn't be so—I don't know—*that*." She rolled her hand at him, grimacing out of the corner of her eye.

He ignored her and shoveled down the cold oatmeal. Not a grain of sugar or dollop of butter gave the muck flavor, and it rolled down his throat like half-dried glue. On his last bite, a horn blared. He downed a huge glass of water in a chain of glugging gulps and wiped the last droplets from his lips before plopping the empty glass on the table.

Ryley sprinted for the door first. Quinn scooted from his own seat and stood. Sleep still dulled his thoughts, but with each breath he took, they came clearer. He didn't know why, but he knew he could beat this test because he knew he could beat the Watkins.

"Quinn?" Patty's voice was oddly soft.

Quinn paused. "Sorry, thank you for breakfast, Patty."

"You'll never do well." She wrapped her icy words in a velvet tongue. "This test has been a long time coming. Ryley knows what's really being tested today, but you have no idea what this is about. You don't know how important this test is to our boy, how this will finally change me and Ollie's lives forever. We've spent years preparing Ryley for this. What have you done? Nothing. I've seen your studying, how you draw geometry like you're some little Einstein and think you know what it really means. I'm burning it soon as you walk out this door. All of it. You'll come back to nothing because that's all you deserve."

He swallowed. "You don't know I'll fail. I might pass."

"No," she said with a chuckle. "I do. You'll fail. You'll fail because it's impossible for you to pass. We made sure it was." She brushed a wide, shiny fingernail over her eyebrow and pursed her lips. "Ollie's done with you, you know. He doesn't need to keep you here after the test. Once Ryley aces it, well, you just won't be worth the trouble anymore."

"Is that why you took me in? So I could do his homework and his chores while he studied for—for whatever this test thing is?"

"No, no. That was just a happy byproduct of you being dumped into our laps." Patty batted her long lashes. "We took you in because they made it impossible for us to refuse. But after today, that won't matter. After today, you won't be worth much at all, and we'll make it our mission to find a way to toss you back into whatever garbage bin you crawled from. Think about that while you take your test."

Quinn clenched his jaw. He spun, running through the living room and out the front door. His body shook. He sniffled and wiped his nose. His feet crunched on the gravel while a crisp August wind cooled his burning cheeks.

A van waited in the drive, an old clunker of a car with a dent above its back wheel and a cracked windshield. Quinn slid the door open. Ryley waited inside, buckled in the front row. A redheaded girl with a face full of freckles and round glasses sat beside him. A mouse of a boy with greasy hair plastered above his blinking eyes sat in the middle row. In the last row sat another girl with feathers woven in her blond locks and a look in her glimmering eyes that said her mind never spent much time in the world where she lived.

The driver craned his neck around and glared at Quinn. He was middle-aged with a scraggly, hay-blond mop drooped over his wide ears. "You're late," he rasped, his smoky voice laced with an accent that could only come from Brooklyn. "Get in, boss, the wind's cuttin' right through my sweater and this heater's giving me agita."

Quinn jumped inside and closed the door. He took a seat beside the mousy boy and tucked his hands into his lap while the driver turned on the radio. The engine rumbled, and the wheels squealed. They rolled down the drive, the Watkins' home shrinking behind them.

"Where are we going?" Quinn asked his neighbor.

The boy frowned, his arrowhead nose shrinking into a wrinkled wedge. "Didn't you know?" His high voice had the air of someone who knew it all but would never waste his energy sharing his knowledge because nobody would understand him anyway. "Up north in Potsdam. There's a testing center at the university there."

"Have you—have you studied? I don't exactly know what the test is about."

The boy snickered. "Of course I studied. My mom and dad said it might be the most important test I ever take, because, you know..."

"No, I don't know."

"So you can't...?" He traced a circle with his finger.

"Draw? Do sign language? I can draw pretty well, but I don't know sign."

The boy scooted closer to his window with his lip curled like Quinn reeked of hot garbage. "You're probably one of those, then."

"One of what?"

"Either you'll find out or you won't. It all depends on your score." He crossed his arms and stared out the dust and snow-coated pane. "Listen, I really need to get in the right headspace. Do you mind?"

Quinn leaned against the cold seat. He hadn't studied a single thing. He had no idea what was even on this test. Literature? Algebra? Biology? If he just knew, if he just had a hint, maybe he could find a way to prepare.

The girl behind him tapped his shoulder. He swiveled around and forced a smile. She grinned back, her teeth happy rows of porcelain. She brushed a golden braid behind her ear and leaned on her elbows. "You worry too much about it."

"But I haven't studied. I don't know what I'm doing or even what this is all about."

She rolled her eyes. "Who cares? Don't let the stress get to you. You just have to, I don't know, *flow*. Like I do. I'm Hydrangea Grace, by the way."

She thrust a hand capped by multicolor fingernails at him. He took it, and they shook. "Quinn Lynch. That's an interesting name, Hydrangea. Like the flower, right?"

Her eyes lit like fresh stars. "Exactly! My mom's kind of obsessed with flowers and pretty things, and the hydrangea's her favorite. It's a mouthful, though, so really only she calls me by my full name. You can totally call me Heidi. Everybody else does."

"Nice to meet you, Heidi. Do you…do you know what's on the test?"

The mousey boy whipped around and jabbed a needle of a finger at Quinn's new friend. "I swear I'll tell if you tell him. You know we can't. It's against the rules to tell anyone who may be—you know."

"You're such a little weed, Billy." She stuck out her tongue and reclined against her seat, yawning. "Sorry, Quinn, I can't. We get in big trouble if we do. Big trouble. Maybe after the test though, depending on your score. Like I said, don't worry about studying. It's the only test in the world that isn't really about what you know. It's about what you can do, that's what matters. That's what they'll be looking for."

"But why can't you—"

"Hey!" The driver snapped around, glaring at Quinn. "Be quiet back there. Billy, Heidi, you know the rules. No fraternizing until after the test."

Ryley turned and pressed a finger to his lips. "Do you have to ruin everything?"

Quinn swallowed the angry ember smoldering in his throat. He crossed his arms and slammed against the seat with a huff. The Watkins had done a brilliant job of keeping Quinn in the dark. He glared out his own window.

They turned onto a two-lane highway walled by mottled evergreens stretching to the horizon.

4

Pop Quiz in Potsdam

Several other vans arrived at the State University of New York at Potsdam exactly when Quinn's arrived. Students poured out of sliding doors, some more quickly than others. The school itself looked like the picture-perfect college campus. Long brick buildings two and three stories tall surrounded an inner campus crisscrossed by wide sidewalks. Their driver ushered them with the other tittering lines of kids to the largest building, an old colonial hulk three stories tall with grand, arched windows and a white clock tower capped by a small dome.

"Welcome to Satterlee Hall," their driver said, grabbing the bronze handle. He pushed the dark doors apart and motioned inside. "Your test'll be in the first classroom on the left. Go on now, and good luck. I hope all youse got plenty talent to go around."

He herded them inside, and they spilled into the hallway, feet clicking and clacking and tapping on the polished tiles. Ryley reached the classroom first and rushed inside. The line followed him like they'd been chained at their ankles.

Quinn rolled his wrists until they popped. Something about the motion eased his nerves, like twisting a soda cap a little at a time before taking a drink so it wouldn't explode. He sat in the back desk in the very back corner and stared at the pencil and answer sheet waiting for him.

Quinn squirmed in his desk. It was an old wooden thing with *Jessica* carved near the top beside a rough heart, and its stubbornly thick plastic seat dug into his back. He traced the girl's name with his fingernail and tried not to think about how much he hated the Watkins for doing this to him.

Other kids from other vans filled the classroom, seven columns and five rows. The heater next to Quinn rumbled and belched hot air across his cheek. He sighed, grabbing the pencil with white knuckles.

Not a single one of his classmates would tell him what the test would be about, no matter how hard he tried. For a brief moment, he even considered asking Ryley but decided the boy would either lie or tell him some twisted version of the truth meant to make him do even worse.

The classroom door parted and smacked the wall behind it. A man entered, papers tucked beneath his arm. He wore a grey sweater and coal-grey slacks that matched the round grey eyes peeking from the messy mop of his midnight hair. "Good morning students! My name is Egon Pennington, and I'll be your administrator on this clear, crisp morning. And what a beautiful one it is, isn't it? Autumn should be such a delight this year."

Quinn frowned. What an odd man, to be so cheery yet dressed like he'd never seen a color before. A woman entered shortly after wearing glasses high up her long nose and hair pulled into a tight biscuit of a bun atop her head. Her pantsuit shimmered blue as a mountain lake, and her heels clicked on the linoleum with each confident step she took. She grabbed a seat by the door and placed a plain leather briefcase in her lap.

Egon clapped his hands. "And this is Ms. Cynthia Doyle. She'll be ensuring a fair and accurate test taking experience for all, and I assure anyone who might be considering less than scrupulous methods for passing this test, Ms. Doyle's eyes can make hawks jealous." Egon shuffled through his papers, his shoulders dancing to a tune only he could hear. "Now, let's get started."

He traced a little square with his index finger and snapped. The blinds on the windows dropped and blocked the morning light. Quinn jumped as one smacked the windowsill. He stared at the wobbling blind and blinked. "How?" he whispered, whipping around.

Ms. Doyle lurched from her seat. "Mr. Pennington!"

"What? It was bright," he said, a sheepish smile on his cheeks.

She cleared her throat and shot quick glances at Ryley and Quinn. "Because, Mr. Pennington. We have guests. The ones from Tupper Lake."

His face paled. He swallowed. "You mean—in this test?"

Ms. Doyle sighed like Egon was a pup she'd just watched tinkle on the rug. Students traded glances, searching for the mysterious guests from Tupper Lake. Quinn slid deeper in his seat.

Egon cleared his throat and grabbed the papers. They trembled like insect wings in his unsteady grip. "Let's—let's get started on the exam, then! There are no right or wrong answers on this test. We're looking for the answers we need, and that can change according to the wind, really." His gaze settled on Quinn. "Or the person."

"So what happens if we're what you're looking for?" Quinn asked, startling himself. The words tumbled out like they'd been pulled on a line.

The class snickered. His cheeks blazed, and he slouched so low, any further and he'd slide onto the floor. Everyone now knew the boy in the back with the loose hoodie and worn jeans was the guest from Tupper Lake.

Mr. Pennington licked his lips and forced a smile. "Why, ah, you get to live at a very fine school and learn some very fine things."

"Live? At a school?" The words lit up Quinn's thoughts like fireworks.

Ms. Doyle cleared her throat. "That's enough. Everything will be explained once you successfully pass the exam."

"And if we don't pass?" Quinn asked. "What happens then?"

"Then you won't need to ask any more questions, because we'll have no answers to give," she snapped.

He straightened and nodded. Pass this test, and the Watkins would become a memory. No more slaving away for Oliver. No more insults from Patty. No more torture from Ryley.

Quinn squeezed his pencil. He wanted freedom. He'd do anything for it. He believed in himself, and no matter what happened, he'd make sure this morning would be his last with the Watkins.

* * *

Quinn dropped his pencil with a sigh, leaning against the stiff chair so it dug deep into his back. The answer sheet stared at him from beneath the dulled nub of his pencil. His answers tattooed the sheet with little black bubbles, many erased over and over again before the he finally settled on a choice.

The other children finished long before Quinn, Ryley first among them. The boy sat with a smile split like a happy cat's when it sees a mouse. For his part, Quinn thought he knew some of the answers. After all, he'd studied geometry for hours upon hours. Yet, the test he had just taken wasn't over the kind of geometry he recognized or understood, even though something about it felt annoyingly familiar.

He knew mathematics and how to calculate curves, lines, and angles, but nothing the test asked made sense. Every answer was off by just a hair, and in math, a hair off ruins the whole thing. It was like the test spoke to him using a language Quinn thought he'd always known, but the first time it came his turn to use it, he realized he'd gotten the whole thing wrong.

Ms. Doyle peered at him through her spectacles. The glare hid her eyes, but he felt them just the same. Quinn swallowed and maneuvered himself behind the column of students and out of her sight and waited for Mr. Pennington to address the class.

Minutes passed. The small clock behind Mr. Pennington's desk ticked in a steady beat.

Quinn shifted uncomfortably. The oversized glass of water from breakfast had worked its way through him, and his bladder begged for a bathroom break. He inhaled through his nose and clenched his teeth.

A small bell on Egon's desk rang. On cue, Mr. Pennington and Ms. Doyle rose. They marched lockstep down each aisle, collecting answer sheets in perfect unison. Mr. Pennington came to Quinn last. The man cast a weak smile and hesitated, his fingers dancing over Quinn's answers.

"I hope I passed," Quinn said. "I really do."

Mr. Pennington's pale cheeks reddened, and his knot of an Adam's apple bobbed down his throat. He slipped Quinn's paper into the pile of others and smiled weakly. "Ms. Doyle will make the announcements during lunch." He turned, but paused before he shuffled off. "It's not the end of the world if you don't, trust me on that. All you can do is hope you tried your best."

"Thanks, Mr. Pennington."

Egon glanced at the clock, rushing to the front of the classroom. "Thank you all so very much. Lunch has been provided in the university cafeteria. If you'll wait there, we should have your results soon. I'm sure…"

Ms. Doyle stepped forward, hands clasped tightly before her. "…I'm sure you'll all do exactly as you're meant to."

They left the room. Children stood, smiling and slapping each other on the back. Quinn got to his feet and tried speaking with the redheaded girl who rode on the van, but she recoiled like he'd been set on fire and rushed from the room without so much a word with anyone else.

Heidi chewed on a lock of her hair and met Quinn's eyes. She flashed a smile and strolled toward him, weaving between the other students like a ballerina.

"How'd you do?" he asked her.

She shrugged, coiling a blond lock around her finger. "Exactly as I was meant to. That's all we can ever do, right? Most—well, all of us pretty much knew what we were doing when we came here. It's rare to have guests like you, so most years they usually don't even bother having us take the test."

"I think everyone aced it but me. I just—I tried, but I don't know. It was familiar, but different."

"No one aces it, Quinn. This test isn't about right or wrong or letter grades. It's about telling them something about what you are, about what you can do. You'll understand soon enough." She pursed her lips and eyed the ceiling. "Or maybe you won't?"

"I don't get you. Any of you."

"You may soon. Or you may not. I kind of hope you do. You seem like a nice guy, and most of the people who grew up like we—like they did, they think they're better than the people who aren't like them, and that makes most of them about as fun as a face full of poison ivy, if that makes any sense."

"I think it does," he said, scratching the back of his neck. "I've got to run to the bathroom. Meet you in the cafeteria?"

"I'll save you a seat." She hooked her arm in his and led Quinn toward the door. "If you need to go to the bathroom, there's one down the hall and to the right. Just after some faculty offices. The cafeteria's on the opposite end of the hall. I've been here a couple times with my mom. She likes to people watch on years where there's a test, so I know the place pretty well."

They parted in the hallway. With her directions, he scurried to the bathroom and slipped inside. Cracks ran like rivers on a map across the floor's beige tiles, and the stalls were a sad state of bluish grey, the color of a fresh bruise.

He paused halfway to a stall as the bathroom door creaked behind him. Quinn glanced over his shoulder in time for Ryley's backhand to smack his cheek. Quinn stumbled back, blinded, face hot and pulsing. He hit a stall at an angle and winced. Ryley slammed his hands against Quinn's chest and pressed him against the wall.

Quinn shielded his face, still reeling from the ambush. "What're you doing? Stop!"

Ryley grabbed Quinn's hoodie and shoved him harder against the wall. Quinn struggled, but Ryley had more than a few pounds on him.

"What did you do?" Ryley asked, leaning into Quinn's face.

"Nothing. What're you talking about?"

"No one in there will talk to me. They act like I'm some kind of freak. I'm not a freak. I'm not like you."

"I didn't do anything. I—I just took the test like everybody else."

Ryley laughed. "And I bet you failed. Mom and Dad said you would. They said you'd never beat me." Ryley kneed Quinn's groin.

Quinn doubled over and coughed. A deep ache flowered in his stomach.

Ryley laughed harder. "You're so pathetic. You're never going to win at anything, not while I'm around."

Quinn clenched his teeth. He breathed through his nose and stared at the floor. He hated Ryley. *Hated* him.

"And you know what?" Ryley asked. "Now that I've taken the test nobody needs you anymore."

Quinn glared at the cracks in the tile, the pain from Ryley's knee fading from his stomach. "I…"

"That's right, nobody needs you. You're going to youth detention. I'm going to make sure of it. I think I'll kill a squirrel and hang it somewhere around the house. I'll blame you. They'll believe me, of course, because I'm me and you're you. Dad'll send you straight to juvie. How do you like that?" Ryley grabbed Quinn's hair and wrenched his head up. "How do you like that, orphan boy?"

"If I pass the test—"

"You won't pass the test, stupid." He laughed, shaking his head. "You don't get it. Only one of us can pass the test. That's what they said. Both had to take it, but only one can go, and I know for sure it's me. I'm done with you. Done.

No matter what happens, you're not going to that school and you're not staying with Mom and Dad. Understand?"

There was nothing Quinn could do. His blood pressure rose, his heartbeat pounding. Ryley had ensured he suffered, not because Quinn deserved it, but because that's what Ryley wanted. They used Quinn. They tortured him and they used him and now they'd throw him away. "I…"

"I'm going to have so much fun at the new school. I'm going to learn it all. Then, I'm going to find you, and I'm going to make you kiss my shoes. I'll show you what you missed, and you'll know then and there just what a nothing you are compared to me."

A tear slid down the bridge of Quinn's nose and collected on the tip. He clenched his fists. His blood ignited, and he snapped, punching Ryley's cheek just below his eye. The boy gave a satisfying yelp and fell on his back. His cheek blushed from cherry to plum and swelled.

"Then I guess there's nothing stopping me anymore, is there?" Quinn bent over Ryley and grabbed the boy's hair like Ryley had done seconds before. "I never wanted to hurt you. I—I tried to be your friend. You wouldn't let me. You made every day worse than the last. But I'm done with it, Ryley. I'm done with you and your stupid mom and your ignorant dad. Done. If you're not afraid of fire now, come at me again and you will be. You know what they say about me. You want a taste of that?"

Quinn tore out of the bathroom, the door swinging behind him. It was like he'd been carrying a car around and just then threw it off his shoulders. If his life as he knew it was about to end anyway, he wanted Ryley to remember that moment forever.

He passed the faculty offices and froze. The walls ended in windows that ran from Quinn's waist to the ceiling, giving him a clear view of who or what might be inside. He happened to notice Ms. Doyle and Mr. Pennington arguing in the last office. Egon waved his arms around and pointed outside. Ms. Doyle shook her head and yelled something muffled.

Frowning, Quinn tiptoed toward them. A door next to their office hung slightly ajar. Ducking beneath the walls, he slid beneath their office window and came to the empty office. Its door widened with Quinn's smile, and he padded into the dark room before quietly, carefully closing the door. The adults' voices drifted through a vent above a chair. Quinn hopped onto its thin padding and stood on the balls of his feet, listening to their argument through a vent spotted with rust and covered in a thin layer of lint and dust.

"Cynthia, I need you," Egon begged. "I don't know if I'm strong enough to fight them off."

"You know I can't leave the results here. What if something happens?"

"Like what?" Mr. Pennington asked, guffawing. "The children are all in the cafeteria eating. I need your help before they break the barrier. If those misfits do break through, these test results won't mean a thing, and if we truly have the potential one among us, that makes keeping them safe our highest priority."

Their conversation paused.

"Do you think it's really him?" Cynthia asked. "Something's off about him certainly, but if it's that I cannot say."

"Which one? Lynch or Watkins?"

"Watkins, who else? If one of them is the potential, it's him. It was clear that the Lynch boy didn't know what he was doing. He has no talent. He's not one of us."

Quinn's fingers dug into the metal vent. Her words were icy daggers that sunk deep into his chest.

"I'm not so certain," Egon said. "Sometimes, it's the less obvious ones you have to keep an eye on. They're smarter than you think, and I could see sharpness in Quinn's eyes when I took his test. He had the look of someone with talent in his eyes if you ask me."

"I guess we'll see once we scan the results—or more accurately, once the briefcase tells us who has the talent and who doesn't," she said.

"Help me take care of these misfits first, Cynthia! The drivers are doing their best, but there's too many of them. We can't cover the entire school grounds. We need you. I need you. Please."

A lull fell over their words. Quinn leaned into the vent, pressing his ear onto its sharp metal slats.

"Very well." Cynthia sighed. "Let me hide the tests. The briefcase should finish tabulating the results by the time we return."

Shuffling sounds drifted through the vent, followed by the click of a shutting door. Quinn waited a few extra seconds to ensure both teachers had left, all the while wondering what their conversation meant.

Satisfied they no longer occupied the office, he crept from his hiding spot. Part of him wanted to tell Heidi what he heard. Part of him wanted to follow them and see these misfits for himself.

…And part of him wanted to look inside the briefcase.

The thought crossed his mind like a sprinter tearing through the tape at the finish line. It beckoned him to their office, teased him with something so powerful Quinn could never resist its pull. And so, he slipped from the office where he hid and snuck to the door beside it.

Quinn exhaled when the doorknob twisted and the door parted at his push. He snuck inside and found the briefcase hastily shoved in one of the desk drawers. Crouching in a dark corner, Quinn grabbed the case and popped it open with trembling fingers. The answer sheets lay in a neat stack on the bottom while the lid bore an intricate geometric design etched into the leather. The symbol gleamed like it held the colors of a rainbow inside it, a spectrum washing over his fingers as they probed the shapes.

His gaze wandered to the first answer sheet. The pattern of the case reflected unnaturally brightly over the results. He checked the name. Not his. He flipped to the next sheet. Same pattern, same bright reflection. Not his name. He checked another, and then another, all with the same result.

Quinn peeked above the desk and into the empty hallway. He knew they would return any minute, and he still hadn't found his test. He thumbed through the papers and spotted Ryley's answers. Like the others, it reflected the case's pattern, but unlike the other kids, Ryley's paper blazed like a fire made of rainbows.

"No, it can't be…" Quinn wiped sweat from his brow and dried his shaking hand against his hoodie. One sheet remained below Ryley's. Quinn sucked in his breath and slid Ryley's paper aside.

The answer sheet sat against the case's leather back. No sign disturbed the paper. No brilliant lights leapt from the page. It was just a paper filled with all the wrong answers with Quinn's name scribbled in messy letters at the top.

"No. Please, please no." His heart sunk into his stomach.

The test should do something. It had to do something. If it didn't, he'd be stuck with the Watkins. Ryley would tell his parents what Quinn had done at the school, and he'd be on his way to youth detention that night. Tears watered his eyes. His chin trembled. It wasn't supposed to happen like this. He should be free. He deserved to be free.

He leaned over the case, cupping his head in his hands. "I give up. I just give up. I don't even care anymore."

Quinn took a deep breath. Something sharp poked his stomach. He winced, digging into his hoodie pocket until he clasped a pencil he must've forgotten he put inside his pocket. He pulled it out and rolled it in his fingers.

For most kids, the pencil was nothing more than an ordinary pencil with a dulled point and a pink eraser cap. For Quinn, it was the chance for freedom. Gritting his teeth, he quickly switched his name and Ryley's on the answer sheets. His heart beat so furiously he feared someone in the cafeteria would hear it. The room felt approximately as hot as the sun's heart, but Quinn smiled anyway.

Trembling with a witch's brew of terror and excitement, he stacked the tests into a neat pile. He shut the briefcase, its brass latches clicking together. He shoved it into the third drawer without a sound and padded to the hallway. No sign of the two teachers appeared beyond the office window.

"All clear," he whispered. Quinn slipped out and shut the door behind him.

Quinn forced down the lump in his throat and shoved his hands into his pockets. He marched down the hallway to the cafeteria, practicing a cool smile as he went. His conscious whispered its disappointment, but Quinn ignored it. By the time he found Heidi munching on a sandwich with the other kids, he'd convinced himself no one else could the guilt his heart screamed with each beat. Quinn took a seat and listened while Heidi chatted about the gardening techniques used in Kuala Lumpur and the wildflowers growing on the slopes of Machu Picchu. He smiled and nodded like he cared, but no matter how hard he tried, he couldn't keep his eyes from darting toward Ryley.

His foster brother glowered in a corner. Shadows hid his eyes. His cheek was a ripe plum. He stared at Quinn, unmoving, unblinking, exactly like he had the first day they met. Maybe today would be their last.

5

Goodbye Ryley, Hello Wimbly's

Cynthia Doyle click-clocked into the cafeteria with Mr. Pennington in tow. Strands of Ms. Doyle's hair fell in rebellious tendrils from her otherwise immaculate bun, and her pale knuckles had a peculiar hint of red blushing their smooth knobs. She smiled and slapped the briefcase onto a table facing the children. Opening it, she cleared her throat and surveyed the group from behind her round spectacles.

Quinn clenched his shirt. He licked his lips and listened.

"Let's get through these results, shall we?" she huffed as she took a deep breath.

Mr. Pennington clapped, his fingers tapping one another like nervous children at a dance. "Please do, Ms. Doyle, please do."

With the briefcase open, only Ms. Doyle and Mr. Pennington could see what lay within it. But Quinn knew. He knew, and it electrified him and terrified him at once.

Cynthia grabbed the first sheet. She held it to one of the fluorescent lights and nodded, scanning the room. "Billy Holcomb?"

The snotty boy with greasy hair stood, chin lifted. "Yes, ma'am?"

She pointed to her right. "Please stand here."

He nodded and scurried to her.

"Hydrangea Grace?" Ms. Doyle lifted a brow.

Heidi scooted from her chair, flashing her bright eyes. She patted Quinn's back. "Good luck," she whispered.

"Ms. Grace…" Cynthia gestured toward Billy. "Please join Mr. Holcomb."

Heidi did as she was told. She clasped her hands behind her and smiled like it was her first time seeing snow. Ms. Doyle continued through the stack of sheets, naming each child as she went. She called, they stood, and each one joined Ms. Doyle on her right. Sheet. Name. Join the rest. Sheet. Name. Join the rest. The cycle repeated until thirty-three children stood on Ms. Doyle's right and Quinn and Ryley waited in their chairs.

Ms. Doyle took a deep breath and adjusted her glasses. Mr. Pennington swallowed, and his knotty Adam's apple bobbed. Quinn snuck a peek at Ryley. The boy sat like a statue, his chin high, his purpled cheek shining like a medal on a soldier's chest.

Cynthia held the second to last sheet up to the light. A rainbow gleam reflected on her glasses. She stiffened, head snapping to attention. She and Mr. Pennington traded glances, and their lips parted in little pink ovals of surprise.

"Mr. Lynch, to my right," she said.

Quinn bolted from his seat. Adrenaline rushed through him, and his heart beat like a frightened hummingbird's wings. He clenched his fists and smiled as he took a place beside Heidi.

"I knew you could do it," Heidi said, her unruly hair tickling his ear.

Ms. Doyle held the last sheet to the light but hesitated instead of speaking.

Egon peeked over her shoulder. "I suppose that's that then," he murmured.

"Yes, I suppose it is," she said, clearing her throat. "Well then Mr. Watkins, to my left."

Ryley glared at Quinn with poison in his perfect eyes. He rubbed his swollen cheek, his chin quivering with the ferocity of a scorpion's tail. Standing, Ryley strolled to her left without so much a word spoken. Quinn and the others watched. Not a peep slipped from a single pair of lips.

The shiny polish of Quinn's success dulled, and an acid-tipped needle twisted in his heart. He hated Ryley for everything he'd done, but seeing his tormenter standing alone in his crisp outfit, perfect hair, and red-and-purple shiner, Quinn pitied him. This was an escape for Ryley, too, and Quinn had doomed him.

The van driver burst through the cafeteria doors and wiped sweat from his brow. "What a lousy day. I shoulda staid in bed. All's clear, though."

Egon's shoulders slouched with his sigh. Ms. Doyle nodded. "Thank you, Rodney. If you would please take Mr. Watkins back home."

"Mr. *Watkins*, you said?" Rodney's pace slowed, his wide eyes blinking. "There's a surprise."

"Indeed. Please escort our guest home." The words were sweet and courteous, but the way she had called Ryley guest told everyone that a guest did not belong among them.

Ryley balled his fists. He stared at the driver with an iron jaw. "I go home alone?"

Ms. Doyle eyeballed Quinn. "Unless there's something you desperately need at the Watkins' residence, Mr. Lynch, I think it best you come with the rest of us immediately. It's, shall we say, in your best of interests. Everything has been prearranged for this eventuality, and we would like to get going as soon as possible."

"Yes—yes with you," Quinn said, the words bubbling from his lips. "I never want to go back there. Never ever."

Rodney the driver patted Ryley's shoulder. "Okay Mr. Watkins, time to go."

"But you don't understand. I practiced so long! If you just let me—"

Rodney's eyes flashed like a cat's gleaming from the shadows, and he thrust out a hand that had a faint glimmer of a shape across his palm. "You gotta' come wit me. I don't got the time or patience to deal with punks today."

Ryley relaxed, and he swayed, slack-jawed. He took Rodney's hand, and the driver ushered the boy toward the exit. "G'day kids. G'day Mr. Pennington, Ms. Doyle."

Ryley's feet dragged over the tiles. Rodney opened the exit and tugged the boy through, and they both disappeared through the swinging door.

Ms. Doyle shut her briefcase. "Well then. Welcome all of you to your first year of learning how to use your talent. Many of you are familiar with what's yet to come." Her gaze lingered over Quinn. "Some of you may not know as much, but you will learn in time. Please form a single-file line and follow Mr. Pennington. He will take you the rest of the way while I stay here and tidy up a few things."

They formed a line and shuffled outside. Rodney's van, the one that took Quinn from the Watkins and brought him there, barreled down the lane with Ryley inside. Its single working brake light brightened at a stop sign, and the van squealed to a halt. It turned and vanished beyond a line of shops and from Quinn's life—hopefully, forever.

Quinn shook. His knees felt like water balloons. His gaze glued to the street corner. Freedom. This was freedom. He'd never see another Watkins for as long as he lived. He inhaled and smiled, ignored as he was by the others in line.

They walked to a school bus the color of an old banana peel. Rust splashed dark splotches on its sides, and several windows were left open even with the whistling winds and rumbling grey clouds.

Mr. Pennington opened the door, but it jammed halfway. He grumbled, grabbing its edge and forcing it apart. "Two to a seat, please," he said, smoothing his sweater with a smile.

One by one they squirmed inside. Quinn took a springy seat at the back with Heidi. Billy Holcomb sat across the aisle with the quiet redhead. Mr. Pennington closed the door and started the bus. It rumbled, vibrating Quinn's cracked green seat. The vehicle lurched, and they were off.

Quinn spun to Heidi and slid to his knees. "Can you tell me where we're going now? What is this?"

Heidi bit her smiling lips. "We're going to Wimbly's, that's where we're going."

"Who's Wimbly?"

Billy laughed from his perch across the aisle. He grabbed a lock of his oily hair and swept it aside like a prince might sweep aside a commoner. "Not who, *what*. The Wimbly School of Arts Arcana. It's near St. Alban's in Vermont. Very prestigious. Only a select few of the most talented of us are accepted." He side-eyed Quinn. "But I guess maybe that's changing these days."

"Don't be such a grease ball, Billy." Heidi nudged Quinn and leaned toward his ear. "Don't take what he says too personally. Kids who grow up in talented society have a totally skewed view of kids without talent. He and the others'll warm up to you after awhile, you'll see." She smiled and rotated on her knees until she faced him. "So you're from Tupper Lake?"

Quinn nodded. "Yeah. You're not?"

"Nearby. My mom, ah, she's not like most of the other kids' parents. She, ah, pretty much keeps to herself. I don't mind though. I like being different, you know? The world would be such a boring place if all the snowflakes looked the same." She winked, the corners of her smile teasing her ears.

"Yeah, I guess that's true." He frowned and quickly glanced around to see if anyone eavesdropped on their friendly chat. "Heidi, I was wondering…"

She giggled, playfully pinching his chest. "Go ahead, ask me. I know you've been dying."

"Is this…Is this…?"

Heidi bounced on her knees and grabbed his shoulders. "Say it, c'mon."

"A school for magic?"

"Bingo!"

"It's kind of hard to believe." He peeled Heidi from him and crossed his arms. "I thought Ms. Doyle and Mr. Pennington were a little off. And when I heard them talking about misfits—"

"Misfits?" Heidi's hands slapped back onto his shoulders, and she leaned uncomfortably close. "There were misfits there?" she asked. Her playful tone had cooled into something oddly serious.

Billy Holcomb and the quiet redhead lurched toward him. They scooted close, trapping Quinn in their tight, wide-eyed huddle.

"Y—yes." He shrank from their stares and pressed his back into the cold metal siding of the bus. "They said they had to fight them off I think. What's a misfit? Some kind of gang? Evil magicians?"

"Magic's such a pretty, enchanting thing," Heidi said. "Like flowers for the soul. You're born with the seeds, you nurture them, and they grow into a beautiful garden. But like any garden, it can get weeds. Weeds choke out the flowers. They kill the seeds. A misfit's like that. They're weeds, and we're seeds."

Billy nodded so hard Quinn thought his head might fall off. "What we have, the ability to cast spells and make enchantments and do all the amazing things magicians do, it's all because we're born with talent. People who are born with talent, we're called magicians. The mythical creatures you've probably heard of before like elves and dwarves and gnomes and all those beings are also born with talent.

"But misfits aren't born with talent. They gain it by stealing it. They gain it through torture." He glanced around before leaning closer and dropping his voice into a whisper. "They torture power from talented folk and use it for themselves. But they don't become like us when they do it. They're changed. Dark. They become witches and warlocks, vampires, werewolves, goblins, and other awful things that stir up trouble in the world. I can't believe there was a misfit attack and we had no idea. My mom's going to kill the principal when she finds out."

"Don't go tattling, Billy," Heidi snapped. "We're just fine. Keep it to yourself and keep an eye out, that's all. It's not like the misfits can hurt us anyway. They'll never be able to touch us as long as we've got the principal protecting us. He's way more powerful than any of them."

"Yeah, but you've heard the rumors. People say the misfits are on the move again." Billy eyed Mr. Pennington. "I overheard my mom talking. She says it's different than the other times, and that they might have already found their king, and when they get him, they'll crown him. You know what the prophecy says. Once he's crowned, that's when he'll come calling all the children of arcana and torture the talent from us and the days of the talented will end. Mom's even heard the principal found out who it was and made sure he got him to Wimbly's before the misfits got to him. All the most respected magician families are up in arms about it."

Heidi leaned over, jabbing her chin toward Billy. "So the Holcomb's must be just fine and dandy with it, shouldn't they?"

Billy's face reddened and his eyes narrowed. "My family's just full of respected talent. My dad—"

"Lighten up!" Heidi's fingers lanced out, tickling deep into Billy's sweater. His eyes widened, and he choked on his giggles as his face reddened like a ripe tomato.

"St—stop!" he squealed.

"Your parents are too scared of a silly legend and you're too mean to a perfectly nice stranger." Heidi withdrew her wriggling fingers. "We're born with talent, Billy. It doesn't mean we deserve it. That's something my mom says we should all remember."

Silence settled. Quinn stared at Billy. The redhead bit her lip.

Billy twisted away, mumbling something as he glared out the opposite window. The redhead swallowed and stared at the knot of her fingers resting in her lap.

Heidi rummaged in her pocket and pulled out an index card. She smoothed the paper, frowning. "I need a pencil. I think I lost mine."

"Why?" he asked.

"Want to see a spell? I'm sure you're dying to see your first one. Most of us don't know much about casting yet, but some spells are so easy you don't have to worry about lighting your fingers on fire or turning your friend into a frog."

Quinn had his pencil out and in her hand in a heartbeat. They crowded one another, staring at the blank card. She drew a rough circle with a square inside it. "Magic's not about newt eyes and cauldrons and wands and stuff. It's about geometry and using the secret shapes of the universe to make nature do what you want."

"Geometry?" A smile inched across up his lips. Geometry was one thing he could do, and he could do it well.

She nodded. "Arcane geometry, actually. Everyone on this bus is born with talent, right? Well, our talent isn't what lets us create spells. It's just like the key that opens a locked door. Get it?"

"Yeah, I think so."

"Good. Talent with magic and skill with spells are like a fingerprints. Everyone's different, everyone's unique." By then she had an intricate pattern scribbled on the card. She regarded the drawing with lips swept into a crooked pink raisin and brows knotted together. "Mom says I have a lot of natural talent. My skills need some practice, though. I've never been too good at drawing straight lines or perfect curves, and harder spells require a lot of complicated pattern-tracing. I kind of get distracted after the third or fourth shape."

Heidi lost part of her smile, and her voice drifted. She stared at the geometric pattern on her card as if it might leap from the paper and shame her any second.

Quinn pointed at the spell. "So what's that, then?"

Her smile snapped back like a rubber band. "Once we get good enough, we'll be able to trace the arcane geometry without a card, but until then, sometimes it's easier to draw the shape instead of just doing it all from memory. Might be awhile until I do it from memory for me. I'm not good."

"Your drawing's not so bad," he said.

"The better you draw or trace the arcane geometry, the more powerful your spell becomes. So while having natural talent is important, the best magicians are really skilled, too. Want to cast it?"

He recoiled like the card was a hissing spider. "No, no, you do it. It's your spell."

"Okay. Here goes…" Heidi inhaled. She licked her lips while she traced the pattern, pressing her palm onto the card when she finished. Soft blue light flashed beneath her hand. She lifted it, the pattern once on her card now shining and spinning in a wild whirlwind of shapes over her palm. A tiny star drifted from the center of her design, sputtering silvery light no brighter than a matchstick.

Quinn stared, leaning toward the flickering magic. "Amazing."

The star darkened. It spat a sad flare and died in drifting sparks. Heidi frowned. "See? My geometry's awful."

"Have another card?" he asked.

She pulled one out and handed it to him. Quinn set her card aside and redrew the pattern with almost machine accuracy despite the bouncing, jostling bus. His arcs were graceful, his lines rigid. He finished and handed her the card. "Now try."

Heidi traced the pattern and pressed her palm against the paper. She lifted her hand, and the pattern swirled. It blurred and flashed. Quinn shut his eyes and shielded his face. Even then, light flared around him and easily burned through his shuttered lids.

The light blazed and vanished as quickly as it came.

Quinn rubbed his eyes. A bright spot followed his gaze, burned into his eye like he'd stared straight into a camera's flash. "Sorry," he said, blinking.

Heidi cleared her throat, and shook the last light of the spell from her palm. "Wow. You're good. *Really* good. I've never even seen an experienced magician draw a spell that well."

Billy peeked around Heidi's shoulder, his travelling companion popping up beside him. Two more children appeared from the seat ahead, and then two more until the entire busload was gawking at Quinn and Heidi.

"Who did that?" someone asked.

"It was the Quinn Lynch kid," Billy squeaked. "His first try!"

Quinn swallowed. "No, I—"

"It's true," Heidi said. "I watched him draw it!"

Quinn shifted under the weight of their stares. He glanced at the bus's skinny rearview mirror. Mr. Pennington's grey eyes glared in the reflection, boring into Quinn like a diamond-tipped drill. "Students," he said, his voice calm and serious, "enough casting. If someone mucks up their spell and makes me crash, they'll earn a quick trip to the principal's office. Trust me when I say you do not want to cross that man."

* * *

Ryley opened the front door, and it groaned on its hinges. He stepped onto the floorboards. They squeaked. He swallowed. His mother jumped from her seat, arms parted for his hug. His father's eyes widened, a smile spreading lips normally flat and hard as a week old pancake.

"Well?" Oliver asked.

His mother embraced him, lifting Ryley to his toes. "Tell me you're going to Wimbly's! How well did you do? Did all your studying pay off while we had Quinn do your normal schoolwork? Where is Quinn anyway? Did they just go ahead and get rid of him for us?"

Ryley locked his jaw and lifted his chin. "I didn't get in."

Her hug loosened, and he dropped to his feet. She rotated and left a clear path from Ryley to his father.

Oliver stood. He crossed his arms and frowned. "What do you mean you didn't get in? They were supposed to take all the talented kids." His voice rose in a quivering, fiery arc. "You had talent. You have talent. That's what they told us, promised us, why they gave us the books, why you can do your little light shows."

"It was Quinn's fault. It had to be, Dad. I did everything right. I answered the questions just like they instructed. I could feel the magic, I swear! I know I did everything right."

His mother tapped her oily nose. "Could it have been Quinn all along? Might everything have been a lie?"

"No!" Ryley's eyes watered. "He's nothing. He had no talent. He cheated. I know he did! That should be me with them, not him."

"Don't you dare shed a tear," his father snapped. "Don't you dare be weak. I didn't raise you that way. Get to the dining room. Your mother's got dinner ready for us."

Ryley sucked in a breath and forced his tears down. He followed his parents to the dining room. His mother had cooked a turkey roasted a perfect shade of honey brown. Buttery corn and potatoes topped with fried onions and flecked with fresh chives teased his nose with their rich scents, and his stomach answered with a rumble. Dinner would help take his mind off his humiliation. Dinner would help him forget Quinn for a few minutes.

His seat scraped along the kitchen tiles. He sat, grabbing a plate, but his father yanked it from him and stared like a robot at his wife. "Patty, he gets Quinn's dinner. This dinner's meant for a winner."

Patty opened her mouth. His father's face tightened. She nodded, taking a cup of oatmeal from the counter and sliding it to Ryley. He stared at the lukewarm slop. There'd be no butter in it. There'd be no sugar. His chin quivered.

"You'll do an extra set of chores tonight," Oliver said, his voice flat as a frozen lake. "Patty, you'll have him do at least two extra hours of regular schoolwork from now on. We can at least try and make him less than nobody, no matter how hard it might be now that we've wasted so many years on a lie. I suppose we were misled from the beginning, when they showed up at our doorstep with him wrapped in a blanket, telling us he'd make us rich if we just took care of him, made sure he studied and passed the special test when it came around. You were supposed to pass that test, Ryley. You were supposed to pass it, and when you did, we were supposed to move to Manhattan and never worry about a thing again. Now I see why your real mom and dad never wanted you. They must have known the truth."

Tears blinded Ryley. "What—what are you saying? I'm adopted?"

"Unlike you, I didn't stutter," the man said.

Ryley wanted to shove a fork in his father's eye. His blood boiled. He stormed from his seat and bolted through the front door. Dark clouds drifted in thick tufts and dusted the dying grass with their shadows. He charged into the trees, crying, hating. Crooked branches snapped against his shoulders and sliced his tear-stained cheeks. This was Quinn's fault. It was all Quinn's fault. Ryley hated him. He hated him more than he'd ever hated anything.

"Wipe your tears, Ryley," a woman cooed. "It's not as bad as you think."

Ryley jumped, choking on his sob. He twisted to the sound. A strange woman reclined against a thin pine. Her hair glittered like trapped sunlight even though clouds obscured the setting sun. Her round eyes were blue as a glacier and just as cold. Shadows darkened around her, like her own gave others power and frightened the light, but despite her frighteningly beautiful appearance, her voice was as smooth and warm as Christmas morning with a stocking full of presents.

"Who—who are you?" he asked, wiping his face.

"I'm a friend," she said with a smile, "and a teacher, too."

"I don't need a teacher."

She straightened and arched a perfect brow. "Really? I beg to differ. You need a teacher because you're special, Ryley."

"But the test—"

"Don't worry about that." She slid her knuckles across his cheek and flicked his tear from her finger. "They can't see what I see. They don't know what I know, and I know you're special. I know you want to learn secrets. I know you want to hurt the ones who hurt you."

His pulse quickened. His fear ebbed. "Quinn. I want to hurt him really badly."

"You will." Her smile widened. "But first, let me teach you how to cause a little trouble."

$\mathfrak{S}$traight to the $\mathfrak{P}$rincipal

The bus rumbled like an old smoker through Upstate New York and crossed into Vermont. They travelled around Lake Champlain and rolled into a town called St. Albans, a crumb of a city whose welcome sign was overly proud of its seven thousand residents. Most children would be unimpressed. Not Quinn. Coming from Tupper Lake, a place where half as many people claimed a home, it was a shining metropolis.

Quaint people walked quaint streets lined by quaint buildings. The bus passed a car dealership with a single line of used cars angled in the sloped parking lot. Downtown slid by on the opposite side, a wall of old brick buildings and small shops with swinging signs hanging over the wide sidewalk.

Quinn pressed his hand against the windowpane. Cold air seeped into his palm, and his breath fogged the glass. He turned to Heidi and grinned. "So this is it? Where is Wimbly's?"

"Well, not quite. Wimbly's is on Woods Island on the lake." She looked over Quinn and pointed out the window. "Look, you can see Champlain now."

The bus turned the lane, and the town thinned into a bunch of old houses dotting the road. Leafy evergreens hung pinecones like ornaments from their branches. Lake Champlain appeared beyond them, a long, flat, mirror of the cottony-grey sky. Their bus followed the shoreline, and the street lost its pavement, preferring a chalky gravel coat instead.

The bus sighed and squealed to a halt. A sign nailed to an old tree told them they'd reached Shantee Point and warned in all capital letters against trespassing any further. A spiral similar to the one Quinn saw on the briefcase was carved onto the wood.

The bus shuddered. Quinn watched Mr. Pennington clench the wheel. They barreled past the sign. Gravel crunched beneath the bus's tires. A few moments later, they reached the water's edge.

Mr. Pennington bounced from his seat and opened the door. He motioned outside, a cool wind tossing his dark, unruly hair. "A little longer and we'll be on school grounds. Please step outside and wait for me at the shoreline. Do *not* use the platform before I have everyone gathered."

Egon's glare settled on Quinn. He shifted, frowning beneath the man's weighty stare.

Heidi nudged him as they filed toward the exit. "Why's Mr. Pennington got it out for you? I know I'm not the only one who's noticed he kept staring toward the back."

Quinn shrugged. "Beats me."

Billy snorted as he struggled with his coat zipper. "Duh, he probably thinks you're a misfit. If they really did attack us during the test it makes sense, doesn't it? You're the only different one, after all."

"You're such a snot, Billy." Heidi rolled her eyes, threading her arm around Quinn's. "Don't pay him any mind. I know you're not a misfit, for what it's worth. You've got a good soul in you, and misfits don't have those."

"Thanks," Quinn said. "Make sure to tell everyone."

Heidi giggled, and they stepped outside.

Quinn's shoes crunched in the round river rocks and pale grass. Water lapped a few feet away against a shoreline of peppercorn stones. At the water's edge, where Lake Champlain's tired waves caressed the earth, a circular platform inscribed with an intricate pattern waited.

Heidi squeezed Quinn, bouncing on her toes. "See that rune? I wonder what it's going to do. I hope it turns us into birds. I've always wanted to be one. They get a view of fields and gardens we never do, and my mom never let me fly around."

"Not even if she watched you?"

Heidi's eyes darkened. "Especially then."

Quinn inhaled and watched Mr. Pennington weave his way through the crush of students inching toward the platform. The man stood before the stone circle and raised his hands. "Step onto the rune one at a time. This is a complex spell, and as Wimbly's first years, affectionately referred to as fish by the rest of us, you're just not at the level you need to use it properly. Therefore, I will. Once I transform you, you will wait overhead until I join you. I will lead the flock to Wimbly's, and when we're there, will show you where to land. Remember to watch for nighthawks and eagles. I'd hate to have a fish eaten before their first day of class."

Heidi squeezed Quinn's arm. "Birds! I knew it. I'm so excited."

"I'm actually kind of afraid of heights."

"Don't worry. When you're a bird, there are no heights, only where you can go and what's below the water."

Egon pulled a girl with crooked pigtails onto the platform and traced a pattern with his finger. He knelt, pressing his palm onto the stone. The pattern sparkled and flashed. Quinn stared, wide-eyed, as the girl shrunk and twisted. She raised her hands, and her fingers extended into dark blades. Her arms bent, feathers sprouting from her pale cheeks like a shimmering beard. She cocked her head, her eyes shifting to large, round orbs, her nose stretching into a mottled beak. Her chest swelled and sprouted a coat of spotted feathers.

She chirped, hopping around the stone circle, now no larger than a baseball. Mr. Pennington snapped his fingers. "Yes, yes, it's all very exciting. Please, take flight and wait for the rest of us."

The bird flew from the circle, wheeling on the breeze coming from the lake. One by one the rest of the students transformed into birds and circled over the shoreline, chirping and spinning and diving in a wobbling ring. Quinn came last, Heidi waving as her fingers sprouted into feathers and she took flight.

He stepped onto the stone circle. His heart raced. Glancing into the sky, he watched the circle of birds chirp excitedly. All Quinn could think of was how high they flew and how far the fall would be. Just imagining the world from that height turned his stomach into taffy and made his palms moist.

Quinn caught Mr. Pennington's cautious stare even though the teacher quickly hid it with a smile. Quinn knew the look. He'd learned how to read people who hid their fear and loathing behind a mask called common courtesy. He knew what nervousness looked like, how it widened eyes and twitched cheeks.

"I'm afraid of heights," Quinn said as he stared straight into Egon's eye. "Why are you afraid of me as I am of them?"

Egon coughed and brought his fist to his mouth. "Non—nonsense, Mr. Lynch."

"I'm not what you think—"

Mr. Pennington traced the symbol and slapped the platform. Quinn's body twitched and shifted. His bones and organs rearranged. Feathers tickled his skin, and Mr. Pennington grew into a giant. No—not a giant. Quinn had shrunk. He chirped, bouncing on the rock, his tiny talons clicking on the stone.

He flapped his wings, and the ground fell away. Wind encased him, and he rose. He felt the breeze's current coax him higher like a friend he always had but never knew. Quinn braced himself for the terrifying height, but when he looked down, the bird he'd become felt no fear because he knew the wind was more solid and safe than anything the earth could offer.

Mr. Pennington-as-a-bird darted into the ring's center. He flapped his wings and sped over the lake, their ring breaking into a line behind him. Wind sang its own song in Quinn's ears. It tickled his wings, lifting him, speeding him over a rippling sheet of grey glass.

This morning, he'd been an orphan and a prisoner of the Watkins'. This afternoon, he was free, a child of a hidden world where magic ruled and boys could become birds by stepping on a stone.

They reached an island coated in trees with a single great hill rising in the center. Buildings appeared on the top of the hill, their colonial arches and columns apparent even from Quinn's great height.

Mr. Pennington descended at a sharp angle, and the line followed. Quinn prepared to land, but something gave him pause. An instinct tickled his thoughts, not an instinct of his own, but one of a bird's.

Curious, he rose, scanning the island. Nothing. He turned toward the mainland, and there, flapping in the sky was a single blot against the quilted grey. Was it a bird like him? His instinct went from a tickle to a roar. He tucked his wings against his feathered chest and darted after the others, piercing the sky like a feathery comet.

Mr. Pennington waited next to the platform with the students clustered around him. Quinn landed on the rock, and Mr. Pennington traced a pattern that returned Quinn to his human form. The man glared at Quinn with features that could have been carved from the same rock as the rune. "Mr. Lynch, I told you to keep up. Flying off like that is incredibly dangerous. The next time you feel the need to wheel around the sky, you ask a teacher to accompany you. Understood?"

"I'm sorry, Mr. Pennington. There was just—well, was someone behind us? Maybe Ms. Doyle?"

Egon's brows knotted. "Don't be silly, she's still back at the campus making sure—I mean, cleaning up. What are you talking about? What did you see?"

"It's probably nothing, but I—uh, I thought someone was behind us. A bigger bird, I guess." He turned, staring at the opposite shore. No spot blotched the cloudy sky. "Or maybe I was seeing things."

"I'm sure you were, I'm sure you were." Mr. Pennington inhaled and shook his head. The other students exchanged glances, shifting on their feet and tightening their coats.

"Could it have been a misfit?" Billy asked. "Did he really see something? If there is I really need to speak with my parents. If Wimbly's isn't safe anymore they should know."

"Of course you're safe," Mr. Pennington snorted. "This is Wimbly's. We have the most powerful principal of all the other schools and one of the oldest, most respected magician librarians in magical society. If a misfit has ever cast one of their wicked spells or gained tortured power in their heart, one of those two would know about it as soon as they even thought about this island. You are magical society's future and its greatest resource. We certainly spare no expense in your protection."

Billy flashed Quinn a sour glance. "And what about the misfit. What about—"

"Mr. Holcomb you are exhausting! Enough of that." Egon clapped and wheeled around. "Welcome to the Wimbly School of Arts Arcana. You stand at the most esteemed school in the magician world, a place of knowledge and power unlike any other. Follow me, please, and try not to gawk or point at dwarves, dryads, yetis, or ogres. Make that a double warning for the ogres. Those folk are very sensitive."

They followed in a single line and passed a long, three-story building painted white and lined with tall, rectangular windows. Old brick chimneys sprouted from its roof like weeds while a tiered dome rose like a wedding cake from the center.

Heidi nudged him. "That's the administration building where the faculty lives. The library's next to it." She pointed to another colonial structure to the side of the administration building. It was a brick square ten floors tall with a high roof capped by a platform deck and arched rails. "And across from it are the classrooms."

Four long, two story buildings sat in neat rows beside the library and administration buildings. A manicured brick courtyard walled by polished iron lampposts occupied the space between them.

"Where do we sleep?" he asked.

"At the base of the hill where the athletics, cafeteria, and study halls are. Some of the classrooms need plenty of quiet, so they moved the noisy stuff downhill to avoid accidents and distractions from older students. This is the Hilltop. They call the dorms and everything else the Glen."

Quinn spotted a woman wearing a pink and blue flannel scarf. Her auburn hair hung in waves over her shoulders, accentuating the splash of freckles on her rosy cheeks. She spoke to three men no taller than Quinn with great round bellies and noses to match. Freckles that looked suspiciously like stones dotted their cheeks, and unless Quinn's eyes needed checking, their beards were braided granite and limestone.

He grabbed Heidi and pointed. "Are those…?"

"Dwarves? Yeah, they visit sometimes from Newfoundland and teach classes on stone shaping in exchange for jewels. They're always looking for more gems, and they specialize in using their talent to shape stone. Everybody wins."

The woman speaking with the dwarves caught Mr. Pennington's eye and waved. She quickly bade the others farewell and scurried to the line of students shuffling across Hilltop's expansive courtyard. She grinned at Mr. Pennington and took his hand.

"Are these our newest fish, Egon?" she asked.

He nodded. "Some of the new class. Students, this is Ms. Callahan. Ms. Callahan, these are our fish from the Potsdam district."

Her eyes sparkled, brows arching. She scanned the line. "Excellent. Just who I was looking for. Is there a Quinn Lynch?"

The line of children turned like well-trained soldiers and fixed their eyes on Quinn. Heat filled his cheeks, and he slowly raised a hand. "Yes, ma'am."

"Hello, Quinn," she said with a cocked smile. "Would you please come with me? Principal Ward would like to have a quick word with you. I'll take you to the boy's dorm once we're finished. Good day, fish. Good day, Egon."

Ms. Callahan extended her hand. Quinn took it, and she plucked him from the line. Quinn glanced behind him at the gawking students. A few traded whispers while he was still in plain sight. Others grimaced and shook their heads. Heidi waved, and Billy scowled. Mr. Pennington clapped and strolled away, and the line lurched after him.

Quinn and Ms. Callahan entered the administration building. It smelled faintly of aged wood and floor polish and had a very old air about it. Persian rugs covered its floorboards while wrought iron chandeliers with thin, swooping arms lit the room. He followed Ms. Callahan through the building to a waiting area with plush green couches and a worn leather chair watched after by the portraits of men and women wearing wigs and coats like they had in the American Revolution.

In the room, an enormous woman with a tight bush of graying hair and two round, dinner plate eyes crouched over an oak desk. The desk would have been big for any normal person but was hopelessly too small for her. Two nubby knobs bulged at her hairline, and her lower lip protruded like she'd just come back from the dentist. She eyed Quinn from the behind the thick lenses of her oversized glasses and smacked her lips oddly loudly when she noticed them approach.

"Hello Rita," Ms. Callahan said. "Is Principal Ward inside?"

"Yes," Rita replied in a voice rough and deep as a rolling boulder.

Quinn froze. He'd never seen an old woman so big, so rough, and so muscular. Rita stared at him, her eyes more inhuman each second he stared into them.

Ms. Callahan grabbed his arm and gently ushered him toward the door. "Ogres don't like it when you stare, you know. Let's be nice and respectful, shall we?"

Quinn's guide slowly opened a tall door covered in carvings of ivy that wound over interlocking geometric patterns. Quinn paused before the doorway and wiped his sweaty palms on his hoodie. As the door's hinges groaned, he realized they must have known his terrible secret. They knew he cheated. They knew he switched tests with Ryley, and the principal had come to throw him out on the street or turn him into a frog and toss him in some swamp where he could be forgotten.

"Am I in trouble?" Quinn asked.

She pursed her lips and furrowed the fiery arches of her eyebrows. "Should you be?"

"No?"

Ms. Callahan laughed, and her frown disappeared. "Please, let's not keep the principal waiting."

Quinn padded inside. Two tall wingbacks faced a desk with carved lions' paws for feet. Silver and brass candelabras with ornate, curvy arms dripped wax from the flickering candles they held. Velvet drapes hung in burgundy waves from polished golden rods, hinting at arched stained glass windows behind them. From what Quinn could see, the stained glass formed dazzlingly intricate, interlocking geometry of every shape and color imaginable.

Ms. Callahan took a seat in one of the wingbacks, and Quinn sat in the other. He folded his hands into his lap and squeezed his fingers. He swallowed, his throat as dry as an Arizona desert.

She unwrapped her scarf and tossed her hair behind her shoulders. "Principal Ward? I've brought Quinn Lynch to see you as requested."

The chair behind the desk shifted. It rotated, creaking. Quinn stiffened. He clenched his jaw.

A man middle-aged sat in the chair's confines. His hair was dark as oil and just as slick, splashed with a river of grey flowing from his hairline to his ear. His eyes burned a blazing blue rimmed by glowing white. He sat with a chin Quinn doubted ever dipped and a smirk desperately tugging at the corner of his mouth. He interlaced his fingers, placing them on his desk. He studied Quinn with eyes that searched, eyes that never missed a detail, from the threading of Quinn's shirt to the single strands of hair growing on his head. They were eyes with infinity inside them and an eternity to ponder it all.

"Hello, Quinn Lynch. I hope Rita didn't scare you. Ogres are actually very kind, misunderstood creatures, and they've got an added bonus of being immune to spells so they make ideal guardians to those who treat them with the dignity they deserve." He talked in a soft and deep voice, his words spoken from a tongue that knew just what to say and when to say it. "I'm Donal Ward, the principal here at Wimbly's. It's a pleasure to finally meet you."

"Finally, Mr. Ward?" Quinn fought back tears. They knew. They had to know.

Principal Ward nodded. "Call me Donal. And yes, we've been expecting you. It's not often someone with such talent goes unnoticed for so long. We're very lucky to have found you at just the right time. Before any misfits did that is."

Quinn exhaled and slumped in his seat. This was about the misfits, not the test. They didn't know. His secret was safe. "Yes—I heard they attacked while we were taking the test."

"I'm sure you've heard a lot of things and have many questions."

"Like about the misfits? Magic? I've got a lot of questions. From what I've learned so far magicians are pretty bad at giving answers that make any sense."

Donal snorted in a way that was very unlike a principal and slapped his desk. For a man whose very presence betrayed his power, he acted more like Peter Pan than some mighty magician. "So true, Quinn, so true. It's the nature of the arcana world, to be a little cryptic. We're like dragons, us magicians, and knowledge is our horde. It's not easily shared with outsiders, especially ones who traipse into the middle of our excruciatingly well-defined lives and introduce a little chaos. If there's anything that a magician hates more than misfits, it's something that interrupts the natural order of things as they define it.

"You, my friend, cause a certain sense of unease in the talented. You see, a few of the more superstitious among us suspect you may be a certain kind of misfit. Not yet, of course, but soon they believe you will become one. They call him the Misfit King, the boy blessed by the three paths who will come calling all the children of arcana—and not in a good way."

"Am I—do you think I could be the one?" Of course Quinn knew it wasn't really him. Ryley was the one they wanted, and if this Misfit King really was a danger, maybe Quinn should to do the right thing and tell the truth before someone got hurt. Maybe now that he knew about their world, they'd have to keep him in it and he could still be safe from the Watkins.

"I don't believe in prophecies and neither should you," Donal continued. "We make our own destinies and walk our own paths. Believing in a prophecy means you give up that freedom to choose what's right. No, prophecies are for cowards and fools who fear to make their own decisions." He smoothed his hair and leaned against his chair. "But even if I did, you have talent, Quinn, and talent is inherited. Misfits are made by…other means, and as far as we know it's impossible for anyone to have more than one path of magic inside them. It's simply your skill and talent combined with your rather unfortunate history—"

"—I didn't start that fire! I swear I didn't."

Ms. Callahan cleared her throat. Quinn melted into his seat. "I'm sorry."

"No apology necessary," Donal said with a wave that could care less. "I believe you if you say you didn't. However, your past is quite colorful and people love to connect two dots no matter how ludicrous the line between them ends up looking. Someone with your talent needs the proper training regardless of what some silly warlocks or witches might be cackling to anyone who will listen."

"But if I can't be this Misfit King, why are they scared of me?"

"The thing is, Quinn, is that sometimes myths take on a life of their own. Give enough weight to rumor and tomorrow it's fact. That makes you a target. It makes you infamous in both the right and the wrong circles. I don't know how we missed your talent for so long, but I'm glad we found you when we did. There were certain old, silly rumors about a potential Misfit King making their rounds around magician households, and you can see how they might have gained the weight they needed when whispers of a powerfully talented, unlearned magician somewhere in the Potsdam district started circulating."

Donal sighed and pinched the bridge of his nose. "So, we searched, and we found you. We even implemented that silly test to get you into the open. There was some confusion whether or not it was you or your friend Ryley, but the test sorted that out. We have the one with talent, not the misfits. All will be well no matter how hard those rascals wish otherwise. I suspect you'll become a very accomplished magician with your level of raw talent, and you'll make us all very proud. That's really all that matters."

Quinn's throat thickened, and he forced a smile. "That's good." He frowned, looking at his knees. "What would've happened if they had found me first?"

"Nothing good." Donal's face hardened. His eyes flashed, and his fists trembled. The candles on the candelabras around him flared, their flames twisting. "The misfits despise the world the magicians have created. They feed on chaos and love corruption. Many of the greatest calamities in history have a powerful misfit pulling the strings behind them. The misfits hate the weak, despise the humble, loathe the poor. They are liars and cheats, beings of uncanny evil, all of them. Count your lucky stars they didn't find you. With talent like yours, they'd tie you by your ankles and—"

"*Donal Ward.*" Ms. Callahan's eyes were wide as bowls, and she spoke through clenched teeth. "You're scaring him. It's okay, Quinn." She reached for his shaking hand and gave it a reassuring pat. "You're safe here."

Principal Ward relaxed. "Yes, apologies. It's my charge to protect this school from them and to instill the ideals of proper talented society into our students. I'm sorry from taking you from your home with so little warning, Mr. Lynch, and should you need to contact your foster family for any belongings you have, you are of course more than welcome to do so. But I hope you understand the urgency of your situation and why we needed to keep you safe."

Ms. Callahan stood. Quinn leapt to his feet and nodded a little too enthusiastically. "Thank you, Donal. I just—one last question."

"Yes?"

"Do the misfits know you have me here? Do they think I'm still the Misfit King?"

The principal shrugged, swiveling his chair away from Quinn so he face the stained glass. "I don't believe in the prophecy and I don't believe they do, either. They're looking to spook people. It's what they do. But yes, they do know you're here, and even ignoring the prophecy, someone with your level of natural talent would make you an easy target without our education and protection."

"What about my foster brother? Will Ryley be safe?"

"The misfits are only interested in you and probably know your situation as well as we do. Considering that, you think they'd ever bother trying to use him as leverage?" He laughed and shook his head. "From what I hear, your foster family would be more likely to join the misfits voluntarily than not."

Quinn didn't reply. Instead, he followed Ms. Callahan out of the office, wondering how long his lie could last, terrified saving his own life might have doomed Ryley's. At least the misfits thought Quinn was the Misfit King. As long as they thought that, they'd leave Ryley alone. He took a deep breath. Everything would be fine. He had this under control, and then, once he had the chance, he'd fix it all.

A Solitary Night & Busy Morning

Two hulking, six-story dormitories connected by a long, single-story commons formed a giant H in the center of the Glen, a place for sleeping and socializing for all students attending Wimbly's. Like the administration building, brick chimneys poked from the dorms' angled roofs like rigid mushrooms. A few rectangular windows dotting the dormitory walls shined like gold sapphires against the backdrop of the high trees of Woods Island. The air vibrated with laughter and the low thrum of flapping tongues trying to outdo one another.

Quinn sniffed and caught scents of bread freshly baked with hints of yeast and warm cream. He licked his lips, glancing at Ms. Callahan.

She patted him on the back. "Don't let Donal scare you. He's like an oyster, really. Just a crabby shell with a soft inside." She scowled at the dorm's rose-colored doors. "But there's no pearl when you crack him open, though. Trust me on that."

"Thanks, Ms. Callahan."

"Please, call me Maisie." She bent, resting her hands on his shoulders. "Let me know if you need anything at all, okay? I'm the school counselor, so if anything at all's troubling you or making you upset, you come to me. I promise whatever's said in my office doesn't leave my office."

Quinn nodded. He wondered how much her promise meant to her if she knew he'd cheated on his test and Ryley was really the one they wanted—the one they feared—the one still out there, ready to be used by the misfits for their dark prophecy.

He shook the dark thoughts from his head and smiled. "So where's my room?"

"Fish are on the first floor. Through the doors, to the left. Follow the sturgeon lamps." She stood and turned toward the path to Hilltop. "Good night,

Quinn. Remember, if you need anything, my door is always open."

Maisie disappeared up the wide, crooked walk leading uphill. The polished green lampposts lining the walkway sputtered alive and cast soft light beneath the trees' thick weave of branches.

Quinn turned. He inhaled, puffing his chest, and opened one of the massive doors. It groaned like an old whale and parted, and his chest deflated with it. Warm air rushed over him like a crashing wave, and he blinked. Down the hallway he went, step by measured step. Age had warped the floorboards just enough for his feet to feel them bend beneath his footsteps.

Turning left, he came to a single, wide door set in an alcove of inset arches. Intricate geometry was carved into the door's pale green face, the loops and angles forming a leaping geometric sturgeon.

"Here goes nothing," he whispered.

Quinn opened the door to a long corridor lit by neatly spaced bell lamps held in the mouths of brass sturgeons. Between each light there were smaller doors colored like the one he stepped through. Quinn walked into the hallway, and the sturgeon door shut behind him.

A boy shaped like a half-melted marble teetered into the hallway, licking chocolate from his fingers. He spotted Quinn and nearly choked on his own tongue, staring with two round eyes and open, watery lips. "It's—it's you."

"Do I know you?"

"No—no, and I want to keep it that way."

Quinn shoved his hands into his pockets and forced one foot after another. No matter what lie he told or what life he lived, it looked like he'd never escape a bad reputation. "I'm not what you think I am. I'm not the Misfit King."

The boy laughed. His second chin bounced as the first one rolled into it. "Of course you're not, not yet. But everybody knows where you come from, about how your parents didn't have the talent but somehow you do. You can't just get talent—one of your parents has to have it. Talent's tortured from someone born with it and shoved inside you, or you get it by completing the trial, and there's only a single instance in all of history that someone's gotten magic that way. A fish like me or you could never survive something like that. You must've tortured the talent from somebody and somehow got past the school's spells. Everybody knows it's true."

Quinn hesitated, frowning at the boy. "I didn't know someone's parents had to have talent for them to have it too."

The boy pointed down the hall, his face squished like a hungry newborn. "Magicians have magician kids and misfits have misfits kids. Now go. You're in the back. The way back. Don't ever talk to me again, for both our sakes."

Quinn wanted to tell the boy he wasn't a misfit and could never be the Misfit King, that he hadn't tortured a magician's talent because he had no magic at all. Instead, he marched down the hallway, his glare glued to the floor. No reason to start an argument with a stranger.

At least he'd earned a valuable gift from their conversation, information he could tuck away and use to find the solution to his peculiar pickle of a predicament. He needed all the knowledge and secrets he could get his hands on if he was going to pull this off. Quinn paused, a cockeyed grin inching up his cheek. On his walk down, he wondered how he'd keep up the charade of having power when he had none.

Maybe, just maybe, if they really did think he was the Misfit King, he could use it to his advantage. If they wanted a misfit, he might just be obliged to give them one if it kept the other kids off his back.

He'd also learned about a new way to gain magic. The trial. With only one person in history to have successfully done it, it seemed a long shot. But even a long shot was better than no shot at all.

Quinn glanced over his shoulder. The round boy peeked from his room but darted inside when their eyes met. Quinn chuckled and turned a corner to another long hall. He walked to the last door on the right, tucked beside a dead end with cobweb corners and a crack reaching to the floor like a bolt of lightning. The door itself was a sad, dingy thing with peeling paint and a brass knob spotted with rust and a deformed by a dimple. The sturgeon lamp beside it popped and sputtered.

It was such a pathetic door. But even a pathetic door at Wimbly's was world's better than the most perfect door at the Watkins' house. No matter how much the paint peeled or light sputtered at his new school, he could sleep knowing Oliver, Patty, and Ryley would never be waiting on the other side.

Quinn opened his dormitory door. On the left side of his room, there was a dingy bed with a faded blue quilt, a desk with a single lamp at least four times Quinn's age, and an old wardrobe with a bent door and three drawers—one of which sorely needed knobs.

The right side of the room mirrored the left, both halves divided neatly by a skinny window. But instead of an empty bed, the other side featured a familiar, scowling boy. The ever-present frown already wrinkling his puckered face deepened when he recognized Quinn. Billy Holcomb crossed his arms, and his mouth pressed into an angry line. "It's all your fault I'm here, you know. Everybody thinks because I came from Tupper Lake and talked to you on the bus we're friends."

"Good to see you too, Billy."

Billy huffed. He twisted toward the wall and slammed his head onto his pillow. Not another word passed between them. Quinn reclined on his own bed, staring at the ceiling. He closed his eyes, and they did not open again until morning.

* * *

Maisie Callahan didn't often get angry. As school counselor, she couldn't. Donal, however, loved testing that theory like a boy with a stick swinging at a fat beehive. She dropped Quinn off at his dorm and stormed into the administration building, blowing past Rita, who was scratching her nubby horns and glaring at the crossword puzzle on her desk.

Maisie tore into Donal's office without pausing for Rita's permission. "Donal, you melodramatic fart. You'll scar him for life or at least give him nightmares!" She slammed the door, and several of the candelabras shook.

Principal Ward had left his desk and stood soldier-straight before a yellowed map, cradling his chin. He grinned and shrugged. "Life's no fun without a little melodrama, and we're certainly in melodramatic times these days. He needed to feel the danger of his situation. We can't let him even consider reaching out to the misfits. You know there's only so much we can do, so much we can shield him from. He will be tested, and when he is, I want him to remember my words and fear what misfits and their torture bring."

"That's ridiculous. You should be kinder. He needs to feel welcome and wanted. He's an orphan, remember? Our spies said his life with that family of psychopaths was hard enough. Cut him some slack and try not to purposefully give him nightmares."

"It's your job to be the warm and cuddly one, Maisie. It's my job to make sure there's never a Misfit King to take the throne."

Her blood ignited. "Ms. *Callahan*."

She knew he'd called her that on purpose. He got a rise out of seeing her cheeks flush from the memories it stirred up.

"Sorry, sorry. Old habits, Ms. Callahan. Now's not the time to go easy or gentle on the boy. He's got enormous potential, and we need all the talent we can get. We've been lazy. We thought we finally broke them after the Great Wars—"

"You're showing your age. No one calls it that. World War One and Two, remember?"

He rolled his eyes and waved. "—But they were just slinking in the shadows. They're not slinking anymore."

Some of her anger ebbed. She drew to his side and stared at the old map. "Are you worried?"

"About this school? Not with us here, not with our considerably powerful librarian and I guarding us. There's simply not any way a misfit could get onto Woods Island without us knowing, much less get to any of the students. We can't stay in here forever, though. The children certainly won't be able to."

"Is it that bad?" she asked, squinting at the map. "Show me."

He traced a symbol and flung it at the map. A glob of mist exploded on the paper, and shimmering ruby beads coalesced in the vanishing haze. The shining spheres rolled around the crinkled paper, spreading over the seven continents. They swirled in patterns and settled on the locations of the misfits Donal could identify with his spells. He'd never be able to spot the more powerful ones, but those he could find were a good indication of what danger lurked around them.

Maisie gasped. "No wonder the testing center was attacked."

The ruby lights formed a vortex swirling around a single point. A shrinking, empty sphere centered on Lake Champlain.

"Indeed. I don't know what part Quinn has to play in this. He's no misfit—not yet—but they obviously believe there's something special about him. I just don't understand who could be gathering them in these numbers. There hasn't been a misfit that powerful since her, and we both know she's long gone."

Maisie winced at the mention of the woman. She believed Donal when he said he'd taken care of her decades ago. Still, Maisie only knew of one misfit so powerful and so evil she could have gathered her brothers and sisters in such large numbers.

* * *

Quinn woke to a soft rapping at the door. He rubbed sleep from his eyes and yawned. Billy's bed was neatly made and completely empty. Quinn swiveled off the mattress and checked his wardrobe. It contained a stack of navy sweaters with pressed button-ups, khaki slacks, a down coat, scarfs, and mittens and woolen caps for the coming winter. The first drawer contained rolled socks and folded underwear. The second had towels and washcloths. The third, gym clothes, shoes, and belts. He grabbed a towel and washcloth. They were downy soft and—warm? Quinn pressed the towel to his cheek. It was fresh, like he'd pulled it from the dryer seconds before.

A tub of toiletries waited for him in the hallway. The sturgeon lamps blinked like a runway, leading down the hall. He followed the empty corridor and its blinking lights until he came to a bathroom with steamy plumes rolling like loose tongues from an open doorway. The hiss of running water whispered softly in his ears.

He found a locker and slipped into his towel. He padded across the tiles, a grid of tiny cream squares coated in sweaty beads. Not a single soul disturbed the steam.

Quinn turned a corner and found the showers. Thick, rolling bellies of steam poured from the doorway. He stepped into a tiled rectangle room with a sturgeon mosaic in its center. A pipe ringed the walls, sprouting showerheads that shot streams of water at gulping drains beneath them.

The opposite end of the room vanished behind a twisting wall of steam. Quinn inched to the far corner so the soupy haze hid him from anyone passing by. He hung his towel and began his shower, smiling as the hot water rolled down his cheeks and soaked his hair.

Someone else padded into the room. Their feet splashed on the pools collecting in the floor's dimples and uneven tiles. Quinn wiped soap and water from his eyes and peered into the steam, but whoever it was must have taken up residence near the doorway. Sighing, he leaned against the wall and stared at his toes as rivulets of hot water poured from his hair.

"Look who we have here," a boy said. "It's the Weasel, waiting for the rest of the showers to empty out so he doesn't get embarrassed?"

Quinn jumped. He blinked, scanning the fog. The boy's voice was unfamiliar. It had a cocky tone like the words were spoken through a sly grin by a sharp tongue.

"Leave me alone, Porter," squeaked Billy's unmistakable voice. "I haven't done anything to you. Nothing at all!"

Quinn took a deep breath of the thick, moist air and straightened, edging toward Billy. The voice that must have been Porter laughed. "Look at you making demands, Weasel."

"My name's Billy."

"But you look like a weasel. So I'm calling you Weasel. And by the end of the year, even the teachers are gonna be calling you Weasel. Understand?"

"But—But, I...I don't like—"

"Why can't you speak up?" Porter asked, snickering. "What's wrong? Speak about as well as you make friends?"

Quinn took another step. Silhouettes appeared in swirling patches. He swallowed and paused his advance.

"You can't bully me," Billy said. "My mom said it's not allowed."

Quinn slapped his forehead. His roommate had to be the most clueless kid at Wimbly's, and that included Quinn. He inched closer, the silhouettes darkening with each careful step. Steam rose around him like a ghostly cloak with curling fingers.

Porter snorted. "Now, now, Weasel..." The bully hissed, his tone softening like a snake slithering toward its dinner. "...Is your mom here? Would she appreciate you talking to your classmates that way, because I don't think she would. Maybe I should teach you a lesson in manners."

"No!" Billy squealed. "Please."

"I know! I'll wash Weasel's mouth out with soap, just like Mommy would. Pinch his nose so he can't breathe out his little mouth. That'll force it open nice and wide for it's washing."

"P—Please, Porter...I haven't done anything." There were tussling sounds, squeaky footsteps over we tile. "No...!"

Billy Holcomb hadn't shown Quinn an ounce of kindness the entire time they'd known each other. But Quinn couldn't let a bully torture his roommate, even if Billy hated him. So Quinn clenched his fists. He took a deep breath and marched forward, glowering at the shifting figures.

"Hey!" Quinn burst through the fog, steam unfolding from his shoulders like a fly breaking from a Venus flytrap.

Porter had Billy pinned against the wall. Billy's naked body trembled like a wet eel. The bully turned just in in time to catch Quinn lunging at him. Porter stood about Quinn's height with swept hair hanging limp above his eyebrows and lips that rested in an old bulldog's snarl, a snaggletooth peeking from them.

Porter dropped Billy as Quinn slammed into him, his forearm pressed against Porter's soft neck. The boy grunted. "G—Get off!"

Movement shifted from the corner of Quinn's eye. Billy trembled on the shower floor, a column of hot water a barricade between him and the world.

Quinn smirked, bringing his attention back to Porter. He leaned in and glared at the wide eyes blinking just beneath the boy's bangs. Porter's cheeks reddened, and he coughed. "Who—who are you?"

Hot breath poured from Quinn's nostrils. A drop fell from Quinn's nose and landed on Porter's chin. "Now you listen to me," Quinn whispered. "My name is Quinn Lynch. Maybe you've heard about me? I'm just dying to find someone to torture at school, being the Misfit King and all. If I ever..." he pushed his forearm harder on the boy's windpipe. "...*ever* hear you call him Weasel again, I think I know the first person I'm coming to when I'm crowned king. Got it?"

Porter's lips quivered, flashing his snaggletooth. "You—you're not a misfit. You can't scare me."

"You don't know what I am. I promise you don't."

Porter's eyes flashed wide enough to show the fear within them. He glanced at Billy, suddenly depending on his victim for support.

Billy's eyes darted between Quinn and Porter before he found his voice. "I've heard rumors, Porter. They say his parents died in a fire. They don't know how it happened, but they say he did it."

Quinn lifted his arm from Porter's neck and motioned for the doorway. The boy massaged his scarlet throat and coughed. He lurched toward the exit and propped his arm against the doorframe while he took a few deep breaths. He glowered beneath the crook in his arm, his eyes glittering in the steam. "You never should've done that. Watch your back, Quinn, because I'll be watching you."

"Watch your talent, Porter. It'd be a shame if you lost it in an accident."

Porter's scowl twisted, and he ran from the showers. Quinn exhaled and wiped his soaking hair from his brow. A smile broke his lips and he rocked on his heels. "That was easier than I thought. This Misfit King thing's really got people on edge."

Billy trembled like he showered in ice and not steaming water. Rolling his eyes, Quinn extended a hand. "You know I made all that up, Billy. Don't look so silly."

"So you're not the Misfit King?" Billy eyed his hand. "You're not even a misfit?"

"No, but if he thinks I am and leaves us alone, why not let him think it? No one's going to call you Weasel anytime soon. That's what matters, right?"

"You know he'll make sure everyone believes you're a misfit." Billy grabbed Quinn's hand and wobbled to his feet. "Nobody messes with Porter Price. Nobody. They say he's got a snaggletooth because he's one-sixteenth werewolf on his dad's side."

Quinn shrugged. "I'll keep an eye out for any bullies howling at the moon. Besides, I'd take my chances with the Misfit King and not the boy with a werewolf tooth. Thanks for playing along back there, by the way. You didn't have to."

"I don't think I had a choice. People aren't going to like you, you know. A few people weren't sure. They will be now."

"I know," Quinn said, sighing. "But I'm used to people not liking me. I'm used to staring and whispers and all that. Even then it's miles better than where I came from."

Billy grabbed the towel hanging by his showerhead. He wrapped it around his waist and plucked his tub of supplies from the slick tiles. He backed toward the door, lips twisted to the side like he was searching for words playing hide-and-seek on the tip of his tongue. He paused at the exit and shook his head, his lips untwisting in a grin. "You know, that was pretty awesome. See you in the commons?"

"See you in the commons."

Billy darted from the showers. Steam rolled in lazy waves over Quinn's shoulders and swirled in thin tendrils around his arms. He stared at the exit, a toothy smile inching up his own dripping cheeks. He'd won Billy over. If he could get through to him, then he could get through to anyone. Now he had two friends at Wimbly's and a reputation that would hopefully keep people off his back. It was shaping up to be a very good day.

Ms. Velvets First Lesson

"You can do it. Draw the circle, Ryley. Draw it better this time."

Ryley clenched his jaw. She was infuriating at times, always smiling with her perfect lips and her blond hair that could make a doll jealous. She stood before him in a trench coat and polka dot button up and an air that said she couldn't care less.

"I'm trying," he said, teeth clenched. "It's harder than it looks."

"The better you get at it, the stronger you'll be. I'm only hard on you because I want you to succeed. Do you want to be a winner or not?"

Ryley drew another circle onto the card. He glared at the curved, dark line. Everything was cold. From his numb, pink fingertips to his sweat-soaked toes. He wasn't sure if it had been the rainstorm or her, but regardless it took another second before he finished the intricate overlapping geometry. The pattern completed, he smiled, straightening. "Did it."

Ms. Velvet arched a silky eyebrow. "Somewhat primitive. Weren't you supposed to be practicing your geometry all these years? What have you been doing? Or should I be asking who's been doing it for you? It was a mistake to keep Quinn around you. I realize that now. Instead of being the magician you should be, you're barely able to draw a simple circle. Pathetic."

An inferno lit his throat into a burning column. He hated her so much. But she was necessary. He'd never get Quinn without her. He'd never make Quinn suffer without her. "I think it's pretty good," he murmured.

She laughed in twinkling, needling notes that crawled under his skin like hungry worms. "Go ahead then. Cast it. Cast the spell and let's see how good you are."

Ryley splayed his fingers. His knuckles cracked and ached, his own blood fighting off an odd cold that turned his digits into popsicles. Licking his lips, he traced the design he had just drawn. Scarlet lines remained wherever his fingers drew the geometry. After a few excruciating moments, he'd completed his pattern. It hung suspended in the air, lingering so he could trigger the spell.

"What are you waiting on?" Ms. Velvet asked. "Afraid? Afraid your geometry might ignite your skin? Melt your bones? Set fire to your eyes? You're tragic, Ryley, and it's because you're afraid. Do it!"

His arm trembled.

"Do it!"

Ryley slammed his hand over the symbol. It flashed matchstick red, and a line of fire lanced through his bones, burying in his heart like a snake's fangs. He cried out, flinging his palm toward the streambed beside them.

Water shivered and burst into hissing flames. For a brief, glorious moment, the streambed became a twisted line of roaring blazes. Steam rose into the treetops, and his fire receded.

Ryley relished the fading heat and let it sink inside him like a happy memory. He cast the spell. His smile split like a lazy crescent. Serves her right for testing him, the witch. She better be careful. He got stronger every day. Soon enough he'd be unstoppable.

"Well?" he asked, crossing his arms over his puffed chest. "What do you think about that?"

Ms. Velvet reclined against an oak. She buffed her nails against her blouse, its brass buttons gleaming behind the loose flaps of her trench coat. His blood pressure ignited as hot as the fire he'd just summoned. "Were you even paying attention?"

She glanced up, surprise painted on her face like a dollar store mask. "Oh? You mean that little Boy Scout campfire you just spit out over the water? I think I caught a flicker of a flame from the corner of my eye."

"What?" He stomped toward her, fists furious bricks beside him. "That was my best one yet. It nearly burned the stream away!"

She straightened and pitched forward as he came within arm's reach. Her fingers wrapped around his neck. Her grip was a clamp of ice tearing into his muscle. Ryley buckled, crying out.

"Going to teach me a lesson?" she asked with a yawn. "Don't be silly. You're nowhere near me. Not even close, you see. Keep practicing, though, and maybe you'll be able to summon a fire that'll do more than light a cigarette. Now get inside. I'm sure your dear parents have dinner ready for you by now, and you know how they hate it when you keep them waiting."

She released him. Blood flooded back into his throbbing neck. He struggled to his feet and massaged his throat. "Are you coming tonight?"

"Of course I'm coming tonight, my darling. I come every night. I have to make sure you don't worm your way out of your obligations, now don't I? Or have you decided your little light show is enough, that you can take Quinn out with your ugly circles and childish flames? If you really want to be the Misfit

King you're going to have to do much better than that. Now should we keep them waiting any longer?"

"No," he said, his nails biting his palms. "Let's go."

Ms. Velvet nodded and flashed the hollow smile of someone who'd lost her heart a long time ago. Her fingers traced a sophisticated pattern. She flashed her palm, and her body faded. All but her brass buttons and eyes remained, broken by the arc of her polished teeth. "After you."

Ms. Velvet vanished, but Ryley still felt her. Her eyes were weights strapped to his shoulders. Every bitter breeze was her breath tickling his ear, and every shifting leaf or cracking twig her footstep. When they first met, he wondered if she was even real. After awhile, he stopped caring. The burnt earth from his spell proved that even if she wasn't real, the things she taught him were.

He traipsed toward the porch, footsteps crunching on the dead grass. The wind stung his fingers and nipped his bones, but the water he ignited with his spell put a smile on his face no icy breeze could wipe away.

Inside, he cleaned his shoes on the rug and dashed upstairs. Ryley ignored Quinn's old room as he ignored everything that reminded him of the filthy orphan. Quinn didn't exist there. When Ryley finally got his way, he wouldn't exist anywhere else, either.

He flung his thick fleece coat over his bedpost and washed up, carefully fixing his hair. The part had to be perfect. Not a single strand could ever be out of place. He'd do everything he could to be flawless, to be better than the stupid house with its peeling siding and leaning porch. This home was for his parents, not for him. Ryley was meant for better things, and soon, they'd understand that.

His mother's voice—no, his false mother's voice—spewed an order from downstairs. Her voice sounded to Ryley like a broken sewer pipe and had about the same appeal. He grimaced, glaring at his own reflection. Without Quinn there, Ryley took the brunt of her giftwrapped insults while his father showered him with disappointment when it should have been confetti. If they only knew.

Ryley made his way downstairs and walked to the kitchen, chin high. He paused just beyond the doorway and stared at the table. "What's wrong with my seat?"

Three seats surrounded the worn table, the old oak surface scratched and pockmarked by sweaty glasses. His false mother and father sat at their seats, Patty with a fistful of mashed potatoes on her fork and Oliver calmly slicing strips of his pot roast.

Unlike their seats, the one reserved for Ryley had been shortened, inches taken from each leg. Oliver motioned at the mangled seat, his greasy knife glinting beneath the kitchen light. "That's your place, Son. You'll use that one for as long as I say. Now sit and eat dinner, and remember to thank your mother for all the hard work she's done preparing this meal for you."

Patty beamed a smile, a glob of buttery potatoes collecting in her serpentine lips.

"How depressing," Ms. Velvet whispered, her breath like softly beating butterfly wings against his neck. "Look at them. Look how they mock and tease you, how they disrespect you."

"I—I don't understand. Why?" he asked, standing behind the chair. It barely came to his waist. Sit in it, and he'd be level with the tabletop.

"Why?" The tone of Oliver's voice could have chilled ice. "I know what you've been doing out there."

Ryley swallowed. "What do you mean? I did my chores, all of them."

"Oh, you do your chores. You do them every day. But what about after they're done? What about those times you wander off in the woods? What about then?"

"I…I…" His voice trailed as he searched for an excuse. He could tell them about Ms. Velvet, tell them he was practicing magic, learning the secret shapes of the universe that gave him power over it. It's what they wanted, after all, a son who would bring them fame and glory. But Ryley wasn't their son. That was a knife they'd buried in his heart when he came home from the test. Now, he'd use it to cut them.

Ryley gripped his seat. He pulled it from the table and sat, the wood lip coming to his collar. "It's a better place to study schoolwork, that's all," he said in his warmest, sweetest tone. "The outside air helps keep me awake. I want to do well in school, I really do, Dad. I'm going to get out of high school and go to college, and I want to make sure you don't have to pay a cent."

He swallowed his cringe. Calling Oliver his father tasted like spoiled milk poured down his throat. Oliver's gaze narrowed, his eyes disappearing in the taught folds of his thin skin. Mr. Watkins opened his mouth, but Patty dropped her silverware, and spoke before he had the chance. "Now, now, Ollie, I think it's good he goes outside. Keeps it nice and quiet in here. He's such a little gnat when he's in the house, always interrupting what I'm doing. Let him stay out there. Gives us more time to have a little peace."

Oliver mulled on her suggestion. He glared at Ryley with poison in his eyes and sharp words on his lips.

"He really doesn't like you." Ms. Velvet's voice drifted to him, carried on a quiet breath. "They don't like you. They could never really understand what it's like to have what you have. They're strangers, useful fools to get what you need and nothing more. Take their abuse and make it your strength."

Ryley inhaled, clenching his silverware. The table was so high it forced him to cut his food with his elbows angled to his ears.

"But I love you, Ryley," she continued. "I love you and I want what's best for you. Stay patient. Stay determined. You will be strong soon enough, and then, you can make them all pay. Starting with Oliver and Patty Watkins."

Oliver accepted his wife's advice with a nod. Ryley's false father turned his attention to his pot roast. Ryley ate quietly, careful never to let his smile slip.

Arcana 101

Quinn adjusted his backpack. Its buttoned flap barely held the thick, laminated schoolbooks stuffed inside it. Like his cleaning kit, he and Billy found their schoolbags packed and waiting outside their dorm when they returned from the showers.

The walk to the Hilltop with his roommate was brisk even though the trees blocked the shivering winds blowing from Lake Champlain. September had finally come, and September in Vermont kissed the trees with a cool breath that turned their leaves rich shades of gold and brown and sent a few of their leaves falling like rusty snowflakes.

Quinn halted halfway up the path when he spied movement in the trees. Lumbering beasts stalked quietly within the forest, their coats of fur blending almost perfectly with the surrounding woodland. He peered at the furry creature wearing an orange scarf and watched it sniff a pinecone with an upturned nose. It smiled, bearing two rows of wide, flat teeth and munched on the pinecone like Quinn might snack on a juicy pear.

"Yetis," Billy said. "Principal Ward has them clear the snow around the island during the winter so we don't get buried in a blizzard, and they get all the pinecones, acorns, and tree bark they can eat."

The yeti spotted Quinn and Billy. It grinned with bits of pinecone stuck between its teeth and waved a hand that could clutch Quinn's head like a baseball.

Billy waved and shouldered Quinn. "Wave back. You don't want to be rude to a yeti, do you?"

Quinn waved enthusiastically. The yeti rumbled a happy grumble from its throat and continued with its snack while they continued toward Hilltop.

"What other creatures are on the island with us?" Quinn asked.

"All sorts. You'll get your chance to see them if you keep an eye out. Maybe even have a conversation or two. Most of the magic races are pretty shy around people, even talented magicians like us."

Quinn and Billy's first class, Arcana 101, was in the first building on Hilltop. A tall red door framed by a magnificent façade of false columns greeted them. It swung open and closed as fish in giggling groups of two and three filtered inside.

Like most students Quinn encountered, the young magicians at Wimbly's avoided him like cheese with a nose-wrinkling mold hidden in the back of the pantry. He wasn't wanted, but he wasn't quite worth the trouble of getting tossed out. One or two of his classmates would glance his way and bend their lips to another's ears, whispering a not-so-secret suspicion Porter was probably already hard at work spreading. If they only knew what Quinn really was, they'd all laugh him off campus.

Quinn made his way through the halls. Faint trails of vinegar and pine tickled his nose, reminding him of the same floor cleaner Oliver and Patty used. But the Watkins were behind him, and soon, the smell would remind him of Wimbly's instead. Sucking in a deep breath, he strolled into class with the widest smile he could manage.

Heidi waved from her desk, her bright eyes shining. The silky feathers woven in her loopy locks had an odd way of setting her apart from everyone else's dull clothes and manicured hair. In a way, she was just as out of place at Wimbly's as he was, and it brought them closer for it.

He scooted next to her and plopped his book upon the oaken desk while Billy took a seat beside him. Students trickled inside, meticulously avoiding Quinn and his friends until all but a single empty seat remained in the class seconds when Mr. Pennington wandered through the doorway.

Egon carried a stack of books piled to his chin. He'd worn a drab outfit when Quinn first met him, but now he was a colorful splash of argyle diamonds and worn leather patches on his elbows.

He dropped the books on his desk and jumped at the sound they made, tittering like this was his first day as much as theirs. He swept his hair from his eyes and scanned the classroom.

"Looks like we're all here. How wonderful, just wonderful. Welcome to Introduction to the Art Arcana 101. During my class, you'll learn the history of magic, its founding principles, and its basic usages. I know for many of you the history is already second nature…" he glanced at Quinn, quickly smoothing the grimace on his lips. "…And for others it may be brand new. Suffice it to say, no talented magician can ever achieve greatness without a firm grasp of the basics.

"So while this may be your first class, and the spells may be achingly simple compared to what your parents and older friends might cast, without a complete understanding of the simple, you'll never grasp the complex. Plus you're liable to blow yourself to bits, and trust me when I say yetis hate cleaning students off the walls."

The children snickered and shifted in their seats. Mr. Pennington wore a trophy-worthy smile topped with a wink, and his stiff posture relaxed.

"Teach us a spell," a student squealed. Several children nodded in agreement.

Quinn pressed his chest against the desk. He didn't want to miss a single detail, a single shape or line or curve in the spell's geometry.

Mr. Pennington arched a brow. "A spell? So, maybe you want to learn how to light the air on fire?"

He traced a pattern and splayed his fingers. Brilliant flames erupted around his hand, roiling and sizzling. He swung in an arc and his fingers left a fiery trail behind them. Students clapped. Quinn's eyes widened. Heat from the flames came in waves and warmed his cheeks even though he sat in the back.

"Or maybe you want to be a master of ice and chill the hottest fires?" Mr. Pennington traced another symbol. He slapped the ribbon of fire and it dazzled, the hot tongues bursting into blue and white crystalline shards. The classroom applauded and filled with cheers and laughter. Egon's ice burst into a cloud of snowflakes and drifted toward the floor.

"Or perhaps you'd like to fly amongst the clouds? Kiss the stars and tap dance on a thunderhead?" Egon traced two patterns. His eyes flashed like streetlamps, and he rose above his desk. He pushed off the desktop and drifted down the center aisle until he reached the back wall. Quinn twisted around, craning his neck to watch the wonders Egon's fingers brought to life.

Mr. Pennington snapped and settled to the ground. He shrugged. "Can't do any of it if you don't know the basics."

"Tell us," Quinn said.

The teacher glanced at Quinn, his only reply his flaring nostrils and taught throat. Quinn didn't know if Egon had a particularly strong hate of misfits or was so frightened by them he feared Quinn would morph into a demon and shove a fireball down the man's throat. Either way, Mr. Pennington's look sank Quinn into his seat.

"In due time, hopefully all your questions will be answered." Egon scurried to his desk, his worn oxfords clicking on the wood. "But first, today's lesson."

He spun and reclined against the desk's lip. "Today we begin by learning about the three paths to magic."

The class groaned.

"I know, I know. No fireballs today, children. Anyway, the first path is talent. Everyone here was born with talent because either their mother or father or both had talent. Talent gives the other magical races their power and prestige as well. Without it, no elves or gnomes or even ogres would exist.

"Talent is why you can draw arcane geometry and cast all the wonderful spells we magicians cast. It's why you can alter the fabric of existence and do things that nature and the mundane humans think impossible. We are the glorious talent, each of us. We are the true magicians of the universe, and it bends to our wills."

A dark, spidery arm shot up. Porter. Quinn rolled his eyes.

"And misfits are the false talent!" Porter craned his neck around and flashed a grin at Quinn. "They're evil leeches."

Mr. Pennington pursed his lips. "Indeed they are. They're certainly not the kindest bunch of magical beings you'll ever meet."

"Do you really have the bones of the first misfit in the library?" Porter asked.

"We brought a very powerful misfit's bones to the library once but decided it deserved a more appropriate in a deep, dark grave. Such things of power shouldn't be near young children. The library has many curiosities, Mr. Price," Egon said. "And the answers to many a fish's curious questions. I hope you spend more than a few hours there in search of your own."

"It's all just artifacts and old histories." Porter snorted and leaned against his seat. "I want spells. How're we supposed to fight the misfits with history books? And what about the Misfit Ki—"

Egon's wave cut him short. "Let's not go off on tangents. Those are for Arcane Geometry 101." He paused for laughter but frowned when only Quinn caught the joke and snickered. "As I was saying, the talented are the pure magicians, the ones born with magic in their blood. But that is not the only way to gain magical prowess. There is a darker way, a forbidden way. The way of torture can steal talent from a magician's soul and place it inside a mundane person. Torture gave the evil things of the world power. It's what makes witches and warlocks, and it's how the dark races of elves, goblins, trolls, and many others were born.

"And while a misfit is blessed with magic once they receive torture, they, ah…" He paused, his lips twisting. "They are changed. Tortured magic is dark. It corrupts the souls who wield it. They become a thing of hate and anger. They gain a hunger for destruction, for death of all things unlike themselves because they no longer see the beauty of the order and balance of creation. No curse can make you into a witch. No hex can transform you into a warlock. Only one ritual can make a boy or girl into such an unsightly being, and that is the path of torture."

Billy raised his hand. "What happens if a tortured magician isn't killed? What if they survive?"

"Scared they'll come get you?" Porter asked, lashing out his tongue.

Egon cleared his throat. "Now, now, Mr. Price. That's a good question, Mr. Holcomb. If a magician who's been tortured dies, the talent is forever in the misfit who took it. We're not exactly sure what happens if a talented magician survives their torture. The, ah, misfits are very thorough in their methods. Very thorough. Although it's theorized the magician could regain his magic by force, we're not entirely sure." Mr. Pennington folded his arms like he'd been put in an invisible freezer and stared into space.

The class watched their teacher lose himself in memory while Quinn's own thoughts wandered. If they made misfits by torturing magic from natural-born magicians, how could Ryley ever be their potential king? He already had talent. A dark thought gave him pause. Donal said the Misfit King was one blessed by the three paths of magic. If the misfits found Ryley and tortured someone's magic into him...

Quinn swallowed the thought and straightened. He was being paranoid. Ryley was safe. Donal said so. Despite the chill racing down Quinn's spine, he told himself everything would be okay.

Mr. Pennington jerked up. He chuckled nervously and clapped. "And now we come to the third way, the path of trial. The most mysterious and most powerful of the three paths."

Quinn perked up.

"Neither good nor evil," Egon continued, "the trial brings out the talent latent in all living things through a great test—a torture of the self. It's a mixture of talent and torture, but bound together. Gaining magic through this path is somewhat of a mystery. I've spent years studying books and theorems in our library, and still, it's unclear how the trial actually works. Not even the librarian with all his wisdom and power and many years knows the secret."

"But there has to be some way," Quinn said. "What did the one who succeeded do? What was their trial?"

The entire class turned, angled eyes glaring. He flushed and leaned against his seat. Mr. Pennington cleared his throat and smiled. "Yes, one person has succeeded in the trial. As to what he did, that's something you'll have to ask him yourself. What better way to learn of the trial than from the one who underwent it?"

"He's alive?" Quinn asked.

The class snickered.

Egon quieted the other students. "Indeed he is. He's very much alive, but good luck prying the secret from his lips. If you're curious, you're welcome to try. His name is Donal Ward, and he is the principal of Wimbly's."

* * *

Mr. Pennington dismissed the class after a long lecture on the origins of magic and the superiority of the talented magicians over all other magical and non-magical creatures. Hearing him drone on and on about how the talented considered themselves the shepherds of society irritated Quinn. Maybe it annoyed him because at some level, he knew it was wrong to think that way. He suspected it annoyed him because they considered talentless people—people like him—less than them. He'd spent his life feeling less than everybody else. He didn't want to at Wimbly's.

Quinn shoved his book into his canvas backpack and slung it over his shoulder. Heidi and Billy flanked him, and together, they shuffled out, a stream of students breaking around them like a rushing river breaks around a rock.

Heidi fidgeted with a feather behind her ear. "The trial sounded interesting, don't you think?"

"Yeah, it did," Quinn said. "I had no idea Donal was born without talent."

"You know," Billy chimed in, "they say trial's the most potent way to get it. It's why Principal Ward's so powerful. It's why the misfits are afraid to attack Wimbly's. They don't have anyone who can beat him. Maybe that's why they're looking for their Misfit King, so they have someone who can face him and can steal the secrets in our library."

Heidi rolled her eyes. "As if the librarian would ever let them. He might not be able to go outside, but take a step in and he'd roast each and every one of them."

They walked outside and into a cloud-painted sky. Billy hugged his book against his chest and squinted at the administration building. "I've always wondered how the principal did it, but my parents say he won't tell anyone. Probably afraid of it getting to the misfits."

"I heard he's embarrassed by it," Heidi said with a shrug. "They say he fell in love with a misfit." She leaned closer to Quinn and Billy. "While he was with Ms. Callahan. That's how he figured it out."

"What?" Billy's mouth could have held an orange with room to spare. "How do you know that?"

"People talk. I'm better at listening than everybody thinks. It's their fault they see feathers and flowers in my hair and think that's all that's in my head."

Quinn stared at the administration building. His gaze drifted to the mysterious library with its secrets and tomes and powerful librarian. He needed answers, but he needed to go about finding them as smartly as possible. "I think we should find out more about it."

"Check out the library then," Heidi said. "It's a great place to start."

Billy blew a leaf circling toward his nose, his dark eyes steadying on Quinn. "What's it matter? We've all got talent anyway so it's not like it's useful. Unless you're trying to figure out how to get more than one path, which is something only a misfit would want."

"Just curious is all." Quinn forced a smile. He bounced on his heels and twisted toward another classroom building. "We've got Arcane Geometry 101 next. Should we go before we're late?"

Billy ambled toward the next building, but Heidi lingered back with

Quinn. Her fingers played with her coat, and she stared at her feet. "Quinn?"

He paused, hoping he hadn't made his new friends suspicious. "Yeah?"

"You were really good at drawing your geometry. Really good. I—I…I need a tutor."

The tension twisting in his chest unwound with his smile. She wasn't suspicious. She needed help, and in a way, the help she needed might help him, too. He patted her shoulder. "You need help drawing?"

Heidi blushed, and she traced a sloppy circle with her shoe. "I'm just not very good at it."

"Of course I'll help you, Heidi. Want to meet up at the library later?"

Her shoulders slumped and she exhaled, twisting one of the feathers dangling next to her jaw. "Thank you, thank you, thank you! I'm actually starting a floriculture club at the greenhouse so I won't be able to get away for a while. How about we meet at one of the study halls soon? They're the only place fish can actually practice spells without supervision. I'll let you know when."

"Sounds great. I'm happy to help."

She started after Billy but paused. "Quinn? I almost forgot. I checked out a book but it ended up being the wrong one. If you're going to the library later can you put it back for me?"

"Sure."

She dropped her pack and rummaged through its contents. Heidi pulled out an old, cracked book, its frayed cover the color of a weary camel. She tossed it to him, and he turned it in his hands. It was a boring little book with a boring title on enhancing bloom quality using arcane geometry. Quinn slipped it in his pack. "Got it."

"Thanks. I really appreciate it. You're not anything like what they say, you know. You don't have to help me, but you do anyway."

"Don't get all mushy on me," he said as they headed to the next class. "We need to get inside. I want us all to sit together."

He shoved his hands into his jacket and glared at the bricks passing beneath his footsteps. Quinn believed he was a good person, somewhere deep down inside him. And yet a voice softer than a cricket's sigh whispered he was nothing but a cheater. A loser. A misfit without magic who would use his friends however he could if it meant keeping his secret safe.

10

Not Just Any Ordinary Librarian

Classes ended and dinner eaten, Quinn readied himself for a night at the library. He waited in his dorm, chatting with Billy about their first assignments while he practiced calculating and drawing several spells he knew would blow everyone away if by some miracle he'd ever cast them. The designs were intricate and beautiful and mesmerizing. Something about them pulled him in, and no matter how complex they became, they always left him wanting more. One day, maybe they'd do something, but for now, they were nothing more than pretty lines on paper.

Billy slipped from the room and headed for one of the study halls. Quinn finished another shape and smiled, leaning against his chair. Cast it, and he'd leap into the sky like the world's mightiest grasshopper, so high and so far he'd make a superhero raise his eyebrows and nod approvingly.

Closing his eyes, Quinn imagined the frosty air nipping his cheeks, the snowflakes flitting madly around him as his dancing fingers tickled a cloud's belly. One day. One day soon.

Quinn stayed in his room until midnight. Billy had told him that the library never closed its doors because magic never took a night off and some of the best inspiration for spells came late at night. Hopefully that late and so early in the school year, few students would be nose-deep in dusty tomes. Quinn wrapped himself in a jacket and stole out the dormitory, grateful no one lingered in the hallway to imagine all the horrible things the Misfit King might be sneaking off to do.

Outside, the lampposts wore gold halos around their rounded heads and kept the dark from slinking onto the winding path to Hilltop. The walkway ended at Hilltop's wide courtyard. He kept to the perimeter, circling the back of the classroom buildings on his way to the library. He reached the last classroom building, his breaths steamy clouds puffing from his lips.

Quinn took a step from behind a classroom building, toward the last stretch of open air between him and the library, but a set of low whispers gave him pause. He frowned, darting into the building's shadow. He crouched at the corner and peeked beyond its edge.

Ms. Doyle and Mr. Pennington lingered beneath a light illuminating the old structure's pale siding. Ms. Doyle huffed, tapping her heel on the courtyard bricks. "I would've found them by now, Egon. Between our spells, Principal Ward, and the librarian, you and I both know no misfit could slip onto the island. Quit letting old fears make new worries for you."

"That's what you say, but you and I both know sometimes the impossible is imminently possible when magic is involved. Do you know what Quinn told me? He said he saw something following us from the mainland. A speck against the clouds. It could have been them, Cynthia. They're watching him." Mr. Pennington clenched his fists and cast his gaze about the sky like it might rain witches on broomsticks any second. "He might not be the one yet, but they want him and they'll do everything in their power to make him theirs. The boy's got talent. He draws powerful spells. If they're not planning on torturing the talent from him, they're planning on shoving someone else's inside along with it. All that raw power will make him unstoppable. Evil. And sleeping soundly next to all the other children."

Ms. Doyle laughed and swatted the air. "Please. We're not even sure if that would work. No one's ever heard of someone drawing on two paths of magic. It's why Principal Ward doesn't believe the prophecy of the Misfit King can ever come true. No one, not even him, has figured out how a single person can be blessed by the three paths, much less two."

"We rely too much on Donal and the librarian's power. I've heard rumors from the townsfolk across the lake. Odd things are happening, dark things. The misfits are gathering." Egon ran his fingers through his hair, shivering from a chill carried on his fears. "Why would the misfits gather unless they were preparing for something? Why would they attack us like they did unless they desperately wanted one of our students?"

Quinn leaned against the corner, risking light breaths through his nose. The librarian was clearly more than just a babysitter of old books, and despite Donal, some of the faculty still believed the misfits were more than just annoyances. Talented magicians' powers might not be all they cracked it up to be, even though the magicians all clearly believed no one could truly be their equal.

"That's easy enough to explain," Cynthia said. "They want Quinn's talent, and they're going to flock around us like a bunch of half-starved vultures out for road kill until we convince them they can never have it. They're mad we got him first. That's too bad for them but I don't see how it's earth shattering. We'll survive this. They'll lose interest in Quinn and find another potential to crow about to keep them relevant when the truth is we broke their backs when we broke the Nazis."

"I don't know. I just really don't know." Egon fidgeted, knots flexing in his bony jaw. "I'm trying to be fair, but I've seen other potentials before and Quinn's different. Something about this whole situation doesn't sit well with me. He has a thirst I don't see in the other students. There's something dark in it, Cynthia."

Ms. Doyle sighed. She pushed her glasses up the strong bridge of her nose and placed a hand on Egon's shoulder. "You're a worry wart, my friend, but if it's that important to you, then I'll keep a closer eye on the boy. My first impression of him was wrong after all, so perhaps you're seeing more clearly than I am."

"Thank you, thank you." His shoulders slumped but quickly straightened. He pinched the collar of the shirt beneath his sweater and smiled. "I'll rest better tonight. Join me inside? I've drawn a new transformation spell for a peregrine falcon I think might even impress Maisie, but I want to show it to you first."

He extended his elbow, and she threaded her arm through it. They turned, facing the administration building. Quinn watched them trail toward it while he hid behind the corner. Quinn stood. He exhaled and brushed off his hands.

"Wait," Ms. Doyle said, halting in her tracks just before she passed beyond the lamppost's light.

Quinn's breath caught. He twisted behind the building and pressed against its siding.

"What is it?" Mr. Pennington asked, his voice drifting beyond the corner.

There was a long pause. Quinn stiffened. His feet begged to flee, but he planted them to the ground and stood as a statue.

"It was nothing, Egon." Ms. Doyle's laugh was like polished china clinking. "You're making me paranoid. I swear, by the end of the school year you'll have us all watching our backs."

"I hope it won't come to that," he said. "But it never hurts to keep one's back very well observed."

They continued chatting, their voices drowned by a slow tide of silence. Quinn waited another minute just to be sure they wouldn't spot him. He clenched his jaw and counted. On three, he sprinted for the library, dashing through the intermittent light cast by the courtyard's lamps.

Unlike most other buildings on the campus with their wide, proud doors, the library had a single, narrow door of stained oak set into an alcove of white arches. The bronze handle was old, its latch a heavy weight that begrudgingly opened for him.

Quinn pushed, and the door parted wide. He slipped inside, shutting the door behind him with a cringe-worthy clunk. The sound the door made quickly slipped from his thoughts when his eyes adjusted to the light.

"Holy cow." Quinn's slack-jawed gaze drifted upward.

Outside, the brick library was fairly tall, being a ten-story rectangle with a flat roof. Inside, it was impossibly taller, with row after row and floor after floor of bookcases spiraling into a ceiling that ended in the pixel of a golden square.

The main floor was a grid of talon-footed desks. Each one sported a bronze lamp with emerald shades placed neatly beside porcelain inkwells and silky swan quills. All but one desk sat unoccupied, the library's only other guest the solitary redheaded girl he'd rode with on his ride from Tupper Lake. As far as he knew, she still hadn't said a single word to him or anyone else.

She eyed him, the amber threads of her hair glistening in the lamplight. He smiled. She buried her face in her book and twisted away.

He padded into the library, looking for a book directory or any kind of direction. Each bookshelf had a label with its subject drawn in looping calligraphy. One of the nearby shelves declared it contained all things botany. Smiling, Quinn strolled into the aisle, pulling Heidi's book from his pack. He checked the reference number. His eyes darted from the number to the shelf, from the number to the shelf. He traced a finger along the many leathery spines until he came upon a small void in the otherwise closely packed tomes in the library's musty corner. The book fit perfectly in the space. It looked comfortable, hugged between its scholarly brothers and sisters.

"Now where to?" he asked one of the books. "I don't have any idea where to start."

"Welcome to the Wimbly Library," a voice said, soft and hoarse as a deathbed whisper.

Quinn whirled around. A hunched geezer stood before him who had to be older than the dirt beneath a fossil. Skin sagged in puffy rings over his sharp cheeks. Liver spots dotted his brow, and the library's gold light reflected on his round, hairless head. A lavender blindfold covered his eyes, and he wore a navy pea coat with smooth buttons that partially hid a dust-colored vest fastened up his neck. The old man grinned, flashing a smile that had lost more than a few of its teeth.

"Is this your first time here?" the man croaked as he leaned heavily on a black walking cane.

Quinn nodded.

The blind stranger waited, light breaths whistling from his hairy nostrils. Quinn blinked, glad the man couldn't see his cheeks reddening. "I—yes, yes it is."

"I thought as much. I always love feeling the wonder shining from children experiencing my library for the first time. Makes my day, it does. I am Nehemiah Crawford, Wimbly's Librarian, Proprietor of Knowledge and Other Unexpected Things." He extended a hand so covered in spots it was almost purple.

Quinn took it, gingerly. "It's nice to meet you, Mr. Crawford. I'm—"

Nehemiah latched on and shook Quinn's hand with shocking strength. "Quinn Lynch, I know. A handshake can say more than any tongue, dear boy."

Quinn yanked his hand away, squeezing his fingers into a fist. He cleared his throat and glanced around the towering structure. "How's it bigger on the inside than on the outside?"

"Maybe it's the same size and you're just a little smaller. Or maybe it's taller than it seems outside because you aren't looking from the right angle. Things only exist because of how we perceive them, and we each perceive things differently."

"Well, okay…" Quinn scratched his head, searching for a quick exit from their conversation.

"What can I help you with so late at night? The witching hour doesn't usually get popular until Halloween." He leaned close, supported by his walking stick. "Something nipping at your thoughts you might be too afraid to seek while the sun's up? Hexes and curses giving you sleepless nights?"

"Not that at all, Mr. Crawford. I just couldn't sleep and wanted to study."

Nehemiah chuckled, his petrified windpipe clacking like two wooden blocks rolling downhill. "Lies are much easier to spot when you don't have eyes to see the imp's lips, I say. Speak plainly or take your chances alone. I'll tell you now, though, you'll have much better luck asking for my help than doing pirouettes through bookshelves for that one book that might spill the secret you seek."

The librarian saw so much for seeing nothing. Lie and Nehemiah would pluck his words from the air and smack him with them across his cheek. Quinn couldn't keep what he wanted a secret from everyone, and something about the librarian put him at ease. "I want to learn about how people get magic. The three paths."

Mr. Crawford's lips pursed into a wrinkled raisin. "You wouldn't be curious about torture, would you?"

"No!" Quinn stepped forward. His nose nearly touched Nehemiah's stump of a snout. "Trial," he whispered, glancing toward the reliably silent redheaded girl. "I'm interested in the trial."

"Ah," Nehemiah straightened. "A fascinating topic. We have many tomes on the trial, although I suggest you would learn more by going to Donal. Why read secondhand accounts and scholarly musings when you can ask the only living magician who's actually done it?"

"Because…" Quinn stared at his feet, his shoe toying with the chestnut floorboards. He didn't know what to say. He feared the man's blind glare would dissect his words like a frog in an eager science class. "Just because…"

"Hmm." Mr. Crawford chewed on Quinn's muddled words. "You know most of the faculty would frown upon a student—especially one as young as you with the reputation even my wrinkled ears can't deny hearing—poking his head around the histories of the paths of magic. Such curiosities are often overlooked when there are more exciting subjects in your schedule. Unless, of course, a student might be interested in alternative methods of gaining magical ability? Perhaps in bringing a friend into arcana's fold?" He leaned closer. "Or perhaps in increasing one's own *raw power?*"

Quinn's mouth dried like a pond in the desert. He chuckled, rubbing the back of his neck while he wilted beneath Nehemiah's hidden glare. "That—no, that's silly. I just want to learn. That's all. I want to learn."

"Do you?" He arched a silvery caterpillar eyebrow. "Well then, that's something entirely different. I'll be honest with you, Quinn. It's against my oath as a librarian to prohibit any from seeking knowledge within these walls. That oath also compels me to report to the administration any peculiar students who are interested in peculiar subjects. If you want to learn about how individuals gain magical ability outside of being born with talent, ask Donal. You can look here if you must, but either way, the principal will find out, and he's liable to treat you more kindly if it's under honest and open circumstances than nosing around my shelves in the dead of night. Do you understand?"

Quinn nodded.

"Good."

Quinn no longer wondered how the man saw without seeing. He could feel Nehemiah's stare, and it came from all around him.

"Now, you're a curious student," the librarian continued, "but you've yet to open a curious book. Let's leave it at that and keep this between us. I like you. I can feel that you're special in some way. You have a—satisfying aura about you, and I am hardly satisfied by an aura these days."

Despite the man's pleasant words, Quinn couldn't help but slouch. His trip was a complete waste. "Thank you, Mr. Crawford. I'll go now since it's so late."

"So soon?" Nehemiah smiled, the broken wall of his teeth flashing. "I thought you wanted to learn something?"

"I—I do." What was this old man getting at? The library with its stale air and towering ceiling held no answers for Quinn. "But you just said—"

"Follow me. I want to show you something very few students and practically no fish have ever had the pleasure of seeing. But you need to. I feel you need to sure as the sun knows it can't sleep below the horizon for eternity. As I told you, I'm not simply a librarian. I'm also a proprietor of knowledge and other unexpected things."

Mr. Crawford led him to a rolling library ladder hooked onto a brass railing. Flipping his walking cane into a loop at his waist, he grabbed the low rungs and hoisted himself onto the ladder. His back cracked, and he winced, rubbing his backside. "Climb onto the low rung. Make sure to hold on until we stop."

Quinn grasped the rung below Nehemiah's polished black loafers. He frowned, swiveling to the grid of desks in the center. The redheaded girl had vanished, leaving him and the odd librarian alone amongst the books.

"Don't be afraid," Mr. Crawford said, a clattering chuckle dancing in his throat.

Quinn's knuckles whitened as he squeezed the rung. "What—"

Nehemiah flicked a pattern etched onto the ladder. It shot up, racing past the library's lower floors. Quinn screamed, latching like a tick onto the rung. Wind whooshed through his hair, drowning his voice. Floors turned into a blur of shelves stocked with cinnamon and scarlet spines. The tiny square of a ceiling expanded so fast Quinn knew they'd slam into it before he could take another breath.

They reached the topmost floor, and the ladder halted. Quinn's heart was a boxer's glove pounding against his ribs and his arms trembled like they'd just been pulled from a frozen lake.

Peeking down hadn't been the best decision he ever made. The library desks were spots against a cracker-sized floor, their lamps glowing specks dotting the wood.

"I'm going to fall. I—I can't do heights, Mr. Crawford. Please. Please don't let me fall." He squeezed his eyes shut and gripped the ladder with every part of his body that could wrap around it.

Nehemiah grabbed Quinn's arm. He plucked him from the ladder and swung him over the railing with more strength than a man his considerable age and condition should ever have mustered. "No one's ever fallen in my library and I don't aim to break that record tonight."

Quinn's feet came down on a worn Persian rug. It ran the length of the walkway bordering the atrium, the ceiling of which bore a brilliant crystal chandelier. Its looping crystals hung in gentle arcs, and within it, tiny points of light shone like stars trapped within the infinity of reflecting glass.

Not a single bookshelf occupied the top floor. Each of the four walls had a single doorway that stood easily three times as high as Quinn was tall. Over each door hung curtains the color of a deep, calm sea.

"What is this place?" Quinn asked, edging from the railing. "Why bring me here?"

Dust swirled in the light like curious sprites come to greet their newest visitor. Mr. Crawford slid his walking stick out and hobbled toward one of the curtained doorways. "You said you want to learn. I've brought you to a place where you can do so. This is the first floor of the library, and we are headed to the North Door."

"But it's on the top. How's it the first floor?"

"Perspective, boy, perspective." Nehemiah pulled the curtains apart with a gold braid, revealing the warped door painted a dull black behind it. Carved into the warped and crumbling wood was an intricate latticework of geometric spells. Curves and intersecting angles formed an immense, hypnotic pattern that Quinn swore moved the longer he looked at it. The door swung inward the farther the curtains parted, revealing an inky black beyond.

"Where does it lead?" he asked.

"To learning, that's where. The North Door's a place to learn about yourself and where the path you walk might lead you. It's true I'm forced to tell the faculty if any student reads about torture or trial from a tome. They never said anything about leading a student through a door and letting him discover if that subject is one he should be seeking."

"But how will I know?"

"When things start making sense—which, I must warn, may not be tonight." He tapped the doorway with his cane. "Now are you going to walk through, or are you going to stand there and pepper me with questions all night? Some might call it rude to keep an old man up so far past his bedtime."

Quinn swallowed. He had no idea what to expect on the other side of the doorway. The wood was old, older even than Nehemiah, who Quinn suspected might have more years than his rattling bones and spotted skin revealed.

Calming his nerves, he stepped into the doorway but paused beneath the massive frame. "I'm scared."

Mr. Crawford's hand pressed gently between Quinn's shoulders and ushered him through. "Good. We fear most what reveals the truth about ourselves. What you see," he whispered, his breath washing over Quinn's cheeks, "is yours to see. Just remember that all things are a matter of perspective."

Quinn stepped into a dark room. The light behind him vanished.

11

A Turning Point

He watched Ms. Velvet carefully inspect the spell scrawled onto his card. The cloudy morning had departed by noon, giving her and Ryley the afternoon to practice under a crisp, pale sky with a horizon streaked by the ruddy pastels of a tired sun.

At her feet lay the pile of Ryley's shredded spells that came before. He rocked on his heels, staring at the perfect curves of her jaw, the elegant, cold bend of her lips, the furrow of her brow that Ryley quickly learned would never wrinkle no matter how angry she became whenever he let her down.

She had to like this spell. It was perfect, like her. Every line curved just as it should. A computer couldn't have drawn the intersecting angles better. Ms. Velvet's lips pursed. He leaned closer to her. This had to please her. It just had to.

"You're making progress," she said, nodding. "Your spells are finally starting to resemble something slightly more complex than a blind, drunk monkey's halfhearted scribbling."

Ryley smiled and reached for his perfect spell. "Thank you, thank you. I knew this was the one. I knew it had to be. The lightning it casts could tear through a wall easy! Just imagine what it will do to Quinn when I cast it on him."

She cocked her head and yanked the spell from him at the last second. "What do you think you're doing?"

Ryley recoiled, edging closer, his hand trailing hers like a fish on a line. This was his perfect spell. He deserved to cast it. He deserved to feel its power boil inside him and leap into the world in all its violent glory. "What am I doing? What're you doing? It took me eight hours to finally draw that spell. I want to cast it." His chest tightened. "I deserve to cast it."

Clucking her tongue, she slipped the spell into her trench coat. "I don't think so, Ryley. I need this."

"That's not fair. You're not being fair when I've done everything you asked. Let me cast it." Heat rose in his throat and spread into his temples like a fire creeping into the branches of a tree. "Give it!"

He never saw her cast the spell. A force like a raging bull slammed into his stomach. His feet left the ground, and he smashed into a tree with a flash of pain that bit deep into his back. Wincing, he cried out. Ms. Velvet's form appeared through his tears entombed in an aura of writhing shadows.

"Ryley, what have I told you about talking back?" Her voice was calmer than the sky and a thousand times as frigid.

"I—I—" Words abandoned him. He disappointed her. His temper got the best of him, that angry little hissing demon in his soul that whispered the most awful things, told him to take and break what he could and blame all others. He hated it. He hated himself because it was a part of him, but most of all he hated that he disappointed her.

"It's alright, it's alright." Ms. Velvet stepped toward him, her cloak of shadows swirling like a mass of snakes and tentacles. With barely two inches between them, she pressed a startlingly cold finger to his lips. "You must remember, what magic you learn is mine. What arcane geometry you draw is mine. What spell you cast is mine. Everything that you were, everything that you are, everything that you will be is mine, my darling.

Her face twisted in what Ryley could only describe as a beautiful snarl. Her eyes darkened into voids, her cold finger now blazing hot. "...My displeasure is your downfall. I will give you everything you ever wanted. I will give you Quinn and let you toy with him using every spell I've taught you. But disappoint me, fail me, move so much a finger in a way that gives me pause, and you lose everything. Do you want that?"

"No! Please, no. I'm so sorry, Ms. Velvet. You can have the spell. I'll—I'll never do it again, I swear. I swear with everything inside me it won't happen again."

She smiled, her dark eyes sinking into his thoughts like fangs. Her breath was colder than midwinter's wind against his cheeks but he loved it anyway.

"Good," she said. "Do not forget the lessons you have learned today."

Sighing, she released him. Ryley slumped to the ground in a coughing fit, his body a shivering bean hunched beneath the tree. Ms. Velvet polished her nails against her trench coat and turned in the direction of Oliver and Patty's home. "Get up, Ryley, your false father's coming."

As Ryley stood, Ms. Velvet's body dissipated, the last remaining traces of her existence her cold smile and polished blue eyes. No sooner had she vanished than Oliver Watkins burst into the clearing. The breeze made his thinning hair look like wraithlike fingers strumming his forehead. His eyes were dark, and his chin flexed beneath his flat lips.

"What's all this commotion out here?" he asked, marching toward Ryley.

Ryley raised his chin, fists clenched behind his back. "Nothing. I fell. There's icy mud."

"Really, now." Oliver dug his boot into the dirt and kicked. Soggy bits sprayed Ryley, more than a few slapping against his face. "It seems like there actually isn't any ice in this particular mud, it being September and all and things don't get that cold here that early. If you're going to lie to me, Son, you need to at least try and be creative."

Son. The word from Oliver's lips crawled beneath Ryley's skin and sent a shiver down his spine worse than ten thousand nails against a chalkboard. Somehow, Oliver knew how Ryley despised the word when his false father spoke it. Ryley could practically see the smile creeping over his smug features.

"I'm sorry," Ryley mumbled.

"Sure you are. You know I know what you're really doing out here, don't you?"

"You do? I, ah, I didn't know you did." Ryley nearly blurted out Ms. Velvet's name but held his tongue at the last second. She was listening, watching, always watching, and he feared disappointing her if a nothing like Oliver Watkins learned too much.

"Of course I do. I'm not blind. You're out here practicing those shapes they told you about, the ones you studied before the test they told us you would pass. You remember that one, right? The one Quinn passed but you somehow failed?"

"I do." The demon in Ryley's soul whispered the worst things about his false father. It very nearly made Ryley smile.

"You failed!" Oliver shouted. "Why do you practice something you know you're no good at?"

Ryley's fingers twitched. Burning his false father to a cinder would be the third simplest thing he did today after brushing his teeth and putting on his socks. The spell would be quick and painless—on Ryley's part. Oliver might disagree.

"Don't do it," Ms. Velvet whispered. "Bare his punishment."

"Why should I?"

Oliver's face darkened. "Because I asked you for an answer."

"Because you're mine," she hissed.

Ryley relaxed his hands and inhaled. He smiled wide as he could manage. "Because one of the other test-takers said there might be another test coming up, and that if anyone didn't make it then, they might make this one."

The words caught Oliver off guard. For once, his taught features slackened. He regarded Ryley, blinking as if his eyelids could filter the truth from the lie. "Another test? Why didn't they tell us about it?"

"It'll be a surprise test. Harder than the last one. A kind of last chance to prove yourself, so I—I want to practice as much as I can so maybe I can pass. Don't you see? If I pass, you get everything you wanted. Isn't that right? That's how your deal worked. I pass, you get taken care of. Maybe it wasn't the first test they wanted me to pass. Maybe it was the second one."

Ms. Velvet's twinkling chuckle tickled his ear. "You're tongue's not just forked, it's silver, my darling. I love it."

His false father's chin swept to the side, eyes still locked on Ryley. "A second test, huh. Then I guess it's best you prepare."

Ryley's knees nearly buckled with his sigh. "Thank you, thank you so much."

Oliver turned and marched toward the house, but paused between a set of old oaks just before the forest swallowed his lanky frame. "You'll practice until eleven every night, including weekends. Weather's no excuse, either. You've got plenty of coats, and I suspect the snow and *muddy ice* will keep your head clear."

"You won't regret it. I'll make you proud."

"I could care less if you make me proud. I want you to make me rich." Oliver disappeared, and his crashing footsteps receded until Ryley heard nothing but his own thoughts. Any other kid might be afraid of the darkening sky, the lengthening shadows, the wind's ghostly howl as it sifted through the trees. Not Ryley. Ryley didn't fear anything, because Ms. Velvet was always with him, and he was hers.

* * *

A dim light lit the other side of the North Door in palest blue. Quinn squinted, the shimmering disc of the sun peeking from the horizon's edge. The blanched sky blushed to a ripe tomato-colored band, revealing a wide valley carpeted with flowers pink and purple and every shade between. They blossomed in soccer ball bushels over broad emerald leaves.

Quinn plucked a pink blossom, rolling its springy stem in his fingers. He recognized the flower, not because he knew flowers well, but because he knew the girl this one was named for. "A hydrangea? What's she got to do with this?"

The ground—the room—the world—wherever he was shifted like he was the center of it all, spinning like a top until what lay behind him faced him.

Forgetting the meadow of hydrangeas, he stared at the sorry structure squatting a few yards away. Once it had been a home with a nice patio, a white door, and a lovely, well-tended garden. Whatever beauty it had was gone, replaced by scorched siding and crumbling lumber blackened by a blaze. The door was ash and charcoal. The windows were glistening, melted lumps hanging from the broken sills like lifeless tongues. The roof flirted with complete collapse, its shingles warped and bent and twisted. Only the brick chimney stood tall despite the soot caking its neck.

"Why are you showing me this?" Quinn asked, face twisting in a snarl. He spun around, but the doorway had vanished and only an empty, flower-painted valley stretched to the pale horizon.

He faced the home. His home. His true home, the one consumed by a fire that ended his parents' lives. The fire many believed he started.

Whatever magic gave this room life coaxed him toward the porch. It guided his feet, tugging him closer like a carnival ride through a house of horrors. At first he struggled against his own footsteps, but the enchanted pull overpowered the icy pit of terror swelling inside him.

Chin trembling, he stepped over the collapsed doorway. Inside, floorboards bent and twisted. Black threads and ashen patches were the sad remains of the many rugs covering the floor. Morning sunlight speared angled gold columns into the living room and lit the morbid scene with warm colors.

The magic pulled him through the room. It guided him down a hallway. His pulse raced. His footsteps creaked. He reached the end of the bent, broken, and blackened corridor. A door waited there. It inched open, creaking.

"Please," he whispered, "don't show me this. I don't want to see it."

The sun crested the horizon, its white-hot face shining through a broken window opposite the door. Quinn shielded his eyes and stepped through.

Blinking, he lowered his arm. Sunlight still blinded him, but he could make out two figures standing back to back in the room's center. One faced him while the other faced the window. In the corner sat a bed, the only unburned, perfect part of the home. His bed. The bed he woke in to a wall of firefighters pointing at the used matchbook in his hand.

Slowly his eyes adjusted, giving him a clear view of the room and its occupants. Ropes bound the two figures' wrists and ankles to one another, and their heads dipped low enough to hide their faces. Even with the head low, Quinn recognized the boy he faced because he knew him better than any other. He saw him every time he'd seen his own reflection.

Enthralled, Quinn edged to his eerie counterpart. "No, no, no. Stop it, please," he said, tears polishing his vision. "Let me go. I want to go."

The magic yanked him. He grabbed the boy that looked like him and lifted his chin. Quinn gasped, staring at his own face like he'd reached through a nightmarish mirror. The other Quinn, the false one, had an intricate pattern drawn on his face in ash. Tears coated the boy's cheeks, and his eyes were dull porcelain orbs.

"You're me," Quinn said.

Bound Quinn remained silent and still as a statue. Quinn pulled his hand away and circled toward the second boy. The second boy's familiar features needled his memory and sent the hairs on Quinn's arms rising. The boy's combed hair bore a smooth line of a part. Not a single strand dared straying from its proper place.

"No," Quinn said. "Not you."

The boy lifted his chin without Quinn's help and opened his eyes. His pupils simmered like paper in a fire. He cocked his head, flashing the embers of his hungry glare.

"Not you. Not *you*," Ryley hissed, his voice a mocking echo.

Quinn stumbled back. He hit the wall, palms pressed against the crumbling wood. "This isn't real. This can't be real."

"I'm coming for you," Ryley said, his handsome lips parting in an icy smile. "And then everyone will know the truth."

Ryley vanished. False Quinn vanished with him. The house crumbled into dust. The flowers wilted. The sunlight died.

Quinn stared into an impenetrable black. He squeezed his eyes shut and listened to his thrashing heartbeat. Nehemiah warned Quinn he would learn something there, and he had. Quinn learned Ryley was coming for him, and if he didn't do something about it, Ryley would kill him.

12

Hatching Plans & Stoking Rumors

"That old crackpot let a student through the North Door?" Donal asked, shaking his head. His blazing eyes shifted from the stained-glass windows of his office to Maisie, the flames on the many candelabras following his gaze.

Maisie sighed, sliding her fingers from her temple to her chin. "Said he felt the student was special, that he needed to learn something."

Donal laughed and strolled to the window behind his desk. He considered the velvet curtains. "These drapes are getting dusty. Remind me to have Rita get them cleaned."

"Curtains? Really?" Maisie clenched her jaw. Donal's vanity would get him killed one day if his ego didn't do them all in first. "What about the librarian?"

"Nehemiah thinks his farts are special if they're ripe enough to curl a page. You know as well as I there is no magician in the world more powerful than a school's librarian. Unfortunately for him, he's bound to his little tower of bookshelves until the sun gets tired of the world and swallows us all up. He's bored, and he's stirring the pot of these rumors like a warty old witch on Halloween."

"That's disgusting, Donal. Wimbly's principal shouldn't talk like that."

"Apologies, Ms. Callahan." He slid his hand down the curtains and brought it away, rubbing his fingers as if the drapes hadn't been cleaned in a generation. "I'm still reeling in shock from learning the North Door's been opened and a fish of all students has been allowed to pass through. Who was it? No wait, don't tell me." He spun around and snapped, looking very much like a boy and not like a principal. "Quinn Lynch?"

"The one and only."

Donal groaned. He fell into his chair and propped his irreverent feet upon the long desk. Maisie slid into one of the wingbacks and rubbed her palms against its cool leather. Her redheaded informant had an excellent knack for keeping her abreast of all the rumors and whispers working their way through the student body at any given moment. This year, they all swirled around the boy from Tupper Lake.

"The kids are talking," she said. "They say Quinn's the Misfit King come to torture all the talent from us…that he's going to be blessed by the three paths of magic and become unstoppable. It doesn't help that Nehemiah took him through a door. A library door can reveal many closely guarded secrets for those allowed to pass through. If Mr. Crawford aims to lead him through all four, Quinn could have all the knowledge he needs to make the prophecy come true."

"Yes, yes, the Misfit King is the one blessed by all three magical paths. That prophecy is so melodramatic." Donal smirked, his smile deepening the crow's feet fanning from his eyes. "But then again, all old wives' tales tend to have a flare for such things."

"Did you know Porter Price told Egon that Quinn attacked him in the showers and started going off about how he was the Misfit King and how he'd make Porter suffer? You know how atrociously paranoid Egon is of misfits. I'm surprised the poor guy hasn't tried to cast a new pair of eyes in the back of his head so he can watch his own back."

"Or at least summoned a couple eyes to watch Quinn while he sleeps. No doubt he's hard at work trying to convince other faculty members of his theories." Principal Ward rolled his hand, signaling her story onward.

"They say you let Quinn into Wimbly's because you were scared of him. Everyone's heard about the mysterious fire that killed his parents. It's easy to connect dots when there are only wild imaginations filling the space between them. Everyone fears he's got the power of talent and torture inside him already. His natural talent is fooling us and hiding the torture beneath it. The way some of them make it sound, he's already got an army of dark elves, warlocks, witches, and trolls waiting across the lake."

"Really?" Donal laughed and laced his fingers behind his head. He rocked in his chair, lips edged in a thin smile. "I wonder if this rumor started after Porter got his wallop in the showers?"

"Glad to hear you're not completely unaware of everything happening at the school." So he did know more than he let on. Maisie wondered what annoyed her more, his playing ignorant, or his carefree smile despite the mess this school year was becoming.

"Regardless," she continued, "now that Quinn's been through the North Door it won't be long before the rumors take on a life of their own. Parents are going to start calling. If they think Wimbly's isn't safe anymore, they'll almost certainly demand their children back before the winter solstice."

"Now that would almost certainly be a shame." He slid his feet from the desk and scooted forward. "These children are in far more danger out there than in here. Part of me wonders if these are just silly rumors spread by children or if there's a darker motive behind it all. There's nothing misfit about

Quinn, but if the real misfits can stir up enough trouble and get the kids out into society, they'd be easy pickings."

"You should let me investigate. If it really is nothing, I'll have wasted my time. And if it isn't, we'll be better prepared for what's to come."

"No." For the first time during their conversation, a hard look of concern flattened his lips. "No student or faculty member is allowed to leave the campus during the school year. That's the rule. It's especially enforced this year with the uptick in misfits we've been seeing. With Nehemiah and I, I don't care if there's an army of ten thousand of them led by their mighty Misfit King riding a six-headed harpy. No misfit is getting on this island, and I refuse to let them scare me into making rash decisions."

"Donal, that rule about staying put during the school year hasn't been in force since the first years of Wimbly's founding. All of us have left the campus many times before, and you deciding to enforce it now only feeds the rumors. You're keeping something from me—from us. I haven't decided if it's something that genuinely concerns you or if it's something you did to stir up trouble that's biting you in the butt and now you're too embarrassed to admit it."

She watched the hellion inside him glitter in his bright eyes, and her lips went slack. She had no doubt he had a plan cooking she would absolutely hate. "What awful, horrible, vile plan is that pink cashew of a brain trying to form, Donal?"

Principal Ward flew back in his seat, hand splayed over his chest. He spun his chair, and it swiveled slowly, circling until they came face to face again. "Why Maisie—"

"Ms. Callahan."

"Sorry, forgive my cashew of a brain. While you were so lovingly tearing me down, you gave me a grand idea."

"And what is that?"

"As I see it, we've got three problems on our hands." He raised a finger. "The students believe Quinn's only here to learn about the trial so he can go through it himself and become the next Misfit King." He held up another finger. "The misfits are going to try and get the kids out of Wimbly's so they can pick them off one by one." He raised a third finger. "If the misfits do succeed at spreading rumors or sowing a little chaos—and let's be honest, that's what they do—parents will happily fulfill the misfits' fiendish desires by taking the children home. All our problems stem from rumors. Our magic protects us, but no spell can stop whispers once they've been given wings. All we can do is let our own words take flight and hope they gobble up the smaller gossip flocks."

Maisie folded her arms and tried her best to look at Donal like the child he was. "More rumors? You've got to be kidding me. Our situation's already bad enough."

He winked. "I'll sprinkle a few reports of misfit encounters increasing throughout New England, maybe have a few fictional homes attacked or something. I'll send a response out on the official channels stating how unfortunate the attacks have been and how thanks to Nehemiah and I, Wimbly's remains free of misfit magic. Parents will be begging me to keep their kids on the island after that. They might even beg to come here themselves if things really get bad enough out there."

"But there was one misfit worthy of fearing, Donal, one misfit stronger than the rest, whose tortured magic could go toe-to-toe with any magician of talent and maybe even you." Maisie looked away, staring at the map nailed to the wall. Even thinking about the woman drove needles into her heart and made old scars itch. "If there is a Misfit King, then she's the one behind it all. Count on it."

There was a long, painful pause between them, brought by memories of a time when Maisie believed in a world with better people.

"But she's gone," he whispered, his boyish charm and light tone replaced by a soft and steady voice. "She fell with the Third Reich, I promise you a thousand times while crossing my heart for extra measure. And if by some miracle she ever did come back to life and threatened a single hair on any living being, I guarantee not even a golden thread of her own would remain. You know that Ma—Ms. Callahan."

"You should let me investigate. I can do this."

"But I can't. I need you here, not out there chasing ghosts from our past."

He'd never give her permission, his voice told her that. Maisie shook her head and tried to drown him with the disappointment in her eyes. "Then what about the first problem? What about our would-be Misfit King?"

"I'm not too concerned with that at the moment," he said, the heavy air lightening, the candelabras brightening. "But I think we should do our best to make sure Mr. Lynch remains quite ignorant of what the trial entails. As long as that liver-spotted cantaloupe of a librarian quits making my life difficult with his ridiculous feelings and magical doors, we should be fine."

"You realize if things get too heated with the misfits, Quinn will become the students' scapegoat. You're juggling fire on very thin ice. Don't let another innocent get hurt because of your actions."

Donal winced like she'd flung the words at him on daggers. Some of the glitter in his eyes dulled, and he straightened. "He'll be fine, Ms. Callahan. You saw his test scores. You've seen the geometry he can draw. That boy's got both skill and talent. I doubt even the fourth year students would mess with a magician like him. And with you and I keeping careful watch, I have no doubt in his safety."

For her own part, Maisie wasn't convinced they saw the whole situation. Donal was just too confident in his own skill. But she wondered how long he and Nehemiah could keep Wimbly's protected. Magic was as fluid as the wind.

Whatever stopped the misfits Friday might shatter Tuesday. No, Donal didn't believe Quinn could be the Misfit King, but Maisie held one or two doubts of her own that required something more than soothing words.

Any other faculty member wouldn't dare break the principal's edicts. But Donal Ward was no ordinary principal, and Maisie Callahan was no ordinary faculty member.

Standing, she slung her scarf around her neck. She flipped her hair behind her shoulders and strolled to the door, pausing with her fingers on its cool handle. "Good evening, Donal."

"Good evening, Ms. Callahan."

13

Secrets, Studies, & a Dryad for Spice

Days came and went in mostly quiet study. Thoughts of the North Door and its eerie vision faded from Quinn's mind. He tried asking Nehemiah what the vision meant, but the ancient librarian wouldn't hear a word of it. The vision, Nehemiah told him, was his alone to keep. Sharing it with others would only cloud its true meaning.

So Quinn lost himself in his studies instead. Arcane Geometry 101, Introduction to the Art Arcana 101, Early Magical Literature of the Talented—he had too many classes and too few hours to memorize each letter on every page. Still, he devoured as much as he could, burying himself in books that were one of the disappointingly few welcoming things he'd encountered at Wimbly's.

He faced another problem soon, one that seemed so far away at first but drew nearer despite how much he tried ignoring it. Soon, they would have their first practical in Mr. Pennington's class. He'd be tested on what he learned before all the other students, and that included spell casting.

Quinn tapped a pencil on his desk, eyes narrowed at the spells begging for freedom from their paper prisons. Index cards covered his small writing table like shingles on a roof, each spell an intricate, complex enchantment he couldn't cast if his life depended on it.

He finished drawing a circle around his latest masterpiece. Trace the pattern, and he'd blast a ball of energy at his target so fast it'd rip them from their feet and send them flying. Quinn adjusted the angle of a set of interwoven triangles, intensifying the light of the orb. Might as well blind them, too, so he could set up for another spell while they recovered. If he could actually cast some of these spells, he might be pretty good in a fight. Smiling at his creation, Quinn blew the rubbery bits of his eraser from the card and pictured the victory playing out in his imagination.

Something clacked against the windowpane. He jumped, nearly falling from his seat. Another object tapped against the glass, light as a twig blown by stiff breeze.

Pressing his hands against the window, he searched what lay beyond. The sun had long since set, the only light penetrating his dorm the fixture nailed to the outside wall. A girl stood in the lamp's light. Her familiar, feather-woven hair and sunrise smile made his own lips curl toward his cheeks. The feathers in her locks twisted in a light breeze, her colorful patchwork jacket powdered with snowflakes from the first snows of October.

Heidi waved, tipping on her toes, and he waved back. Quinn had wandered into the greenhouse just yesterday and seen the wonders she'd performed with her floriculture spells. In barely more than a month at Wimbly's, the greenhouse had become a spring that never ended. Flowers bloomed in every imaginable color, shape, and size like some rebellious army fighting against the approaching winter.

She motioned for him. He held up a finger and slipped from the window, grabbing his coat and school bag. He darted outside, weaving in and out of students chatting who did their best to pretend he was covered head to toe in poison ivy.

Outside, Heidi skipped to him, hanging her mittened hands around his shoulders. She pecked him on the cheek and giggled. "Good evening, Mr. Lynch!"

Quinn blushed, prying her from him. It wasn't a romantic kiss, but even so his stomach fluttered. "Hi Heidi, what's up?"

She pulled him close, leaning to his ear. "Study hall? Remember what we talked about? I—I'm having a trouble with some of my basics and we've got Mr. Pennington's practical coming up. Help me out?"

He nodded. She grabbed his hand and led him alongside the commons. Linen clouds allowed broken starlight to the island. Lake Champlain bathed in the silvery light, stretching it into squirming caterpillars over the waves. Quinn and Heidi passed frosted fields where groups of third year students played acrobatic soccer games with thorn-coated dryads. Alchemical globes ties to red and white balloons lit the edges of the field and reflected in the dryads' round, amber eyes. Their bark-like skin creaked and stretched, their knotty branches of hair twisted like dreadlocks behind them.

"What's it like to play a dryad?" Quinn asked.

Heidi shrugged and paused by the field. "Once we hit our third year, we'll learn how to enchant our bodies. Playing matches with the dryads helps you figure out the best way to do that really fast. They're very good at kicking the snot out of you if you aren't careful."

One of the dryads kneed a third year in the stomach. The boy went flying and smacked the ground, rolling like a log that nearly took his teammates out.

"But that's not legal," Quinn said.

"It's a different type of soccer." Heidi took his arm, and they continued past the field. "Think of it like a mix of sports and self-defense. If you can walk away from a soccer match with a team of dryads without a bruise, then you could pretty much go head on with anyone and walk away with a smile."

"Is it really that dangerous out there for…for us?"

"It used to be a lot more dangerous. Some people say it will be again. My mom says life is like a tide, and that if we're smart we'll learn to recognize when it's low and high, and that way we'll keep from drowning." She stared ahead, lips pressed into a little thoughtful line. The look faded as they approached a long line of doors spaced evenly along the rocky shoreline. "Here're the study halls. I'll find one that isn't being used."

Quinn had never been in one of the study halls. Not because he didn't want to check out the mysterious row of doors that spanned the shore, but because the spells inscribed on the door required a talented magician to unlock them. Students said the halls were worlds within their world, hidden pockets enormous enough to practice any type of magic the magician desired, but safe for an untrained, unsteady hand.

Heidi found an unlocked door. She grinned, twisting the knob. "I already have the perfect setting for our practice. It's so pretty."

Humming, she parted the door and spun inside. Quinn followed on her heels, the door clicking behind him. It was dark on the other side, like the door Nehemiah sent him through. His heart twisted at the memory while his imagination drew Ryley's features in the blackness.

"How're we supposed to study in this?" he asked, hoping his voice sounded calmer to her than it did to him.

Heidi giggled, and it echoed like a fairy in a forest with a trick up her sleeve. "Watch this."

She turned. Dim light framed her form in faded grey. Pulling a card from her pocket, she traced the pattern scrawled over its surface. The symbol flashed, and a midday sun blinked on, turning their pocket of a world into brilliant blue. A meadow formed, orange and yellow wildflowers popping from grasshopper colored grass like bubbles in a soda. Fat, lazy bees buzzed from petal to petal. Butterflies with shimmering wings like delicate ball gowns fluttered on a cool breeze. The sun kissed his cheeks with warmth while a cool breeze ensured the kiss would never burn.

"Wow," he said.

She stretched her arms, smiling at the blazing jewel of the sun. "Perfect! Mom drew this one for me. Don't you love it?"

"It is very nice. Is this—real? Are we somewhere, or just inside the door?"

"Does it seem real to you?"

"Yeah, it does," he said with a shrug, glad that her spell had chased away all the shadows. A bumblebee buzzed by, its furry, banded body bobbing in the breeze.

"Then that's all that matters." She peeled off her jacket, scarf, and mittens and tossed them onto the meadow. "Now, let's get to studying. Mr. Pennington's going to test us on the elements, and no matter how hard I try, I can't seem to get them down. My fire couldn't light a candle. My ice couldn't cool a cup of tea. I've sneezed harder than my best wind spell. I need help, Quinn."

Quinn dropped his bag beside hers. He pulled out his cards and fanned them like a poker hand. There were so many spells that waited so long to be used.

His leap spell drew his eye to it like that one overly eager kid in class who had to be called on every time the teacher wanted volunteers. Quinn had spent most of his time crafting that spell because heights scared him almost as much as someone discovering his secret.

Not having something solid beneath his feet, that floating feeling fluttering through his stomach, the dizzying amount of empty space between him and the ground—it weakened his knees just standing there thinking about it. But cast that spell, and he'd never fear falling again.

He handed the spell to Heidi. "Try this one. I've put a lot of work into it. Get it down and other air spells will be easy."

"Hmm." She held the card up to their private sun. A butterfly colored like an early sunrise landed on her shoulder, its great wings flexing and shimmering. "Looks like it's not just an air spell, but also with some movement mixed in? Looks like…maybe a jump? Knowing how well you draw, I'm a little scared to trace it."

"I call it the hopper. Why don't you try casting it?"

"It won't—it won't hurt, will it? If I fall?"

It probably wouldn't hurt. But how could he know? It wasn't like Quinn ever experimented with any of his spells. He knew the shapes. He knew how they interacted. He believed in himself. Still, he'd never actually used one, and making Heidi into his guinea pig twisted his heart into a knot.

"Well…" his voice trailed, and his mind searched for an excuse. "It shouldn't, but…"

"You mean you haven't even tried casting this yet? What if I, like, I don't know, disappeared or flew into space, if space even exists in this place? What if I just disappeared forever? Totally not cool." Her lips puckered, and the butterfly on her shoulder took flight. "You could've made me hop into the sun, Quinn! Give me a spell you know works—one that won't kill either of us if I cast it."

He stared at the deck in his hands. He wanted to give her a spell, any spell. He knew they worked, believed they worked. His gaze flicked from his spells to her. Her head cocked, and she rested her hands against her hips. Every instinct he had told him to just give her a spell, any spell, and lie. Another lie piled on all the others. But his life was full of lies and half-truths. Add another one and he'd choke. Worse yet, he might take someone innocent like Heidi down with him. She deserved better after being the only one at Wimbly's who tried to be his friend.

Her eyes narrowed. "Quinn?"

"Maybe we should use one of the simple ones in the books," he said, his voice tumbling.

"We can't use those for the test, though. These have to be unique." She stepped forward, her voice edging higher. "Which spells have you used?"

"I…" His eyes watered. He didn't want any more lies. Keeping them wrapped around his heart was a poison, but the thought of being kicked out of school, of being forced back into the Watkins' house with Oliver and Patty and Ryley, turned his stomach more than any lie ever could.

"Quinn." She stood before him and folded her arms. "You haven't cast any of those spells, have you?"

He blushed, stepping back. His chin rested on his collar, and he lowered his spells. "I haven't, because—"

"You can't," she finished. "It's why you let me cast the spell on the bus, even though if you really had talent you'd be jumping at the chance to cast your first spell. I've never seen you volunteer to cast a spell in class. Everyone talks about how totally amazing you are at *making* spells, but I've never heard someone talk about seeing you *cast* one." Her eyes widened, and she stumbled back. "Are you—are you really a misfit? Is that why you haven't cast anything, because you know the school's spells would go off if you used misfit magic?"

"I'm not a misfit!" He lurched forward and grabbed her hands. "You have to believe me, I'm not. I'm not anything. I can't cast magic." He sighed. Ten thousand weights slung over his shoulders turned into balloons that drifted away. "I'm just—normal. Talentless. I couldn't use magic even if I wanted."

They stood before each other without a word passing between their lips. Even the buzzing bees quieted and the breeze lost its cool caress. Although a weight lifted from him, his world lost some of its charm, like a brand new car after its first scratch.

"And that's the truth. I'm not a misfit, much less the Misfit King. I'm a nobody who's pretty good at drawing and lying, and that's it."

"Why'd you do it?" she asked, her voice as soft as the butterfly wings beating around them.

"I hated my life before Wimbly's. My foster parents hated me. They made me work and clean for them. Every day they told me I was worthless, I was stupid, and I was trash." Quinn wiped his wet eyes with his arm so the hot tears wouldn't spill. "And then when the test day came, they told me they'd send me to juvie if I didn't pass. You—you don't get out of that, Heidi. Not until you're old enough to go to prison. It's how the system works, and I couldn't let it beat me."

He stared at his feet, at the tangerine and banana colored blossoms brushing his pants. Even though he couldn't see it, her stare swallowed him. Quinn couldn't face it—face her.

"So you switched tests with Ryley," she said. "While Ms. Doyle and Mr. Pennington were distracted by the misfits."

He nodded, slowly. "Don't worry, I'll tell Principal Ward. I'm sorry for lying to you, Heidi. I really am. It's just Ryley was such an awful person. I've never met a misfit, but I bet you he was worse than them even without having tortured magic inside him."

Quinn turned. The old oak door waited a few feet away. He swallowed, heading for it. The door loomed. He reached for its brass knob.

"Wait!" Heidi shouted.

Quinn paused, fingers resting on the knob. He glanced over his shoulder.

"I can keep a secret if you can." She rushed toward him. "Maybe together we can keep it from the rest of Wimbly's until we find a way to get you some magic."

"But why? Why would you help me when this could get you in trouble?"

She laughed, her cheeks reddening. "Have you seen me? Do you think anyone thinks the spacey girl with feathers in her hair and a flower for a name could be trouble? Please. We can do this if we work together, Quinn. Your skills, my talent. Together we can totally figure this out."

"Two fish, one magician. I like that. But what about Ryley?"

"Sounds like he was pretty nasty. As long as everyone keeps thinking what they think of you, the misfits would never need to bother with him. Once we figure out how to put some magic in you, that's when we'll tell them about Ryley." She straightened her arm, thrusting her hand toward him. "Keep the secret safe, deal?"

Quinn took her hand, a slow smile growing on his lips. "Deal. But—what about the practical?"

"That's easy. We don't technically learn enchantments until third year, but my mom happens to specialize in them and they're basically all I've been casting since I was five. With some creativity, we'll fool Mr. Pennington."

They shook. Heidi giggled. "Let's get started. Give me that hopper spell."

He gradually took out his spell cards. "Why? Aren't you afraid of it?"

"Would you have cast it if you could have?" she asked.

"I've never wanted to do anything more in my life."

"Then that's good enough for me." Heidi grabbed the spell. Holding it before her, she traced the design. An emerald flash lit her palm, and a wave of power billowed from her body. Slowly, she twisted toward Quinn, teetering on the balls of her feet. "What now?"

"Jump, and good luck. Break a leg."

Heidi cocked her head. "You think you're so funny, don't you?"

"I know I am! Now jump, Heidi."

She swallowed, bending at her knees. "Here goes…"

"Jump!"

Heidi sprang. It started like any jump. Her feet left the ground, and she slowed two feet up as gravity stalled her rise. But then, a blast rocketed from her heels. She zoomed as if an invisible hand had tossed her in a graceful arc over the blanket of grass and swaying flowers.

Quinn's eyes widened, his mouth hanging open. "Heidi!"

He sprinted after her. She spread her arms and twisted, embracing the sky with closed eyes. She soared on a long arc until she was a speck against the pale sky. Quinn chased her, but his feet were slow and painfully average compared to a spell cast by a talented magician. No wonder the talentless were practically invisible to them. If a boy or girl magician could cast a spell like that, Quinn wondered what a trained, experienced graduate of Wimbly's could do, or what Donal or Nehemiah could accomplish.

Gravity nipped Heidi's toes and tugged her down. She landed in the distance, bending onto her hands and knees in a cloud of grass and flowers. Her back lifted and lowered with her heavy breathing.

Quinn reached her a moment later, his own breaths heavy, cold sweat sliding down his neck and moistening his collar. He leaned over and patted her back. "So how was it?"

She inhaled and snapped straight. Her cherry cheeks glistened, and her lips spread in a smile that would have shamed the Cheshire cat. "Amazing! I—I can't even describe it." Giggling, she grabbed his shoulders. "Quinn, I have a feeling this is going to be an amazing year."

"Even with our little, uh, secret?"

"Especially because of our secret. Now get out another spell. We're just getting warmed up."

.

14

What Goes Around...

By the end of their time in the study hall, not even the false midday sun could keep sleep from weighing on Quinn's eyes. Heidi panted and leaned on her knees. Sweat glistened on her brow, and strands of blond hair plastered against her cheeks.

"I think that's good for today," he said.

She nodded, stretching. "I think you're right. It has to be way after midnight. I'm going to be a total zombie tomorrow."

"At least it's Saturday and we don't have class."

They grabbed their winter clothes and their schoolbags and walked toward the door. Heidi paused before it and wiggled into her jacket. "You should spend the weekend trying to find out everything you can about the trial."

"But how? They're watching me, and Nehemiah will tell Donal if I go looking for a book."

She leaned against the doorframe, tapping her chin. "Well, we know Nehemiah likes you because he took you through the North Door. Why not ask him if there's anything else he can do? Maybe there're more answers behind the other doors, or at least some clues. The library's usually got hardly anyone in it on a Saturday anyway. You'll have the place to yourself."

"Good idea. I'll go talk to him, then. You ready to go? I'm beat."

"Right." Heidi grabbed the knob but paused before she opened the door. She spun around, eyes lit up. "I've got another idea."

"All I want to do is sleep right now. Can it wait?"

"No, not that, silly. It's about the trial." She slung her pack around and pulled out a book bound in red leather. "I checked this out to study for our last test in Mr. Pennington's. It's a complete history of Wimbly's."

Quinn frowned, plucking the book from her outstretched hands. The leather was soft and flexible against his palms. "Thanks, but what does school history have to do with the trial?"

She clutched his forearms and flashed her eyes. "Because, Quinn, this book has extensive biographies on every faculty member the school's ever had, including Principal Ward. Maybe there's something you can find out from it."

"Awesome." He tucked the book in his bag. "I'll look over it tomorrow."

"Good, just make sure you return it tomorrow, because I don't want a late fee. I hear Nehemiah gets really creative with how he handles students who keep his books too long. Oh, and when you do start studying make sure to read Principal Ward's section out loud first thing. It's an enchanted book."

"Why? I can't use magic anyway."

"You can't use most types of magic, but this is an enchantment for anybody, even a talentless boy like you." She winked above her lopsided smile. "I promise you won't be disappointed."

He shrugged and followed her out the study hall. The mystical meadow blinked out behind them. Cold air whistled over Quinn's hot cheeks and cooled his sweaty body. Snow drifted from the clouds, thick enough now to choke the starlight from the sky and transform Lake Champlain into a black table. Heidi hummed a little tune and skipped toward the dorms.

"The girls' dorm's on the other side of the field. I'll catch you later," she said.

"Let me walk you back at least! You don't know what's out here."

"Please, I know exactly what's out here. Go to bed, Quinn. Make sure you tell me how things go with Mr. Crawford."

She disappeared beneath a trail of snow curling in the breeze, her twinkling hum fading into darkness. Quinn turned and stared at the glass face of Lake Champlain, its opposite shore glowing with the few silver and gold lamps of the town of St. Albans rising above the treetops. It was a dark scene, bleak by most standards, but for Quinn, it was the most beautiful thing he'd seen in years. For the first time since he lost his parents, he had a real friend. A friend who knew the real him without any lies or exaggerations hiding the truth like winter's clouds hid the stars. He stretched his arms and gazed at the sky, spinning in a circle and laughing.

Something crunched softly behind him. Quinn froze, his world spinning despite his steady head. He twisted around and glared down the row of doorways. "Who's there?"

Shadows and swirling snow curtained him in a close circle like dancers with daggers in their gowns. He stared for another second, his heartbeat suggesting his feet follow its pace. It was after midnight. He was exhausted, and his mind was playing tricks.

Quinn headed toward his dorm. He kept to the center of the empty soccer field, bobbing balloon lights illuminating either side. He reached centerline and paused. Something nagged his senses. Eyes watched his back. Spinning, he faced the presence he knew skulked on the edge of the field's lights. His breaths were little steam engines puffing from his lips.

A figure strolled from the shadows and into the dim field, finally revealing who followed him. Porter. The boy stood there, arms folded across his bulldozer chest, his lips snapping in a smile that was a freshly sprung mousetrap and his snaggletooth the cheese. In the distance, in the dark, a stranger might have mistaken him for a stocky gargoyle.

"Hello, Quinn," he said as he casually unfolded his arms.

Quinn glanced left and right. The field was empty, the balloons their only spectators.

"Looking for a place to run?" Porter asked.

"What do you want, Porter?" Quinn swallowed and slowly stepped back.

Porter shook his head and mirrored Quinn's steps. Quicker than a heartbeat, Porter's fingers danced in a flaring symbol.

Quinn twisted around in a desperate sprint for the darkness. Roots exploded from the field and lashed around his wrists, yanking him to a standstill. He tugged and pulled, but with each sinewy root he snapped, two more took its place. The roots lifted him and rotated his body toward Porter like a string puppet. They curled around his ankles and bound his legs. They stretched his arms until his shoulders ached. Quinn clenched his teeth and glared at Porter as the boy laughed and rubbed his hands like the glee in his eyes might heat them.

"Not so brave when it's not on your own terms, are you?" Porter paused a few feet away and shook his head.

"Let me go!" Quinn struggled against the roots, but his binds tightened.

"You won't be getting out of that, sorry. It's one of the drawbacks of using magic. When someone's got your fingers all wrapped up it's kind of hard to cast a spell. Once we learn enchantments, there're ways around that. Too bad we don't learn enchantments until third year. But you'd have known that if you didn't grow up talentless."

Quinn relaxed, and the plants loosened enough to dull his burning wrists. "What do you want?"

"Not much." Porter turned his back to Quinn. "What you did in the showers really wasn't cool. Not cool at all."

Porter twisted around. His nose wrinkled in a snarl that pulled his lip up his snaggletooth like a long knife flashed halfway from its sheath. The boy traced a quick, blazing sign. Air solid as a fist slammed into Quinn's shoulder. He grunted, and his lungs deflated as pressure exploded against the back of his eyes. He doubled over and gasped.

Porter laughed. "What's wrong, Misfit King?"

Quinn lifted his head. "Don't—"

Porter flashed a sign, and another invisible knot slammed into Quinn's stomach hard as a steel-capped boot.

Tears filled Quinn's eyes. He gagged, writhing in his binds despite their tight hold. "Please, stop. Please."

"Don't worry, this spell won't leave a mark. Your wrists and ankles might get a little red and purple from the roots, though. Haven't quite mastered how to keep someone bound without leaving some bruises. Not yet, anyway." He drifted nearer, whistling, and grabbed Quinn's hair, just like Ryley grabbed it in the bathroom on test day.

With a painful yank, Porter forced Quinn's bleary gaze up. "But the air spell, see, I've got that one down. You thought you were so smart, ambushing me in the showers, trying to save Weasel. But really, you're not that smart. You're new to the magician world, and you thought you could just walk in and take over the place because some stupid kids think you're the Misfit King?" He patted Quinn's cheek. "Just because I spread a rumor doesn't mean I believe it. I'm not as big an idiot as Mr. Pennington. You caught me off guard in the showers, that's all. You may have talent, but you grew up talentless. You're no better than they are to me, and you never will be."

Quinn's shoulder and stomach throbbed. He sucked the snot up his nose and blinked, trying to regain his swirling senses. He clenched and unclenched his fists and ground his teeth. He was trapped, and not just by the roots. Even if they weren't there, even if Porter challenged him to a fair fight, Quinn could never defend himself. In a sick way, Porter had helped Quinn by binding him.

Porter clicked his tongue and stared at his prey. "I hope this teaches you a lesson. You'll never really be like us. No matter how hard you try, no matter how good you become, you'll never be like the true talented magicians at Wimbly's." Sighing, Porter brushed his hands on his legs like they'd been covered in dirt. "Let's get a few more hits in before we head back to the dorms. Sound good?"

"This is wrong, Porter." Quinn glared at the boy, meeting his darkly twinkling eyes. "I never hurt you. Not once."

Porter shrugged. Quinn braced for the attack.

But before it came, a sigh slipped into the field from the shadows. A voice broke into a high-pitched cackle. Porter glanced around and took a step back. Quinn thought it might be another of Porter's tricks, but the look in the bully's eyes told another story. Milky mist poured around them like snake's tongues, slithering through each blade of grass and coiling around their ankles.

Porter snarled at Quinn. "How are you doing this?"

"I'm not doing anything. Get me out of these roots. Now!"

Porter stumbled back. "No, it's a trick. It's some stupid trick you thought up, I know it."

"Porter, I swear it's not me! Please, let me go. Please."

Something hissed deep within the gathering mist. Porter spun toward it, casting one of his air missiles at the sound. His spell punched a hole in the grey, but it reformed in the space of a breath. The boy panted, his hands clenching and unclenching.

The creature hissed behind Porter, a black shape writhing in the fog. The boy twisted around and launched another spell, punching another hole that quickly vanished.

Quinn struggled in his binds. He was trapped, first by Porter and now by their invisible enemy. "Porter, let me go. We need to get out of here!"

Hisses came from all directions. Mist swarmed in unnatural tendrils, serpents barely visible within the cloud. The snakes slithered toward Porter, baring their ghostly fangs from eyeless heads.

"No, get away!" Porter's eyes were full moons of panic that swallowed Quinn. "You really are a misfit, aren't you?"

Porter wheeled around and sprinted beyond the muted light of the bobbing lanterns. The mist closed around Quinn, the snakes within it swaying side to side like a soupy hydra. A silhouette appeared beneath the snakes, calmly standing within its misty folds.

"Don't hurt me," Quinn begged. "Please, I haven't done a thing. I'm not even what you think I am."

"I know," Billy said. Quinn's roommate stepped into view. His proud smile and bright eyes gleamed beneath the curtain of his greasy hair. "That's obvious from you being wrapped up in roots from head to toe."

The mist thinned, pulling apart like strips of cotton. A smile dared inch up Quinn's lips. He laughed, and his shoulders slumped. "Billy, it's you. I—how, how'd you know I needed help?"

Billy flashed a sign and a smile, and a slim, flaming dagger sprouted in his fist. He kneeled by the roots and began sawing through them with his summoned blade. "I've overheard some of what Porter's been planning on doing, like teaching you a lesson and showing the Misfit King what's what. I think it was his plan all along, to make everyone think you were the Misfit King and then beat you up. He'd be the real king here because nobody would mess with someone who could take you on and win. So when it got late and you still weren't back in our room, I got worried."

He cut through the first rope, and Quinn's arm fell. An achingly wonderful rush of blood pounded through his wrist and into his fingers. "You came out here all by yourself? That's, that's—"

"Not something you thought I'd ever do in a million years?"

Quinn nodded. Sheepishly.

Billy smiled and sawed through the binds on Quinn's other arm. "You're right. But ever since you helped me in the showers, I started seeing things differently. I've, uh, I've always kind of relied on my parents for everything. I never..." his lip trembled, but he swallowed, and his lip stiffened. He went to work on one of the leg binds. "I've never really had any real friends before.

I can't remember the last time someone was nice to me, and it made me feel good. I knew something bad was going down, and I knew if I was in trouble, you'd do the same for me. I guess I just want you to know I'll always have your back. It's what friends do."

The last of the roots shriveled and fell from Quinn's ankle. Quinn struggled from the nest of knots and stood, kicking the withering plants away. "You really saved me back there. It took guts—Porter's really good at casting a spell fast. That was some pretty amazing magic you did. I bet he's gonna need a new change of pants when he gets back to his room."

Billy waved dismissively and turned toward their dorm. "Please, he just snuck up on you is all. Everybody knows you're one of the best magicians on campus, maybe even better than the any of the fourth year kids. My spell was just a little illusion. Shows you how tough Porter is though, doesn't it?"

Quinn rubbed his wrists and splayed his fingers. Billy had just confessed how much it meant that Quinn was his friend. If Billy truly did care for him, if he really was a true friend, maybe he would understand his secret like Heidi understood it. "Billy, there's something you need to know."

Billy paused and faced Quinn. "What's that?"

"I…I just wanted to thank you for everything. I'll pay you back, I promise."

Billy laughed. "Pay me back? That's not why we're friends."

"I know." Quinn started to suspect he was more of a coward than he thought. He'd always imagined other students cheering at his spells. He'd always told himself that he was a good, honest person. He'd always believed that he would do the right thing. Not being able to tell little Billy Holcomb the truth made all those things seem like something a silly kid would think. But Quinn wasn't a silly kid anymore. He was a cheater who snuck his way into a world where he didn't belong.

15

Hello, Old Friend

She pulled the rusted gate aside, and it protested with a long creak. Maisie paused, glancing around. No animals disturbed the abandoned lot. No birds took flight from the wall of trees. It hadn't been too difficult to find Quinn's old home in Indian Lake, a splotch of a town hidden in a basin within the Adirondacks. Most homes in the small town were in various stages of disrepair, with cracked foundations and peeling siding as common as the chimneys and window units.

Quinn's family—his real family—had lived on the northern edge of Lake Abanakee, a lake so still and flat it could have been mistaken for the sky had the frosted evergreens surrounding it not reflected in blurry triangles along the water.

Tightening her jacket, she stepped onto a gravel drive dusted with light snowfall. Winter had deepened, and most of Wimbly's was already begin to disappear beneath the snowfall. Farther south, though, it had yet to collect in much more than patches. Taking in the eerie site, she would have preferred Wimbly's calming snows to the dark, needled evergreens with their old pinecones and tired branches.

Around the driveway's bend, she found the remains of Quinn's home. It waited like a grave in a forgotten cemetery, a burnt and broken husk hidden amongst the trees. Most of its roof had blackened and collapsed. What glass had been in its windows lay melted or shattered along the porch. Great charcoal bruises darkened its siding where flames had eaten through the walls. Only the chimney remained standing tall, despite the soot and burnt timbers coating its neck like a morbid collar.

Donal would be furious if he knew she'd left the campus to investigate Quinn's past. He expressly forbade any student or faculty member from leaving the island. And for good reason. The misfits gathering in covens or murders or whatever they called their groups these days might have spotted a less talented magician. But Maisie wasn't like most magicians. She was an elder, old as Donal and as powerful as any of her kind. She could've waltzed through a group of misfits with a pointed cap and a glowing wand and they would have scattered like roaches beneath a falling boot.

"Now, what clues have you left for me?" she wondered. Donal didn't believe in the Misfit King, and his stubborn pride wouldn't let him see the danger lurking on their doorstep. No such thing clouded her judgment. Quinn and the misfits were bound up in something very old and very dangerous, and she needed to know what.

If any clues still existed there, they'd be long cold and hidden to human senses. Maisie rolled her shoulders and stretched her neck, preparing a complex transformation, her favorite subject among the magical arts.

She traced a complex pattern using both hands, expertly interlacing and drawing invisible shapes until the satisfying snap of energy flowed from deep within her chest and into her tingling fingers. The pattern flared before her, and the magic spread through her arms. It worked its way through her body and warmed her skin. Maisie shrank, coming to all fours, her wool jacket and scarf now the coat of soft black fur of a housecat.

Her smell sharpened, the scent of pine overwhelming her nostrils. Each flake of snow was a vibrant shock of ice against her paws. Color lost its luster, but it was more than compensated for by the sharpening of every detail of the world around her.

Pawing onto the porch, she sniffed the old wood. It carried a hint of wet mold and smoke even after so many years exposed to the elements. She leapt over the broken door and landed on the floorboards softer than a leaf in autumn. Maisie searched the living room, nose and whiskers scouring the ground. Nothing. She prowled through the house until she came to the last room at the end of a long hallway. She'd never been in this home before, but she knew the room from Quinn's record.

The door hung ajar, so Maisie leapt through the gap. Deep black coated the walls. Wood crumbled like bits of old charcoal. The roof piled onto the floor, its timbers shattered like broken fingers. Only the room's corner remained unharmed by fire, an odd refuge against the inferno where an old mattress and broken metal bedframe sat partially collapsed.

The fire marshal report said the team found Quinn huddled in the corner, matches in hand, passed out from smoke inhalation. The official report couldn't determine where the blaze started and so did not officially blame Quinn, but finding him with used matches in his hand left little room for doubt.

"There's got to be something in here," she whispered, sniffing around the timbers. Maisie sensed nothing more than a fire and all that came with it. And yet, the relatively unharmed corner of the room was wrong in every way. Any normal fire should have killed the boy long before the fire department arrived.

Flames had eaten a hole into the crawlspace between the floor and the foundation, just where Quinn's bed met the fire's edge. Maisie leapt within the crawlspace, her enhanced feline vision illuminating the dark space in bright lines. She sniffed. She searched. She even pawed at a few things. Still, Maisie found no evidence of misfit magic. Maybe Donal had been right.

Frustrated, she made her way back to the hole in Quinn's room. Slats of light filtered through the wood. Dust and dirt coated her paws. She'd be a mess when she returned to human form, but at least she could leave with some measure of peace knowing the fire had simply been a fire and nothing more nefarious despite what her instincts screamed.

But then her vision caught something that gave her pause. Odd lines etched on crumbled, dust-covered boards. They might have been nothing—but then they might have been something. She inched closer to the collapsed wood until she stood mere inches from them. Sharp angles, gentle curves, both interlaced. Half a spell remained. Half a spell any elder magician would recognize.

"No, it can't be." Maisie's heart fluttered. She recoiled from the spell as if it might leap from the boards and sink fangs into her body. Donal had to know this. Donal needed to know this. She leapt from the crawlspace and darted outside. Shaking her fur, she dropped her transformation, claws elongating into red-knuckled fingers, legs stretching and thickening, the world losing some of its intoxicating clarity.

She cracked her knuckles and took a deep breath. She prepared a spell that would transform her into a thrush so she could fly back to Wimbly's when she realized she was not alone. Forgetting the spell, she prepared another one, a deep seed of dread sprouting in her soul.

"Hello, Maisie," a familiar woman said. "It's been so long. Too long, don't you think?"

Maisie wheeled around, adrenaline and instinct already putting the spell into her fingers. Ms. Velvet stood on the house's patio, wrapped in a trench coat with brassy buttons, her golden hair curled in a style that hadn't been popular in over half a century. The witch smirked, her fingers waggling the last of her own flashing spell.

Maisie finished casting, and her skin hardened into granite. A sword sprouted from her fist, crackling with white flames. It hissed as a blast of ice screeched around her. Maisie cut it with the fiery long sword, shards of ice splitting in two hissing rivers around her blade.

The ice blast dissipated, leaving a thin veil of steam between her and Ms. Velvet. The woman smirked, lightly clapping. "Better prepared than I thought you'd be. Looks like babysitting a bunch of spoiled talents hasn't made you too soft around the edges."

"So you do have something to do with this," Maisie said through the wall of her teeth. "I suspected as much. Haven't you learned your lesson by now? You'll never win. You'll never have your king, and you'll never have Donal."

Ms. Velvet's features hardened. Shadows gathered around her shoulders, and she stepped onto the patio's stairs. "I think that's something we both have in common, from what I hear."

"I'm not with him by my own choice. You're not with him by *his*." Maisie backed away from the woman. Letting that viper within arm's reach could prove fatal.

"And what a blessing that turned out to be," Ms. Velvet said. "Look at me now. Look what I've become."

Maisie pointed the burning blade toward Ms. Velvet. Its heat washed against Maisie's cheeks and over her stiff arms. "You're nothing but a monster, even if you do call yourself the Witch Queen of the West. You torture magic from innocent, talented magicians and put it into—"

"The undeserving talentless? Please. The normal people I choose to receive the gift of torture put it to far better use than you filthy magicians."

"Normal people would never agree to participate in the torture rituals. Normal people have a moral compass, unlike you and your kind. You're a pathetic, empty doll that's wandering aimlessly in the woods, looking for something that might make that black heart of yours beat again."

Ms. Velvet looked around, her red lips parting in a sharp curve. "I think I'm not the only one who's lost in the woods, Maisie."

"Why are you here?" Maisie tightened her grip on the enchanted weapon.

Ms. Velvet circled Maisie, and Maisie circled her. They were like two blazing suns bound by gravity's chain, locked in a dance that threatened each other's destruction.

"I was about to ask you the same. Shouldn't you be at Wimbly's under Donal's...protective care? I thought you talented folk didn't wander from the castles you built. It's a shame, too. While you've been tending to your walled gardens the world's been changing in the most pleasing ways."

"You didn't answer my question."

"Because I'm not your student." Her eyes flared, and so did the shadows writhing over her body. Her wicked look faded into a twinkling chuckle. "But I forget myself. I'm not here to fight you. I'm here to ask for your help."

It was Maisie's turn to laugh. "You've got to be kidding me."

"I'm serious. Deadly serious. Join me. Donal broke both our hearts. Why stay with him? Come with me, and together we'll bring a new age of magic to the land. Help me create a new race of magicians, and torture will become a thing of the past. I want to combine the blood of misfits and magicians, Maisie. A hybrid will unite the paths and end our long war. The reign of the talented is waning. Soon, it will be a memory."

"Hybrids are impossible. Misfits have misfit children and magicians have magician children. Besides, if you're so inclined to end torture, why was it committed here? I recognize the arcane geometry when I see it. Why was the spell etched into the burnt wood beneath Quinn's bedroom?"

Ms. Velvet sighed and pinched the bridge of her nose. "Why did you have to see that, Maisie? You're such a nosy little thing, always the thorn in my side. It was a necessary procedure to ensure I meet my goals. There are prices to pay and sacrifices to make in every war. You understand more than most I'd think."

So Ms. Velvet did commit the torture ritual there. It explained the fire. It explained the spell. "You tortured the talent from his parents, didn't you? But why leave him untouched—unless you really do think he's your Misfit King. Did you—did you torture their power inside him?"

She smirked, licking her teeth with her pink tongue. "How frustrating it must be to stand before the truth yet never have it farther from your grasp. Such is the curse of a mortal life, one not even a magician may evade. Everything you know is a lie. You have no idea what's coming."

"I'll never let you have Quinn. No matter how hard you try, no matter how close you get, I'll do everything in my power to keep him from you."

"Oh, you're such a mighty moral beacon, Maisie, and I believe your words, although I admit you still don't quite have a grasp of the situation—something you're not unused to." She laughed, and the shadows quivered around her.

Ms. Velvet had kept that particular dig for this moment. Maisie knew it.

"His parents' death," Ms. Velvet continued, "was just the first part in a very long-laid plan that's only unfolding enough now. You're beginning to grasp the gravity of your situation, and if you're any kind of clever, you'd realize how very far behind you already are."

"You killed them. He's an orphan because of you!" The flames on her sword reacted to her rage and flashed an almost blinding white, searing her knuckles. Ms. Velvet was toying with her, plucking at her emotions and trying to prod a reaction. She wanted a fight. She'd wanted that fight for decades.

"Quinn's no orphan." Ms. Velvet waved her hand, and the flames on Maisie's sword parted like curtains on a stage, framing the witch's smooth chin and frozen smile. "He has a family. He might not know them yet, but he will, very soon. He will be known by all children of arcana soon enough."

Maisie's heartbeat thundered, and her blood was more of an inferno than her blade. Sweat beaded on her temples, and the scarf once warming her neck now felt like the coil of a hot stove. "Let's end this."

Ms. Velvet's lips formed a little o of surprise. "Really? How lovely. I've been itching to kill the woman who took Donal from me."

"You took him from me. Don't twist that, misfit."

Ms. Velvet lifted a hand and traced a pattern. As she did, her nails became long claws. Her blue eyes darkened into pits. Shadows thickened around her in an ever-growing black aura. Massive raven's wings sprouted from her back, connecting at a thick, feathery collar. Her shoes became black talons, and fangs slipped through her crimson lips.

Maisie stiffened. She locked her arms and took in a deep breath.

Ms. Velvet licked her lips, her muscular harpy form trembling in anticipation. Maisie feigned casting a spell. Ms. Velvet moved to cast her own. Maisie flung her flaming sword at Ms. Velvet. The Witch Queen of the West screamed, lurching from the fiery, razor-tipped comet racing for her chest.

In the instant Ms. Velvet took her eyes away, Maisie traced a pattern and cast a spell. Her body burst into a cloud of dark brown and beige feathers of a peregrine falcon. Wind screamed a welcoming roar as she took flight. She shrieked, her call tearing the air while Ms. Velvet's roar faded below. The harpy form was made for intimidation and battle. The peregrine form Maisie took was a sleek, simple vessel no other bird could hope to catch.

A flash lit the ground. Maisie tucked her wings and rolled. A blinding bolt grazed her chest. She winced, swallowing the pain. She beat her wings with the full force of an elder magician whose very soul boiled with scorching adrenaline and arcane power. They were all in danger: Donal, Quinn, and every student and teacher at Wimbly's. She must warn them. Nothing else mattered.

She pierced a low cloud and leveled out, the senses of her falcon form tugging her toward Wimbly's on an invisible line. High winds carried her with minimal flapping. Her chest throbbed. Her shoulder trembled. The acrid stench of a burn turned her stomach. She ignored it the best she could, even though a pulsing black ebbed into her vision.

Ms. Velvet had returned. For so long they believed the woman defeated along with her misfit army in those last days of the Second World War. But somehow, she survived. Not only that, she had a plan long in motion, one centered on Quinn, one she'd kill to keep a secret. If only Donal had been true to Maisie. If only he'd never strayed to the blonde sipping a martini at a smoke-filled bar in Paris. If only he'd realized the monster Ms. Velvet would become when he broke that blonde's twisted heart.

16

The Esteemed Roderick Shellhouse

Quinn sat at his desk, tapping the bright red book begging for his attention. *A Brief History of the Wimbly School of Arts Arcana*, by Roderick Shellhouse. His fingers slid across the soft leather. Pinching the cover, he parted its pages and scanned the book's many chapters. He paused when a page caught his eye and grinned. Mr. Shellhouse had scrawled Principal Ward's name in bold, curling calligraphy across the top of the page.

He glanced at Billy's empty bed. His roommate mentioned going to one of the dryad soccer games so he could study their combat techniques. Even though being Quinn's friend made Billy about as popular as head lice, the boy didn't mind. Facing Porter Price conquered the last timid ties holding Billy back, and now the world was one great big oyster cracked open.

"Here goes nothing," Quinn said, licking his lips. He cleared his throat and said in his most commanding tone, "Principal Donal Ward."

Tiny shapes swirled around Donal's name like bees around a hive and Quinn had gone for some honey. The book trembled and bounced like a jumping bean on his desk. He scooted his chair against the door and stared awestruck as the book took on a life of its own.

Its covers spread wide. Long, paper arms sprung from the pages. Fingers covered in calligraphy wiggled and grabbed the desktop. A man popped from the rapidly thinning book. He sported a flattened bowler hat and mustache folded into angular curls. The origami stranger pulled his torso out, his stomach folded in lanky squares like a loose accordion. He plucked his feet from the last pages, and the book's leather cover folded into his shoes.

For a moment, he regarded Quinn without a word passing between them. Quinn eventually found his wits somewhere on the floor and opened his mouth, but even then he struggled for any words.

Sighing, the man grabbed his bowler hat and swept it in an arc. "Good day to you, my curiously-confused friend. Come to learn the wonders of the Wimbly School of Arts Arcana? Or perhaps you would like to learn how to simply speak at all? I must warn you that I am strictly a historian and not a linguist. You'll have to inquire in the library for the appropriate book if speech is what you seek."

Quinn's jaw hung loose. He blinked, the back of his chair still leaning against the door.

"Maybe you're under some kind of curse?" The man rubbed his angular chin with papery fingers. "I can't do much about that either. Speak up, or I'm going to fold back up and take a nap while you look up the definition of common courtesy."

"Who—wha—what…" The words stumbled from Quinn's mouth like bricks down a hill. He gripped his seat and scooted forward. "Who are you?"

The man replaced the bowler hat atop his head and hopped from the desk. "I'm Roderick Shellhouse, at your limited service. I'm not *the* Roderick Shellhouse, of course, but rather a facsimile enchantment for the exclusive purpose of assisting inquisitive readers such as yourself."

"But you *are* the book."

"Indeed. Roderick was aware the subject itself might be a little dry for the tastes of excitable young students, so he thought adding me might spice up your research and give your reports some necessary flair."

Quinn grinned and stood, slowly approaching the paper man. "Cool. So you're like an audiobook."

"That is a rather rough approximation for such a carefully constructed, complex creation such as I. I see by the particular chapter you named that you're curious about Wimbly's most unique and fascinating faculty member." He cleared his throat and stared at Quinn down his folded nose. "Donal Ward was born in Mullingar, Ireland. His parents, Patrick and Shannon Ward, immigrated to the United States in 1905 to escape certain unscrupulous debt collectors. They boarded the *Merriweather*, whose captain was Alan O'Ma—"

"Wait!" Quinn raised his hands and stepped forward. "Stop. Do you…can you answer questions, or do you just recite everything in the book?"

Paper Roderick's mustache wiggled. "Of course I can answer questions. As long as the information is referenced in my pages or the original Roderick noted it within his memory at the time he wrote the book, I'll know the answer. That's all, though. I can't tell you what might be on certain tests if that's what you're aiming for."

"No, not at all. I'm, ah, I'm doing a report. But it's very important. *Very important.* Understand?"

"Is it now?" An eyebrow arched up Roderick's forehead.

"Yes." Quinn swallowed the excitement racing up his throat. "I'm doing a special report on all the principals of Wimbly's."

"Wonderful!" Roderick rocked on his heels, his body bouncing like a spring at the folds of his waist. "I've got plenty of information to go around about all of them. It's understandable you'd want to start with Principal Ward, as he is your current principal."

Quinn nodded as eagerly and wide-eyed as he could manage. "Thank you so much for your help, Mr. Shellhouse. Okay, first things first..." Quinn took a breath, thinking of how exactly he might pry anything useful out of the gasbag when it struck him like a shooting star on a dark night. " Did you say Principal Ward was born on 1905? I knew magicians were old, but that old?"

Roderick nodded. "He was less than two when he came to the United States."

"People can't live that long. That'd make him over a hundred!"

"You don't know much about the world of magic, do you? Magic is a powerful thing, and the better you are with it, the longer it sustains you. Lady Catrain Ashdown of Amesbury, first headmistress of the Amesbury Sanctuary for High Talent, lived long beyond a talentless person's years before she became a librarian. Records indicate her advanced age did nothing to soften her temperament, much to the chagrin of the school's students. She was also the first and only magician to be both principal and librarian, but that is another story altogether."

Quinn nodded, pretending like he truly pondered the information. He'd attended Wimbly's long enough to realize that having magical powers extended a magician's life, so the information didn't exactly blow him away. Not wanting Roderick to slip into another long-winded conversation, Quinn tried guiding the paper man to the information he actually wanted. "But I'm sure Lady Catrain was a talented magician, correct?"

"Yes of course. Talented magicians from the early years were quite powerful indeed. Have you spoken with your librarian yet? Some say his power rivals even that of Principal Ward's. Nehemiah Crawford was born in—"

"Hold up, Mr. Wikipedia!"

"My name is Roderick Shellhouse."

Quinn rolled his eyes. "No, it's this website. It's—it doesn't matter. How has Donal lived so long? He wasn't born with talent. He survived the trial."

Origami Roderick stiffened, his folds and creases flattening into a stiff board. "I'm afraid I don't know details of the trial. Not to say I didn't try. Principal Ward wouldn't let anything slip no matter how hard I pressed him. Are you sure you don't want to hear more about Nehemiah Crawford? He's got quite a colorful past as well."

Quinn took a deep breath and forced his most believable smile. "No. Thank you, but no. Mr. Shellhouse, I can tell you're a very smart man."

"Of course."

"And you don't miss a thing."

"I have won several awards for my insightful research."

"Then I'm sure you must have heard something, anything that clued you in on the trial. As a thoughtful and detailed person, you have to have some kind of theory you noted when you wrote the book."

Roderick strummed his squared fingertips over his chin. His flat head dipped, staring at the floor. "I did have my theories, and not even Donal Ward could keep every detail completely secret…"

This had to be what Quinn needed. He rushed forward, hoping he looked as excited and desperate as he felt. "Please, Roderick. How can I do a good report if I don't have all the facts? I'm here to learn, and I hoped you wrote your book so students who wanted to learn actually could. The fact that you're, ah, you're enchanted like this shows just how much the real you wanted others to know what you know. So tell me." He edged so close his breaths rippled Roderick's papery clothes. "Tell me, please."

"I suppose…I suppose you are correct." Roderick stood to his full height, his flattened fist pressing against an equally flat chest. "Let it be known that Roderick Shellhouse believed no fact should be hidden from a magician who sought it!"

Roderick began his speech while Quinn jumped onto his bed and folded his legs against his chest. "As I said," Roderick continued, "Donal kept mum on most details pertaining to his trial no matter how many times I asked. The particulars he guards with an iron will, and I daresay even his mother would have known the secret had it been her dying wish. I did, however, discover a few vagaries that might relate.

"While conversing with Donal about his life during the Second World War, we broached a subject of a more…personal nature. He spoke fondly of a woman who felt fondly of him, but as most stories of love amidst war go, things did not end as they hoped. Donal made a mistake, one that cost him dearly in more ways than one. He lost his love and made a great enemy. He said it was a funny thing, a talentless man such as him surviving four brushes with death only to lose the one thing that saw him through them. He looked very sad then and said power isn't worth the enemies it makes or the hearts it breaks."

"And you think his brushes with death might have had something do with the trial?"

Roderick nodded. "Indeed I do. I inquired as to those brutal encounters. When he refused to detail them or any individuals involved, I suspected there was more than a romance gone sour at work. But who and what were involved? And what enemies did he make from it? I did not know, so I cannot say."

Quinn squinted at the opposite wall. Four brushes with death. Four battles. Four spells. Four monsters. Something pushed Principal Ward to his limits four different times and nearly killed him. It was an important clue, but Quinn doubted he'd gain anything from risking his life four times in a row. No, he still missed a piece, and he suspected it had everything to do with the enemy Donal made. "Anything else?"

"I'm afraid not."

"Well, it's something. Thank you, Roderick." Quinn unwound his arms from his legs and slid from the squeaky mattress. "If you could go ahead and fold back up into a book that would be great. I don't think you'll fit into my pocket like that."

The paper man huffed, recoiling. "What? No other stories on Donal? No tales of other members of the esteemed Wimbly's?"

"You've been a lot of help, Mr. Shellhouse, but I think it's time to turn you back in." Roderick's paper eyes looked at Quinn with a heaping helping of suspicion. Quinn grinned innocently and looked up at Roderick with wide, round eyes. "I loaned you from a friend, and you're almost late. Nehemiah is never happy about late returns."

Mr. Shellhouse's features relaxed. "Oh my. I'd hate to be on Nehemiah's bad side. Perhaps you should check me out again and learn the tale of Nehemiah Crawford? One day soon, I hope?" His tone was more hopeful than anything as he back-flipped over the desk and his body folded in on itself. He folded again and again until a simple scarlet book remained.

Quinn wriggled into his jacket and tucked the book under his arm. He knew much more about the trial than he had ten minutes before. He couldn't help but smile, knowing he was hot on the trail of a mystery that had hidden from the magic world for centuries. Having a talentless kid like him on the edge of figuring it out, that heaped a helping of warm pleasure on Quinn's heart.

* * *

The library stole the breath from Quinn's lips each time he stared into its impossibly tall ceiling. Row upon row of book after book rose into the soaring pillar, the collective knowledge of magic and the history of the people who used it contained within books that seemed to be as plentiful as the stars on a clear summer night.

Thankfully, he found the Wimbly's history section on the third floor. *A Brief History of the Wimbly School of Arts Arcana* fit snuggly in its slot.

"Until next time, Roderick." Quinn smiled, tapping the spine.

"Hopefully not any time soon, eh?" Nehemiah's rattling chuckle burst like a firework in his ear. "He's a bit long-winded, don't you think?"

Quinn choked down his heart before it leapt from his throat. He fell into the opposite bookcase, and it began a slow, dangerous wobble. Nehemiah clucked his tongue and steadied the case with a snap. He smacked his cracked lips and favored his cane. "Careful now."

"You scared me!" Quinn wiped his brow and forced a few calming breaths. "I nearly jumped over the railing, Mr. Crawford. You know, for a blind man, you're just a little too good at spotting things. Is that blindfold around your eyes just for show?"

Mr. Crawford flashed the two silvery brows that rested like caterpillars over his lavender band. "This is my library, Quinn. I know everything that goes on in it. I feel everything, every book, every page, every breath a student huffs as they rush upstairs to bring a book back hoping it isn't past due so I won't turn them into a toad or curse them with warts."

"My book's not late, is it? Please don't turn me into a warty toad. That's— that's just harsh. I only wanted to learn something."

The librarian grinned, flashing the broken wall of his teeth. "Books are funny things. Books have within their pages the secrets of all creation. If we would only take a moment and sit with them, then they would gladly tell us their story. Don't worry, you won't be hopping out of here today."

Quinn backed away from Nehemiah and folded his arms over his chest. The old librarian's tone had an eager edge to it, and for the first time since he'd met the man, Quinn wondered if Nehemiah's help might come with a price tag. Quinn had lived in more than enough foster homes to know better than to trust strangers and their promises.

"So what's your deal, Mr. Crawford?" he asked. "Why do you keep helping me? I'm not completely stupid. You're going to get something else out of this too, aren't you?"

The librarian considered Quinn through his lavender blindfold. He took a deep breath and exhaled, his nostrils expanding. "Would you walk with an old man and let him tell you a story?"

Nehemiah's tone softened, the sagging lines of his skin deepening and the hobble in his step worsening as he turned toward the outer walkway. Reluctantly, Quinn followed. "Don't think this gets you off the hook. I won't let you get me kicked out of school."

"Kicked out? How nefarious do you think I am? Kicking you out of Wimbly's is the last thing on my mind, you have my word." He held out a crooked arm. Quinn took it, and they walked toward one of the bookshelf ladders.

Nehemiah cleared his throat. "Sooner rather than later, this library will be considered ancient. But it is not the only library for talented young students of magic. Every school in the magic world has a library of its own with someone like me looking after all the books and artifacts inside it. We librarians are a rare breed, selected from a very young age, younger than yourself even, because we have a level of talent within us that only comes along once in a generation. That talent is carefully nurtured until our eighteenth birthday."

Nehemiah paused, his tongue wetting his lips. They moved like words were on them, but no sound followed.

After a few moments of awkward silence, Quinn tugged on the man's arm. "Nehemiah? I can't hear you."

Mr. Crawford jerked, straightening. "Oh? Oh yes, my apologies. At times I lose myself in my own memories. As I was saying, once we turn eighteen, we're bound to our library until either time ends or the world does. We collect knowledge, we decipher arcane secrets, and we build floor upon floor until our libraries are so tall on the inside they become something like you see today. And while we age as all things must, we do not pass from this world into the next. We grow as our library does in power and in knowledge, but we will never die."

They reached the ladder. Mr. Crawford's shoulders slumped, and he sighed. "But there's a price to pay, yes indeed. There is always a price. We are walled within our own library, a prisoner of the knowledge we so lovingly keep. This is the librarian's curse. I can know everything but can experience nothing of the outside world. I have the power to reshape minds, to raise the dead, to snap my fingers and summon a mighty storm, yet I am bound body and spirit within these walls where I can do nothing but dust old shelves that are forgotten by nearly all who wander through my hallowed halls."

"You're stuck in here forever? Seriously? There's got to be something that can get you outside. The whole point of magic is to do the impossible."

"Astute observation. There may be a way to escape my binds. If the library's destroyed, some theorize it might free me. No one knows for sure, as no misfits have ever destroyed one. The principal may summon me from time to time when the need is great and the danger is real." His nose wrinkled in a scowl and he smacked his lips. "Rather like a dog chained to a post, don't you think?"

"It almost sounds worse to me, to have all this power and not be able to do anything with it. To know it all and not be able to do anything about the things you care most about."

"That is why I call my life a curse and not a blessing." He slipped his walking stick through the loop on his belt and grabbed a ladder rung. Twisting, he reached for Quinn. "Coming?"

Quinn took his hand. Nehemiah's skin was soft and thin, each bony ridge beneath it pressing against Quinn's palm. He stepped onto the ladder, his feet flexing over the rung. Quinn knew what came next. He tightened his grip and closed his eyes. His black world roared as wind poured over him, the ladder speeding fast as a rocket toward the distant ceiling.

A boyish urge to sneak a peak teased his lids, but he ignored it. Instead, he waited to open his eyes until Nehemiah swung him over the top floor's railing.

After a few very deep breaths punctuated by a heart beating so fast Quinn worried it might burst from his chest, he collected his thoughts and faced the librarian. The old man leaned on his walking stick, an impish smile teasing his cheeks.

"So…" Quinn cast a quick glance over the long drop, and immediately regretted his decision. He spun to Nehemiah and swallowed the last of his lingering vertigo. "That's an interesting story, but it doesn't explain why you're helping me. Do you want freedom? I know you're smart and I know you conveniently see a lot for a blind guy, so you've probably heard what everybody says about me. If it's true, I am the Misfit King, I could hurt everybody at Wimbly's. Probably more than that, even."

Nehemiah struggled against his widening smile. His lips twisted and bent like ribbon in a strong wind until his wheezing, wild cackle split them apart.

"What's so funny?" Quinn asked.

"You're no Misfit King, Mr. Lynch," he said as he wiped a nonexistent tear from his cheek. "Not one at all."

So many people had assumed Quinn was the Misfit King ever since Ms. Doyle grouped him with the other talented kids that Quinn had taken his assumed identity for granted. If Nehemiah saw through it, maybe others did, too, and that thought made the library suddenly much less comfortable. "You don't know that. I—I could be him. Maybe if I really wanted, I could."

The librarian ambled along the walkway toward one of the three doors Quinn hadn't yet stepped through, the old man's chuckle softening like a dying echo. "The prophecy says the Misfit King is one blessed by the three paths of magic. As I've already told you, I feel everything inside my library. So when something that I normally feel from every student is conspicuously lacking from one peculiar student, it's easy to spot. Some things are painfully obvious even if you've never seen a hair or hiney since ships sailed on wind and all honorable folk bent a knee to the King of England."

"So you know!" Quinn raced after the man, cold sweat collecting on his palms. "Please, don't tell them. You can't. If—if I go back to the Watkins, they'll kill me. Ryley will kill me. He'll hate me for what I did. Don't tell them and I promise I'll make it better—"

Nehemiah clapped a hand over Quinn's mouth. "Lad, you cracked easy as month old bread. I suggest you remember to keep that secret a little safer if you want to stay here. Any other faculty member or student finds out and you'll be expelled and memory wiped before the next sunrise. Understand?"

A firm nod from Quinn and Mr. Crawford lowered his palm. "Good. My lips are sealed in the matter. You may not have talent, but that doesn't mean you're not special. Trust me when I say having talent's not all it's cracked up to be. Most talented magicians these days have sticks so far up their butts they're burping bark. They think they're better than normal folk. They've forgotten that without folks like you, they're not so special anymore. Even Donal's lost his way. I thought him special once." Nehemiah sighed, and it came from a deep place. "But now I think I misread his soul. He is a good man, but not the one I thought. That is why I want your help to show the talent something Donal's failed to. It's time for us to change, Quinn. I'm so very tired of the way things are."

They paused before the curtained doorway, its massive velvet drapes shimmering like butterfly wings. Quinn turned to the librarian. Learning he shared his secret with Nehemiah, and that the old man would help him keep it, warmed Quinn's heart in the best ways. "Thank you, Nehemiah. I want you to know I won't let you down. I'll figure out the trial. And when I do, I'll make everything right. I swear."

Nehemiah leaned over and squeezed Quinn's shoulder. "And I believe you. I told you I felt there was something special about you, Quinn. You're here for a reason, and it's greater than what you think. I want you to achieve your dreams, because in some ways we share the same one. The mere fact we speak before the South Door after you've lived through so much and gone so far shows how great your potential is."

"Thanks, Mr. Crawford. I—it's hard, being talentless here. I've always been lonely, but…" his eyes watered. He'd always been an outcast, been mistrusted and regarded with a suspicious eye. He wiped his tears and swallowed any others that might make their way into his eyes. "I'm just glad someone believes in me is all."

Nehemiah smiled and lightly patted Quinn's cheek. "Blessed be, boy, have pity on an old man and save him from his tears. How about you see what lay beyond this door of mine?"

"What will it show me?"

"The North Door you traveled through revealed things yet to come. The South Door you stand before illuminates things we've forgotten."

Quinn swallowed the lump of knotted energy clawing at his throat. He stared into the darkness as Nehemiah drew the curtains. Quinn stepped through, and the curtains swept closed behind him.

So Close, Yet So Far

Her wings spread over the brisk rivers of wind rushing through her feathers. The crisp, moist clouds cooled her burning chest and soothed her throbbing shoulder. Each time she beat her right wing it pounded from Ms. Velvet's parting kiss of pain.

Just a little farther, she thought, fighting her body's failing strength. *I must warn Donal. Everyone at Wimbly's is in danger, and it's up to me to keep them safe.*

Tucking her wings, she darted from the clouds, a dark arrow hidden by the overcast night sky. Patchwork farmland dotted with snowdrifts sewed a quilt hemmed by leafless trees. Near the horizon, Lake Champlain glittered against the street and city lights of Burlington, a city just south of St. Albans. An hour or two of flight and she'd be safe at home where a faculty member with full use of both hands could cast the complex spell required to mend a human body.

She sped over Lake Champlain and crossed from New York into Vermont. Thick mist drowned Burlington's rows of brick homes topped with squat chimneys. Streetlights glittered like burning cinders in the fog, their electric bulbs placed in neat intervals by talentless people who feared the night. Maisie's shoulder twitched, an intense flash of pain flaring through her neck. *No, not now. Please.*

She tried spreading her wing, but it refused her request, and she drifted lower. A flaming, nail-covered hammer pounded against her shoulder. Her falcon eyes watered. Her wing folded against her chest despite her best efforts. Once comforting winds became wild torrents that forced her down.

Maisie twisted side to side. Her world spun. By some miracle she spotted a steeple rising above the jewel-studded mists, its cross-topped roof pleading for her. Taking in a last, deep breath, she swelled her chest and sped toward the structure. Maisie forced her injured wing out, and her shoulder ignited.

Her wild screech pierced the sky—one that would send children scurrying into their blankets while concerned parents peeked between curtains.

The steeple swelled larger as the wind howled louder. Archways supported the pointed wizard cap of the steeple's roof and exposed the canopy beneath. Bracing her body, she raced toward an arch, dropping her transformation just before she passed beneath it. Maisie's feathers vanished. Her body stretched and regained its human weight.

And then she slammed into a pillar. A bright flash stole her sight. Pain blasted her back. If she could have screamed, she would have, but no breath remained to bring it out. Instead she lay there, shuddering, staring at the pointed ceiling in a freezing layer of her own sweat.

Half blind, burnt, and disoriented, she crawled to her hands and knees. She struggled to her feet as her burnt arm lost its feeling. *Not good.*

A door waited beneath a small ramp. If prayer ever had an appropriate place, it was there and then. Maisie sent one out and tested the doorknob. It swung open. She laughed and limped into the church. "Remind me to do that more often, will you?"

She half-ran, half-tripped down a narrow circular stairwell that ended behind an organ in the sanctuary room. Long, velvet pews lined the tranquil place while a towering cross and pulpit ever watched those who took a seat.

Maisie made her way down the center aisle. Her feet plodded quietly over the burgundy carpet. A steel chain secured the double door exit. No particular religion claimed her soul, but she respected all of them regardless. Under normal circumstances she'd never damage the property. But these weren't normal circumstances.

Maisie glanced over her good shoulder, and smiled at the tall, silent cross. "Forgive me. I think—I'd hope you understand." She turned to the door. Tracing a symbol, a twisted whip of lightning lanced from her finger and struck the chain. It broke one link clean in half, and Maisie unwound it from the door. She burst outside, inhaling the cold, damp air.

Since Burlington neighbored St. Albans, Maisie had the good fortune of knowing the city well. It so happened that the hospital lay not far from that very church on Pearl Street. She floundered down Pearl, each step a painful flash that threatened to collapse her right ankle. She gritted her teeth and walked onward, ignoring the fire in her step.

Despite her sorry state, she couldn't help but laugh when she thought of Donal's face if he saw her then. The finger-wagging she'd get for disobeying him would certainly fuel gossip for days to come, but what did she care? Ms. Velvet confirmed all her suspicions. The Witch Queen of the West had somehow returned, and she would use Quinn to further her own dark goals, the likes of which undoubtedly included taking revenge on Donal and Maisie.

Campus lights appeared through the fog like a hundred welcoming lighthouses. Maisie forced her footsteps, one after another, one after another. The Fletcher Allen Healthcare building drifted from the fog. She stumbled through its wide ER doors and collapsed onto the scuffed linoleum. Nurses rushed toward her, their clipboards clattering on counters and conversations cut short.

A woman clutched her, the nurse's eyebrows a knitted v of concern. "Miss, what happened?"

Maisie swallowed, and it felt like she'd dined on ash and embers. "Burned. Accident."

Another nurse went to a knee beside Maisie. He had arms like firefighter and palms hardened by calloused hills. He scanned her body before flashing her a smile. "Looks like you went through the ringer. We'll take good care of you, though, so don't you worry about a thing. Think you could tell us what happened? It might help."

Of course she couldn't really tell them. Not unless she would rather wake up strapped to a hospital bed or worse, a straightjacket. "Can't remember. How bad—how bad is it?"

His smile widened in a practiced way. "I've seen worse. How about we get you onto a bed?" He looked at the other nurse. "Lindsay, get a doctor. I'll get her to a room."

"Wait!" Maisie grabbed Nurse Lindsay's arm with her good hand. "St. Albans. Please, I need you to call my emergency contact there. I have…" she winced, pain flaring along her neck. "…It's important you get a hold of them. Understand?"

Lindsay shot a quick glance to the male nurse before nodding at Maisie. "Okay, what's the contact information?"

"His name is Donal Ward. You must tell him exactly what I say. *Exactly*. Tell him I've been called away on family business. Tell him I'll be back as soon as possible."

Maisie gave Nurse Lindsay the phone number to Wimbly's. Rita would be there to answer the call even this late at night. Maisie's excuse might not work. Rita would believe it, but she doubted it would delay Donal much. Still, she had to try. She had fully expected Ms. Velvet to chase her, but when the witch didn't, Maisie knew the woman planned to spring a trap using her as bait.

The nurse scribbled the phone number on her palm but hesitated instead of darting off to make the call. "I don't know if I can lie, but—"

Maisie flashed a symbol that flared within both nurses' eyes. They nodded like wooden puppets and accepted her command. Donal needed to stay at Wimbly's. He needed to protect Quinn and the other students from Ms. Velvet and her misfits now more than ever.

Lindsay scurried off while a few more nurses swarmed into the gap and gently lifted Maisie onto a bed. The hospital sheets and thin mattress invited her with a rough embrace that somehow soothed her anyway. Harsh fluorescent lights lost some of their painful glare. Her rolling bed clicked over the tile, the scrolling lights a lullaby for her exhausted eyes.

"I'm so tired," she said.

The male nurse leaned over her. His hand gripped hers, soft as a newborn grips its mother. "I need you to stay awake. Can you do that?"

"For a little while longer, I guess I could."

"Good. That's all I need."

Maisie continued staring at the ceiling. Someone would be there before sunrise to get her. She hated admitting it to herself, but she hoped Donal wouldn't be the one. She must look awful in such a sad, wounded condition, and she never wanted him to think her anything but beautiful.

* * *

Lindsay Day marched with more determination than most soldiers on the battlefield. She clasped the beige phone behind the front desk. An annoyingly persistent voice told her she shouldn't lie to the voice on the other end of the line. Not only was it highly unorthodox, it went again every ounce of her ethics.

Then why did she pick up the phone? Why did she press it to her ear? Why did her finger move to dial the number scribbled on her palm?

"Excuse me," a woman said.

Lindsay furrowed her brow, glancing at the stranger from the corner of her eye. "One moment please."

"Yes, that's all it should take."

Lindsay had never used the term dolled up before, but it crossed her mind when she saw the woman. The stranger wore a coffee-colored trench coat with large buttons and dark leather gloves. A blue hat with a shiny blue bow wrapped around the brim sat angled atop her polished blond hair.

Nurse Day gawked as the woman's fingers traced an intricate pattern that glowed wherever her fingers went. Never had she seen such a hypnotic, intoxicating symbol. It flared, and Lindsay's thoughts shifted. This woman was nice. Lindsay liked her. She'd do anything for her. "What can I do for you? Please, tell me. I want to make you happy."

The woman smiled and flipped her collar. "How sweet of you to be so accommodating. What's your name, my darling?"

"Lindsay Day. What should I call you?"

"How pretty. You may call me Ms. Velvet, and all I need for you to do is keep typing that number on your hand. A horribly rough and hideous-sounding woman will answer the phone. When she does—"

"Tell her the message the woman gave me? She was lying, you know."

Ms. Velvet's face darkened. "Don't interrupt me again."

Lindsay's eyes watered, and her hand shook. How disgusting of her, to interrupt such a beautiful, perfectly sweet lady. "I'm so sorry. Please, forgive me."

"As I was saying, a woman will answer the phone. Deliver the truth instead of the lie when she asks why you've called. Tell her that you were here, that a wounded woman came tripping through the doors in an awful state and told you to lie to Donal Ward. As a stand up, ethical nurse such as yourself, you just couldn't do it. That's all I need from you. That's all I need and you'll make me ever so happy. Is that too much to ask?"

"No, no of course not." Lindsay smiled, lost in the strange woman's round eyes and centerfold smile. "Anything else? I can do anything you want. Anything at all."

"Just do this for me, and if I need you again, then I will let you know." She turned, hands slipping inside her trench coat pockets. "Oh, her name is Maisie Callahan. Make sure you tell them she looked simply horrendous. Vile. Disgusting." Ms. Velvet snarled, but even then Lindsay doubted anyone else had looked so perfect. "Just make sure they know what a sad creature she appears to be."

Lindsay wept as Ms. Velvet left. Never in her life had she been so miserable watching Ms. Velvet stroll through the ER doors. A part of her would never be complete again without that woman in her life. She would chase after her, of course, but first, she had to make the call.

Nurse Day dialed the number. The other end rang. A deep voice, hardly recognizable as a woman, answered. "Wimbly's, how can I direct your call?"

"Hello, my name is Lindsay Day. I work at the Fletcher Allen Hospital in Burlington. I have a message for Donal Ward. A very ugly woman named Maisie Callahan's been in an accident…"

13

The South Door

When Quinn had stepped through the North Door, he found himself in a valley full of hydrangeas. But beyond the South Door, no flowers bloomed. He stood in a gravel drive, surrounded by trees leaning toward him. Their pinecones gazed like curious eyes within their nettled branches. Quinn knew those trees, and he remembered the gravel-covered drive. Although the memories blurred like he watched them on a screen of cloudy glass, he could never forget the home he came from.

He edged down the driveway, each footstep crunching on the loose gravel. A glance behind him revealed the closed and barred gate. He rounded a gently curving corner and came face to face with his house. It sat there, windows reflecting a warm spring sun, porch free of a single speck of dirt or fallen leaf, siding a fresh coat of powder blue, and a single, white whicker rocking chair nestled in the porch's corner. No flames marred the home's surface. No fire scorched its roof. No soot stained the chimney black.

Even Quinn's veins trembled at the sight. Licking his lips, he stepped onto the porch. The boards squeaked and shifted beneath his footsteps. The screen door's curved handle was cool and smooth, and the hinges gave a satisfying groan when he pulled the door wide. It had been so long since he'd seen his mother and father. He knew without knowing they would be in there. For the first time since the fire, Quinn would see them.

A warm light and crackling fire illuminated the small living room. A candle coaxed the sweet perfume of fresh rain and linen through the space—his mother's favorite scent, lit every Saturday while she read bent books with yellowed pages. He smiled, passing his hand over the flame. A book lay in her oversized grey recliner. *Where the Wild Things Are.* His smile widened. She read this to him often. When he was young, he loved this book more than any others. He'd wanted her to read it to him that day…

The fire. Quinn blinked, looking around. This wasn't just any day from his memory. It was *the* day. The day it all ended. The day the flames took them from him. The day a little boy lost everything he'd learned to love.

"Mom? Dad?" Quinn rushed into the kitchen, his heartbeat quickening. His stomach twisted so hard he thought it might flip inside out. The kitchen, with its diamond tiles and off balance white stove, was empty. His father's mug with the quadratic equation written around its porcelain face idled on the counter while steam rose from the coffee filling it. Creamer sat beside the mug, droplets dotting the dark countertop.

Spinning around, he dashed into the hallway. He checked the master bedroom, but it too was empty. He passed his father's study, the old desk littered with pyramids of mathematics textbooks and stacks of students' papers. No living thing disturbed the thoughtful clutter.

A single door waited at the hallway's end, the door Quinn knew this nightmarish vision would end through. His footsteps were feathers on the floorboards, his heartbeat a drummer against his ribs. He clasped the doorknob. Twisting, he pulled the door wide.

* * *

"*What*? The South Door?" Donal clenched his jaw, his blood approaching a boil. Was Nehemiah trying to give him a stroke? He strummed his fingers along the desk, his breath flaring his nostrils. "Are you sure that senile fool let Quinn through the South Door?"

Cynthia nodded. The burning candelabras reflected off her round spectacles, her lips a flat line. Egon mirrored her nod with a dramatic flair, his fingers combing through his messy mop. "Positive," Egon said, "Cynthia's been keeping an eye on the boy at my request. I really think he's up to something."

Donal's blood reached its boiling point. "You had her keep an eye on him? Are you the principal of this school and I've not been informed of the change, Egon Pennington?"

Egon flinched. "No."

"No? No what, Mr. Pennington?"

"No, *sir*."

"Thank you for that teaspoon of respect. It's taken the bite out of some of the bitterness I'm tasting at the moment." Donal strummed his fingers on his armchair and let the firestorm of his thoughts settle. He shouldn't blame the teetering, paranoid teacher. This was his lapse, not Egon's. He'd let his desire to be seen as an equal overtake his authority as principal. In good times, it worked. In times like these, it invited chaos. It invited a darkness misfits would only too happily use for their own ends.

Cynthia pursed her lips. "Principal Ward, we're all aware of Mr. Pennington's peculiarities, and please accept my apology on his behalf that we watched Quinn without your approval. I was wary first, but I've concluded that Egon's suspicions are warranted. While I haven't personally witnessed Quinn doing anything wrong—and trust me when I say I've had my sights on him for quite awhile—you must admit the shine Nehemiah's taken to him is unnerving. The librarian should be meddling with his books, not with our students. The librarian is a creature of power. He's not like the talented. Not since he was bound to the library."

Donal scooted from his seat. He turned, glaring at the stained glass windows peeking through his thick curtains. He had no idea if she knew how the words she said were double-edged blades buried in his heart. He'd heard them before, spoken from mouths poisoned by a well of hate, a well with waters that fed the worst wars the world had ever known. Not only that, but if talented magicians thought Nehemiah different than them, it only made Donal wonder what they thought of him, a talentless magician who through some stroke of luck entered the ivory tower of their world.

"But it makes no sense," Donal said, shaking his dark thoughts. "Why has Nehemiah taken an interest in him? What are we missing?"

"I don't know." Cynthia sighed. "I really don't."

"The misfits want him," Egon softly added. "I've heard reports of them stepping up encounters outside our sphere of influence. Parents are worried. They think their kids are safe here now, but…"

Donal rolled his eyes. Those were his rumors, the ones meant to keep the children corralled at Wimbly's where they'd be easier to protect. Donal faced the two faculty members. "Egon—"

"Please." Egon leaned onto Donal's great desk, his voice a low, trembling whisper. "You know the prophecy. The Misfit King is the one blessed by the three paths. I think they'll try and torture someone else's talent inside Quinn if they haven't already. At the very least he's in danger. At worse, he's already one of them, Donal."

"Now Egon—"

"Donal, what if they've put the torture within him and he just doesn't know? That might explain why it's undetectable. If it's never been used, maybe his natural talent is hiding it. I think they've carefully orchestrated this while they gather power. Quinn might not know it yet, but I'm convinced he is the one who will be unleashed by the three paths, and then they will crown him king and come calling all the children of arcana."

"And how do you expect him to learn about the trial when I'm the only one with that information?" Donal asked.

Cynthia stepped next to Egon, trying her best to maintain a neutral tone even when the minor movements of her chin and shoulders betrayed she'd already seen the logic in Egon's thinking. "Are you positive, Donal? There are no others who might put the pieces together?"

Donal briefly clenched and unclenched his fists. This felt more an interrogation than a plea for help. They did not respect him, and no matter how hard he tried, they would never see him as one of their own. The time had come for Donal to disappear and Principal Ward to take the stage. "Listen, both of you, and listen well because I will not repeat myself."

The candles flared and the candelabras shook. Behind him, the stained glass windows rattled like they held a hurricane at bay. "I am the rightful principal of this school, and there are none who will overstep my authority."

Egon leaned harder onto the desk. "But—"

Donal cut the air with a rigid hand, and the many candles burning atop the candelabras flared with an angry hiss. He took to his feet and planted his hands on his desk so he came eye level with Egon. "Do not interrupt me again, Mr. Pennington. I am intimately aware of the misfits and the ways of their magic and how Quinn might somehow be linked to their plans. But what would you have me do, throw the boy out? Lock him up? There's nothing I can do that I'm not already doing. Meanwhile, two of my most powerful teachers have been spying on a boy, one who came to us with no true family, no friends, and not a single rusted penny to his name. There are few who remember what I do, fewer still who saw first hand the ruin of fear's cold grip when the world bathed in the fire of the great wars.

"If Quinn is the Misfit King, I swear to you my most sacred vow I will hand him a golden crown and bow before his throne before I become the monsters of our past. You forget yourself, Egon Pennington." His glare flared, shifting to Ms. Doyle. "You forget yourself, Cynthia Doyle. You dance on a ledge above oblivion, and I fear your fall will doom us all. I am your principal. Overstep your authority even an inch one more time and you will find yourself a real monster to contend with on this campus."

Egon's face lost its color. Even Cynthia, normally carved from granite, lost her hard edge. Donal shook his head, collapsing into his chair with a sigh. The candles dimmed and the candelabras stilled. "You're both good people," he said, pinching the bridge of his nose, "but you've got to remember why you teach here in the first place. This is a school, a place for enlightenment and learning, not a courthouse. Don't put him on trial."

Egon's head dipped. "I hadn't realized, Principal Ward…"

Cynthia clasped her hands before her. "My apologies, Principal Ward."

"Just—have a little faith." He rotated his chair toward the multicolored windows. "We are done here."

They padded from the room, softly closing the doors behind them. Donal's gaze flicked to the map on his wall. His tongue-lashing brought a small level of comfort and released some of the bottled tension that had been rising with each new misfit that gathered around the island.

Winter had fallen early and with a heavy hand. If Donal could keep things together until spring, he knew passions would thaw. Still, he felt his carefully spun web slipping. Too many spiders plucked at threads holding the same fly.

Other students had come before with powerful talent and the skill to draw equally powerful spells. But something made Quinn different than all of them. Something set the boy apart. The misfits knew it. Nehemiah knew it. Now, Donal knew it too.

Tracing a pattern, he flung a spell at the map. The ball of mist exploded over the weathered paper. Ruby lights blinked like scarlet stars against the continents. They swirled around the map, slowly forming a glittering hurricane with its single, calm eye centered over Wimbly's. "It's not too late, is it?" he wondered.

Rita's heavy knock tore him from his thoughts. "Sir?"

"I'm busy, Rita. Can it wait?"

"No." She burst—or more accurately squeezed—through the doorway, nubby ogre horns peeking from the bush of her graying hair. Her thick lip protruded the way it always did when something disturbed the shallow pool of her emotions.

"What's wrong?" he asked.

"Phone call from Burlington. A nurse from Fletcher Allen called—"

Donal lurched from his seat. "Maisie!"

"She's hurt. And ugly."

* * *

Quinn's mother and father surrounded a small bed tucked into the corner of the room. A bulge nested deep in the bed's puffy blankets. His mother rubbed his father's back. "He looks so peaceful," she rasped, her voice accented by her exhaustion.

"Are you scared?" his father asked.

"For him, yes. I can't help it."

Quinn's eyes watered. He choked on a sob and edged into his bedroom. "Mom? Dad?"

They ignored him. He reached for them anyway, but the magic of the South Door held his feet, the vision a painful tease poking his heart.

His father held out his hands and traced complex—familiar—patterns. Wherever his fingers went, a glowing line remained until an intricate symbol hung suspended before Quinn's bed.

Breath caught in Quinn's throat. He fought the South Door's hold, but it kept him still. His parents knew magic. All this time, he assumed he only knew how to draw shapes. It never crossed his mind he might have inherited his skill. And now, staring it in the face, he hated himself for not realizing sooner. "I—I never knew. Dad!" He reached for his father, but his feet held him as a statue. "Let me go! I want to see them!"

The magic of the South Door refused.

His father nudged his mother, and she traced another spell, the glowing lines her fingers left like the tracks of a graceful skater across a freshly frozen lake. "Your spells were always so much more beautiful than mine," she said.

"Not as beautiful as you." He leaned over and kissed her cheek.

A shadow flitted across the window. His parents traded glances.

"They're here," his father said. "Our magic will hold. Don't worry."

His mother nodded. His father nodded. They pressed their hands against their spells, and the patterns flared. Quinn watched, dumbstruck, at the unfolding scene. His parents knew magic. All along, they'd known how to cast spells, and he had no idea. Yet somehow, he couldn't cast a spell to save his life.

Quinn shuddered. An icy hand reached from his stomach to his heart. He knew that two talented magicians should always have a talented child unless someone took that talent from that child. No wonder he loved geometry. No wonder he had such a steady hand.

He was born with talent. The misfits came for him. They tortured the talent from him, but thanks to his parents' spell, they couldn't kill him. Instead, the misfits framed him for the murder of the only people who ever really loved him.

Another shadow flitted across the window. A loud crack echoed down the hall. A light flared outside, rattling the pane. His father grabbed his mother. "Stay close, they've got us surrounded."

"They're going to get him." She turned toward the hallway. Her tears were tiny glass beads sliding down her cheeks. "I wanted to see him grow up. I wanted to wave goodbye his first year at Wimbly's. We won't have any of that."

"We knew when we hid him this might happen. All we can do now is believe in him. You've got to believe in him."

"I wanted one more night. I'm scared our spell will fail. Are you sure it's strong enough? If they break it—"

"I swear to you there is no misfit magic they can cast that will break our spell," he said. "No talented or misfit could ever hope to break it."

Another force slammed the windowpane. Cracks burst from corner to corner. Footsteps pounded in the hall behind him, followed by an ear-splitting cackle. He turned and locked the door, but knew it wouldn't hold. "No, no, no. Go away! Leave them alone!" His voice tore his throat. Tears wet his cheeks.

If he tried hard enough, he could warn them. He spun around and found them standing inches away, holding one another's hands.

"Quinn." his father smiled despite the sadness in his voice. "It's okay. You'll get through this."

Quinn's tears turned his world into swirling watercolors. "You can see me?

I'm sorry. I—I should have done better. I lied and cheated, but—"

His mother clasped his cheek in her soft palm. "You look so very handsome."

"But—how—why…" Words failed him. He grabbed her wrist. "I miss you."

"I miss you too, my little wild thing."

A great force slammed the door. He glanced behind him. Its wood cracked, long lines of splintering violence drawn against its face. Quinn's mother pulled his chin to her. "There's not much time left. We can't keep them out much longer."

"I want to help you. Let me help you."

His father clasped Quinn's shoulder. "You can by winning. They're going to take your talent, Quinn. They're going to take it because you're very special. You're very powerful. You're different, and both sides will fear that."

"My talent? Is that…is that what this is about?"

He nodded. "The misfits need someone with your power for their prophecy because yours is a very rare power. But we've seen more than they have. We know more than they do, and while they'll win today, there will be a tomorrow when they lose. I am warning you, Quinn, things will be much worse before they're much better, and when you think things are over, that's when they've just begun. Prepare yourself."

"But what can I do? How do I stop them?"

Flames snaked their way through the floorboards. Black smoke slithered up the walls. His mother coughed. "They're under the house. It's done now."

She reached into her shirt and pulled out a locket on a silver chain. She slipped it over his neck, the cool metal a reassuring weight over his shoulders. "This is yours now. Keep it safe. Tell no one you have it."

"I don't understand. What do I do with it?"

"When danger swirls in all directions, this will be the sword and shield you need to see you through it. Don't open it until that time comes." She leaned in and kissed him. "I love you."

His father played with Quinn's hair while the man's gentle eyes fought against his tears. "I love you. Goodbye, Son."

A blaze erupted in the room. And then, the South Door went dark.

19

The Witch Queen of the West

She flexed her fingers through bandages wrapped so thickly her fingers looked like wiggling albino cocktail wieners. Maisie giggled, wiping the drool slipping from her lips.

They'd taken X-rays, and afterwards some silly, talentless nurse told her that during the mysterious accident, several ribs had been fractured and her shoulder and right arm suffered severe burns. Stupid Ms. Velvet, with her stupid spells that burned her arm and made Maisie practically face plant into a church's steeple.

If only she could use both hands. Curing a wound even this severe wouldn't make a second year student bat her eyes. Maisie wiggled the fat white sausages of her bandaged fingers. She considered casting the healing spell with one hand but decided against it rather than risk turning her arm into undercooked bacon.

She grinned, imagining the look on Donal's face if she waltzed into his office with her arm sloshing in a Ziploc like old leftovers. Maisie hadn't seen Nurse Lindsay since their conversation on the ER floor, and her current mental state and useless hand made the prospect of compelling another nurse about as likely as a snowless winter in Vermont. For now, she would listen to the rhythmic beep of her heart monitor and rest her weary eyes, tucked into the corner of a dark room where she could smile at nothing and everything out the rectangular window.

"Ma—Maisie?" Donal's voice trembled like he'd choked on a chicken bone.

She turned from her windowpane. Donal stood beside the bed's powder blue curtain, his strong features framed by his black hair with its shock of grey. Red rimmed his blazing eyes, his usual arrogant boyishness absent within them. A new, harder man had taken Donal's place, one who the real world had finally teased into the open.

"Oh, don't be so sad, you big mope." She waved, the heart monitor clipped over her fingertip suddenly reminding her of a fairy's motorcycle helmet. Maisie snickered. Fairies didn't ride motorcycles. The ones she knew preferred the train.

He leaned over her and clasped her hand in his. "Maisie what happened to you? I told you not to leave Wimbly's. I ordered you."

"Wimbly's?" The name echoed in her cotton head. "Yes, I was going there, wasn't I? Then there was Ms. Velvet and she hit me with a lightning bolt. Can you believe that, Donal? A lightning bolt! Nearly fried me like a chicken. But Egon showed me this wonderful new transformation into a peregrine falcon and I got away. If it weren't for him, I might really be fried."

"Perhaps I'll thank him sometime soon, then." His features contorted, and he glanced away. "She burned you bad and they've got you doped out of your mind."

"You know I didn't want you to see me like this, but *shhhh*, don't remind me when my meds wear off. I. Will. Kill. You."

Donal laughed, his trembling fingers caressing her temple. "You still look as beautiful as the day I met you, you know that? Hold on while I heal those wounds of yours and flush those medicines out. Try not to murder me when you find your wits."

Maisie's heart fluttered, heat rising in her cheeks. "Do you really think I'm beautiful?"

"I'd never think otherwise." His fingers danced as they traced the spell.

"You know I love you, Donal. Even though you're such a—"

"Hey!" The male nurse barged into the room, clipboard pressed against his chest. He spun Donal around, interrupting the magic. "What are you doing in this room?"

"That's Donal," Maisie said, laughing like a little girl. "Careful, he's likable—I mean, liable to break your heart."

The hard line of the nurse's jaw flexed. "Donal Ward? The one you wanted us to make sure didn't come?"

Donal turned to Maisie, his bright blue eyes shadowed by a scowl. "Excuse me?"

"Because I didn't want you to leave the school, silly. If Ms. Velvet's back, they're in danger. We're in danger. Quinn's in danger because…Oh yeah! Torture at his home. The ritual was committed there. They must have taken it from his parents. Now get out of here, Donal, and let me get some sleep." She yawned, stretching. "I'm very sleepy."

Principal Ward rolled his eyes. "How loopy are you? It's impossible she's back, Maisie. I swear. It just isn't possible. Believe me."

The nurse cleared his throat, a strong hand twisting Donal around. "Torture? I don't know what's going on here but I'm calling the cops. You need to get out of here. Now."

Donal swatted the man's hand and cast a spell that dulled the nurse's eyes and sent him walking like a zombie back into the hallway. Returning to her bed, the principal traced a spell with both hands so complex she couldn't help but stare in awe at the glowing lines. A tingle raced up her injured arm while a warm pulse filled her back and shoulders.

Maisie raised her wounded hand. Her bandages evaporated like steam over boiling water. Her burn swirled like paint on a canvas, the skin smoothing until it was soft and pink. The dull ache in her bones subsided, and her senses snapped into brilliant clarity. "Don't think for one second I meant the words. I was doped up on painkillers," she snapped.

His shoulders slumped and he pressed his head on the bed's support rail. "You're alright. Thank God." He glanced at her, eyes glittering with a boyish charm. "But don't you worry, I love you too."

She ripped the heart monitor from her fingertip and it protested with an annoyingly loud beep. "You shouldn't have come, Donal. I told the nurse to tell you specifically not to come."

"But Maisie—"

Maisie hopped off the bed and muscled past him. She couldn't believe she just told Donal she loved him. If she remembered her doctor's name, she would have throttled the man for turning her brain into morphine porridge. But she didn't know his name, and there were more important things afoot. "If you're here it's because she wants you here and this is a trap. We need to get back to Wimbly's. Now."

Barreling through gawking nurses, doctors, and wide-eyed technicians, she reached the lobby with Donal trailing, doing his best to calmly hiss her name.

The automatic doors parted, and she exhaled as a rush of icy wind cooled her burning cheeks. Maisie walked into the parking lot and traced an intricate symbol. Snowflakes swirled around her in a thick column and coated her skin. They piled in layer upon layer. Instead of bitter cold, she felt her body embrace the enchanted snow's shifting warmth. With the spell finished, she stood before the hospital clothed in an ivory jacket and matching pants and boots. "I look like a snow bunny. I hate this spell."

"I think you look good," he said.

She whirled around and shoved a finger against his chest. "Don't talk to me, I'm mad at you."

"You are impossible, Maisie Callahan, you know that? The nurse sounded very worried about your accident. What did you expect her to do, break every ethical obligation she had and lie for you? Why is nothing I do ever good enough? How far do I have to bend before you forgive me? Will I need to break before you do?"

Her brows knitted together and she took a deep breath. "We can talk about it when we're back on campus. I assume you took a faster means of travel than turning into a bird and flapping to the hospital?"

He nodded, motioning toward the edge of the lot. "Around the side of the building."

"Good," she said. "Because every minute we're away from Wimbly's the more danger those kids are in. I was right to suspect something about Quinn. He's special. He must be. I don't know why, but the torture was committed at his home. They must have taken it from his parents but spared him. Why? What part does he play in Ms. Velvet's plans?"

Donal ushered her through the parking lot. "Ms. Velvet," he grumbled. "I suppose I didn't clear all the medication from you. Maybe I need—"

They turned the corner and froze. Sitting on an olive green Chevy Bel Air, the 1950's antique the principal so lovingly called Claire, waited Ms. Velvet. She reclined with one leg crossed over the other wearing an hourglass trench coat and blue hat.

Donal's choking gasp broke the silence. "How…" His voice rolled into an unsteady whisper. "You shouldn't be here. It's—it's not possible. After all that I went through, you can't be here."

Ms. Velvet looked up. The streetlight arching over his car bathed her in cold fluorescent light. Her round eyes lit like fireworks, and she smiled as if two old friends had just arrived for a barbecue. "Donal, it's beyond amazing to see you! When I saw this car, I knew it had to be yours. I bet all the kids these days think you're such a fuddy-duddy rolling around in a fossil like this." Her predatory glare shifted to Maisie. "Good to see you're looking healthy. Let's hope lightning won't strike the same place twice tonight."

"Why you—" Maisie lurched forward, the perfect spell already tingling on her fingers.

Donal's arm lanced out and blocked her advance. "Don't let her get to you." His voice was low and eerily calm, like a green-tinted thunderstorm hiding a cyclone in its belly. "What do you want, Ms. Velvet?"

The misfit witch smirked, hopping from the car onto the frosted pavement. "I just wanted to see you, Donal. It's been so long since we last met, don't you remember? It was that day you ripped out my heart and flushed it down the drain. That day you left me bent and broken and dying in a hotel lobby. You know, I never really understood why you did it. She's not particularly pretty…"

"Don't bring her into this," Donal said. "She has nothing to do with it."

"She has everything to do with it, you silly, doll-dizzy man, because without her, you never would have overcome the trial, and you never would have made me who I am today." Ms. Velvet strolled forward, her footprints pockmarks in the snow.

Donal and Maisie scooted back. Maisie grabbed his shoulder. "What does she mean? What did I have to do with your trial?"

"You mean he didn't tell you?" the witch laughed, chin thrown toward the sky as she danced in a circle. "I shouldn't be surprised. We both know he can keep a secret better than you or I ever could."

"Shut up, Velvet!" Donal tensed. Raw power vibrated through his veins and sent a tingle down Maisie's fingers.

Forms appeared on the parking lot's edge. They stood beyond the artificial lights, masked in a shadow and falling snow. Something perched atop the streetlight, its eyes glowing like hateful embers. "Think of something fast, Donal," Maisie whispered. "We're surrounded."

"Planning on leaving so soon?" Ms. Velvet asked. "We haven't even gotten to the fun part yet. Don't you want to know about the trial? Don't you want to know why he couldn't do it without you?"

"I…I—" Maisie's gaze darted between Donal and Ms. Velvet. She didn't know the game the Witch Queen of the West played, but the twinkle in the misfit's eyes said a truth waited on her forked tongue.

Ms. Velvet licked her lips. "There's only one way to pass the trial, you see."

"You know nothing of the trial," Donal spat.

"That's where you're wrong, my darling. I was fortunate enough to torture an incredibly longwinded historian named Roderick Shellhouse who just happened to put one or two things together about the trial. He believed the trial was split into four parts—four spells, if you will. Specifically, ones so dangerous they must be made solely to end a life."

"Donal, what is this?" Maisie asked. "She doesn't really know, does she?"

Donal laughed, shrugging his shoulders. "If that was the trial, you'd have done it to others by now. Clearly it isn't."

"You're right. I tried and tried and tried, but to no avail." Ms. Velvet pulled her leather gloves off and stuffed them in a pocket. "I realized I was missing something. You knew of magic when we first met, but you didn't know how to cast it, not even after you broke my heart in hopes of mending dear Maisie's.

"Even after I became the Witch Queen of the West, you still couldn't cast a spell to save your life. It wasn't until after you tricked me, said you really did love me when I had come to end your life that you gained power. It wasn't until after you dropped my guard by slipping me a tasteless poison that you succeeded with the trial. To think, it was in front of me the whole time! Surviving four deadly spells and sealing the deal by killing the one person who hates you more than any other. It's poetic, isn't it?"

"But you're still alive," he said, the edge in his voice considerably dulled.

"Oh, you killed me. I walked the pale fields of death and saw many of my misfit sisters and brothers, each one begging for a second chance. In those fields, a voice whispered in my ear and promised me new life and vengeance if

I'd bind my soul to service. All I had to do was crown the true Misfit King, and I would have all that I desired. Now here I am, back amongst the living with more power than even a talent-born magician. I may even be as strong as the great Donal Ward, thanks to my master."

Donal tensed, his breath catching in his throat. Maisie clutched his arm. Her fingers dug into his bicep. "It's not true, is it?"

Donal didn't answer. Ms. Velvet laughed, and it was one of pure joy, one that had waited generations to bubble from the pit of her soul. "Of course it's true! It's why he never told anyone, not even you. I told him I hated him, that I wanted him dead more than any other in the world. He told me he loved me, and in that brief moment before I realized what was happening, I drank his poison." Her eyes hardened into cold spheres. "And you know what, Maisie? I believe he loved me then, *and I believe he does now.* Maybe he even loves you. It's too bad we both know Donal's only true love is his own power. Discovering the magic world sealed that for him. There's no denying it."

Maisie shuddered. She squeezed Donal tighter.

"Don't believe her," he said.

She did anyway. Maisie knew him too well. It hurt, hearing someone besides her own inner voice speak the words, but Maisie wouldn't let the revelation destroy her. Her heart closed to Donal long ago, and not even the Witch Queen of the West pecking at the scars could truly harm her using him.

Movement flickered in her periphery. The creature on the streetlight stiffened, its glowing eyes narrowed to slits.

"Donal, there are so many of them…"

"Things are about to even out," he said.

A low, long rumble echoed from above. Maisie frowned.

Donal relaxed. "Took long enough."

Ms. Velvet looked into the sky. "What the—"

A massive form slammed on top of Donal's car, smashing the automobile into a glass-and-steel pancake. Ms. Rita the ogre roared, the sound vibrating into the deepest parts of Maisie's bones. Ms. Velvet barely had time to turn when Rita's tree trunk of a forearm smashed into the woman's torso, flinging her screaming clear across the parking lot. Misfits waiting in the wings charged, hurling fireballs, ice lances, and crackling lightning at their new adversary. The creature from the streetlight pounced, but Ms. Rita swatted it like a fly, and it disappeared into the night.

Rita was a blur of strength and muscle. She thrust herself before Donal and Maisie, her thick arms and wide body absorbing the spells as easily as a brick wall absorbs a snowball.

Donal grabbed Maisie and swung her onto Rita's back while he hooked his arm around her neck. "Good thing Ms. Rita's immune to magic, huh?" He grinned in his usual boyish manner, oblivious to the fact that their world collapsed around them.

"Can we go now?" Maisie ducked beneath a column of fire roaring over Rita's shoulder.

Donal tapped Rita and yelled into her ear, "Let's go home, please!"

"Right." The ogre squatted, and her great body swelled and muscled hardened. She sprang, soaring over the parking lot in a leap that could have crested a skyscraper.

Gathering Storms

A few tense days passed at Wimbly's since Maisie and Donal returned. Mum was the word from the faculty, but rumors spread regardless, whispers of a misfit attack that could have killed both teachers and the return of a powerful enemy. Principal Ward locked down the campus as winter fell in icy curtains and covered the ruddy colors of Woods Island in thick and downy white.

Quinn sat amongst the wildflowers of Heidi's study hall illusion and watched a bumblebee buzz by. Escaping to the hall proved a feat unto itself. Some of the older and braver students tailed him everywhere he went, hoping for a hint of the true Misfit King to show itself. Teachers kept an even closer eye than normal. He'd known they watched him for a while, but now something more than idle suspicion or curiosity glimmered in their eyes.

Donal—Principal Ward, as he now expected everyone at school to call him—had summoned Quinn to a meeting earlier that day with him and Maisie. They explained their theory that Ms. Velvet tortured the talent from his parents but spared him for some as-of-yet unknown purpose. Quinn tried his best to play along, to gasp when they paused, to shove his hand into his pocket and pinch his thigh so hard his eyes watered, to agree that no matter what anyone said they believed he was too good a kid to be the Misfit King.

He just had to keep telling himself it would all be over soon. He'd finish the trial and come completely clean, and even if they did expel him, at least he could find his own way instead of getting forgotten in juvie somewhere.

Heidi plopped beside him, playfully nudging his shoulder. "Try not to look so depressed. You'll make the flowers wilt."

He forced a smile and stared at the door leading to the real world. "Everybody has it all wrong. They think Ms. Velvet tortured my parents when it was really me they took the magic from. It's hard, knowing you've got the answer to a question everyone else is getting wrong. They're going to hate me when I tell them."

"Some people will, and some people won't." Heidi wrapped her arms around her knees and propped her chin upon them. "I bet it was tempting to tell them just to see the look on their faces when they found out a talentless boy outsmarted all the precious and powerful talented magicians…"

"Every time Mr. Pennington looks at me it's like I'm about to claw his eyes out and cook them for dinner. I almost tell him the truth then, each time. Just to see his face." Quinn smirked and ripped a tuft of grass from the ground. "Do you think I did the right thing keeping it a secret?"

"I don't know," she said, her voice a shaky whisper. "I guess you have to just, like, believe in yourself and know it'll all work out. That's what I keep telling myself anyway."

Quinn shifted to his knees. "I wish it was that easy. Sometimes I wish I was more like you, you know. Nothing gets to you. You always see the bright side of things. It's nice."

She smiled, but there was sadness in it. "You know, Quinn…" she took a deep breath and rocked forward. "Maybe it would be better to give up. Maybe it would be better to tell them the truth, to get it all out in the open. The magic world's not all it's cracked up to be. Between the talented and the misfits, sometimes I just—I just don't know who's worse. I was excited when I came to Wimbly's. The kids here are mean, though. They think they're better than me. They think I'm stupid because I can't draw very well. I don't like it, and I don't want to be like them. I don't want you or Billy to be like them either."

They were the last words he expected her to say. She'd usually been so eager to help, so happy to see him succeed in whatever he planned. But that had changed, and now he saw a struggle in her eyes. "What's wrong? Something's bothering you."

"I don't know. I'm just scared I think. You're my friend, Quinn, and I don't want you getting hurt. It feels like that's where this is all going. That's what the butterflies and bumblebees think when I ask them, and butterflies and bumblebees hardly ever agree."

"We'll be fine, don't worry…unless…" He turned to her, forcing her eyes to his. "Is it the practical? Are you worried about it? If you're not okay, we won't go through with it. I'll pretend to be sick or something. Considering how terrified Mr. Pennington is of me, I don't think he'll mind."

"No, no," her smile lost its sadness, and she inhaled, her somber tone disappearing on the breeze. "It's not that. Sometimes I just get a little spacey is all. Ready to practice?"

He grinned, putting aside her odd words, and they began their practice. Quinn drew the spells and coached Heidi on each bend and angle and curve until she was almost as perfect at tracing the patterns as him. Then, she in turn would enchant his fingers, and like a puppeteer with a doll whose strings funneled magic, she cast the spells through him.

Quinn enjoyed playing the puppet, although he knew it only made him that much more desperate for the trial. His fingers danced and wagged, and from them flames whipped or wind roared or blazing orbs shot into the sky before exploding in a thunderous boom. Each spell she cast through him brought him closer to the answer. Deep inside him, he knew it to be true.

In a few days, they'd take Mr. Pennington's winter practical. Despite the nerves tangling in a giant ball in his stomach, Quinn never felt more confident than he did then, and soon, he'd have everything he ever wanted.

* * *

Ryley's spells came easier to him each passing day. He finished his latest masterpiece, an intricate tapestry of triangles and diamonds that would make even the bravest magician kiss his feet and beg for mercy. He handed the card to Ms. Velvet. A bead of sweat slid down his back as he watched her examine the card. Ryley hoped—no, he prayed, she would love it.

Ms. Velvet's features lit like a Christmas tree with the pride in her eyes and the joy in her smile. "Oh, Ryley, this spell is just perfect. Your skills are astounding. You're going to make me so pleased so very soon."

The freezing winds and endless snow falling in waves like an old witch's hair couldn't keep the warmth welling within him. She approved. She loved him.

"It's a particularly nasty one," he said. "I'm very proud of it. I can practically hear Quinn screaming from it right before he turns into an ice cube." Ryley closed his eyes, heavy breaths pouring from his nose. He shuddered, losing himself in the image of the orphan writhing at his feet. Ms. Velvet's silky palm cupped his cheek, and he opened his eyes to her loving smile.

"Yes, very true. Looks like just by seeing the spell it might cause a few years' worth of nightmares for the boy. How delightful. How has your other practice been going? Have you been working on your dueling spells?"

He nodded enthusiastically. "There's not anyone who could beat me. I'm that good."

She arched a brow and tucked her hands into her trench coat. The snow parted around her as if it feared landing on her shoulders. "Are you now? Let's not get too cocky. Remember, Quinn's been practicing, too. He's very good."

Ryley laughed, and it was a real, deep one. "Quinn's got nothing on me. He can't even use magic. I'll wipe the floor with him Ms. Velvet, you'll see. He won't even know what's coming."

"Of that I'm certain." She stepped beneath a tree so weighted with snow it looked like a cotton umbrella suspended over her perfect head. "Still, I fear you might not do as well as you think. He's made so many friends at Wimbly's. Did you know? He's quite popular with the students. The girls giggle about him. All the boys say he's their best friend. It's sad, really, thinking how that could have been you all this time. But here you are, stuck in this miserable little winter wonderland of your false father's while Quinn's tricked everyone at school to think he's you and you're him."

Ryley's heart twisted into a burning knot. Quinn shouldn't be at Wimbly's. He shouldn't even exist. The orphan should have just crawled into that fire and burned with his parents. "I'm going to make him pay. I don't care who his friends are. He's going to pay for what he did."

"He's even got a little girlfriend now. She's a pretty thing with blond hair I hear. Gets along with everyone, even the yetis."

"Yetis?" Ryley rushed forward. "There are yetis there?"

Her eyes lit up and drifted toward the charcoal sky. "Have you seen a yeti before? They're all over the campus, clearing the snow for the students while they munch on pinecones, as yetis tend to do. They're beautiful creatures—" she caught her breath, her lips puckering. "It's so unfortunate you haven't seen one. The wildest things around these parts are squirrels and rabbits, and if it's anyone clearing snow, it's you. How terribly boring."

Ryley spun and kicked the snow, Ms. Velvet's silvery laughter echoing behind him. He traced a symbol, the pattern flashing through his red-tinged vision. Flames erupted around his fists, hissing and crackling, defiant of the winter. His fiery fists slammed the snow and ice, throwing up steam. His hands ached and his arms trembled, but he didn't care. Quinn stole everything from him. Ryley had never seen a magical creature. He didn't have a girlfriend. He didn't have friends. He didn't even have parents anymore thanks to the stupid orphan.

Ryley cried, beating the ground like it was Quinn's face. The flames roiled. Their hot tongues seared his cheeks. Despite the fire, he smiled, beating harder, his tears turning into laughter. His fists throbbed. His arms burned. Still, he beat the ground, a laughter sprouting deep within his belly and spilling out his throat. He hated Quinn. But he knew Quinn's secret, and soon, the world would know the truth. Then, Ryley would make them love him, and Quinn would be a memory.

* * *

Even though Donal's spell healed her wounds days ago, the whole ordeal left Maisie exhausted both physically and mentally. She washed her face, brushed her teeth, and put on a fresh change of clothes. She kept her interactions with the principal to a minimum, meeting with him only once since their encounter with Ms. Velvet so she could break the news of her discovery to Quinn.

It tore the poor boy up. It would have torn anybody up, spending so many months at a school where so many believed such horrible things about him. And then to find out the misfits took his parent's talent and framed him for their murder…

Sighing, Maisie put her hair in a loose ponytail and stepped into the hallway. Principal Ward wouldn't let her avoid him any longer. He had summoned her, Cynthia, and Egon to his office. For what, she could only guess, although something told her it had something to do with the trial.

Maisie left her room and headed down the sweeping stairs to the first floor. The faculty slept on the top floor of the administration building, and while their rooms were larger than student dorms, most people would consider them sparse at best. Talented magicians tended to shun lavishness because it invited attention. Not just from the misfits, but from the talentless as well. Magicians thrived best when the world let them lead from behind. It was a good system, an orderly system.

Downstairs, Rita perched like a mountain over a desk comically small for the ogre's body. She adjusted her oversized glasses and nodded at Maisie. "Morning."

"Good morning, Rita. Thanks again for saving us from the misfits."

A low rumble rolled from Rita's thick lips, a sound signifying she didn't think much of the feat. "You're welcome. Dirty things."

Maisie smiled. She envied the ogre, the steady, strong creature, immune to the things that brought so much trouble to her own life. She'd trade her magic in a heartbeat for a set of nubby horns. Inhaling, savoring a last, fleeting moment of peace, she opened the office door and strolled inside.

Instead of two leather wingbacks facing his desk, four of the chairs faced one another with a pedestal table placed in the center. A silver tray of tea and cream was placed onto the table, steam rising in sweet tendrils from the pitcher. Egon, Cynthia, and Donal sat in the wingbacks. Their conversation paused as she entered, and their eyes acknowledged her arrival.

Cynthia nodded, pushing her glasses up her nose. Egon smiled through tight lips and took a sip of tea. Donal's blazing gaze met Maisie's own. The immaturity she typically saw within them had vanished, replaced instead by worn and weary eyes resting above dark rings.

"Good morning, Ms. Callahan," he said.

"Good morning to you too. I hope you're all enjoying an especially early winter. Usually the snows don't come this heavy until New Year's, but it's not even November and the kids are making snowmen tall enough to trick the yetis."

As adults tend to do, they discussed the weather over their tea despite the dark thoughts she knew waited just beneath their nods and polite smiles. The conversation came to a lull, and Donal shifted, propping a leg on his knee and holding his chin in the crook of his fingers. "I suppose it's time we all had a particular conversation I've been strenuously trying to avoid for a very long while."

Cynthia poured another cup of tea with a surprisingly steady hand. "I think that might be wise considering our current deteriorating predicament, Principal Ward."

Egon nodded, a lump travelling down the peachy pipe of his throat. "Yes, indeed."

"If that's what you think's best," Maisie said.

"First things first…" Donal cleared his throat, staring at the map on his wall. "The misfits."

"The misfits," they echoed.

"They're gathering," he continued. "Their numbers have only swelled since the year began. Now that the self-styled Witch Queen of the West, also known as Ms. Velvet, has summoned every witch, warlock, werewolf, troll, goblin, and whatever else she could pluck from under a bridge or inside a sewer pipe, I think it's time we prepare for the worst. I doubt Lake Champlain has ever seen so many of these tortured creatures surrounding its waters, including those first dangerous days of the school's founding. If it weren't for the combined power of Nehemiah and I, I believe they might have already attacked."

Donal let the words sink in as Egon flicked a quick glance at Cynthia. The woman kept her own gaze on Donal, acknowledging the admission with pursed lips and a terse nod.

Maisie exhaled and locked her fingers over her lap. "What can we do about it? Most of the students' parents have already gone into hiding. The other schools are sending help our way, but with so many misfits between them and us, they'll have an army to fight through before they can reach us. They've got us surrounded. We're cut off from the outside, and if this blizzard doesn't bury us, then the misfits surely will."

"We let this happen," Egon murmured. "I tried warning—"

"No you didn't, Egon," Cynthia snapped. "You and I blamed Quinn for a true misfit's own evil plans, and Principal Ward was entirely correct about our behavior. We were so worried about casting Quinn as our enemy we didn't see the real one hiding in our shadow. I'm of the mind that Quinn's been her pawn all along, that he was a distraction for us while she set the real plan in motion. We fell for it like a bunch of prideful fools, and now she's twenty steps ahead while we're scrambling to catch up."

"We all could have done better," Maisie cut in, Egon gripping his teacup with white knuckles, his glare glued to the liquid inside it. "Principal Ward could have heeded warnings sooner. I could have researched Quinn's upbringing much more closely before he came to us. Egon could have been less suspicious of the boy, and you could have worried more about the misfits outside of Wimbly's. Nobody sitting in this office has done a perfect job. Let's move past what was and start figuring out how we get the children through this unharmed."

Cynthia and Egon relaxed while Donal flashed a thankful smile. She returned the smile and nodded toward the principal. "What are your thoughts on Quinn and the prophecy? Knowing what we know now, do you think Ms. Velvet really believes he is the one?"

"I'm still not prepared to call Quinn the Misfit King or believe much of anything she claims." Donal turned to the stained glass windows. Snow twisted in dark flurries on the other side of the colored panes. "It just doesn't feel right for some reason. And if Ms. Velvet truly has been planning this for years, we may be playing into her hands by coming to that very conclusion. That's what she's good at, distraction and sleight-of-hand. Just when you think you know what she's going to do, she plays the ace up her sleeve."

Egon placed his tea onto the table and straightened. "I know I sing a tired song with this. Believe me, I'm tired of fearing it myself. I know I was wrong to think so poorly of Quinn, and I'm ashamed I did it."

Cynthia reached over and gently patted his hand. He smiled, squeezing hers. "But more than anyone in this room," he continued, "I have studied the prophecy of the Misfit King and how it came to be. The things happening around us—the rising tide of misfits, the endless winter, a boy born of fire, sole survivor of a dark and deadly magic—we cannot deny these things point to a great change that's come upon us. I fear the less we do, the less we shape events and the more they carry us along. We are the talented. We shape the course of history, not the other way around."

Ms. Doyle placed her tea next to his and slid to the edge of her seat. "There's reason in his words, Principal Ward. None of us place any guilt on Quinn. I swear to you he is innocent in all our eyes. That doesn't mean we shouldn't take certain precautions to guarantee he stays that way."

"Precautions…" Donal cracked his knuckles, his jaw steel. He turned from the curtains, lost in his own thoughts. "…Yes, we all must take precautions."

Maisie sipped the last of her tea, cradling the warm cup in her hands. She took a deep breath and dove into the subject they'd avoided until then. "There's another piece we're missing, and this whole prophecy with its kings and misfits has everything to do with it." She looked square in Donal's eyes. "Did she have it right?"

He cleared his throat, his gaze meeting hers. "Who? About what?"

"You know what I'm talking about. The trial. Does Ms. Velvet know how it works?"

Both Egon and Cynthia gasped, the weighty air in the principal's office shattering like a glass slipped off a butler's tray.

Egon found his wits and spoke first. "She actually knows how to perform the trial? Do we know if it's worked on a misfit? Does it make them more powerful? Could they actually go head to head with a magician then?"

"Calm yourself, Mr. Pennington. It's not as easy as you think." Donal took a sip of his own tea, regarding each of them with steady eyes. "What I say in this room doesn't leave it. I need more than your words for this. We'll bind each other to secrecy as long as we live. Understand?"

They eagerly agreed. Principal Ward traced a slow, looping spell that glowed like a knotted serpent chasing its own tail. Maisie mirrored his movements, the warm flow of magic welling from her heart and speeding down her arm. It ignited her fingertips with a satisfying shudder, and her own spell came alive. Cynthia and Egon cast their binding spells last, and together they sealed the secret until the last of them lived.

"She had it pretty much spot on," Donal admitted, staring at the fading afterimage of his spell.

Egon leaned onto his knees. "So how does it work?"

"The trial has two phases. In the first, the potential must survive four spells meant to kill them. During the Second World War, I was captured by a particularly cruel warlock named Franco Donati who, like many of the evil men those days, wanted to test the limits of what the human body could conceivably survive." He glanced at Maisie, his eyes struggling with the emotions the memories brought to the surface. "I had not gained the power to manipulate magic yet, but I knew something had changed within me.

"Thankfully, Maisie saved me before Franco turned me into ash. Since I knew the secret of your—our world, she couldn't very well send me back into talentless society knowing about magic, so we stayed together and fought with the other magicians and magical races. That leads us to the second phase of the trial. Once you cheat death four times, death demands a payment. You must find the one who hates you most…" His voice trailed, his gaze drifting to the carpet.

"And you must destroy them," Maisie finished. She leaned against her seat, memories of their night in the parking lot still fresh as a stitched wound. "Donal poisoned Ms. Velvet when he discovered what she had become. She died, hating him more than anyone else in the world."

"And yet Ms. Velvet lives today," Ms. Doyle said. "How do you have the power of the trial?"

"Someone resurrected her." Donal's glare narrowed, burning like stars sunk into shallow pools. "They are the true enemy. Not even I could resurrect a person once they've passed. There is a force out there, hiding, waiting, and I fear our part and Quinn's is but a small piece of a larger puzzle. We need to discover who brought the Witch Queen of the West back and how we can stop them both before it's too late."

Maisie knew rehashing his past must torture him, but they needed to address their current issues instead of playing dimensional chess with the future. "And we will. But first, what do we do about the misfit attack we all know is coming?"

"That's the easiest of our solutions," he said. "From now until this is resolved, Wimbly's will be teaching one kind of art." The principal stood. He strolled to his windows, staring out the multicolored glass. "Prepare yourselves, and inform the rest of the faculty. Until further notice, Wimbly's will be making warriors."

Snowball Fight!

Friday, October 30th finally arrived, the day of Mr. Pennington's practical. Quinn and Heidi had practiced daily, spending long hours together in the study halls. So much time they spent with one another, their performance became second nature. Quinn knew Heidi's spell just as soon as she began casting it through his fingers, and he would move his body in a way that could convince even someone as trained as Mr. Pennington that he cast it. No doubt they would at the very least fool the other kids in class.

The winter storm broke long enough to give Wimbly's some rest from the endless snow. In preparation for Halloween, orange and black ribbons hung in loose curls from the walls. Jack-o-lanterns floated on bat-shaped balloons throughout both Glen and Hilltop while a constant layer of mist swirled over the grounds. Outside, yetis dressed like ghosts or goblins wrapped lampposts in shiny orange tinsel. Despite the misfit rumors, despite the fear laced in every whisper and sideways glance cast his way, Quinn couldn't keep the smile from his lips and the bounce in his step.

Quinn and Billy walked outside and found Heidi waiting by their dorm. A carved pumpkin carried by a bat-shaped balloon floated by, its stubby wings struggling to keep the jack-o-lantern afloat.

Billy laughed and poked the pumpkin. It grumbled and spit orange and black sparks before howling like a wolf at a full moon. "This is my favorite holiday, you know."

"Why's that?" Quinn asked, trying not to grab them both and sprint to Mr. Pennington's class.

"Because on Halloween you get to pretend to be something else. My granddad never liked it, said it was like a misfit Christmas. I think he just told me that though because he was afraid of getting scared."

"I'm in it for the treats," Heidi said. "I hope we get buckets of chocolate."

"The tricks are pretty fun, too." Billy winked at Quinn. "I bet Quinn and I could trick you real good. Better be on the lookout."

Heidi snorted. She tucked a feathery lock behind her ear and glanced at Quinn. "I'm better at tricks than you might think. Maybe you should be the one looking out, Billy Holcomb."

Quinn picked up his pace, filling his lungs with the crisp winter air. "I think we should get the practical done before we worry about trick-or-treating."

Heidi caught up with Quinn, her nose squished into a wrinkled wedge. "It's…it's in front of the whole class. I'm so ready to get it over with, but I wish it would go away at the same time. I made some chamomile tea earlier and it's helping, but I can get kind of crazy under pressure."

Poor Heidi. Quinn opened his mouth, searching for words of comfort, but Billy burst between them and spun around so he blocked the path.

Quinn and Heidi stopped in their tracks. "What?" she asked.

"Listen." Billy planted his feet and lifted his chin. He pointed a confident finger between her eyes. "You've got to learn to believe in yourself. I saw you practicing in the greenhouse the other day when you thought no one was watching. Your training with Quinn's paying off, and you're getting really good. You can beat this, easy. I know you can."

The dark cloud over Heidi thinned, and her eyes brightened. "I kind of didn't expect that from you. Thank you."

"We're friends, aren't we?"

"Yeah…" A smile tiptoed up her cheeks. "Yeah, I guess we are."

"Good. You know it might be hard to believe, but I was pretty much afraid of everything and everyone before this year."

"No kidding?" she asked through the corner of her mouth. Quinn chuckled.

"Well, I'm not anymore. Quinn showed me I don't have to be. He stuck up for me even though he didn't need to. Without even using any magic, he scared off one of the worst bullies in the school. And when Porter tried to get Quinn back, I beat him all by myself. Quinn didn't even lift a finger or trace a single spell, I swear."

"I believe you. I really do."

"Then believe in what you can do, too. Look at us. We're probably the most unpopular kids at Wimbly's." He pointed to a group of girls who detoured from the path instead of walking by them. "No thanks to our friend Quinn the Misfit King. But even though we're not popular or people think we're weird, who cares? I actually like being different. I like being friends with Flower Power and the Misfit King, and I hope you don't mind being a friend of Weasel's."

"They really call you two that?" Quinn asked.

Billy shrugged and nodded. "I'm fine with it. My mom says if they're talking about you then that means you're doing something right."

"Flower Power's kind of pretty anyway," Heidi murmured as her gaze drifted toward the clouds.

They made it halfway to Hilltop when Quinn noticed some commotion in the woods. He stopped and stared through the dense pillars of rough bark. Porter Price's familiar voice drifted through the forest and tickled his ears. "Hey you big idiot, over here!"

A confused growl replied. Snow and leaf and pinecone burst in a cloud, followed by a group of harsh giggles. Heidi puckered her lips, and her hands balled into trembling fists. "Those jerks. They're picking on a yeti!"

Common myths claimed yetis stalked the snowy mountains of faraway places and preyed on unsuspecting travellers, but like most myths, the truth was far different. Though the beasts could make a stranger shake in their boots or run for shelter, yetis were avowed pacifists and lovers of nature. Some even said that in their homeland in the Himalayas, it wasn't uncommon to find a yeti tending to a monk's garden or resting against a temple enjoying a cup of bark tea.

Billy dashed into the woods before Quinn and Heidi could say another word. "I'm not having it!" he shouted, darting through the trees. "Nobody beats up on a yeti. It's not right. Like kicking a puppy."

"I like Billy more every day," Heidi said as she chased after him. Quinn took off after her, a little more nervous than his friends appeared to be.

Despite the heavy snow, the trees grew close enough together to provide plenty of clear ground. Being so small, Billy wove easily through the forest and soon disappeared behind a curtain of low branches.

Quinn caught up with Heidi. "I'll have to tell him soon," he said between breaths. "I can't keep our—my secret from him forever."

Her cheeks reddened, and she glanced down. "I know. I should tell you not to, but…I know."

They finally burst into a clearing, arms raised to protect themselves from the last slapping branches. A group of other first year students danced around one very confused yeti and taunted it with snowballs and ugly names.

The creature had a snowy white coat like most its brothers and sisters save for a splash of ashy grey ringing its right eye. The fish students called it horrible names and pelted it with snowballs while the beast moaned and pleaded in its growling tongue. Its large, round eyes darted from student to student until they came to Quinn, and he saw the tears well within them.

Porter Price stopped his ring of lemmings, and they spread into a wall between Billy, Quinn, and Heidi with the yeti on the other side. Porter flashed his snaggletooth beneath his smile, his breath cold puffs beneath his cherry cheeks. "Look who's come to save the day. It's Wimbly's regular gang of misfits."

Hi *Weasel*," he said, putting a venomous accent on the name. "Did you a grow a pair or something? Shouldn't you be hiding in the Misfit King's shadow, wishing he gave you half the attention he gives his airhead girlfriend?"

"Hey!" Quinn marched forward. "You better watch it."

All the students except Porter stepped back. The bully glanced behind him. Seeing the others retreat, he took a defiant step forward. "They might be scared of you. I'm not. What you gonna do about it?" His beady glare caught Heidi in its crosshairs, and he laughed, pointing a crooked finger at Quinn's friend. "I mean, look at her. She's talking to a freaking butterfly. How ditzy can you get? Flower Girl? Hello? Earth to idiot!"

Quinn glimpsed Heidi cradling a monarch butterfly colored like a tropical sunset, its wings flexing over her knit mittens. Her lips whispered words he couldn't hear. Her eyes betrayed how much she cared even for something so small as an insect.

"I don't care what you think about them." Quinn crossed his arms. Things could get ugly fast, but his reputation was a suit of armor, and he'd outsmarted every single talented magician at Wimbly's since day one and had no reason to think he couldn't keep the game going. "You mess with them, you mess with me."

Billy nodded so hard his chin bounced against his jacket collar. "Yeah, and you don't pick on the yetis. You know they've done nothing to you. Stop throwing snowballs and leave the poor guy alone. It's mean and you know it."

Porter brushed his fingers through his hair and laughed. Encouraged by his display, his friends clustered behind him, fingers out and spells ready like an Old West standoff. And there Quinn stood with a gun and no bullets.

"I'm not leaving it alone, Weasel," Porter spat. "You think it cares? They're just big stupid monkeys. They serve *us*. We're the talent. We're the best."

The yeti made a sound that was half growl, half whine. It looked at Quinn and his friends, head cocked to the side. Yetis might not cast spells or carry on conversations. That didn't make them simple or stupid.

Porter bent over and gathered a mound of snow the size of a bowling ball. "There're seven of us and three of you. Two and half if we're being honest about Heidi. Make a move and you'll regret it." He looked over his shoulder at a girl with straight bangs and square shoulders. "Katy, throw the yeti a pinecone. I don't want it to see what's coming."

Katy nodded, pulling a pinecone from her coat. She tossed it at the yeti, and the creature plucked it from the air like an apple hanging from a low branch. It regarded the pinecone as if it had taken a lifetime to find, and all the confusion and anger vanished from its eyes.

And then Porter's snowball slammed against its cheek. The beast cried and dropped the pinecone. Shards of packed snow fell from the yeti's furry jaw as it searched frantically for its missing treasure with a snow-blinded eye.

"You're a bully!" Billy lurched forward, his fingers tensed. "You can't do that. It's cruel!"

Porter and the children readied spells, Porter's dark smile secure in the numbers around him. "I'm the best of the best, a talented magician everyone wants to be like. I can do whatever I want."

Just then, Heidi's butterfly floated into view. It landed on the yeti's shoulder. Billy's fingers stopped wiggling, and for a moment, even the other students forgot the spells dancing on their fingertips. Quinn frowned and turned to Heidi. "Everything ok?"

"It will be," she said, rocking on her heels with a smile wide as a crescent moon tipped on its back.

Porter laughed at the butterfly before he zeroed back on Quinn and the others. "That's the best you can do? You two and your hippie think you're so special. You're not. We're better than you, all of us. Even if you're talented, you'll never really be one of us."

Behind him, the yeti pursed its great lips. It blinked at the butterfly and nodded. More quietly than a falling feather, it bent and began scooping great mounds of snow into an ever-growing ball.

Porter spread his arms, blissfully oblivious as he ranted. "Nobody here likes you. Nobody here wants you. I thought we made that clear, but I guess you need a little more encouragement. The hurting kind of encouragement."

The yeti lifted a mound of snow above its head so large calling it a snowball wouldn't do it justice. It was a snow*boulder*.

Heidi stepped between Quinn and Billy. She wrapped her arms over their shoulders and leaned between them. "You're wrong about that, Porter. In fact, I imagine at least half of those people standing behind you'll regret being your friend sooner than you think."

"Guys…" Porter began a spell. "Let's get—"

A deep, savage growl interrupted his casting. A shadow fell over Porter as the snarling yeti stood to its full height. Porter's eyes widened, and he slowly turned. The yeti let loose an earth shaking roar and plopped the snowball right on top of Porter's head like a scoop of ice cream on a bully-shaped waffle cone. If the look in the yeti's eyes was any indication, it was just as satisfying.

Porter's friends scattered with their screams and fled into the forest. Porter dug his way out of the snow, crying and screaming, and scrambled from the laughing beast. The bully dashed away, practically tripping on his own feet. "This isn't through," he shouted. "You know it's not!"

The yeti waved goodbye to its former tormenters. Heidi doubled over and tried to smother her laughs within her mittens. Billy burst out laughing, clutching his stomach and falling back into a tree trunk. Quinn grinned and crossed his arms. "How'd it know, and why'd it do it?"

"My butterfly," Heidi said. She straightened and skipped to the yeti. The gentle giant cooed as she wrapped her arms around its waist. "They're not stupid, you know. They just don't talk like we do. Wild things from nature, they don't speak in normal languages like we do. They speak with hearts. Butterflies are one of the few creatures that can do both. I just told it to tell the yeti what to do."

The yeti patted her head. She smiled and bowed before rejoining the others. "For some reason, the practical doesn't seem like such a big deal anymore."

Billy headed back the way they came. "Feels good, doesn't it? Facing them like that, even though they were stronger, we were smarter. The three of us, we can do anything if we're together. Too bad I didn't get a chance to cast anything though. I had the perfect spell."

"Yeah," Quinn said, "too bad." He and Heidi shared another glance, and they headed back the way they came.

A Different Kind of Test

Arcana 101, Mr. Pennington's class, took longer to fill than usual, a good portion of those trickling in covered in snow and dirt and fallen leaves. Porter stalked in last. He shoved his hip against Quinn's desk hard as he could and took his seat, refusing to face the group who just humiliated him. Quinn knew what it meant. A boy like Porter couldn't allow a slight like that to go unanswered.

Egon regarded the stragglers with an arched eyebrow and puckered lips. Scratching the back of his head, he shrugged and turned to his board. "It seems some of you have been practicing before class. I have some unfortunate news, though. There will be no winter practical."

Heidi clapped. Billy pouted. Quinn felt something between relief and disappointment. After practicing so long and hard, he'd almost looked forward to showing the students what the Misfit King could do.

"Now, now," Mr. Pennington continued, "let's not be too hasty. While we won't be having a practical, per say, we will be having another kind of magical test. In light of recent events outside of campus, Principal Ward has declared that it is in every young talented magician's interest to focus more on the, ah, more aggressive arts than is typical for our students—especially first year fish like you."

Billy perked up. Heidi slouched. Quinn waited, holding back his judgment until he knew what kind of new event their teacher had in mind.

Mr. Pennington cast a spell at the oversized chalkboard. It spun into a vertical rectangle and parted, winds billowing from the opening like a leviathan's yawn. "I've created a special training area on the other side of this doorway much like the study halls you're used to. We will file in and spend the day doing some light dueling. Don't worry about harming one another. While a good hit might smart, this room will temper the meager spells of fish like yourselves and ensure nothing but a few light bruises are your battle scars."

"Why now?" Heidi asked, not waiting for him to call on her raised hand.

Egon rotated and frowned. His glaze flicked to Quinn and back again. "Because that is what the world requires of us. It's no longer useful to anyone to deny the rumors, and many of you already know your parents have gone into hiding. They will be safe, just as you will be safe. As long as we have Principal Ward and Mr. Crawford, not even a thousand misfits could harm a single student at Wimbly's."

"Then why are we practicing?" Heidi persisted, her voice flat. "If we're safe, why do we need to learn how to hurt people?"

"Because, Ms. Grace..." Egon sat on the lip of his desk. "...We cannot stay at Wimbly's forever, now can we?"

Another hand shot up. Egon acknowledged it. A boy with blond hair and big hands grabbed the lip of his desk and leaned forward. "Are you afraid, Mr. Pennington?"

"Of course not." Mr. Pennington laughed in a most unconvincing manner. The students traded glances, many of which ended up on Quinn.

Billy leaned over. "Don't worry about what they think, we've got your back."

"I hope so," Quinn whispered. The class stood, and they shuffled single-file into the dueling room.

The room itself was a bottomless abyss. Above the void, two columns of floating arenas connected by a sloping rope bridge bobbed in a light breeze. High webbing that would catch any student before they fell ringed each platform. Mr. Pennington paused at the head of the line. He traced a wide pattern, moving like a conductor before a symphony, and flung his spell before him. A sky of stars burst over the black blanket, the band of the Milky Way running in a murky streak across the studded sky. A single crescent moon hung much larger than the real moon overhead.

Egon turned to his class and addressed them, pinching his collar between his thumbs. "We'll have three dueling phases. I have assigned partners for each of you—"

"Can we volunteer?" Porter barreled through the line, knocking students into the swaying path's rails. "If we want, can we volunteer, Mr. Pennington?"

"Hm." He tapped his chin, narrowing his eyes at Porter. "At my discretion, I don't see why not. I won't be having any of you partnering with your best friends so you can pull rabbits out of your hats while the other students practice real magic."

"Oh no, Mr. Pennington, I'd never cheat like that." The boy turned to Quinn and smiled. "Quinn, you up for some training?"

Heidi nudged Quinn's back. She leaned to him, her breath tickling his ear. "Don't do it. It's a trap. Volunteer with me."

What she said made sense. Porter wouldn't hold anything back. But Quinn couldn't resist the urge. Part of him wanted that fight, and he needed Heidi to start believing in her own ability. Maybe pitting himself against Porter would finally break her timid streak and show the world how good she could be at magic.

"Sounds like a great idea, Porter," he said.

Egon shrugged. "Fine with me. I don't believe there's any love loss between the two of you so it might make for some good sport." His attention shifted to the other students. One by one, he paired them with their sparring partner.

"Quinn," Heidi hissed. "What're you doing?"

"The right thing." He leaned over, winking. "Make it look convincing, but don't let him win. Who'd care about us if they knew the Misfit King was nothing but a lie?"

"I don't—"

"Heidi, you can do this. I believe in you, and I trust you. Now trust me when I say you've got this."

He felt her tense for a moment, but she relented with a sigh. "I guess you're right. The enchantment I put on your hands during our practices will still be there until I cancel it, so you're ready to go whenever."

"Make it look convincing," he said.

"I'll try. You know this is twice today I'll have saved your butt."

"My butt is very thankful."

They laughed. The puppet, the name of her spell, was a special enchantment that let her channel her talent through his fingers. He'd never technically cast a single spell, but as long as she had full concentration, no one would ever suspect otherwise.

Mr. Pennington paired Heidi with the quiet redhead from the van ride. Heidi waved goodbye and joined the girl at the edge of the class, hidden just where the gateway back to the classroom stood.

Despite most pairs sidling up to one another and shaking hands, Quinn avoided Porter. The first round of duelists spilled into the rings, Billy among them. He sparred a boy named Boyd almost twice his size. In the talentless world, that might have inspired a measure of fear in Billy. But Billy had both talent and courage, and that made him a match for a magician of any size.

Boyd started out by summoning a ring of fire, the flames serpents swirling around his body. Billy laughed like he'd seen better from a toddler and cast his own spell. His body faded into mist. His eyes blanched white. He swirled around Boyd, his body mixing with the smoke of Boyd's fire spell.

Billy's partner cast a missile that thumped through the air. It tore a hole through the ring of Billy-smoke, but Quinn's roommate just laughed in ghostly notes. Like a mad wraith Billy dove, his body transforming into water as it doused the snaking flames around Boyd. The terrified boy tried casting another spell, but the water splashed over him turned to ice. Rings locked around Boyd's wrists and snared his feet in icy grips. Veins on Boyd's temple pulsed. His muscles flexed. No matter how hard he tried, Billy held him fast.

Mr. Pennington watched the duel, all the while nodding at Billy's spells. He clapped, strolling toward the arena. "Duel is done and much faster than I expected. Billy Holcomb, might I say excellent job. Many fish fear transformation without the help of an instructor. What you've managed, especially a complex air transformation like your swirling fog, is a wonderful feat for one so young. The dryads will certainly fear you on the field when you start your soccer matches."

The ice around Boyd melted, and the mist ceased swirling. Billy reformed and wiped the hair from his brow as he gave a bow. "It was nothing."

He strolled from the arena. Mr. Pennington followed his exit with a grin on his face and his hands still slowly clapping. "All of you should take note of Mr. Holcomb. A smart magician confuses his opponent with a diversion and then binds them so they may not cast another spell. Bind a magician, and you make them powerless."

The rest of the sparring partners finished. Round two began, and Quinn followed Porter onto a platform. Even the others duelists in their round couldn't hide the disappointment of missing Quinn and Porter's duel. If Egon had given them the chance, Quinn had no doubt every eye in the room would be glued to his arena. A comet streaked across the sky, and Quinn quickly wished things would work out his way.

"This is stupid, Porter. You won't prove anything." Quinn edged back. His hands went numb. Heidi was ready.

"It's not stupid, it's practice." Porter sneered, edging forward. "You don't scare me, Quinn."

"Funny that I don't. Since you've been calling me the Misfit King I kind of thought I might."

Porter put his hands at the ready. His eyes glinted with a deep hunger. He couldn't accept defeat, and ever since that day in the showers, this had been the moment Porter worked for. Quinn put his trust in Heidi. The bully might have been working for that moment, but so had Quinn and Heidi. Heidi wasn't a warrior. She was kind. But push a kind person far enough and they can go toe to toe with any fighter.

Porter's fingers twisted in an arcane sign. Branches sprouted from the arena floor. Quinn's own fingers moved faster than his eyes could register. He bounded high, flipping over Porter and landing on the opposite side. Thrashing vines slapped at empty space where Quinn once stood, Porter's familiar binding spell looking for its target.

"Nice reflexes," Porter said, spinning around.

"Learn some new moves," Quinn retorted.

"I have."

Quinn tensed as Porter prepped another spell. His own fingers danced, possessed by Heidi's mind, but they moved more slowly than Porter's.

Three violet balls spun around Porter's palm. They rotated faster and faster until three bright bands raced around the boy. He flicked his wrist, and one flung lightning-fast at Quinn. Quinn's own hands moved, but the spell failed and the ball slammed into Quinn's chest. He flew into the netting, a burning sensation blasting over his ribs.

He tried recovering, but the second ball slammed into his cheek before he hit the ground. Ringing filled his ears. His world spun. He hit the arena floor, and the third ball burst onto his side. Quinn gasped, not knowing which way was up or down. His arms trembled. His eyes watered.

His fingers moved despite his nausea, and a flash lit his eyes. There was laughing. Porter laughing at him. His classmates laughing at him.

"Not as fast as you thought you were." Porter's voice seemed so far off. Through a tunnel. Through eternity.

Quinn cast a spell, and a force of air erupted from his body. There was a yelp, then a gasp of several startled mouths. Blinking, he struggled to his feet, his world finally steadying. Porter struggled to his own feet opposite where Quinn stood. Black ringed his eye where Quinn's—Heidi's spell struck.

Quinn wiped his chin and wobbled toward the center. Porter recollected himself much more quickly and flung two bolts of air that slammed into Quinn's chest. Quinn went flying, his senses reeling. He landed on the floor, blinking, trying desperately to make sense of the world in his jumbled head.

Before he knew it, Porter was over him. Thorns sprouted on the boy's fist. He punched Quinn in the cheek, and while the arena protected his body from major harm, he still felt Porter's thorns sink into his chin. Quinn cried out. Porter struck again. Quinn jerked his arms over his face and tried to twist away. Somewhere inside him, he called out to Heidi. Porter hit so hard he couldn't gather the breath to scream. He thought Heidi could do it. She couldn't. She just wasn't a warrior.

A warm spell ignited his fingers. A disc of fire erupted over his body. Porter yelped and flew backwards. Quinn's spell ignited with furious energy. He rose in the air, fire spreading over his body yet not burning it. The fire increased in heat and intensity. Had it not been coming from his own skin, it would have blinded him.

Porter scrambled from the heat, shielding his face. Mr. Pennington shouted. Still, Quinn's fingers wove the complex web of power blasting the arena. A flaming tail scorched the webbing, destroying it as if it had been made of ash. Another fiery tail burned a hole in the arena floor. And then, the fire gathered in a swirling hurricane around his palm, a nova of energy that would annihilate anything it touched.

No, he thought. *Stop, Heidi. How are you doing this? Why are you doing this?*

The fire condensed into a star blazing within Quinn's palm. His class-mates looked on, horrified. He turned to Heidi as his palm opened toward Porter. Mr. Pennington burst onto the arena, his fingers flaring with power as he traced a spell.

Heidi's fingers moved with the grace and ease of someone a hundred times her age. She stared at Porter, unblinking a dark and seething anger rag-ing in eyes that should have been bright and carefree.

Stop, his lips pleaded, the heat so strong he couldn't scream.

The fire around Quinn's palm gathered to a single, destructive point. Quinn realized in one horrible, awful heartbeat that not even the room's en-chantments would protect Porter from its power. He looked away, the last thing he remembered Mr. Pennington's glowing fist racing for his face.

Rising Suspicions

Quinn stared at the ceiling of his dorm and tried not to think about the world outside his little room. Billy watched two enchanted elf figurines battle one another on his desk, their slender bodies performing graceful flips and bends, their curved swords showering the desk with sparks.

Three days passed since his duel with Porter Price. Quinn closed his eyes and replayed the battle as he had so many times before. He remembered the heat on his arm, the wild fire of a star so powerful not even the enchanted room could have saved Porter. Luckily Mr. Pennington made it just in time. The man walloped Quinn on the jaw with an enchanted fist and knocked the fireball to the side, blasting it harmlessly into the background.

Quinn had passed out from the heat. When he woke, he remembered Egon's wide eyes staring over him, sweat glistening on his cheeks, his breaths heavy. There was fear in his eyes. Not suspicion or paranoia, but true fear. No fish should have the skill to cast that spell. If only the man knew it hadn't been Quinn that cast it. When Quinn looked for Heidi, she'd already fled the scene, and he hadn't seen her since.

"You know," Billy said, "you've got to stop beating yourself up about Friday. Nobody ended up getting hurt. You showed Porter what's what. I don't think he'll be messing with any of us any time soon."

Quinn propped himself on his elbows and watched the tiny elves clang their swords against one another. He wished he could tell Billy it wasn't him in the first place. He wanted to tell him it was Heidi, their kind, carefree friend who somehow managed to cast the most powerful spell Quinn had ever seen. He wanted to say so many things. But he didn't. He couldn't.

"I know." Quinn sighed, his gaze sliding from Billy to his feet. "I just…lost it I guess. I could have hurt him, Billy. I never wanted to do that. I don't want people to think that about me. You haven't seen Heidi around any chance?"

Billy shook his head, his lip protruding as he thought. "No, not the entire weekend. She's probably walled up in the greenhouse singing to daisies or whatever it is she does in there. Maybe she's practicing in one of the study halls, trying to get as good as you are at casting."

"Not too sure about that one," Quinn murmured.

A soft rapping at the door disturbed their thoughts. Billy flicked the elves, and they stiffened into figurines. Someone knocked again. Quinn slid from his bed and padded across the cold floorboards. Opening the door, he discovered a package and an empty hallway. At first he thought it must be for Billy—after all, Quinn didn't know anyone who would ever send him something.

On further inspection, he saw his name written on the package along with his room number. He turned the brown rectangle in his hands, gently squeezing and shaking. "I wonder who it could be from?"

"Then open it," Billy huffed.

Quinn nodded and shut the door behind him. He jumped onto his bed, legs folded, and placed the package in his lap. He ran his finger through the taped seals, and they gave a satisfying rip and parted. The rest of the packaging peeled away, revealing a plain white box within. Excited, Quinn opened the box to find a black book nestled in pink tissue paper with a little white folded card that bore his name in looping letters.

He lifted the book out of the box like its spine was gold and covered with polished diamonds. "I love it," he said.

"You don't even know what the book is!" Billy sat on his own bed, its springs squeaking in agreement. "Who's it from?"

Quinn read the card's looping letters.

Hi Quinn,

I'm really sorry about how things got so out of hand. I saw him hurting you and something just snapped inside me. I don't want you to hate me for this, and I hope we can still be friends. If not, I understand.

Heidi

"Heidi. She's saying sorry."

"Oh." Billy tapped his nose, his brow squishing into a wrinkly blanket. "Why would she need to say sorry? She hasn't done anything, has she?"

"She, ah, no, no she hasn't." Quinn bumbled and stumbled on his words. He'd almost let it slip. "You know how weird she can be. She probably thinks she's done something when it's not anything at all."

Billy accepted the excuse, although a wary look lingered in his eyes. He lifted a chin toward the book. "So what's it about?"

Quinn peeled the cover apart. It was an old book, so he treated it with care. Yellowed pages full of scribbled notes and complex patterns filled the book. Circles interlaced one another, lines braided in elegant columns, triangles and squares interlocked in fascinating shapes. He stared at the spells, scratching his head. "It's a spell book."

"Whose?"

"No idea." He flipped through the pages, but there were only spells— many, many spells of such complexity and power that the mere thought of trying to cast them made Quinn's pulse race. Whoever's book this was must have been a powerful magician. A page flipped by and caught his eye. Quinn studied the old spell on it, the realization of what happened during the duel with Porter finally clicking.

Billy scurried over, his shadow slipping over the page. "That's the spell you cast, isn't it? The fireball that nearly blew us all away, it came from this book?"

"Yeah, it did. I, uh, I got it from somewhere else though. Looks like whoever owns this book created it first."

"What a mystery. You want to know about books, though, you know where you need to go."

"You're right. I think I need to take another trip to the library."

* * *

Snow was the state bird of Vermont, but even then Quinn had never experienced a snowstorm hard as the one blasting Woods Island that day. It came down in biting, blinding sheets. He fought against the howling wind, arm shielding his numb cheeks. The crooked path to Hilltop took three times as long to scale than other days, and when he finally reached the library, the storm had stolen most of his breath and left a wet chill seeping through his clothes.

After prying the door apart despite the storm's best efforts, he slipped inside. It banged shut behind him, a few flecks of snow swirling inside and drifting to the floor. Quinn swung his pack onto the nearest desk and pulled out the spell book.

"Nehemiah?" He twisted around, searching the shelves for the old man. "Mr. Crawford? I've come…to learn something."

If the librarian was there, he did not respond. Quinn scanned the first floor. Normally, Quinn welcomed a quiet place to study, but in an empty library coffined by a blizzard, it felt like more of a grave than anything.

"Mr. Crawford? Hello?" He walked toward a shelf.

A cold hand gripped his shoulder. He yelped, spinning around. Nehemiah stood before him, leaning on his cane more than usual, bent like an L tipped on its side. His liver-spotted skin had taken on an olive hue, and his lips were dry and lined with deep cracks. "Hello, Quinn."

Quinn swallowed, instinctively backing away from the walking vision of death that had just called his name. "Are you—are you okay, Mr. Crawford?"

The librarian smacked his lips. His knotty knuckles whitened on his walking stick, and he straightened, if only a little. "It's these damnable misfits, you see. There're some witches messing with the spells I've cast around the school and it's taken a toll on my old bones."

"I've heard." Quinn's gaze dropped to his snow-covered shoes. "I'm sorry. I think it's my fault, because of who they think I am."

Mr. Crawford wheezed his old, dusty cackle and playfully ran his thin fingers through Quinn's hair. "Don't you worry about those misfits! By the time this is all said and done I'll have them so in awe of what a librarian can do they'll be begging to catch my farts for a whiff of power, yes they will."

Quinn snickered. The old man looked like death, but if his spirit felt a strain he hid it well. "That's good to know, Nehemiah." Quinn held the mysterious spell book up to the librarian. "I brought this for you."

"For me? But this didn't come from my library. Are you wanting to make a donation?"

"No." Quinn pulled the book away. "Heidi gave it to me. It's…it's a spell book. We used one of the spells inside it and basically if everyone wasn't completely afraid of me before they're sure terrified now."

Nehemiah's silvery eyebrow peeked above his blindfold. "Ah yes, I heard about your little performance in Egon's arena room. I doubt Mr. Price will be harassing you any longer. Egon spent the better part of three hours in here talking my ear off about it."

"Do you think he hates me?"

"Hates you?" The old man burst out laughing and slapped his knee. "No, of course not! Egon Pennington is a powerful magician, but he's more superstitious than a black cat using an umbrella indoors beneath a ladder. He doesn't hate you, Quinn. He's scared because he lets a prophecy have power over him. You and I aren't like that. We won't let some silly talk of a Misfit King make us shake in our boots, now will we?"

"No, I guess not."

"Now, about this spell book. May I see it?" Nehemiah asked.

Quinn handed him the book. Slowly the old man thumbed through it, his finger sliding over its pages as he mumbled and grumbled in a low whisper. "Interesting."

"Do you know whose it is?"

"Haven't got the slightest idea, I'm afraid. I think it will require a little while longer to study. Do you mind if I hold onto it for awhile?"

Quinn really wanted to snatch the book away so he could run off to his room and get lost in its pages. Instead, he looked longingly at the cover and smiled. "Yeah, take as long as you want. Billy's never seen it before, either and—"

The librarian's shockingly strong hand clamped around Quinn's arm. "You showed this to Billy?" Quinn buckled from the pain and gasped, his own hand clawing over the librarian's. Nehemiah loosened his grip and lifted Quinn to his feet. "I'm sorry, but sometimes I forget my own strength in here. You must be careful what you show others. Wimbly's is safe for now, but that doesn't mean there aren't enemies here. There might not be any misfits on the campus grounds yet, but that doesn't mean the taint of one of those foul beings can't infect other talented magicians like a plague. Misfits have tongues and magicians have ears. That means deals can be made."

"Billy would never do anything for a misfit," Quinn said, yanking his arm from the librarian. The thought irked Quinn almost as much as being yanked around like a little boy. He rubbed the throbbing echo of Mr. Crawford's grip. "He's helped me before. I trust him."

"Indeed, forgive me, then. If you trust him, then I must trust him because I trust you." His shoulders sagged, and his voice trembled. "Things are just so difficult these days, and I'm so tired."

The fire in Quinn's blood cooled. He reached out, patting the old man's crooked back. "It's okay. A lot of people are. I just—I overreacted. I've got a temper sometimes. At least that's what everybody tells me."

Mr. Crawford smiled. "We're more alike by the day! As to your book, I swear to you no other book within this library will be guarded with more love and care than this book. I would burn my entire life's work to the ground before I let it out my hands, Quinn Lynch."

"Okay, okay. I get it. Don't be so dramatic."

Nehemiah laughed, and it carried a hint of warm relief. "Now, you said you wanted to learn something? I believe you may find some particularly interesting information through the East Door. It is the door of dreams and possibilities, of what your heart truly desires. You learned the future through the North Door, the past through the South, and now you'll learn about your own desires through this door."

"But I know what I want, Mr. Crawford."

"Don't be so quick to know yourself. The heart speaks in whispers while the mind roars from mountaintops. You might be surprised how many people don't realize what they truly want. Now, how about we get you through that door?"

The East Door

Quinn stepped through the East Door, the door that would teach him something about himself and his true desires. A meadow appeared, much like the one he and Heidi practiced in, but instead of wildflowers the color of a burning sunset, these flowers were the cool blues and greens of deep oceans and mountain lakes. Heidi stood in the center of the meadow, flashing her usual sunny smile. A cool breeze toyed with the feathers in her hair. She held her hands clasped eagerly before her.

"Heidi? How are you in here?" he asked.

She giggled and danced toward him. "What do you want, Quinn?"

"What do you mean?"

"What do you want?" She reached him and clasped his hands. "More than anything, what do you desire?"

Quinn's brows knitted together. Heidi would never talk like this. The magic of the East Door must have crafted some illusion, and it wanted something from him.

"I want to be a magician," he told her.

"More than anything?"

He squeezed her hands. "Yes, more than anything. Can you tell me how? How do I become a magician? I know there are four parts to the trial. What are they, battles? Tell me what I have to do to survive them and I'll do it."

A breeze whistled around them. She cocked her head and grinned impishly. "Don't worry about that, silly. What you survive won't give you what you need. It's what you destroy that will give you what you want." She reached into his collar and pulled out his mother's locket. Flicking it open, she lifted it to his face.

The tiny mirror set into the frame showed him a very confused reflection. She dropped the locket in his palm. He stared at the jewelry, shaking his head.

"I don't understand. I have to destroy myself?"

"Maybe that and more. This is the secret of what you desire. To gain, you must lose. When the time comes, remember that."

"I still don't understand." She kept speaking in cryptic riddles. The other doors had at least been more straightforward than this one. "Do I need to—"

She pressed a finger to his lips and glanced over his shoulder. Laughing, she twisted and skipped away. "He's coming now. I have to go before I get in trouble. I'm not supposed to tell you this, but Nehemiah said it was okay as long as *he* didn't come, but he's coming now, so bye!"

"Wait! Will I learn everything I need to through the West Door then?"

Heidi paused, glancing over her shoulder. "You will learn who you really are, just like he did."

Quinn whirled around. The exit appeared, the meadow around it fading to black. He turned to Heidi, but the illusion had vanished. The sky darkened. The flowers wilted. Quinn made his way to the door. He reached the doorframe, and a hand burst through the curtains, latching around his collar. A yelp slipped past his lips as the hand yanked him through the curtains.

A shock like a wave crashing on his chest plowed into him, rushing the air from his lungs. He doubled over, wobbling on the walkway. Blinking, his world regained some balance. Principal Ward stood straight and hard, his blazing eyes framed by dark circles so intense Quinn feared they'd turn him into a blubbering puddle of nerves.

The principal leaned down and stared into his eyes. "And what do you think you were doing through that door?"

Mr. Crawford leaned against his walking stick, both hands resting on its polished knob. "Looks like he was in the East Door, Donal."

Donal spun to Nehemiah and shoved a long, straight finger at the man. "You stay out of this. I don't know what your goal is, Crawford, but you're dangerously close to upsetting me with this ridiculous game you're playing. This is neither the time nor the place to fill the boy's head with your delusions."

"Delusions?" Nehemiah shook his head. "Who is the deluded one here? You are the one with false impressions. You are the one keeping secrets from a boy who very much deserves the truth."

Quinn's temperature inched higher, and he edged forward. "What secrets?" His steady stare bounced between the librarian and the principal. "What are you keeping from me?"

"This should be something discussed in private," Donal said, losing some of the hard edge in his voice.

"No, tell me now. What are you keeping from me?"

Donal flashed a stare at Nehemiah that said they'd discuss more later before he went to his knee. "Quinn, you know how Maisie went to your home and found evidence of torture?"

Quinn's stomach turned. "Yes, but you told me already." He could tell the conversation made Donal uncomfortable. A man so powerful wasn't used to dealing with the emotions of children, and it made him squirm.

"And you know we think the misfits tortured the talent from your parents? We think that is what caused the fire. Why they've saved you is anyone's guess."

Quinn knew the look of a lie in someone's eyes after having lived one for so long. "I know, I know. But what do you really think?"

Donal's lips contorted in a wiggling line. Sighing, his head dipped. "We think it might have something to do with the Misfit King prophecy."

"So you really do think I'm him? You think I'm the Misfit King, the one that's going to destroy all the talented magicians?"

His own words startled him as Heidi's echoed in his mind. *What you survive won't give you what you need. It's what you destroy that will give you what you want.*

He tried to laugh off the nerves working their way up his spine and glanced at Nehemiah for support. The old librarian nodded with a warm smile.

"No, I don't think you're him," Donal said. "The Misfit King prophecy, it's honestly a bunch of baloney if you ask me. It's a way for them to scare talented magicians, to make us fear them even when our power is so much greater."

"But you're not a talented magician, Principal Ward. You're not a misfit, either. What do you believe you are? How does someone with the trial fit into a world that's just talent and torture?"

Quinn had never seen the principal so dumbstruck. The man stared at Quinn, his lips parting in a hollow circle. "I'm with the talent…"

"Are you?" Quinn had just about enough of all the talent and torture talk. The talented thought they were above everything, that nothing could touch them and that the world owed them something just for being there. The tortured misfits were warped and evil things, demons and villains and all the dark things in the world. That left everyone else lost somewhere in the middle. He wanted another way. He deserved another way. "I'm so close. Why won't you tell me? Why won't you let the world know about the trial? If you could just say it, there could be another way, a better way. The talent would still be there, but people wouldn't have any reason to fear torture. If we knew the trial, we could just do that. Why won't you do it?"

Donal's features darkened. He stood, straightening his jacket. "And why do you care so much? Why have you made it your one goal this year to find out the truth? What's in it for you, when you're already so talented in magic?"

Words caught in Quinn's throat. He eyed Nehemiah, but the librarian's barest of headshakes told him to keep his mouth shut about the secret. Maybe the librarian was right. Maybe telling Donal would get him kicked out. If they expelled him, he'd never walk through the last door, and by then he realized he wanted that more than anything else.

"Are you afraid of what might happen if I find out?" Quinn asked.

Donal stared at him a long while before he spoke again. "Yes, I am."

"Then maybe there's more to the prophecy than you're willing to admit."

"We'll be leaving now, Mr. Lynch." He faced Nehemiah with a jaw of steel and glared down the strong bridge of his nose. "This library is now closed to Mr. Lynch. He may not enter or leave. You are, for once, commanded to do your job of protecting this campus and nothing else. Don't test me, Crawford, you know what I'm capable of."

Nehemiah smirked, waving dismissively with his walking stick. "You've always been a dramatic fool. To think, the trial wasted on such a selfish narcissist—"

"Enough!" Donal grabbed Quinn's arm and leapt from the railing. They plummeted, Quinn screaming, floor zooming larger each second. Donal tucked Quinn beneath his arm and landed soft and steady as a cat, plopping Quinn and his jelly legs onto the floor. "I will walk you back to your dorm, Mr. Lynch. You will practice combat like all the other students and prepare in the event of an emergency. You are not to return to this library until I give you permission on threat of expulsion from this school and any others in the magic world. Is this understood?"

Quinn clenched his teeth, his jaw steel knots. "Yes. I understand"

But Quinn wouldn't do as Donal commanded. Quinn needed the library. All his answers would become clear through the West Door. He was a boy with nothing to lose and everything to gain, and not even Principal Donal Ward would keep him from what he wanted.

An Unexpected Guest

He traced the finishing touches of his spell with his tongue pinched between his teeth. Ryley laughed, tears in his eyes. He held his most beautiful creation in his hands, a spell that would make anyone stupid enough to become his enemy nothing more than a knife-riddled memory. He lurched from his desk, his card in a death grip. His false father Oliver wanted Ryley practicing outside, but the snowstorms became so frequent and so furious they forced everyone inside no matter how much Oliver grumbled otherwise. Ryley took it as a sign that even nature stuck its thumb in his false parent's eye. The world was Ryley's to take, and soon, everyone would know it.

Ms. Velvet's piercing blue eyes peeked like a serpent above the edge of his card. He thrust it toward her, his heart beating like a thousand drummers. "This is it, the last spell you wanted. Does it please you? Is it everything you wanted?" His hands shook. His eyes watered. He needed Ms. Velvet's approval. Nothing else mattered but the love she gave him.

She plucked the card from his grasp so easily he wondered if his fingers had oil on them. Studying it with a raised eyebrow, she rotated the piece of paper, checking each line and angle, each shape and intersecting point. A smile spread across her lips slow as a creeping vine. "And you know it? You know it by heart? Is it written on your soul, always itching to leap from your fingertips and punish the one who punished you?"

"Yes, yes it is. So you like it?"

"I do. Excellent job, my darling."

A fat, burning tear escaped his eye. He caught it with his sleeve and pulled his shoulders back. "I knew I could make you proud."

"Ryley!" Patty's voice drifted upstairs, and he cringed. "Dinner's ready. Get down here or I'm throwing it out."

"Do as your mother says," Oliver hollered, his voice harder than a ruler slapped against the back of a hand.

Ryley trembled. He clenched his fists, his nails digging into palms that were covered in thick, leathery callouses from endless hours of wintry labor. Ms. Velvet considered him with a cocked head, her tongue sliding across her ruby lips. "I suppose it's time for dinner. But first, tell me, what time is it?"

His lips contorted with the rage that burned through his veins whenever he thought of his false parents or the orphan who ruined his life. "It's time I left!"

"It is?" Ms. Velvet clapped. "Perhaps it's time to start a new beginning for you since we're getting so close to the New Year. Do you know why we celebrate the New Year?"

"New beginnings?" Her question frazzled him, so he hoped he gave a pleasing answer. "So we can make promises about being better for the next year?"

She laughed, and it was like listening to a hymn at church sung by a saintly choir. "From the mouth of babes. No, Ryley, people don't celebrate the New Year for the resolutions they're as likely to break as the sun is to rise. People celebrate New Year's because they've *survived*. That's what the existence of humans is all about. Survival. Their holidays and celebrations are all about having survived a world full of loss, disease, war, and violence. As creatures of magic like you and I, we've moved beyond the simple joy of survival. Our joy blooms from something much more grand."

"Ryley," Oliver shouted. "Are you deaf or just dumb? Get. Down. Here!"

"Our joy," Ms. Velvet continued, "is their destruction. We are their loss, their disease, their war, and their violence. Without us—"

"They wouldn't have any reason to celebrate," Ryley said, the revelation dawning like the sun cresting a high mountain. "We give their lives meaning by making them survive it."

"Exactly, my darling. Now, about your false parents..."

Angry footsteps pounded from downstairs. They reached the stairwell, Oliver's heavy steps creaking louder and louder as he headed toward the second floor.

Ms. Velvet cracked her knuckles. "Unfortunately for Oliver and Patty Watkins, I don't think they'll be celebrating the New Year this year. Do your sacred duty as my misfit and give the humans who find your false parents a reason to celebrate survival."

False father's footsteps halted before Ryley's door. The lock twisted, turning vertical like a clock hand striking midnight. The door swung open. Ryley smiled. A deep, wide rush of joy flooded his veins like water bursting from a crumbling dam.

* * *

Quinn waited outside the study hall doors, hidden beneath a cluster of trees. The wind coming from Lake Champlain had an icy bite, but it was clean and crisp and carried the scents of freshwater and pine. He grabbed his mother's metal locket. Rubbing it gave him comfort, and despite the chilly weather it was a source of warmth.

A yeti hummed nearby, shoveling great mounds of snow from the line of doors spanning the island's coast. It noticed Quinn and waved. Quinn smiled and tossed the creature a pinecone, which it eagerly accepted.

After watching the yetis for so long, he realized they were more like him than any other students at Wimbly's. At first blush they could strike fear in just about anyone. Coats of coarse fur covered muscles tough as living wood. Hands that could crush granite cleared fallen branches and boulders as easy as Quinn handled Styrofoam, and their mouths were so wide they'd have little problem gobbling up a child. Yet despite their size and strength, they were about as harmful as a toothless shark in the desert—they were just like Quinn, a painfully ordinary boy stranded in a world where he didn't belong.

His secret wasn't just weighing on him anymore. It actively dug long, sharp claws into his chest. It gave him dark dreams starring his foster brother, a wicked smile etched on Ryley's face, the boy's eyes burning cinders of a hate that might outlast them both.

Quinn kept telling himself that Ryley was safe, that while he'd never forgive Quinn, he might forget him. But those comforting thoughts thinned and sheared apart like a wet tissue the more the misfit rumors swirled throughout the school. Each new rumor he heard became darker and more disturbing than the last until it became an unspoken truth the misfits would attack Wimbly's any day.

He spotted a girl trudging through the snow, head bent into the wind. She wore a cable-knit beanie splashed with flower pins, and the locks of blond peeking from her hat's hem had several feathers woven in them. Heidi had finally appeared. Finally. After over a week of feigning ill and skipping classes, she'd finally snuck out of her room.

Quinn knew she'd come to a study hall. It was the one place they could speak openly without fear of students or teachers eavesdropping.

The yeti noticed her and waved exactly how it had waved at Quinn. She nodded, motioning toward an empty study hall. The creature hurried over to the door and opened it for her, bowing like a perfect gentleman as she slipped inside.

Brushing off his jacket, he rushed from his shadowy shelter and headed for the door. The yeti motioned that it was occupied and pointed to another.

"It's okay, she's expecting me," Quinn said with a wide and innocent smile.

The yeti shrugged and returned to its snow shoveling. Quinn grabbed the cold knob and twisted. The door flung wide with a particularly hard blast of wind, and he stumbled inside, cloaked in a swirling cloud of snowflakes.

Heidi waited for him in a field of fiery wildflowers. Her back faced him while she gazed at the blue-soaked mountains roughing the horizon's edge. Quinn struggled to close the door, fighting against a wind that desperately wanted to chill the sunny valley. He eventually won the battle and turned to his friend.

Heidi's shoulders sagged. A warm breeze teased her hair as butterflies glided by. "I'm sorry, Quinn. I really am."

He walked toward her. "Why'd you do it? How'd you do it?"

"He started hitting you. He wouldn't stop. I just—I just couldn't watch it knowing I could stop it. I was so angry. I don't think I've never been that angry before." She faced him with tear-polished eyes and puffy cheeks. "I just started casting the spell I found in the book. I don't know what came over me."

"Heidi, it's okay. Nobody got hurt." Quinn didn't fear many things in life. Seeing his friend so upset, though, made him want to scream in terror and bolt from the study hall. "Please don't cry."

She laughed, wiping a snotty nose with her sleeve. "It's more than that. Things aren't—things aren't good, and they'll get worse. I'm not as good as you think I am. I had to protect you, had to keep you safe. I'm afraid what I might do when I have to do it next time."

"There won't be a next time. If there's a practical, I'll fess up. This has gone on too long, and I don't think I can keep it up any longer. People deserve the truth."

"No!" Her face flushed red and she charged forward. "No, you don't understand. No one can know the truth. If they find out you don't have any magical talent at all—"

"I knew something was up!" Billy's voice burst from behind Quinn, and he nearly jumped out of his shoes and ran for the distant mountains.

Heidi's features hardened, and she twisted to the source with a spell flashing on her fingertips. "Billy Holcomb I can't believe you'd spy on us!" She blew the spell from her open palm and wind blasted from her fingertips. It bent the grass and sent flower petals flying. It also peeled away the layers of invisibility from Quinn's roommate, who stood a few feet behind Quinn, arms shielding his squinting eyes.

The wind calmed even though Heidi didn't. Billy blinked and picked a flower from his hair. He flicked it away and balled his fists into shaky peaches. "You two have been lying all this time? I thought we were friends." His eyes flashed at Quinn. "I really thought we were. But you're just like everybody else, aren't you?"

Quinn shook his head. "No, Billy, it's not like that. I just—"

"I don't want to hear it," he snapped, the veins on his temple bulging.

"Friends don't keep secrets from each other like that. I broke the rules for you. I could've gotten beat up for you. And you thought it was okay to lie to me? Even after all that?"

Even Heidi lost her rage beneath his words. Quinn felt slightly shorter than a thimble and desperately wished he could hide inside one and disappear for twenty years. "I know, I should have told you," Quinn said after a few moments of tense silence. "I didn't. You deserved better than that."

"It would've been better if you'd been the Misfit King. I half expected that's what I'd hear when I followed you. When you said Heidi sent that spell book to you as an apology, I knew something was off about the whole thing." He combed his fingers through his hair, lips pressed into a line. "What a mess this is. For all of us."

"I can make this better," Quinn said. "The misfits don't think Ryley's anything. They'll ignore him, and if they didn't don't you think the faculty would have told me by now? I've almost figured out the trial. As soon as I do, I'll get magic. I deserve magic."

Billy laughed and rolled his eyes. "You deserve it? Tell me how you deserve it."

"Because the misfits killed my parents, Billy. They tortured the magic from me and then framed me for the fire that killed my mom and dad. They stole my talent, and then they killed the people I loved and let the world believe I did it. Since then my whole life's been one long torture."

Some of the anger swirling in Billy's eyes lost its fire. He swallowed, his brows pinching together. "They tortured the magic from you?"

"Yes, and I only survived because my mom and dad cast a spell that kept me alive. I'm so close to learning the trial, Billy, so close. If I did, I'd gain what I lost back. I didn't want to tell you because I didn't want you to get in trouble too."

"They'd expel Quinn," Heidi added. "Do you think that's fair? After everything he's been through?"

Billy avoided their eyes, his voice falling to a murmur. "We could all get expelled."

"Listen, I was wrong. I'm sorry," Quinn said. "I swear I'll never keep anything from you again. But I could use your help now more than ever. I want to learn the trial. I want to set what happened with my parents right. And then I want to make everything I've done wrong right again, too. And look at you now! The Billy I met on the van would never have had the guts to go against Porter. You went up against him and you beat him. And the best thing is, he still has *no idea* it was you. You're a hundred times better at magic now that you believe in what you can do."

Billy eyed Quinn, slowly nodding. "I suppose I might be a hundred times better than I was." A smile curved his lips. "And it was fun watching Porter scream like a baby."

"So you'll help us?" Quinn asked.

"Please?" Heidi added.

"Yes, yes, I'll help you, but only because you need it." Billy rocked on his heels, arms folded on his chest like a victorious wrestler just after the match. "The way I see it, since you couldn't cast a spell to save your life, you'll need all the help you can get. Now, what's next?"

A Final Clue

"What are you thinking they'll do?" Maisie asked Donal.

He scratched his chin, staring through the stained glass windows of his office. To most, they appeared nothing more than three beautiful arched windows. For the principal of the school, they revealed much more. One of the rectangular patterns woven into the glass shimmered, revealing Quinn and his two friends walking out of class and into the snowy courtyard.

"They're planning something. I'm not sure what, but it's something." He clenched his teeth. Being so comfortable with the boy had been a mistake on his part. Initially, Donal dismissed the prophecies of the Misfit King as nothing more than rumor. That became more difficult with each passing day.

If only magicians could turn back the clock without consequences, he'd do things differently. He turned around and smiled at Maisie. He'd do quite a few things differently if he could so easily rewrite the past.

"I'm still not sure what Nehemiah's game is in all of this," he said. "To think he let Quinn through the East Door. I'm dumbstruck by it. At least it wasn't the West Door. That door could take Quinn's life."

"If Nehemiah lets him through the fourth door, he must be pretty certain Quinn would survive. Has anyone ever gone through Nehemiah's four doors? We don't even know what it will do."

"Bah." Donal took his seat. It gave a satisfying creak as he pressed his weight into its leathery back. "He's just chained inside that library and it's finally getting to him. I think he's trying to pull rank or at least convince everyone on campus who the real power is at Wimbly's."

Maisie took a seat and rested her hands upon her knees. Every part of her was painfully perfect to him, from the way her knuckles curved, to the gentle fall of her auburn hair and each freckle splashed over her rosy cheeks.

"Donal," she said, her voice losing its normal edge, "perhaps it's time to stop being so dismissive. You're one of the most powerful magicians in the magic world. That doesn't mean you can't be tricked. Pride comes before the fall. Remember that."

He glared at the corner of his desk and shook his head. "So you think Nehemiah's doing more than stirring the pot? That this might be more than him playing politics?"

"It's possible. Whatever it is, we'll be safer doing everything in our power to keep Quinn out of that library. Banning him isn't enough. We need added protection."

Donal swiveled around and stared into his window. He interlaced his fingers and rested his chin upon them. Stained glass shimmered, and Quinn reappeared. The boy stood across the courtyard, staring at the library with eyes that had a certain nervous determination that made the hair on Donal's neck tingle.

Commanding a new vision, the glass shimmered. The library's interior came into focus. A few schoolchildren studied at the long desks, noses buried in their books. His spell shifted up a few flights until it found Nehemiah perusing a book in a dark and dusty corner of his library. The old man paused and lifted his chin. He turned, staring straight at Donal from behind his lavender blindfold. Nehemiah grinned with a bent and broken smile.

Donal shuddered and ended the vision. "Have two yetis guard the library's entrance at all times. Tell Cynthia to keep an eye on it from above and maintain a list of every student and faculty member who walks into that building. I want a daily report. He cannot under any circumstances go through that door and I want to know if any of his friends try to slip through instead."

"Donal…"

He turned. The concern contorting Maisie's features twisted his heart into a thousand fraying knots. "Yes, Maisie?"

"I know we have to do this. Still, I feel as if we're doing exactly what Ms. Velvet wants. We've turned this school into a prison. We've made a little boy into a boogeyman. I'm worried, but I don't know what else we can do."

"Don't be. I'm here. I'll always be here. Things will get better soon and we'll all have a laugh about it. Trust me."

She smiled, but he knew the words hadn't been a comfort. Standing, she slipped into her jacket and coiled her scarf around her neck. "I'll get a couple yetis at the door and let Cynthia know about setting up watch. Have a good day, Donal." She nodded and walked toward the office door.

"Have dinner with me."

Maisie laughed as she grabbed the knob. "Good day, Principal Ward."

"I'm serious. Have dinner with me tonight."

She cocked her head and glanced over her shoulder. "I'm sorry, but no."

Without another word, she left his office. The door clicked behind her. He swiveled to his windows. As with most days since their encounter with the Witch Queen of the West, he stared at the painted glass and watched the shimmering vision of Maisie Callahan as she went about her day.

* * *

Quinn shivered in his seat on the bleachers. "We're never going to get in there with those yetis squatting at front of the door."

Heidi and Billy huddled next to him with a thick wool blanket draped over their knees. Will-O'-Wisps, tiny burning orbs of sizzling blue, hovered around them. The creatures radiated heat and kept winter nipping on the edges. Still, it was downright freezing outside.

Quinn glanced at the other end of the bleachers. Students of every year and skill level huddled in warm, cheering groups as the dryads played a team of fourth year students in a game that was both literally and figuratively heated. A band of empty space, devoid of any student foolish enough to approach the three outcasts, formed an invisible wall around Quinn and his friends. A few students on the edges would glance at Quinn from the corner of their eyes and trade whispers with their neighbors or fidget nervously whenever he moved.

Heidi placed her hands over a Will-O'-Wisp and shivered. "There's just got to be another way."

"Maybe we can bribe the yetis guarding the library?" Billy wondered, lifting his eyes from the book in his lap just long enough to acknowledge them. "Get a couple pinecones or something and they'll be ours."

"No," Heidi said, "Ms. Doyle's been perched up on the roof watching day and night. If we even try to get in she'll know about it."

A dryad player dove into the earth as if the soil were water. It burst beneath the boy who had the ball and head-butted it clear across the field. Students roared and cheered as the dryad high-fived its teammate.

Billy flipped a page on his book, *Otis Gaskin on War & Magic*, and tapped the yellowed pages. "You should see some of the spells in here. Otis knew some major magic. When Wimbly's was first founded it came under really hardcore misfit attacks. They were trying to get a hold on the continent before the talented could set up schools and bind librarians. Back then, before the World Wars, the magicians and misfits were nearly equals."

He slid the book onto Quinn's lap. The large tome was a welcome barrier to the cold. Quinn thumbed through its pages, skimming the complex spells that could summon wonders and enchantments that could turn a seemingly normal person into any number of incredible things. Alongside the spells were certain summaries explaining when Otis created them and why.

Wind whistled through their tight huddle and turned the spell book's pages. The breeze settled almost as quickly as it came, and so did the pages. Quinn furrowed his brow and read the surprisingly detailed description of an early attack. Apparently, Nehemiah hadn't always been a powerful being. When they first bound him to the library, he was much more vulnerable. Otis described a battle with witches and warlocks and their rabid direwolves. The misfits had infiltrated the island shortly after Mr. Crawford's binding ceremony:

> *They came from Cambridge, their cackles piercing the lake's calm waters, the howls of their vile dire beasts splitting the joyous air of Wimbly's campus. The wolves were particularly cruel and wild, each one on its hunches as tall as a man and twice as wide.*
>
> *The misfits planned on using their beasts as a distraction while they cursed our poor librarian to be, the man who so bravely accepted his eternity of servitude to the talented. But we would not let our librarian fall. No, we fought them bravely, the talented casting their wondrous enchantments that lit the sky with blessed works.*
>
> *We drove the corrupted back to the waters and put them from their misery then and there. We plucked them from the sky and sent them to graves beneath the lake. The last, their leader, we found hiding as a yellow birch on the isle's northern end. But none of these birches grew within the northern forest so we found her out before long. Thankfully so, as she hid dangerously close to the tunnel's entrance. I shudder to think what may have befallen our new librarian had she discovered it.*

"There's a tunnel!" Quinn could barely contain his excitement. Nearby students grimaced, sliding farther from him. Quinn rolled his eyes and showed the passage to Heidi and Billy.

Heidi scanned the page, a smile inching up her cheeks. "Who would've thought there could be a tunnel to the library?"

"Tunnel?" Billy blinked, leaning in. He read the passage and cracked his own smile. "What luck! How'd you find this book, Quinn?"

Heidi and Quinn both traded glances. Quinn closed the tome and handed it to Billy. "It's yours. You were reading it less than a minute ago."

Billy laughed and grabbed the book. He examined its cover with a slight headshake. "Nope. Never seen this before in my life."

It dawned on all three at once. The book had never been a lucky find.

"It must have been Nehemiah," Quinn said.

Heidi brushed a feathery lock behind her ear. "He must have charmed Billy the last time he was in the library. Do you, like, remember the last time you went there?"

Billy thought. His nose squished into a wrinkled arrow. "Right before they banned Quinn from the library. I think that's the last time I went there."

"And what books did you check out?" she asked.

The wrinkles on his nose deepened. "I…I can't remember."

Heidi clapped her hands and giggled. "Nehemiah knew Quinn wouldn't be able to get in through the front, so he found a way to get the information to him. So crafty."

Quinn took a deep breath. He watched the soccer game, the dryads furiously attacking the students with every dirty trick they could think of. The magician players countered each one, forming a tight formation around the ball. Another student came from behind their formation running faster than any normal human could manage and kicked the ball so hard the air clapped.

The magician formation broke apart, and the ball rocketed past the dryad goalie. The stands erupted in cheers and furious claps. It was the last game of the winter semester. Tonight, everyone would be celebrating the hard-fought victory.

Quinn glanced at Heidi and Billy, his hand moving to the heavy locket chained around his neck. He squeezed the metal, his blood electrified with excitement. Not everyone tonight would be celebrating. At least three students attending Wimbly's would be sneaking into the library.

A Little Help from an Old Friend

Quinn, Heidi, and Billy trudged through the snow, avoiding both the yetis clearing the main paths between the Glen and Hilltop and the raucous parties celebrating the students' defeat of the dryads. Outside the pathway, deep into the forest, an eerie silence persisted. Branches clawed above them with snowy bundles threatening to burry them in the winter storm's endless onslaught. Shadows danced in eerie patterns like imps planning every manner of tease and trick that would bring the snow crashing down.

Billy could barely hold his arms down in his obnoxiously thick down jacket. Heidi wrapped at least three scarves around her neck and wore a wool beanie with long tassels capped by pink puffs. By the time they disappeared from the campus and made their way through the island's quiet forest, snow painted everything they wore in white.

Tired, frustrated, and shivering, they gathered beneath an evergreen, chests heaving with heavy breaths. Heidi pulled a scarf away from her mouth. Scarlet tinted her cheeks and kissed her nose. "I love Mother Nature and all, but this storm's a killer. We'll never make it to the other side of the island before tomorrow morning."

Quinn took a deep breath despite his aching lungs. Snow seeped into his boots, soaking his wool socks and chilling his toes. At this pace, the storm would turn them into popsicles for a troll before they reached the tunnel. "Is there another way we can take?" he asked.

Billy turned, surveying the billowy snow collecting in high drifts. He tapped his foot, mumbling something Quinn couldn't quite make out. He finished his mumbling and laughed and spun so fast he nearly toppled over. "Why are we walking through this mess anyway? We're magicians! Let's make a faster way if there isn't one."

"Two of us are, anyway," Quinn said.

"For now." Billy grinned and swatted Quinn's shoulder. "We'll get you there too."

Heidi rubbed her mittened hands and cocked her head. "What do you have in mind, Billy?"

"Well…" Billy eyed the snowdrifts. "Walking through this is a pain, so maybe we should stop walking and try something else?"

Heidi grinned. "I think I see where you're going with this."

"What are you two planning?" Quinn asked. "Some kind of spell?"

She giggled, bouncing to Quinn with glittering stars in her eyes. "Of course! You're better than Billy and me at drawing spells. Why don't you give it a try and we'll cast it?"

"I don't know…"

Billy nodded, joining Heidi. He tried crossing his arms, but his ridiculously thick jacket refused. "You've got the skill, we've got the talent. Make yourself useful and draw us something that'll do the trick."

Heidi dug into her jacket pocket. She fumbled with something inside it, her tongue wedged between her teeth. "There it is." She yanked out a folded card and a worn pencil and handed them to Quinn. "Draw us out of this mess."

Quinn bit his glove, pulling his shivering fingers from its protective wool. A frigid breeze blew, cutting through the skin and chilling his bones. His fingertips shook and reddened against the wind, but he grit his teeth and set to drawing despite the cold.

He cradled the paper in his free hand and stared at the blank paper. His hopper spell might send them flying over the island and crashing into Lake Champlain, and he doubted any of them would last more than a few seconds in the freezing waters. They needed something different, something that could travel swiftly over snow and easily weave between the close trees…something like a sled.

Shivering, teeth chattering despite his best efforts, he drew an intricate braid of circles overlaid with sharp-edged diamonds. Once or twice he paused, considering the best way to complete the spell, but within a few minutes, he finished.

It was complex—something only a faculty member or fourth year might have drawn, but Quinn knew it would work. He couldn't cast magic, but that didn't mean he didn't know it better than almost anyone on the island.

Heidi raised an eyebrow and glanced at Billy. "It's scary how good he is."

Billy took the card and grinned as he inspected Quinn's handiwork. "Think how scary he'll be when he can actually cast the ones he draws."

Despite the snowstorm and its icy breaths, warmth filled Quinn's chest. *When he gets it.* They believed in him. They believed in his mission. Quinn swallowed the urge to hug them and mirrored Billy's smile instead. "Go ahead, cast it."

Billy faced a snowdrift piling beyond the tree's protective canopy. He removed his gloves and flexed his fingers, shivering in the wind. The card held in one hand, he began casting with the other. Lines of azure light trailed his fingers like dust from a fairy's beating wings. With each graceful movement, the lines brightened until they flared like a blue sunrise against his palm.

The snowdrift before him shuddered. It swelled and hardened, thick bands of ice weaving together to form a crystalline sleigh. Sharp, icy antlers protruded in front of the sleigh, rising with the head of a mighty white deer that bounded onto the surface. The deer huffed, a snow flurry bursting from its nostrils, a translucent rein fastened around its neck.

Quinn stared at his handiwork. To think in a matter of minutes he had created such an advanced spell—it seemed impossible only a few months ago, trapped in the hell of the Watkins' home. "Before we go," he said, "I just want to say thanks. Both of you did so much for me. You never needed to, but you did. Even when it could have gotten you expelled, you were there for me." He swallowed, trembling from something other than the cold. "One day I'll make it up to you. When I can, I will. I swear."

Heidi pecked him on the cheek. "You're totally being silly right now."

Billy laughed and playfully shoved his shoulder. "Heidi's right. We're your friends. I'd do it all again ten times over if I had to."

"And you don't ever have to make it up to us," she added. When he met her eyes, she looked away and toed at the snow. "That's not how friends work. You don't—won't ever owe me anything. Trust me."

They piled into the sleigh. Billy slapped Quinn on the back and leaned to his ear. "Since you didn't get to cast the spell I think it's only fair you get to drive."

Billy handed the reins to Quinn. The deer's excitement quivered through the straps.

Quinn tightened his grip and took a deep breath. He pressed his stomach against the icy rail and whipped the reigns. The deer reared and shot through the forest. Waves of snow walled them in. Trees bled into blurs of green and white. They wove through tight trunks, their sleigh bouncing off bark and branch in a shower of snow and ice. Heidi squealed and wrapped herself around the rail like a pretzel. Billy whooped, his beanie flying off. Quinn's heartbeat raced. He smiled and leaned into the howling wind, his own excited yell matching Billy's.

The misfits might come to Wimbly's any day and Quinn lived a lie that probably put both his friends at risk of being expelled at best and at worst something much darker. But in that moment, misfits and prophecies and lies and cheats didn't matter, because even though he hadn't cast the spell, he had created it. It was his, and it worked.

Their sleigh reached the island's north side after an hour or so of travelling. Quinn stopped the charging deer, and the sleigh came to a stop. The deer shook its great antlers, and they disintegrated into snowflakes. Its body followed, and then the sleigh itself slowly vanished until only the riders remained standing at the forest's edge along a shoreline freckled with frosty boulders and icy patches.

"Where to now?" Quinn asked.

Billy shrugged. "Well, I'm not, ah, exactly sure. It should be around here if the book was right."

Heidi groaned, tightening her many scarves from a particularly brutal gale whipping in from the lake. "There's got to be some kind of clue. Isn't there anything that could help us?"

"Well…" Billy scrunched his little nose and stared into the trees. "It's a tunnel, so maybe we look for a hill that doesn't fit?"

The forest was a white-sheeted mess of hills rising toward Hilltop. Quinn sighed and buried his hands inside his pockets. "I guess we split up, then. I'll go left, Heidi goes right, and Billy, you take the center."

They searched until late in the night, never wandering too far from at least one of the others. Under every rock, behind every tree, beneath every dark shadow they scoured, but still the tunnel eluded them. Exhausted, they squatted beneath a grove of hemlock trees and rubbed their arms and hands for warmth.

Billy traced a spell that summoned a Will-O'-Wisp, and the blazing orb bathed them in comforting heat. "We can't do this for much longer. It's nearly midnight and still no luck. Maybe they sealed the tunnel after the attack and it's just not there any more."

"Then why would Mr. Crawford make sure the book got to us?" Quinn asked. "It's got to be here somewhere."

A branch cracked not far from their circle. A bolt of adrenaline raced through Quinn's body. Words fled their lips and hid deep inside their bellies. Billy extinguished his Will-O'-Wisp. Heidi tensed and scanned the forest. "There's something moving in there."

Quinn squinted. The only light came from across the lake, and even that was terribly poor. It took a few moments, but he eventually spotted the shifting form swiftly weaving through the trees. Snow-laden branches shook as it passed, dropping their loads of powdery white.

"It's big," Quinn whispered.

"And fast," Heidi added.

Billy cracked his knuckles. "Get ready."

Quinn wished more than anything else in the world he could help them. But as a talentless nobody, all he could do was hope he didn't get in the way.

They backed out of the forest and onto the shoreline. The creature raced toward them, its footsteps silent despite its great form. Snowflakes swirled around Quinn and his friends. He tensed, ready for a fight.

The creature burst from the forest, its fur covered in thick, snowy patches. It shook like a wet dog and stretched, revealing the yeti beneath it. The beast waved, its wide mouth parting in a grin filled with blocky teeth. A familiar dark patch over its eye sparked Quinn's memory. "It's the same yeti we saved from Porter. It must've followed us. Kind of like a puppy."

Heidi relaxed. Instead of casting a spell, she ran at the yeti and wrapped her arms around it. "Exactly like a puppy! It's super cute, isn't it?" She looked up, giggling. "I wish I could take you home with me. I'd put so many bows in your hair."

Billy brushed the hair from his face and laughed. "Of course you would."

"Yetis are so much nicer than most of the students here," she said. "I've noticed this one sneaking around ever since the day we helped him. I had no idea they could follow us through the island that fast. Guess yetis have a better nose than I thought."

"Either that or it just knows the island way better than us," Billy said.

Quinn shoved his freezing hands into his pockets and stared at the yeti. A plan, however, crude, formed in his head. "Heidi, how well do you think these yetis know the island?"

Her eyes widened with her smile, and her own gaze drifted to the gentle giant's happy gaze. "Better than any of us, that's for sure."

"Think you could ask him if he knows of any tunnels around here?"

She let go of her yeti friend and scooped a handful of snow. "Wouldn't hurt to try. Let's see…" She bit her tongue and traced a pattern over the snow. It shifted and trembled, flakes falling from her hand in dusty trails. She drew the last line of her spell and splayed her fingers, and the snow fell away. A butterfly remained in her palm with wings as white as a spring cloud and fragile as a Christmas ornament. She whispered to the insect and motioned toward the yeti.

The butterfly fluttered from her palm, it looped lazily around the yeti. The creature laughed, enjoying the attention from its new friend. The butterfly landed on its shoulder, and the yeti's ears twitched. It cocked its head and listened to something only it and the butterfly could hear.

Once finished with the message, the butterfly took flight and disappeared into the forest. The yeti pursed its lips and stared into the sky. For a long moment it did nothing but think. In fact, it thought for so long Quinn wondered if the creature even remembered what the butterfly asked it. But then the yeti's eyes shot wide. It snapped its thick fingers and twisted around, dashing through the trees.

Billy took off first. "We can't lose it. C'mon!"

Quinn and Heidi rushed after him. They wove through trees and dodged snow disturbed by the lumbering yeti.

Huffing and panting, they eventually reached a depression in the hillside on a particularly shadowy part of the island. A great boulder rested against the hill with exposed hemlock roots growing over its face. The yeti motioned to the boulder, grumbling something that sounded triumphant.

Heidi walked up to the boulder and smiled at her friend. "Good job!"

The yeti bowed. It lifted a finger and grumbled something else before twisting to the enormous stone. It wrapped its arms around it and heaved, a low and mighty growl rumbling from its lungs. Its enormous arms quivered, the muscles bursting with its mighty strength. At first, nothing happened. The yeti inhaled, its growl deepening, and heaved so hard the ground around the boulder cracked.

The stone shifted. Roots snapped. Snow fell upon the yeti's shoulders. A hole appeared behind the sliding rock, the open mouth of a dark tunnel that ran like a serpent into the hill's heart. The yeti huffed, wiping its forehead, and faced Heidi.

She bowed with a giggle and thanked the beast, and it repeated the gesture. Quinn and Billy edged next to Heidi and stared into the tunnel.

"Should we go inside?" Quinn asked.

Billy stepped through first. He turned and flashed a smile. "That was the plan, right? Don't be such a scaredy-cat."

Heidi skipped after him, lighting a small orb to guide their way. "Well since we've got Billy Holcomb on our side, the bravest of all magicians, I guess whatever we find in here couldn't be too scary. Whatever it is, it's sure to go after him first anyway since he looks like such a plump meal in that silly jacket."

"Don't forget," Quinn said, stepping into the tunnel and tasting its stale, earthy air, "you've also got the Misfit King on your side."

They laughed, and the tunnel's exit shrank behind them. Quinn glanced over his shoulder and saw the yeti peer inside. The creature hesitated as if it wanted to impart some sort of knowledge but simply waved instead and disappeared.

ℭhe ℱlight ℵorth

She watched the celebration in the commons slowly thin out. The clock would strike twelve any minute, and once it did, the last of the reveling students would retire. Maisie smiled, savoring the scents of honeyed, warm caramel and cinnamon wafting through the air. Eyeing her coffee, she shrugged and plunked a sugar cube into the mug.

One of the lights reflected in the commons' narrow windows, reminding her of the stained glass ones of Donal's office. He'd wanted to treat her to dinner that night, and she very nearly accepted his offer. Their encounter with Ms. Velvet had stirred old memories, and with those memories buried feelings rose like a loving zombie from the grave.

She took a sip of her sweetened coffee and watched the steam rise from its porcelain mouth. She made the right choice by declining the invitation. Better to be safe and strong than exposed and vulnerable when the misfits waited on the edges of their little island world.

The commons doors swung inward, disturbing a cluster of giggling girls. Ms. Doyle marched inside, weaving between students with a face carved from granite and a jaw set like steel. Maisie caught the woman's glare, and a sinking feeling pressed into her stomach.

Cynthia reached the table and eyed Maisie from behind her spectacles. Maisie savored a last, sweet sip of her coffee, wishing she could dive into the mug and disappear so the world could turn and other people could fight the good fight for once while she enjoyed life.

"Everything okay, Ms. Doyle?" Maisie finally asked.

Cynthia's glasses fogged from the commons' warm air. She yanked them from her face and wiped them over her tight wool jacket. "Not here," she said, replacing the glasses.

Ms. Doyle surveyed the room from the corners of her eyes. Maisie, too, noticed the curious students innocently inching closer to the two teachers, ears wide as elephants. A few of the older ones had probably already cast eavesdropping spells and would quickly relay the words to their friends who'd spread it like a flu in a football stadium.

Maisie slid from her seat, straightening her own jacket and grabbing her scarf. Cynthia smiled and checked her bun for errant hairs. "If you wouldn't mind coming with me, Ms. Callahan, I'd like to go over my syllabus for next semester with you."

"Of course, Ms. Doyle." Maisie smiled as they passed a few familiar students on their way to the exit. Maisie did her best to look relaxed, but Ms. Doyle had never been particularly adept at fibbing, and the woman's tone had probably betrayed them both.

Outside the commons, the air lost its sweet scents and grew frigid and biting. Maisie rubbed her shoulders as they marched out of the Glen and up the path toward Hilltop. Ms. Doyle paused halfway. She scanned the woods with narrowed eyes and breath that poured like smoke from her flared nostrils.

"Ms. Doyle?" Maisie asked, arching a brow.

Cynthia nodded sharply. She turned and grabbed Maisie's hands. "They're up to something, Quinn and his friends. I don't think Principal Ward would want to hear it from me or Egon, but maybe he'd believe it if you told him those students have something up their sleeves tonight."

"Did they try to sneak into the library?"

"No, they haven't gone anywhere near Hilltop. But they're not in the Glen, either."

Maisie cocked her head. A breeze whistled downhill, and she shivered. "Really? How do you know that?"

"I'm not fluent in yeti—you know how oddly emotional their language is—but I can pick up the general gist of their speech." Cynthia leaned close, quickly glancing around before she continued in a whisper. "They said the three children wandered into the forest, that they're looking for something."

"Hmm…" Maisie furrowed her brow. Woods Island held many old rumors, but one particularly old one concerned her. "What direction did they head? Do you know?"

"Yes. North."

Maisie stiffened. Cynthia must have registered the surprise, because her grip tightened on Maisie's hands. "What's on the northern side of the island? Some buried artifact? Some ancient power?"

"No, nothing like that." She pulled her hands out of Cynthia's grasp and glanced north, heartbeat thumping in her ears. "I've heard of a tunnel. It's supposed to be sealed, but we should check it out just to be safe. Egon, you can come out now. I know you're hiding."

Cynthia's cheeks reddened. A figure spun from the shadows, moments ago cloaked in darkness. Egon rubbed the back of his neck, his gaze glued to the sidewalk. "Hello, Maisie. Good to see you out and about even on such a cold night as this."

Maisie rolled her eyes and began a spell that would transform her into a night owl. "Owls, both of you. Follow my lead."

They nodded and began casting their own spells. The three shed human form and took flight. As Maisie rose in wide circles, a boom thundered from Hilltop. It could only be Donal, racing to meet her in true dramatic Donal Ward fashion. Of course he'd been using the stained glass windows to spy on her. Hopefully they were overreacting. No one but a few of the oldest teachers knew about the tunnel. Still, she had to check, just to make sure.

* * *

Donal ordered Quinn to stay away from the library. The principal should have kept a closer eye on the boy instead of obsessing over Maisie. Had he kept his attention on Quinn, he might have stopped him before he reached the tunnel. But no, he just had to obsess over Maisie, just had to watch her day and night like some love struck fool.

At least Cynthia overheard the news before Quinn breached the library's hidden entrance. *What are you up to, Quinn?* Donal wondered. *Don't prove me wrong. Don't try and crown yourself the Misfit King. Show me you're better than what they think you are.*

The wind rushed past his wings, feathers drawing trails of snow that disappeared into the cloudy night. He tucked his wings over his chest and circled the northern end of Woods Island, Maisie and the others joining him as he searched for the spot.

Movement disturbed the forest, caught by Donal's sharp eyes. He squawked, diving toward whatever clue just revealed itself. Maisie and the others followed, a flock of owls darting toward the treetops. They burst through the branches in a shower of snow, surprising a yeti munching on a pinecone.

Dropping the transformation, Donal landed spryly on his feet. He brushed snow from his blazer and glared at the yeti, his glowing eyes reflecting in the confused creature's own wide ones.

"Get out of here," Donal commanded, "before I do something I regret."

The yeti whined, scrambling to its feet. Tears wet its furry cheeks, and its lip trembled.

Maisie rushed to the yeti and cooed a comforting sound. She took its arm and stroked its great hand, speaking in its complex, growling language that was half words-half emotion. "Don't worry, the principal's not as mad as he looks. Best to go ahead and slip away, and I'll treat you to a pinecone myself tomorrow."

The yeti nodded and wiped its cheeks.

"It's okay." Maisie smiled and squeezed its hand. "Before you go, can you help me now and go tell your brothers and sisters at the library to keep an eye out? We need extra help at the door tonight."

The yeti smiled and nodded with the enthusiasm of a child. It bounded into the forest, each step it took crashing through the otherwise still trees until the creature faded away.

Donal exhaled, flicking a few errant snowflakes from his jacket. "You know I can understand yeti fairly well. I did invite them here."

"You were unnecessarily harsh," she snapped. "They're different, not lesser. Don't forget that."

Donal winced and made his way toward the tunnel. "I'm sorry, I was in a rush. That yeti might have just done something horrible, and I forgot myself. You are right, though, they are not lesser. Just different."

Cynthia and Egon followed behind Donal and Maisie. "They're beasts," Egon said matter-of-factly. "Like dogs or deer. You're not mean to them of course, but that doesn't mean they shouldn't know who's master. They respect power, so at times it's appropriate to express dominance. I've read many studies on the subject."

"And their language," Cynthia added, "so brutish. I've always suspected some wise magician bred the violence from them long ago, made them appropriate for laboring and guarding and not much else."

Donal swallowed the biting remark leaping from his tongue and concentrated on finding the tunnel. Talented magicians and their superiority complexes were so difficult to stand at times. However Maisie avoided such stomach-twisting arrogance made him thankful a thousand times over he had her in his life.

They came upon a clearing with a single enormous boulder freshly moved, snapped roots laying around it like the nest of a great dragon and the boulder its egg. Behind the boulder, the tunnel's mouth loomed wide. A light no brighter than a tired firefly pierced the darkness deep within the tunnel. Donal's blood pressure rocketed, and he raced inside.

Spiders, centipedes, and round beetles clawed in the dank soil of the tunnel's low walls. He cringed and tucked his arms close to his chest, ignoring the shiver-inducing thought of a spider dropping on his shoulder, or worse, a clump of wet mud dropping like slop over on his hair.

"Students!" he shouted, his voice a booming echo. "Halt immediately. This is your principal and I demand you halt at once."

The distant light froze. Donal increased his speed. The dim light framed two figures against the black. A small boy with greasy hair and beady eyes, wrapped in a jacket so thick and unforgiving he looked like a stuffed starfish, stood next to a girl who clearly felt guilty about something while she dug her toe into the mud and refused to meet the principal's glare.

Donal halted before the children. He tried straightening, but the low ceiling and tight space made an imposing figure impossible. He huffed, clenching his fists, and cast a light much brighter than the students used. "Where is he?" Donal roared. "Where is Quinn Lynch?"

The girl recoiled, hands pressed against her body. The boy swallowed and met Donal's eyes. "There—there was a door there, but it vanished when he walked into it. We tried finding it again, but it—I don't know, it just isn't there anymore. The tunnel ends in dirt."

"You're too late," the girl said in a shaky whisper. "You're too late. He's going through the last door. I'm sorry, but it'll all be over soon."

"We'll just see about that," Donal grumbled. "Maisie, Cynthia, Egon?"

The teachers shifted behind him. "Yes?" Maisie asked.

"Back to Hilltop. I think it's time I speak with the librarian. He's tested my authority for the last time."

The teachers each nodded and turned. Donal ducked beneath a root and followed them back to the entrance. A sound disturbed them, long off and far away as it was. The teachers froze. Maisie gasped. Donal's throat thickened, his eyes growing wide. "No, it can't be." He twisted to the two students. "What is this? How is this happening?"

The girl's chin dipped closer to her chest. "I told you, you're too late."

She had hardly finished speaking when Donal blew past the teachers, his body twisting form and shrinking into an owl. He darted from the tunnel, glowing lines of his spell leaving a glittering trail behind his wings.

Decades had passed since those alarms sounded over Woods Island. No storm set those sirens blaring. No calamity of nature would make them howl. No, those sirens sounded for one thing and one thing only: misfits had come to Wimbly's.

It Begins

Quinn stepped through the tunnel's doorway and into a large room walled by bookshelves. "It's the library. We made it in," he whispered, turning to his friends.

But instead of a doorway and his friends, he faced a blank wall. He frantically searched for any handhold or sign of the door, but if it had ever been there once, it no longer remained. "Heidi? Billy? Can you hear me?"

Nobody replied. Not so much as a muffled shout sounded behind the wall.

He turned around and took a calming breath. Shelves blocked his view of the library floor, their books like bricks of a fortress wall. He caught a whiff of something odd, something acrid that made the hair on his arms stand on end. A different kind of quiet had settled in the library, not like the comforting quiet Quinn remembered when he was very young, sipping coco before his parent's crackling fireplace. No, this quiet didn't belong. It had been forced into the building and watched Quinn from every shadow and dark corner it could find.

"Mr. Crawford?" he called, but the books muffled his words before they travelled far.

A heavy weight beyond the bookshelves shifted. Metal clinked as it dragged along the floor and broke the silence in a most unsettling way. Quinn froze, his heartbeat spiking with the flash of adrenaline racing through his veins.

The sound repeated, followed by a labored and broken moan. It sounded like Mr. Crawford, but the pain in the voice made Quinn tremble. Whatever caused the pain—it could be anywhere, waiting, watching, and if it could hurt the librarian, Quinn could only imagine what it would do to a talentless boy.

He grabbed his mother's locket and kissed the cool metal. With one last glance behind him, he slipped from the corner and wove between the towering shelves, twisting and turning in the direction of Nehemiah's groan. Each step he took brought with it a stronger and stronger scent. He remembered the reek. He'd hated it since he was five. It was the pungent odor of charcoal, ash, and the lingering flames of a hungry fire.

Quinn stepped beyond the last bookshelf and came to the library's towering atrium. He gasped, backing into the shelf as he surveyed the destruction. Desks once placed in a neat grid lay in smoldering shambles, their polished surfaces cracked and blackened. Chains hung in loose lines from the shelves and coiled together in the middle of the room, the steel cocoon hovering a few feet above the damaged floor. Around the cocoon four spell cards rotated, each one bobbing lazily as they circled their prisoner.

A moan escaped the links. The cocoon shuddered, and the loosest of the binds dragged against the ground.

"Nehemiah?" Quinn swallowed. He inched over the broken desks, carefully avoiding any remaining embers. Seeing the burned desks, the shattered lamps and heaps of rubble, it all brought the memories of his home roaring back. He'd rather be balancing on a pole a thousand feet high than relive that nightmare one more time.

"Quinn…" Nehemiah's voice rasped from his binds. His finger poked out and wagged. "Quinn…help me…"

"Who did this to you?"

"Misfits. Damnable misfits," Nehemiah said. His hand wriggled through the binds, and he clenched his fist. The chains shuddered. The loose lines tightened. Nehemiah cried out, and his hand relaxed. "They've got me trapped. They've slipped enchantments into the library. Wimbly's is in danger, grave danger."

"But why?" Quinn eyed the four rotating spells.

"They—they must be attacking the school. Hurry, Quinn, free me. It's up to you." His fingers splayed, reaching for Quinn. "The spells, they're bound to my chains. Destroy them, and you will free me. It's the only way."

Quinn stared at the swirling cards. Energy surrounded them, energy that roiled with a dark and deadly power that dared Quinn to risk everything to break their hold over the librarian. "How Nehemiah? You know I can't use magic. How can I stop them?"

Nehemiah jabbed a finger at Quinn's chest. "That is all you need." The man groaned, and his hand went slack.

"Nehemiah?" Quinn grabbed the librarian's wrinkled hand. "Mr. Crawford!"

The librarian did not respond. Quinn whirled around and watched the spells pass one by one. Wimbly's depended on him. Nehemiah depended on him. He'd never heard of a talentless boy stopping spells powerful enough to chain a librarian, but he had to try.

First, he needed to test them. Sidestepping the rubble, he made his way back to the bookshelves and slid one of the desks toward the center of the room so it formed an oaken wall between him and the cards. He grabbed a broken chair leg and squatted behind his makeshift fort and closed his eyes. "You can do this. You can do this."

Quinn peeked above the desk. He inhaled through his nose and focused on a spell as it floated before him. At the last second, he chunked the leg at the card. The wood slapped it square in the center, and both it and the other cards froze. Slowly, the spell spun. A warm wave washed over the library. Flames erupted in a brilliant halo around the card.

"No, not fire," he said, swallowing the room's hot air. "Anything but fire, please."

He ducked behind the desk. Sweat rolled down his neck and soaked his shirt. Damp hair plastered against his forehead. Each breath became more difficult than the last. Memories of the fire came roaring back. He slumped against the desk, fingers clutching his hair, head buried against his knees.

He remembered their screams, the fire, flames, and smoke. Glass breaking. Wood cracking. His father traced odd symbols that glowed hot as the fire in his room. Quinn tried getting out of bed, but his mother calmed him. She traced a symbol of her own, and something shot out his window. He cried. He wanted out. She wouldn't let him. He reached for her. She placed a hand upon his cheek. With her other hand, she traced a symbol, and his world went black.

"No!" he screamed. The misfits took them from him, and now they wanted to take Nehemiah and everyone at Wimbly's he cared about. He survived three foster homes. He survived the terror of the Watkins. He outsmarted an entire school of the world's most powerful magicians and the talented students who walked its halls. He was Quinn Lynch, and he could do anything he wanted.

His locket sent an electric tingle racing through his chest. He ripped it from his neck and held it in his open palm. The metal vibrated and expanded into a great disc. Its chain clattered on the floor and straightened into a long, sharp blade. The disc in his hand curved and formed a large, sturdy shield light as feather despite being half his size. The blade sprouted a grip perfect for his hand.

Quinn slipped his arm through the shield straps and grabbed his sword. He lifted his shield toward the heat and inhaled. Dancing orange and red reflected against his shield, and the crackle and pop of burning wood was a timer ticking down the few safe seconds he had left. "Here goes nothing…"

Quinn sprinted from his hiding spot. Fire blasted his shield hot and strong as the breath of an ancient, angry dragon. So hard it blasted him that the flames nearly forced him to his knees. His forearm shook and quivered. His hair singed, and his cheeks blistered.

Still, he fought the fire, knees wobbling, eyes watering. He steadied his legs and forced his weight into the fire. He took one step. Then he took another. He reached a point so hot and so intense it blinded him. At the last, agonizing second, he screamed, forcing his shield up and jabbing his sword where he prayed the card hovered.

He heard a pop, and then a tear. The raging fire vanished, and the room cooled. He lowered his shield and shook the last lingering flames from its shiny surface. Laughing, he stumbled back, arms wide. "Now that's how you do it!"

A few chains binding the librarian fell slack. Quinn whooped. He wiped sweat from his face and steeled himself as the remaining cards began to move. He backed away, watching the next card orient itself directly before him. Lightning arced around the card and cracked like a whip thirsty for a victim.

Quinn lifted his shield just in time. A thunderous bolt smashed into its steel face. His feet left the ground and he soared over the broken desks. He hit a bookshelf and gasped, the air rushing from his lungs. His back ached. His arm throbbed. He coughed, rolling as another bolt tore into the spot he occupied just a second before. Scrambling to his feet, he dove behind another bookshelf.

He braced his shield arm against his side and crouched. He went to the balls of his feet and clenched his jaw. Roaring, he charged into the library. Bolt after bolt slammed against his shield. His arm cried out with each strike, and he feared the next bolt might be the one that would drop his shield. He leapt over a desk, blinded by the lightning, deafened by the thunder, and lashed out wildly where the card waited.

His sword struck true, and a familiar pop and tear cut the chaos of the room. The lightning card fluttered to the ground and caught fire on a burning desk. Another group of chains securing Nehemiah slackened. The librarian groaned, jostling his binds. "Hurry Quinn, you've almost done it!"

"Two more spells," Quinn huffed, racing for cover as the next card faced him. "I can do this."

The first spell heated the room. The second one lashed out with lightning. The third one one sought to freeze it. Every fire extinguished as frost gathered in crystalline patterns along the shelves and coated the floor. Quinn's breath came out in foggy clouds. At first he didn't mind the chill, but the comfort quickly faded when he realized if he didn't stop the spell soon, he'd freeze solid where he stood.

Gripping his shield and squeezing his sword, he barreled from his hiding spot. A banshee wind howled around him. Frost collected on his nose and cheeks. Icicles formed on his shield, and it doubled in weight halfway to the spell. The shield shuddered. Cracks formed along its rim.

Each step hurt. He couldn't feel his toes or fingers. He tried jabbing the spell, but his sword arm had gone completely numb. He only held the weapon because it had frozen to his hand. Shutting his eyes, he dropped the shield and twisted his body so hard his numb arm flung in an arc.

Ice blasted his face. It coated his chest. He couldn't breath, couldn't think. His arm crested the swing, and a third pop and a tear quieted the chaos. Quinn fell to his knees, coughing. The ice slowly melted from his face and body. A deep, awful ache sunk into his bones. He opened his eyes, and another group of chains went slack. Only one spell remained, and it spun toward him.

He had this. He reached for his shield, and his hand clasped it—or what remained of it. Quinn plucked a piece from the ground, staring at the torn straps and bent and twisted shards of what once was a perfect circle.

"Not what I needed."

Quinn sprinted behind a bookshelf, heart thunking against his ribs in deep, panicked beats. He stared at the naked forearm that once held his shield. Flames had seared patches in his shirt. Lightning singed the threads. Ice stiffened the cotton. He doubted whatever spell the last card cast could be thrown back by cloth alone.

Quinn peeked at the spell card. A silver flash zipped toward him. The bookshelf shook, a throwing dagger buried inches from his face. He spun behind the case as three more daggers cut gashes into wooden shelf and leather tome.

The card tossed dagger after dagger, rocking the shelf. Quinn gripped his blade, staring at the reflective surface. He had no shield. He had no magic. Nothing would stop the daggers if he left his spot. Maybe, if he ran fast enough, he could cut the spell more than it cut him.

It all came down to this. He would suffer. He might even die. But what does a boy with nothing have to lose?

His knuckles whitened on the grip. A warped reflection of his sweaty, ashen, and frosty cheeks stared back at him. Tears wet his eyes. "Mom, Dad, I'm afraid. I know I don't talk to you a lot these days, but I miss you. Because I lied all this is my fault." He pressed his lips together and blinked away the teardrops. "But I will make you proud of me. I promise."

Quinn took his sword in both hands and raised the blade. He pressed its flat side against his forehead and breathed, eyes closed, as he savored the cool steel against his sweaty skin. "No more hiding," he whispered. "This is for you."

Quinn's eyes shot open. He spun into the library and bolted for the spinning card. Silver flashes erupted from its surface. Quinn swung. Sparks showered. His blade rang. A dagger whistled past his cheek. A third slammed into his shoulder. He screamed, a hot wetness blossoming beneath his shirt.

His hands shook. His world blurred. A fifth dagger pierced his leg. He cried out and fell to a knee. With his last ounce of strength, he hurled the sword at the card. Quinn fell onto his back and stared at the ceiling, his world spinning and his ears throbbing with his heavy heartbeat.

He reached for the dagger in his shoulder. His shaking fingers graced the hilt, and he cried at the flash of pain it sent racing through his body.

A shadow slipped over him. "Boys were never meant to be pin cushions, you know," Nehemiah's familiar voice whispered through the tunnel of his fear and pain.

"It hurts," Quinn rasped. "I—I'm scared."

A smooth hand graced his brow, brushing aside the hair. "Frightened after the fact? Usually one feels fear during acts of bravery, not after."

"The daggers…"

"*Shhh*…." Nehemiah's face came into focus, lavender band fastened over his eyes. The librarian traced a spell, and a point of cool light erupted from his fingertip. He touched the dagger in Quinn's shoulder, and it disintegrated into a thousand mayflies that flitted toward the ceiling. The scorching wetness of the wound vanished, replaced by a cool pulse that smelled of fresh mint.

Gradually, Quinn's pain faded into memory. He struggled to his feet and inspected the pink skin where his wounds should be. "They're all gone?"

Mr. Crawford nodded, and for the first time since Quinn entered the library, he finally got a good look at the man. His deep wrinkles had smoothed, and his liver spots disappeared. His cheeks had cherry kisses on them, and he stood soldier-straight without the help of the walking cane strapped to his belt.

The librarian smiled, flashing rows of perfect, porcelain white teeth. "Thank you for your help today, Quinn."

"What—what did I do? What was all that?"

Nehemiah turned and ambled toward one of the few remaining bookshelf ladders. "You freed me. You risked everything to free me. There are very few who would do such a thing. Certainly not any of those talented brats who think they run the place."

Quinn followed the man, carefully navigating the debris. "The misfits trapped you. They tried to hurt you, so I just acted. I used a present my mom gave me when I saw her through one of the doors. It saved me."

Nehemiah paused before the ladder. He hopped onto a higher rung and reached for Quinn. "Yes, and you have just survived four very nearly deadly encounters. Ring a bell?"

"You don't mean…"

"Not yet, my boy, not yet." Nehemiah chuckled. "There's still one door left, remember?"

Quinn took the old man's hand. The last time Quinn took it, it felt weak and the skin hung loose over Mr. Crawford's old bones. Now the librarian's hand was soft, the skin springy and the grip strong. Quinn clutched the ladder as the librarian activated its rune. They shot skyward, the ceiling zooming toward them like the beast of a great whale scooping up a prawn.

They reached the top, and Nehemiah plucked him over the railing. The man strolled toward the West Door and waited by its curtain. Quinn followed, pausing before the doorway. "You look different than before, Nehemiah."

Mr. Crawford flashed his brows and chuckled. "I feel much better than I have in quite a long while, thanks to you."

"Will Principal Ward be mad about the mess? Because I'll help clean it up. I promise."

"Don't you worry about him. I'll take care of dear old Donal."

Quinn nodded. He swallowed the lump clinging to his throat. "What will this door show me?"

"It is the West Door. It is the last and most challenging door. When you walked through the East Door, you learned of what your heart desired. It is the door that represents the innocence of youth. Walk through the West Door, and you will face the truth. Walk through this door, and you will have walked the long and difficult path of the trial. It won't be easy, but you will reach the end before long."

Quinn took a step forward. The curtains brushed his arms. "Thank you, Nehemiah."

"No Quinn, thank you." The librarian took Quinn's hand, and before Quinn could say another word, they stepped through the door together.

30

Revelations

Wind whistled through Donal's ears, carrying the blaring sirens across a black, bleak sky. He circled Hilltop, yetis scrambling through the courtyard for the protection of the forest. The poor creatures covered their ears and cried out, confused and frightened. They may look like savage beasts, but in a real fight he'd have more luck with a litter of kittens.

Donal swooped to the ground and dropped his transformation. Casting a spell, he calmed the yetis before they could hurt themselves or trample any teachers and students making their way to the library for its protection, as was the standard drill all students knew in case of a misfit attack.

"All of you yetis, to the forest," he commanded. The yetis nodded and slinked into the trees, disappearing behind snow-laden branches.

The administration building's doors flung wide, and faculty members poured into the courtyard wrapped in jackets, robes, and scarves thrown hastily over their pajamas. By then the first students from the Glen appeared, all wide-eyed from a potent mixture of terror and adrenaline.

He frowned and scanned the swirling mass of grey and black that was the sky. Not a thing disturbed the clouds. No sounds pierced the snowfall save their misfit warning sirens. The enchanted alarms couldn't lie—misfits had indeed breached the island's shores. Yet they held their attack. They waited, just out of sight, just beyond the edge of his perception.

A few of the teachers led a line of shivering students to Donal. He forced a reassuring smile and motioned to the library. "File inside, all of you. Nehemiah will take over once you're in."

He twisted on his heel and marched to the library door. Grasping its looping, wrought iron handle, he yanked the door. It jostled but didn't budge. Donal exhaled through his nostrils. His knuckles whitened on the handle. He pulled harder. Still, the door wouldn't budge.

Porter Price pushed his way to the front. "Mr.—Mr. Ward, why isn't the librarian opening the door?"

"Back in line, Mr. Price."

"The misfits are here! You're supposed to protect us. We're talented, Principal Ward, it's your job to keep us safe from them. Open the door!"

A chorus of agreement slipped from a few of the students. They crushed against the door, a wall of eyes and hot bodies.

Donal grabbed the handle with both hands and yanked with all his might. Even then, the door wouldn't give an inch. "Nehemiah!" Donal pounded on the door. "Open this library immediately!"

Mr. Crawford did not reply. Tension mingled with the rising terror flitting around them, carried by snowflakes that swirled like pale bats looking for a meal. Donal pointed to the nearest teacher, a dwarf stone shaper named Garnet Moldavite. "Mr. Moldavite, gather what faculty's available and keep the students secure. Hold a position against the administration building until—when I get the library open."

Porter's jaw set, and he muscled closer. "It's Quinn, isn't it? He's closed the library on us. He's tricked us. He's the Misfit King, and you didn't do anything about it! We're talented and—"

"*Porter Price,*" Donal roared, his voice shaking the ground. "Fall in line, you spoilt brat."

Porter wilted like a flower in the desert and rejoined a now utterly silent line of students. Garnet the dwarf corralled the students toward the administration building, cooing reassuring words and phrases to the younger ones who had already started weeping.

A flock of ivory owls descended, morphing into Maisie, Egon, Cynthia, and the two young students. Donal wiped an annoying layer of cold sweat from his palms and fixed his hair as Maisie approached. He smiled, but she looked beyond him at the library door. "Not opening?"

"I'm going to kill Nehemiah if Quinn isn't in there doing it himself."

"I thought you didn't believe Quinn was the Misfit King."

"I…" He crossed his arms and rolled his eyes. "I just don't know what to believe anymore."

Cynthia joined them, her steely glare darting across this sky. Her fingers danced in a complex pattern, and a great black hammer erupted from her fist, taller than her by several heads and capped with a block of black steel that radiated heat. "Be on your guard. This is a trap, Principal Ward. I've no doubt of that. Quinn must have been a distraction to get us away from Hilltop."

"Yes," Egon added. He cast his own spell and a broadsword covered in runes appeared in his hand. Arcs of lightning leapt from rune to rune and reflected in his eyes. "This is the boy's doing. He's come. He's finally come to call all the children of arcana."

"Bah." Donal waved them away. "Even if he is what you say he is and even if he does somehow stop Nehemiah, he's still got me to contend with."

"No offense, Principal Ward," Egon said, glancing at the library, "but if he can defeat a librarian then a principal would be a piece of cake, even if having the power of the trial makes you a potent opponent. I hope there are enough talented magicians among us to face such a creature as the Misfit King."

Donal refused to engage the man any further. He had half a mind to fly away and let the talented magicians deal with the attack themselves. It boggled him that he'd ever accepted this position in the first place. He would never be one of them. Even if his power outstripped their own, he wasn't born into it, not like them. He wondered if even Maisie thought of him her equal.

Most of the school had clustered in a shifting crowd within the administration building's shadow. Teachers formed a protective wall around the students with some of the oldest children edging to the front to protect their younger schoolmates.

Clenching his fists, Donal stomped to the center of the courtyard, his veins roaring with rage and power. "Where are you?" he shouted, his voice an echo of thunder. He cut the sirens and opened his senses to the island. "Show yourself, Witch Queen of the West!"

Donal glared into the sky. Wind blew in beats like the breath of a dying giant. Snow swirled around him, tiny flakes melting into droplets against his hot cheeks. At first, he only heard the low sigh of winter wind. But then, another sound joined it. A faint, familiar, twinkling laughter grew louder each passing second.

A form disturbed the clouds, a black mass of writhing shadows. It swept in lazy circles over Hilltop and landed a few yards from where Donal stood. It gathered height and took the form of a human. Ms. Velvet appeared from the black, blue eyes like gleaming sapphires, blond hair swept in a gentle wave over her shoulder, lips so red they could make a rose blush, and a dress of living shadow that searched the ground with a thousand writhing tongues.

"Hello, Donal," she said, blowing him a kiss.

"You made a mistake coming here." He cracked his knuckles and made sure he stood exactly between her and everyone else. "You sealed your fate when you came to this island."

She laughed and strummed her nails against her chest. "How amusing. I was about to say the same thing."

The Witch Queen of the West snapped her fingers. Her dress expanded and filled the space behind her. From it warlocks rose like creatures clawing from a swamp. Their crimson robes swirled like smoke while gold and silver rings weighed upon their bony fingers. Cackling witches burst from the clouds, swooping on brooms of black charcoal, their hands tipped with long, dark nails.

"That's all you brought?" Donal asked, risking a quick glance at Maisie and the others. Egon and Cynthia watched the skies. Maisie's fiery gaze never left Ms. Velvet. Heidi Grace looked utterly defeated even though no battle had begun while Billy Holcomb's fingers danced at his side, ready to cast a spell at the drop of a hat.

"You think your witches and warlocks can take us?" Donal smirked. "Look at the talented magicians I have at my disposal. One of them is worth five of your tortured."

Ms. Velvet grinned. She licked her lips and stepped forward. "You know you're out of place among them. You're a child of the trial, Donal. These talented folk—" She waved dismissively at Maisie and the crowd of students. "—They will never look at you as one of their own. You're a glorified guard dog. You have to know at some level, they would gladly put you up for slaughter if it meant saving just one of them."

"I didn't realize you were such an expert on talented society. You wear so many hats, Ms. Velvet, it's a wonder you ever see your head."

"My, oh, my what a sharp tongue. Arrogant 'til the end, aren't we?" She stepped forward again, flashing her eyes toward the students. "Odd that you would keep them out here in the cold. They're liable to die from pneumonia before I have a chance to get them."

"Well, when I stand between you and them, there's not much for them to worry over. You'll never be able to kill me. You'll never get that satisfaction."

Ms. Velvet laughed, the sound like silver bells gently rocking back and forth. "Kill you? Why ever would I kill you?"

Donal blinked, his anger fading. "But you're here for revenge. That's why you've come here."

"No, it's not." She flexed her fingers and winked. "That's never been the plan."

Enough was enough. Donal's fingers danced, a spell welling within his heart like a flower blossoming in his soul. Hot magic travelled down his arm and toward his hand. He'd take her out with one spell, and then her misfits would scatter in the wind.

The library door creaked open, splitting the air more loudly than any lightning strike could ever hope. Donal paused, and his spell faded. He twisted around and glared at the parting door. From the opening Nehemiah appeared, his rosy cheeks and wide smile propping up the blindfold around his eyes. "Pardon my late arrival, but I had a certain visitor to attend to."

"I was beginning to get worried about you," Donal said.

Nehemiah turned. He reached into the darkness and pulled Quinn Lynch beside him. The boy blinked, eyes casting about at the scene before him. Together they walked out of the doorway and into the courtyard. Nehemiah grabbed his cane and twirled it around as he whistled a happy tune.

Donal swallowed the creeping feeling crawling like cold moss up his spine. "Nehemiah, how did you get out here? You are bound inside your library, the ritual—"

"All in due time, all in due time." Nehemiah continued his whistling, swinging his walking stick and ambling toward the principal. Donal glared at Quinn. The boy flinched but continued pace with the librarian.

Nehemiah and Quinn halted beside Donal. The librarian bowed, and then faced Ms. Velvet. "Witch Queen of the West, come to cause some havoc at Wimbly's, eh?"

Donal nodded. "Indeed. Let's take care of this situation promptly. I'll have words with both you and Mr. Lynch once we're finished. Both of you have put undue danger on the talented, and—"

"Your morals have destroyed you, Donal, and so has your alliance with the talented." Nehemiah shook his head, his fingers clenching his walking stick. "We tried to tell you that you'd never be one of them. They even did their best to show it. Yet you clung to your misbegotten beliefs like a frightened child when the world needs a man."

Donal frowned. "Mr. Crawford, what are you—"

The librarian slapped Donal against the chest with his walking cane. Donal's chest paled and hardened. His arms stiffened. His fingers lost feeling. His feet refused his mind's commands. He twisted around and forced a hand toward Maisie, his fingers already polished marble. She screamed and rushed forward, and although fear and panic twisted her features, knowing she would be the last thing he saw brought a smile to his lips.

* * *

Quinn stared, dumbstruck, at Principal Donal Ward. Nehemiah's spell worked quickly. Within the space of a second, Wimbly's principal transformed from flesh to gleaming rock. The librarian clicked his walking stick on the principal's stony shoulder and chuckled. "I've been waiting to do that for a long time. Now he'll know what it's like to be trapped for an eternity."

Maisie lurched forward, a fiery spell igniting her fingertips. Cynthia and Egon sprinted behind her, their weapons clenched tightly in their grips. Nehemiah thrust his cane in a lazy arc toward the teachers, and the three magicians flew back into the crush of students.

Quinn shook, a pit opening in his stomach. He stepped back and stared at the librarian. "What—why did you do that, Mr. Crawford?"

Nehemiah smacked his lips. He turned on his heel and walked toward Ms. Velvet. "Because it must be done, Quinn, it must be done. I told you the talented needed change. That change is upon them."

"You never wanted to help me, did you? You never wanted me to have the trial."

"Of course I did! I do. But you haven't completed the trial, not yet. You have one more task before you gain the power you seek. That task is at hand."

"But the door—"

"The West Door shows the truth of things. This is the truth of things." He reached Ms. Velvet and spun around, clicking his cane forcefully on the courtyard. "The truth of all things."

Billy inched next to Quinn, eyeing the statue of the principal. "What's he talking about?"

Heidi drew up on Quinn's other side. "I wish it could have ended differently," she whispered. "I'm sorry. Both of you, I'm so, so sorry."

Quinn gave Heidi a blank look. Red rimmed her wet eyes, and she avoided his stare like it might give her measles. "What are you talking about, Heidi?"

"She made me do it, Quinn. You don't understand. She made—she made me do it. If I didn't help they'd punish me. I didn't care at first and played along, but then I did, and when I tried to stop, she told me she'd hurt you."

"Who? Do what, Heidi?"

Nehemiah cleared his throat. "It was such a lonely curse, being bound inside that damnable library, serving Donal and the other principals like I, Nehemiah Crawford, was a lowly slave to their whims. But what could I do? No talented magician would free me, and no misfit could step onto the island without setting off the sirens. No, to be free, I needed someone else, someone no talented magician would ever expect could do the deed I required. Four spells it would take to free my binds, four spells no misfit could or talented magician would carry into my library. I required someone no one else would suspect, but who would have every reason in the world to reach me."

"I never took you a single spell!" Quinn shouted.

"Oh, but you did. Think hard, and the answer may just come to you."

"The books! I…the books…" The botany book. The history book. The spell book. "But I only brought you three books. There were four spells."

Nehemiah smiled, flashing his now perfect teeth. "Sharp as a tack, you are. Ms. Grace had to slip the last one on your roommate when she enchanted him and sent him to my library. I plucked it from him and then tied the spells to my own binds. That sword of your mother's did the rest."

"Heidi?" Quinn spun to Heidi. She backed away. Heidi. Sweet, innocent Heidi, the first one at school who accepted Quinn for who he really was. The friend who eagerly kept his secret. The friend who conveniently slipped so many books into his trusting hands. "You planned this all along?"

She nodded slowly. "I'm so sorry," she mumbled, wiping tears away. "They said they'd hurt you. I didn't want to do it. I never did. I'm not like her at all. You have to believe that."

"But why, Heidi? I thought—I thought you were my friend. You should have gone to the principal."

"I am your friend," she sobbed "I told you that you wouldn't understand. I couldn't say no." Heidi looked up. She grabbed Quinn's hand. "Ms. Velvet is my mom, Quinn. I couldn't say no, no matter how much I wanted."

Quinn wrenched his hand from hers. "Your *mother?*"

He turned to Ms. Velvet. The Witch Queen of the West cast a sly wink and motioned for her daughter. "Come here, Hydrangea Grace. Be a good girl and give Mommy a hug for being such a wonderful enchantress. I was so lucky to have a daughter from such a talented magician as your father. It's too bad he couldn't join the party."

Heidi began a slow, painful traipse to her mother. Quinn had no idea why, but he grabbed her hand and spun her around. By all rights he should hate her for what she did. Yet for some reason, he didn't. Her situation trapped her just as much as his.

"Don't go," he said. "You don't have to go."

Heidi smiled weakly. "I do. I wish I didn't, but I do."

Billy scrambled toward her and grabbed her shoulder. "No you don't, Heidi. Trust me, I know how convincing moms can be. But yours, she's not good. She's not good like you are. Stay here. Please."

Heidi pulled away. "You don't understand. I can't. She'll hurt you both if I don't. Quinn—this is the only way you'll get what you want and make it through tonight. I hope you understand why when it's all finished."

When Heidi reached Ms. Velvet, the Witch Queen of the West grabbed her daughter's hand. The witch snapped, and her shadowy dress expanded. Something within its folds stirred, and they parted like a curtain. Out stepped a boy Quinn's age, wearing the same neatly-pressed scarlet button up and slacks he had worn so proudly on testing day, his hair parted with cold and mechanical perfection.

"Ry—Ryley..." Quinn stumbled back. He glanced behind him, at the crush of students and teachers across the courtyard. Everyone was there: Cynthia, Egon, Maisie, Porter Price and all the other students of the school, all staring at Quinn.

"Yes," Ryley said, his voice booming for all to hear. "Ryley Watkins, the one who should have been here all along. The one whose life you stole. The one you left to rot with Oliver and Patty when it should have been *you.*"

Quinn faced Ryley. The boy stood cross-armed a few yards away, a smug smile inching up his cheek. "Cat got your tongue, Quinn?"

"I—I..." Quinn thought he had prepared for this situation, having spent most nights thinking how it might all play out. But in his imagination, he'd already gained the power of trial and could fight off whatever Ryley flung his way. He never imagined the Witch Queen of the West would have found Ryley. He never imagined the librarian would betray him.

"That's right, Wimbly's," Ryley continued as he addressed the crowd.

"Quinn Lynch is a fraud. He never had any magical ability. He's *nothing*. He cheated his way through school. He cheated all of you."

"I knew it!" Porter Price shouted, pointing a finger at Quinn. "I knew you were different. I knew you were wrong."

"No!" Quinn spun around. "You don't understand. I had to get away. The Watkins were evil. They—they would have done awful things. I just—I just thought that if I could pass the trial, I could make things better." His heart thundered. His stomach might turn inside out any moment. It shouldn't happen like this. It couldn't happen like this. He was being blamed, again, for ruining everything, just like they blamed him for the fire.

Maisie pushed through the crowd. The disappointment in her eyes, they way her lip quivered, it made him feel six inches tall. "And look at what you've done. I stuck up for you. Donal—he believed in you. Look at what that cost him. You've put us all in danger for your own selfish desires. Quinn—I—I can't believe you'd do something so, so *evil*."

"It's not like that, Ms. Callahan, I swear." Tears rolled down his cheeks, hot and embarrassing. "I knew I could get the trial in time. I knew it!"

Ryley gave his best slow clap and stalked forward. "Look at what you've done, Quinn. You've taken down Wimbly's almost single-handed. Soon, because of you, we'll have the other schools under our control, all thanks to the lying, cheating orphan named Quinn Lynch."

"It won't work," Quinn said. "I'll find a way to stop you. I don't know how, but I will."

Ryley smirked. His fingers danced. Thin trails of flame wove an intricate pattern before him. "I don't think you'll see the next—*ooph!*"

Nehemiah swung his cane toward Ryley, and it flung him toward the library. The building's door flew open and swallowed the screaming boy.

Mr. Crawford rocked on his heels, his brows flashing above the lavender band. "Well? Aren't you going to follow him, Mr. Lynch?"

"Why? Why are you doing this?" Quinn asked.

"All things in time, all things in time. I'd say you have just a few more moments to chase Ryley before he recovers. Might I suggest that if you really want the power you've desired, the power that might save all these poor magicians, you make your way into the library and finish the trial. Finish this, and it will be complete."

"I don't trust a thing you say." Quinn planted his feet and glared at the librarian. "I won't do it."

"Meh." Nehemiah shrugged. "If you don't want to, you don't have to. But know this: Ryley Watkins is not a talented magician. He's a misfit, like dear Ms. Velvet here, and just like her, he's very powerful because he took a very powerful magician's talent. You know how misfits are made, don't you?"

"Yes…" Quinn's eyes narrowed. "Through torture."

"Indeed! And you know the misfits tortured you all those years ago because one of my doors showed you as much. Who do you think received your talent? What dark creature was made when Quinn Lynch lost his magic?"

Quinn's knees nearly buckled, and a sick feeling filled his stomach. "You mean Ryley has my talent. He was the one they put it in?"

Mr. Crawford nodded. "And if you want what's yours back, I suggest you go after him. You've come too far to give up now, but if giving up is your choice, so be it. Let Ryley visit all the evil he wishes on your friends. Believe me when I say he will be quite unforgiving."

Nehemiah had barely stopped speaking when Quinn sprinted into the library. Billy screamed his name. Maisie called after him. Spells flashed. He dove through the doorway. The door slammed shut, leaving Quinn alone with the one person on Earth who wanted him dead more than anything in the world.

ॐ1

It Ends

Quinn crouched in the doorway. He tensed, fearing Ryley would be waiting with a spell aimed straight for his head, but neither Ryley nor his spells appeared. Quinn crept from the doorway. He danced and hopped over the rubble littering the library floor, silent as a rabbit trying to outwit a fox.

He never should have chased after Ryley. Nehemiah wanted him here, and for whatever reason, he wanted Quinn to have this fight. The librarian had his own agenda, and Quinn knew now it had been in motion long before he set foot at Wimbly's.

Quinn shook the suspicions from his mind and concentrated on the library. He crept behind a partially collapsed bookshelf and scanned the first floor. The last flames had extinguished from the broken desks, and since no lamps remained, only the light cast by the high ceiling lit the room, dusting the destruction in tarnished gold.

He crawled through his makeshift fort. On the other side, he peeked beyond. A fallen bookshelf shifted, groaning as it slid across the floor. A form rose from within a mound of cracked and broken books. Hunched like a terrible monster rising from a grave, Ryley shoved his way out of the books and strolled to the center of the room.

The boy had hit the rubble hard, and soot and charcoal covered his once perfect clothes. Deep wrinkles crisscrossed his shirt, and the careful part in his hair had become a messy squiggle.

Hands shaking, the boy wiped his shirt and inspected his stained clothing. He checked his hair, a deep, dark scowl twisting his features. Ryley clenched his fists, and his nostrils flared. "Looks like the librarian wanted us to have some quality time together. Come out, come out, wherever you are. I've got a killer game we can play."

His fingers twisted in a grotesque dance, and flames erupted along the veins running from his fingers to his elbows. The fire popped and crackled like they burned on dry wood and not a boy's arms. Ryley admired his handiwork, fire illuminating his toothy smile. "Isn't it beautiful? My spells, they're perfect. I made this enchantment especially for you. I know how much you hate fire, because, you know, your parents burnt to ash in one. Remember that?"

Quinn's body shook. He dug his nails into his palms and concentrated on his breathing. Ryley wanted him angry. He wanted Quinn off-balance.

"Remember?" Ryley swung his arm, and a fiery arc exploded from his fingertips. Scorching flames blasted into a nearby bookcase. Quinn's eyes watered from the heat and stung from the smoke. He pressed his arm against his mouth to block the reek of seared leather burning his throat.

Quinn scrambled from the bookcase and slipped behind another while Ryley laughed at his spell's destruction.

"Feel that?" Ryley asked. "That's power, Quinn. That's my power. It's *mine*, do you hear? It will always be mine. You stole the life meant for me, but you won't ever take my magic. I should have been at Wimbly's. They would have loved me. They all would have loved me!"

His fingers twisted in another pattern that glowed deep green. "Ms. Velvet says she loves this spell the best. She says it shows how powerful I am, how far I've come despite you."

He finished his spell, and his skin deepened to the same shade of green as the magic he cast. Scales sprouted across his fiery arms and made their way up his neck and over his cheeks. His eyes glowed like little yellow points of hate as a long, forked tongue flicked from between his sharp teeth. Quinn knew then that whatever piece of Ryley might have been human vanished with his spell if it had ever existed in the first place.

Quinn looked around for something, anything he might use to fight serpent Ryley. He wiped sweat from his forehead and swallowed, scanning through a thin gap between books. Unless Ryley melted into a wailing puddle if he touched a book, Quinn's chances of stopping his enemy looked bleak at best.

But then he spotted one of the enchanted ladders, untouched by fire and propped against a nearby bookshelf. Nehemiah activated the ladder with a simple tap. Maybe, just maybe, he could use that to his advantage.

He turned his attention back to Ryley. The boy scratched his chin and searched the library with his beady yellow eyes. Quinn waited. Ryley slowly turned until his back faced Quinn.

Quinn sprinted toward the ladder and swiped it from the shelf. He pointed the rune end of the ladder at Ryley and whistled. "Maybe next time you should weave in some better vision in that spell. It's totally understandable, though. Enhanced vision is pretty advanced spell casting. It's not basic like slapping some scales over your skin and turning your arms into sparklers."

Ryley spun around with a sharp hiss. His claws elongated, dripping fiery bits of poison at his feet. "Basic? Look at you, trying to be the brave little hero. You're not the hero. I'm the hero. They'll love me when this is through, and no one will remember you."

Quinn laughed, edging closer. "I'm pretty sure if we took it to a vote, based on looks alone I'd be the hero here. I mean, c'mon, Ryley, how many stories have you heard of the brave demon lizard that tried to kill his foster brother and attacked a school? You're twisted."

"You've got it all wrong. I don't care about those talented brats. I'm a winner, and winners write the stories. When we're done with this place and all the other snotty little magicians, Ms. Velvet will be writing the stories, and they'll all star her brave demon lizard because I'm the one she loves. She told me so."

"I can't believe you don't see it yet." Quinn rolled his eyes and inched closer.

Ryley cocked his head. "See what?"

"This story's not going to end like you think it does. I used to think like you did, you know. But you were my third foster family. I learned after the first and second ones that fairy tales don't have happy endings, that if I want something, I have to make sure I take it before someone else takes it from me. I also learned something else." Quinn took another step forward. His arms strained against the ladder's weight. "I learned people will use you to get what they want. I thought I was smarter, but I wasn't, Ryley. I see it now, though, and I see how they're using you, too. Problem is, they don't need you anymore after tonight, but for whatever reason, they still need me."

Ryley laughed. He cracked his knuckles, and the flames reaching for his elbows flared. "You're wrong. Ms. Velvet loves me. She taught me. She freed me. She'd never let anyone hurt me."

Quinn took another step. A hard jab with the ladder would almost reach Ryley, but in a few more seconds, Quinn wouldn't have the strength to lift his makeshift weapon, much less whack the boy with it. "She doesn't care about you. Nehemiah's the one in charge. Can't you see that?"

Ryley's eyes narrowed. "And what if he is? Why should I care?"

"We don't have to play their game. Let's beat them. We can be better than them."

Ryley considered his words. Sweat rolled down Quinn's back. It dripped from his quivering arms to the floor. His hands would give out any moment.

"No," Ryley said, focusing his poisonous eyes on Quinn. "You're a liar, Quinn. I know you are. You'll never be happy if I have magic and you don't. Even then, we're not better than them, and that's the truth. You know it is."

Quinn tightened his grip on the ladder. He stared at Ryley, unblinking. For the first time since he'd known his foster brother, he saw how much he hated Ryley, and how much the boy hated him. "You're right. We're not."

He screamed and jabbed the ladder at Ryley's chest. His foster brother caught it, claw wrapping around its rune. A light flashed beneath his scaly palm. Hope blossomed in Quinn's heart, and he thrust harder, teeth clenched so hard he thought they might crack any second.

The ladder lengthened. Ryley slid back. He grunted. He scowled at Quinn. Quinn smiled. And then, so did Ryley. His serpent claw twisted, and he shattered the ladder like it had been made of Quinn's hope instead of wood. The boy tossed the broken pieces into the rubble and cackled.

Quinn stumbled back, tripping on a desk and falling flat on his back. He scrambled away, but Ryley cleared the distance between them with a single leap.

The boy grabbed Quinn's shirt, its threads burning and twisting from the fire on Ryley's knuckles. An intense flash of pain burst across Quinn's chest, and he screamed, kicking and swiping, desperately fleeing the hot pain. Ryley roared and tossed him like a doll into a bookshelf. Quinn's head slammed one of the shelves, and for a split second his world blinked out.

It came back into focus as Ryley stalked forward. Flames around his hands erupted into clawed infernos. "Time to end this, Quinn."

Quinn shuddered. He swallowed his tears. No matter how much he hurt, he'd never give Ryley the satisfaction of seeing him cry. Quinn had survived two great fires in his life. Asking fate to spare him a third time seemed too much.

Ryley stood over him, laughing. "Goodbye," he hissed, bringing his hands high over his head.

Quinn braced himself. This was it. He wouldn't close his eyes. He couldn't. He only wished he could have made his parents proud.

Quinn's hands went numb. They lanced out, fingers twisting in arcane patterns. Confused, Ryley recoiled with a snarl. "Stupid. You can't cast spells, you're a nobody—*NO!*"

Light exploded from Quinn's fingers. A beautiful, intricate tapestry flashed. Quinn's eyes widened as he recognized Heidi's puppet spell work its magic. This was why she went with her mother. If she hadn't, she couldn't have saved him.

Ryley splayed his claws and swiped at Quinn's head, but the boy waited too late. Quinn slammed his palms into Ryley's chest, the boy's flaming, serpentine claws an inch above Quinn's face. The heat forced Quinn's eyes closed, and he shuddered from the borrowed power raging through his fingertips.

His foster brother grunted, and his fiery arms lost their flames. Ryley's body twisted and fell to the side. Quinn opened his eyes and scrambled back. Ryley writhed on the floor, his scales melting away, the last of his flames dying in sad sparks. He clutched his chest and flipped onto his back, gasping at the ceiling.

Quinn gathered enough strength to wobble to his feet. He wiped his soaking brow and winced at the burn pulsing on his chest. "Ryley—are you— are you okay?"

Ryley gagged and gasped. His gaze turned to Quinn, and the terror swirling in Ryley's eyes nearly toppled him. Glowing cracks appeared around Ryley's chest and spread throughout his body. They made their way down his arms. They spread up his neck and into his cheeks. The boy reached for Quinn, and then, went still.

A blue orb rose from Ryley's chest. It floated above him, growing brighter and brighter. Quinn shielded his eyes just as the orb slammed into his own chest, and for the briefest of moments, he felt as if he had become everything that ever existed all at once.

And then, he was a boy again. His wounds disappeared. Comforting cool pulsed within his ribs. A current of power filled his veins, and the world gained a clarity that left his jaw hanging. "The trial," he whispered. "I did it. I did it…"

He smiled, but it faded when he saw the pile of ash that was Ryley Watkins. Quinn knew he deserved this magic. It was his, after all. But even knowing that, he felt wrong, like he'd stolen something even though it had been his all along.

The library door swung open. Quinn took a last look at what used to be his foster brother and stumbled outside.

.

The Fall of Wimbly's

A funnel of ice erupted from Maisie's fingers with a satisfying roar before encasing one of the warlocks. The evil wizard flew into the night, screaming. Without pause she spun around, already casting another spell. A witch swooped down, her long, crooked hand reaching for a running student.

"Oh, no you don't!" Maisie roared, a hurricane-force wind blasting from her palm. The column of wind caught the witch and slammed her clear through a window in the administration building.

Cynthia and Egon fought valiantly as well. Egon had transformed into a griffon and tore into a murder of witches. Cynthia used her massive hammer to beat back any charging misfits. Rita the ogre had burst from the administration building moments before, a force in her own right. Her great body absorbed spell after spell, her mighty fists flinging misfits left and right. Other faculty members held their own, blasts of fire, shields of ice, and howling winds keeping the misfit army from the screaming students.

And yet Nehemiah and Ms. Velvet lounged near the library door, completely disconnected from the battle. Heidi stood beside her mother, her fingers weaving a powerful spell that for some reason didn't appear around the girl's hands.

The librarian leaned against Donal's statue, picking dirt from beneath his nails like a bored child at Sunday school. The battle went well for the talented magicians now, but if the librarian and Ms. Velvet joined the fray, Maisie doubted things would continue in the same direction.

A bark troll barreled from behind the library with a roar that shook the earth. Its skin was living bark, its eyes and mouth dark pits full of spiders, snakes, and centipedes. Maisie twisted her hands and fingers into a mighty spell and blew a wind that froze the monster solid.

She marched past the troll, casting spells that turned her skin hard as granite and heavy as solid steel. She stood tall before the librarian and the Witch Queen of the West. "What is going on here, Nehemiah?" she asked. "Is this some kind of game to you?"

Mr. Crawford looked up. "Eh? Just waiting. Should be any moment now."

"Any moment for wha—"

The library door creaked open, cutting her short. Out stepped Quinn Lynch, but the Quinn Lynch before her had completely changed from the Quinn who raced inside minutes ago. Once Quinn had brown eyes, wide and curious and not so different than any other boy his age. But now his eyes glowed with a raging power that was blue as the sea and hot as the sun's heart. Power radiated from his body in gentle waves. The force of his will pressed upon her, and she struggled against it. She knew this power. She'd experienced it radiating from Donal Ward.

"The trial," she said. "Dear God, you've actually done the trial."

Ms. Velvet clapped, bouncing on her heels. Nehemiah nodded approvingly. He raised his hand and snapped, and the misfits attacking the school fled to the shadows and the sky. The librarian smiled, bowing to Quinn. "Welcome back to the world of magic, Quinn Lynch. Tell me, how does the power feel?"

Quinn looked at his hands, dirty and covered in soot as they were. "I've never—I've never felt anything like it."

"None have ever felt what you have." Nehemiah gripped his walking cane. He stepped toward Quinn, slowly circling the boy as he stared at his hands. "Because none have the raw power you have."

"Principal Ward had it," Quinn said.

"Not quite." Nehemiah paused before Quinn. "Donal had the power of the trial."

Quinn ripped his gaze from his hands. "This isn't the trial?"

"Yes and no."

Maisie's eyes widened. Her hand went to her mouth, and she shook her head as she realized what the librarian suggested. "No...it can't be."

"Yes, Ms. Callahan," Nehemiah continued. "Quinn, when you were young, you were blessed with talent. Then, it was tortured from you. Tonight, you gained it back from the trial. You have been crowned, Quinn, because the three paths of magic have blessed you. You are the one foretold by prophecy. You are Quinn Lynch, the Misfit King."

Quinn's face paled. His chin and hands quivered. "But I don't want to be the Misfit King. I'm not—I'm not evil."

"But aren't you?" Nehemiah asked. "Look at what you've done. You're only here because you cheated, ruining one boy's life to make your own better. You lied your way through school, all the while knowing your actions put everyone in danger. Yet you still continued on your merry way. Your friends..." Nehemiah motioned at Heidi and swung his arm in Billy's direction. "...You pulled them into your conspiracy and put them in danger for your own benefit. If that isn't evil, Quinn Lynch, then what is?"

"But," Quinn whispered, his hands shaking harder. "I never meant…why are you doing this?"

"Because I want you to come with me." Nehemiah held a hand out. "Join me. I know the secrets of arcana and can teach you the knowledge I've collected over generations. Be my pupil, and you will do mighty things. This world could be yours, and all you need to do is take my hand."

For a single, horrible moment, Maisie could see the boy consider Nehemiah's offer. She rushed forward, dropping to a knee and taking Quinn's hands. "Don't believe him for a second. Nehemiah's been lying for ages, probably longer than you and I have been alive. This is a plot. You're not the Misfit King. He wants you to think it, but you aren't."

"I never wanted anyone to get hurt," Quinn said, his eyes searching hers. "Please believe me."

"I do," Maisie said. She smiled and brushed a lock of hair from his forehead. "You're not evil. Donal knew that. He saw that. Even when others said so, he believed in you. And you know what? He was right. I believe in you, Quinn. I trust that your heart is good, like Donal did."

Nehemiah cackled. He clicked his walking cane on the courtyard and sighed. "Oh, Maisie Callahan, you're so typical of talented magicians, always having your head in the sand like some wand-waving ostrich. Quinn is the Misfit King! There's no denying it. Three paths of magic blessed him. And clearly Donal's powers of perception aren't too terribly keen. He is a statue now, after all."

Maisie took a deep breath. She patted Quinn on the cheek and rose to her full height. "You're wrong, Nehemiah, and I think you're lying. I'm a counselor for a reason, and it's because I'm very good at reading people." She scowled at the arrogant old man. "And when I look at you, I see a snake trying to sell us its oil. No, Quinn is not the Misfit King. *You* are. You are the one blessed by three paths. Bound by talent, allied with misfits, and teacher of the trial. Quinn is a byproduct of your plans, and because of his power, you fear he'll fight against you so you fill his head with lies while you take away his hope."

Nehemiah strummed his walking cane. He smacked his lips, his jaw clenched like he wanted to swallow something sour but couldn't quite get it down. "You're wrong, and you've interfered quite enough for tonight. Perhaps its time you joined Donal as a monument to the fall of Wimbly's."

Mr. Crawford raised his walking cane, its end flaring with the cursed spell that would turn her to stone. She knew she couldn't fight Nehemiah. She couldn't run or flee. So she turned to Quinn and smiled instead. "I should have been there for you. I'm sorry I wasn't. But you're not the Misfit King. You're not."

* * *

"Wait!" Quinn swatted the cane away. It felt like his heart might leap from his throat and thrash into the night, but he swallowed it down and gathered all his courage instead. "Don't. I'll go with Mr. Crawford. I'm sorry, but he's right, Ms. Callahan. I'm a liar and a cheat."

Maisie's shoulders slumped. Seeing her angry would have been one thing. Seeing her disappointed broke his heart. He walked away from her, avoiding the pained, defeated look in her glassy eyes.

Nehemiah beamed a bright and cheery smile. "I knew you'd see reason."

"Simply wonderful," Ms. Velvet said, turning away. "Come along, Heidi. We've got much work to do."

Heidi stared at Quinn, shaking her head. "You can't do this, Quinn. They're bad people. They'll hurt you."

Ms. Velvet grabbed Heidi's collar and yanked the girl to her side. Heidi slipped, and Ms. Velvet dragged her across the courtyard while her daughter kicked at the bricks.

"Insolent girl," Ms. Velvet snarled, "You'll need some lessons in manners."

Quinn stepped toward them both. "It's okay, Heidi, you don't have to fight anymore."

Ms. Velvet paused. Heidi stopped struggling. "But Quinn…"

"I said it's okay. Tonight's been a bad night, and I know you wish your problems would just *hop* away, but they won't. We have to face our problems. And in the end, if we want to solve them, it'll be us who has to make them hop away."

She frowned, blinking. For the briefest second, her eyes widened. He flashed his own eyes, hoping she realized his plan. Heidi stood, slowly brushing off her jacket. "You're right," she said, turning to her mother. "I'll go. I'm sorry."

Quinn smiled. He turned to Nehemiah. "I want to learn power. I want to learn the secrets of arcana."

"Good." Mr. Crawford spun on his heel. He angled his arm for Quinn to take. "You will take the magic world by storm. You will be a force to be reckoned with. My secrets will be yours, and all will fear the great Misfit King when he comes calling."

"Yes, yes they will." Quinn watched Ms. Velvet pull Heidi toward the courtyard's edge. "Mr. Crawford?"

"Please, call me Nehemiah. What is it?"

"You should know by now never to trust a liar and a cheat!" A spell burst on Quinn's fingertips, flashing in blinding brilliance. He slammed his palm onto the startled librarian, the hopper spell activating on its target, Quinn ramming as much of his newfound power into the spell as he could manage. He shoved Nehemiah before the librarian could react, and the hopper spell rocketed the man into the sky in a blast that sent Quinn flying into the library wall.

Ms. Velvet twisted around, screaming. Heidi's eyes narrowed. Her own fingers danced with the hopper spell, and she slammed her palm against her mother's thigh.

"Why you—" Ms. Velvet roared as the spell activated. The Witch Queen of the West blasted after Nehemiah, her scream fading into silence.

Quinn took a few deep breaths. He pressed his hands into the courtyard bricks, the snow frosting the ground a welcome chill against his sweaty palms. He smiled and let a laugh slip, scrambling to his feet. "We did it!"

Maisie turned. She smiled, though it was only half-hearted. "We did."

Quinn's overflowing joy slowed to a trickle. "For now."

"For now. They'll be back in minutes, I'm afraid."

Heidi jumped to her feet. She ran to Quinn and wrapped her arms around him. "You had me scared for a minute. I thought you'd join them, but then the hopper—what an idea! I bet Mr. Crawford doesn't hit the ground until he's in Canada!"

"I thought Nehemiah might be looking for an offensive spell. He never expected a leap spell."

"A leap spell from you might as well be offensive. He probably still doesn't know what happened," she said with a giggle.

Billy burst from the crowd of students and sprinted across the courtyard. "That. Was. Awesome!"

He reached Quinn and playfully punched him in the shoulder. "Look at you with the glowing eyes. You're a magician now, Quinn, just like you wanted."

Quinn turned in the direction Nehemiah disappeared. He knew, somehow, the librarian would survive. Already he could feel the old man's power thumping like a giant's heartbeat on the horizon. "He'll be back, though." Quinn stared at Maisie. "I can't stay here. You know I can't."

"I can try to keep you safe," she said, but like her smile he knew she only half meant it.

"I know you'd try, but it's not me I'm worried about, it's all the students. Besides, the talented think I'm the Misfit King now. They'll put me in prison. I came to Wimbly's to get away from that and I'm not about to let it happen now. You've got a few minutes. Get everyone out of here."

"What will you do then?" Maisie asked. "The misfits want your power. They'll hunt you down. You can't do this alone."

Heidi straightened. "He's not alone."

"Yeah," Billy chimed in. "He's got us."

"Absolutely not," Maisie said, crossing her arms.

Billy faced Quinn. "Listen, we're in this together. We can't just go back to the way we were before this all happened. No one will ever trust Heidi again seeing as how her mom's the Witch Queen of the West, and I'm guilty by association. If they don't put me in prison they'll use me to get to you. You know that."

"I never meant to bring you into this," Quinn said.

"Get over it, geez." Billy rolled his eyes. "I'm going with you because I want to. It's my choice as your friend. Got it?"

Maisie cleared her throat. "Did you not hear me? Your parents—"

"I'm sorry, Ms. Callahan, but you know I'm right." Billy crossed his arms. "You can't stop us, not unless Quinn wants you to."

Her lips twisted in a frustrated line and her cheeks flushed red. She glared at Quinn. "Quinn…"

"We've got to make things right," he said. "I'm sorry, Ms. Callahan, but we have to go and you have to get the other kids out of here. Nehemiah will be back, and if we're with you everyone's in danger. He'll use Heidi and Billy against me if they stay here. I've got to keep them safe."

An argument bubbled on her lips, but instead of shouting she shook her head and asked, "What will you do, then?"

Quinn glanced at Donal's statue. "There has to be a way to stop Nehemiah. We've just got to find it before the misfits take over."

"Fine." She twisted away and marched toward the other talented magicians. She paused halfway, glancing over her shoulder. "You're right, though. Magicians and misfits will be hunting you. Once you leave the island, you're on your own. Consider this my last piece of advice: No librarian has ever broken the bonds that tie them to their library, and a librarian's power alone is greater than any talented magician's. Don't think for a second that because you gained magic from the trial you'll be his equal. You are a threat, and threat's and equals are two very different things. If you really want to stop Nehemiah, you'll need to learn as much about him and the binding ritual as possible. Good luck, Quinn Lynch. I'm sure we will speak again."

Quinn nodded. Maisie's gaze flicked toward Donal's statue one last time, her brow contorting in a sea of emotions that she quickly tucked away. She reached Egon and Cynthia. Mr. Pennington scowled at Quinn. Ms. Doyle lifted her chin and stared darkly through her spectacles. Maisie turned them toward the children, and together they began casting the spells that would take Wimbly's former students far from the fallen school.

Quinn cracked his knuckles and wagged his fingers. "Ready?"

"So ready," Heidi said.

"Ready," Billy echoed. "Let's go save the world."

Quinn cast his hopper spell. He grabbed Heidi and Billy and stomped hard as he could against the courtyard. Their feet left the ground, and the island shrank into a speck in less than a second. Clouds swallowed them, and the campus vanished. Quinn closed his eyes and said goodbye to the Wimbly

School of Arts Arcana, knowing full well his life and all the danger it would bring had just begun.

Thank you for joining Quinn Lynch on his incredible journey. If you enjoyed *Welcome to Wimbly's,* you'd do Quinn a tremendous honor by rating this book at your favorite online retailers.

Book two of Misfit Magic, *The Horologist's Pocket Watch*, is coming soon! You can visit www.abbradley.com to sign up for release dates and learn more information about this series and my other books.

ABOUT THE AUTHOR

AB Bradley was born in Fort Worth, Texas and spent most of his time growing up there. He did everything most kids in suburbia do: school, sports, scouts, etc. and grew up slower than he liked but faster than he expected. He attended the University of North Texas, where he graduated with a Bachelor's Degree in English.

Currently, AB Bradley writes both professionally and personally, which means he's writing about eighteen hours a day and still loves it more every time he taps a letter on the keyboard. He's a resident of Dallas, Texas and loves Tex-Mex, days by the pool, and creating stories that will stay with you for a lifetime. You can find out more about him at www.abbradley.com.

Made in the USA
Middletown, DE
07 December 2018